I will knock down the Gates of the Netherworld,

I will smash the door posts, and leave the doors flat down,

and will let the dead go up to eat the living!

And the dead will outnumber the living…

~Epic of Gilgamesh

warning

This book deals with a topic near and dear to many of our hearts – the Zombie Apocalypse.

Before you begin to read this book, you need to keep something important in mind..

THIS IS JUST A GAME!

We're not predicting the end of the world. We're not psychic. If we were, we'd use our talents to discover the next great investment or the winning numbers for the lottery. Then we'd retire to a small island somewhere warm and descend into wanton debauchery.

Even we don't believe (most) of what we wrote and you're about to read. It's just speculation on a hypothetical reality. A hypothetical reality that is only slightly less implausible than the programming director at a certain network admitting his or her folly and putting Firefly back on the air.

As appealing as the Zombie Apocalypse is to read about, talk about, think about, or use as a game setting… it's probably not going to happen.

The sad reality is that advances in the field of robotics make the robot apocalypse a far more likely scenario than the zombie apocalypse. Once our robot masters round us up and execute those of us who lack the skills to perform necessary repairs to vital systems and write basic code, there won't be enough of us left to make the zombie apocalypse a legitimate threat to human existence.

Ergo, there is no need to beat people with baseball bats, hockey sticks, or other pieces of sporting equipment. No need to shoot people with any manner of firearm. In fact, I'm going to go out on a limb and just advise you not to use any implement at your disposal to harm, injure, maim, or kill another human being… unless such actions are unavoidable to protect yourself from their attempts to injure, harm, maim, or kill you… Such actions are discourteous and unpleasant… not to mention rude and, most likely, illegal in your jurisdiction.

If you've somehow managed to short-circuit natural selection and learned to read without gaining the ability to distinguish between fiction and reality, don't read any further… seriously… stop reading… You don't follow directions very well either… Your parents must be so proud.

If the above doesn't apply to you, please enjoy.

HIGH SCHOOL
OF THE DAMNED

Created By:	Ben Schultz & Eric Meyer
Primary Text & Development:	Some figment of Ben's imagination
Other Text & Editing:	Nick Miller and figments of Ben's imagination
Some art copyright:	Other World Creations, used with permission
	Louis Porter, Jr. Design, used with permission
	Bradley K McDevitt , used with permission
	Reality deviant Publications, used with permission
	Joseph J. Calkins & Cerberus Illustrations, used with permission
	Skortched Urf' Studios, used with permission
	Richard Spake, used with permission
	Sade, used with permission
	Black Hand Source, used with permission
	Misfit Studios, used with permission
	Jeremy Mohler, used with permission
	Peter Szabo Gabor, used with permission

I took the time to point this out in the Author's note of our first book & game setting *Lady's Rock*, but it's an important item that bears repeating.

When I was younger, I learned so many things at the gaming table, and owe so much of who I am today to this hobby, it's literally mind boggling.

When I was in second grade, I was terrible at math. I used to have to go and spend a half hour every day with a teacher's aide to run through flash cards ad nauseum. No matter how hard I tried, I just couldn't get my facts down. I was reading at grade level, but I'm dyslexic, so I struggled to maintain that. I had no artistic talent. I was overweight, so I was always picked last when we chose teams for gym class. In short, my early academic career was a nightmare.

Then I spent a summer in Oconto at my aunt and uncle's house. My older cousins, who probably did not want me hanging around all that much, were forced to keep me entertained. One night I sat down a quietly watched them play a game that came in a red box with funny looking dice.

I was enthralled by the game. You got to be a different person and do things you could never do in the real world. Of course, I was too young to play with them, but I watched and learned.

When I went home, I begged my parents to buy that game for me. As luck would have it, that was the summer of 82, a bad year to want to become a gamer. Needless to say, my parents were not quick to feed my new found desire to role-play.

My luck finally changed when my cousins purchased the "advanced" version of their role-playing game. I inherited all of their basic boxed sets. Soon my brother and I were living oout our fantasies of slaying orcs, vanquishing dragons, and rescuing damsels.

My reading level improved greatly as I scoured the library looking for source material. My math skills still left a lot to be desired. Midway through my fourth grade year, Mrs. Wagner suggested to my parents that I might need "additional help" in mathematics because I struggled to complete even the basic timed addition and subtraction tests they regularly gave.

My parents refused, and it's a good thing that they did. Because just a year later, role-playing cured my problem with math. The concept of THAC0 had just been introduced. I was complaining about my problems with math and my fear of taking algebra because of them. My cousin Ted pointed out, in that lovely condescending way that only cousins can, that I was doing algebra every time I figured out if I had hit my opponent in the game.

It was a revelation that literally changed my life. It was a remarkable transformation. I went from struggling to pass math to scoring in the top ten percent of the state the following year. All because I realized the thing I had been struggling with in school was no different than the thing I had been doing for fun once school let out.

But the debt I owe to role-playing didn't stop there.

Between my eighth grade and freshman years, I studied Greek mythology. I read both the Iliad and the Odyssey. I owned a copy of Bullfinch's mythology that I paid for by cutting lawn at the greenhouse a block from my parent's house… a task that took the better part of my Saturdays.

My newfound love of learning did not stop there. I was creating new and exciting worlds for my growing group of players to adventure on. I needed to make them believable, so I needed to know more about how planets worked. I needed to know about tectonic plates and continental drift. I needed to know why planets had moons and what role asteroids played in their formation. I needed to know why certain weather patterns happened where they did and when they did. I needed to know more than they were teaching me in school, so I went to the library and I read.

I read for fun too. I fought through Nehwon at the side of Fafhrd and the Gray Mouser thanks to Fritz Leiber. I traveled to distant worlds to learn the secret of life, the universe, and everything with Arthur Dent and Ford Prefect. (The answer is 42, by the way.)

When I entered high school, life changed, but not as much as I thought it would. I still enjoyed hanging out with my friends and slaying dragons, but we also roamed the shadows of Seattle trying to earn Nuyen and gain a reputation as the baddest runners in the metroplex. We flew around South America in gerwalk mode fighting rebels in battle pods.

Oh… and I discovered girls…

That's something that causes problems for many maladjusted nerds, but it didn't cause problems for me. I had placated kings and emperors. I had hit on princesses. I had talked my way out of being court-martialed too many times to count. I had met with Mr. Johnson and negotiated a good rate for my crew.

It didn't matter to me if she was the hot foreign exchange student from Belgium or that soprano with the short black hair. It was just another role-playing experience for me, and those were the challenges I had come to live for.

Luckily, this love for role-playing challenges didn't go away as I grew older. In fact, just recently, I approached a company about the role I wanted them to play in this book. Have you ever tried explaining the zombie apocalypse to non-gamers and asked them to let you showcase their respectable business in your role-playing book? It's a challenge you won't soon forget.

The idea for High School of the Damned hit me one night while I was watching TV. I was taking a break from working on another game for Erisian Entertainment, and I started jotting down some ideas. Before I knew it, I had fleshed out the ideas for High School of the Damned.

The mechanics were already in place. They needed a little tweaking to fit the genre, but it didn't take much. We'd developed the d10 system with the idea that it could be adapted to other genres and settings, so it was just a matter of assigning values to weapons and deciding how many build points you got to start with.

Then a funny thing happened. While trying to come up with the back story for the setting, we realized that the Zombie Apocalypse was more complicated than we had originally anticipated… but not in a bad way.

The first question that was asked and needed to be answered was why zombies were here in the first place. Not the existential "why are we here" but the more important "where the hell did you come from". As we saw it, there were two primary scenarios for the zombie apocalypse – magic or disease.

Either scenario offered its own merits and had its own flaws.

If zombies were created by magic, it would answer a lot of the really tough questions. Cemeteries would give birth to a veritable army of the zombies to plague humanity. Some dark magician or evil priest could easily serve as the ultimate villain… for those gamers among you new to table-top role-playing that would be the "end boss".

Of course, then we had to figure out why they had an insatiable need to eat brains… And we all know that zombies eat brains as sure as we know the sun will rise tomorrow.

If there was no reason for them to crave cerebral tissue, then the bad guy was just a causing suffering for the sake of suffering. While having a villain who's an implacable sadist isn't necessarily a bad thing, I prefer my villains with more realistic goals.

After all, what would he or she hope to gain by killing everyone and turning them into zombies?

Eventually, he would be the only remaining human. Everyone else would be mindless killing machine in search of the one remaining (albeit not properly functioning) brain. When faced with several billion zombies and a dwindling food supply, he's either dead or zombie food. That doesn't sound like a good plan for world domination to me.

Besides, the arcane origin stratagem would require us to ask and answer some of the questions that have baffled mankind since before we discovered fire. We're trying to make a game here, not uncover great philosophical truths about the universe.

As you have probably guessed, option two made more sense. It was not without its own set of problems, however. If being a zombie was a disease, how was it transmitted? What types of creatures could catch it? And why did zombie's crave brains?

That last one was going to be a problem no matter which way we decided to go…

Before we begin discussing the setting in which this game takes place, there is one more thing I need to mention.

The city I am about to present to you really does exist. Most, if not all, of the places I am going to talk about are real.

Though the map of the city is a real, albeit vague, representation of the city, the maps for specific places, however, are fictitious. Even when real maps of the locations are readily available on the internet, we took the time to make up new maps for inclusion in this book.

In this world of heightened security, it would be irresponsible of us to provide everyone with access to a map of any one of Green Bay's high schools. It would be equally (and fiscally) irresponsible for us to (buy the rights to) depict many of the other buildings mentioned. If you want more realism in your game, you can either get more accurate maps from places like the internet or set your game in more familiar surroundings… like the city you grew up in.

We have also exercised creative license with some of these locations and the people who populate them. Some we just made up because it seemed to make the setting more exciting.

It may seem odd to use a real world setting and then manipulate the reality of that location… until you realize that the whole idea of a zombie apocalypse is itself a pretty sizable manipulation of reality… so it seems a bit ridiculous to argue for absolute realism in a zombie apocalypse setting…

Also, whenever (what little we have of) good sense dictates, the names of real people have been changed to protect the innocent… and not so innocent…

At any rate, this note is getting quite a bit longer than I'd like, so I'll finish by saying that I hope you enjoy High School of the Damned. Good luck. You'll need it!

~Ben

Dedications

It would be impossible to thank everyone who had a hand in, not only this book, but everything that we've done. Still, we're going to give it the old college try.

Michelle, my lovely wife. Without your understanding, love, support, and encouragement, none of this would have ever been possible. Thank you for seeing beyond the fat nerd with glasses who always sat by the girls to the fat nerd with glasses that would spend hours on end sitting in the corner of the living room writing. I know Ive already said it, but, if I said it a thousand times, it still would not be enough. I could never have done it without you.

Jack and Maren, my parents. Not only for feeding, sheltering, and clothing me long enough to turn into the somewhat well-adjusted adult that I am, but for continuing to love and support me afterwards. You will never know how much it has meant to me.

Nate, Tim, & Dan, my brothers. We will never know exactly what role you played in making me the person that I am today, but I like to think the unique mixture of love and ridicule has helped make me who I am today. It's a shame that the four of us can't do an activity together anymore, but I'd hate to bring about the very apocalypse I'm writing about in this book.

Kennedy & Kaiden, my children. One of the greatest things about being a parent is the love you get from your children. You'll never know how much encouragement I gained just from your smiles. Oh, and thanks for giving me an excuse to continue to watch cartoons.

Nick Miller: Thank you for all your insight and help making this game what it is today. I couldn't have done it without you.

Pete Figtree. Thank you for reminding me where I first discovered my love of gaming. Though you might not realize it, our emails and your gaming group had a profound impact on this game. I hope you enjoy playing it as much as I enjoyed making it.

The UWGB Gamers Club. I cannot tell you how much you've helped my company grow since we've met. Not only have you purchased my material (or won it… pirated it… whatever…), but you play the game. You talk to your friends. Most importantly, you've accepted both me and my company for what we are… and entertained me during the occasional ill-timed tornado.

Lee Herring. Thank you for helping sort out all of the jumbled thoughts that swirl around in my head, and accompanying me on my treks across the state in search of more players. I might have been able to do it without you, but I didn't have to and wouldn't have wanted to.

Eric Meyer: Thank you for the countless hours of technical support… and help killing zombies. While the technical support is certainly appreciated, I'm fairly certain, helping me to not get eaten is far more important… it was certainly more fun!

Pete Bamke. Thank you for pointing out the things that I didn't think of and for trying to break the things I did think of.

Chris Glassman. Thank you for taking a chance on our company and introducing us to a whole state of fans I might not otherwise have visited.

Chad Knight and Adam Netzler. Thank you for your support and hyping my product. I appreciate everything you've done for me.

Adam Loper. Thanks for making room for us that first year and for inviting us back in the years that followed.

Ben& Beth Dow. Thank you for all your support and well wishes… and for lending me the channeled power of the mustachio.

Aaron Maternowski. Thank you for not sharing the joy found in the little room hidden in the corner.

Our Customers: Finally I'd like to thank everyone who previously purchased a role-playing product by Erisian Entertainment. I wouldn't still be doing this today if it wasn't for the faith you've had in our company. Hopefully, you've had as much fun playing our games as we've had making them. We appreciate your support and encouragement.

Table of Contents

Survivor's Journal

I don't know when it happened. I don't know why it happened.

Maybe the Mayan's were right and the world was doomed to end. We just didn't get the date right when we translated the calendar. Of course, if they were so good at predicting the future, why didn't they see the Spanish coming?

Maybe the religious right was correct after all, and god was punishing his creation for abandoning his laws. The libertarian bastard in me just can't accept that as even plausible.

Maybe conspiracy theorists are right and this is the first phase of an alien invasion. Though it seems a waste to destroy a population you could subjugate.

The government could have been telling the truth when they claimed this is a terrorist plot, but that didn't work for me either First, They don't have the best track record when it comes to honesty. They are the people who experimented with LSD for mind control in the 60s and tried to convince us that the whistleblowers were crazy. Second, if there was a biological weapon this effective, I'm pretty sure we would have had it in a lab somewhere... probably in Colorado where we keep everything else we scold the rest of the world for having.

Personally, I think it was the release of 4ᵗʰ edition. As soon as I saw it I said to myself... and everyone around me... this is the harbinger of the apocalypse.

The sad truth is that it doesn't really matter anymore. As reality has set it, we've stopped asking how it happened or why it happened. We've started focusing on more important things like how are we going to survive...and why should we even bother.

Each of us has our own reason, for wanting to live, or at least not wanting to die.

After years of screaming about their small-mindedness, Bobby finally bought into the hype from whack jobs who think an infallible god created man just so he could hate homosexuals. He's wracked with guilt and trying to atone for the way he was born before he dies.

Gwen and Jerome think they're in love. They believe it's their destiny to repopulate the earth once we've killed all the zombies. Actually... that's what Gwen thinks. I'm pretty sure Jerome is still just trying to get laid. I can't really blame him. It might be the last chance he gets.

Sarah thinks this is just the first phase in Chulhu's awakening as foretold in some book I never bothered to read. She sees this all as a test and thinks those of us that survive will have proven their worth to the elder gods. It's pretty messed up, but we need as many warm bodies as we can get right now.

Matt and Paul are sitting on the roof shooting anything that staggers past the front of the building. Even with the advent of the zombie apocalypse, the number of staggering people hasn't really changed. After all, it is football season, and we are in Green Bay. The only real difference is that these people don't wake up with a hangover... and they want to eat our brains...

For me, I don't really see a point to surviving. It's a war of attrition, and there seems to be a lot more of them than there is of us. In the end, I think humanity is doomed, but I also don't want to be a punk. So I'm fighting because the idea of being eaten alive doesn't really appeal to me and the only other option is unthinkable.

Except that I just thought about it... So I guess it is "thinkable" just not something I want to think about right now. Damn you zombies... Now I have to kill you for making me think...

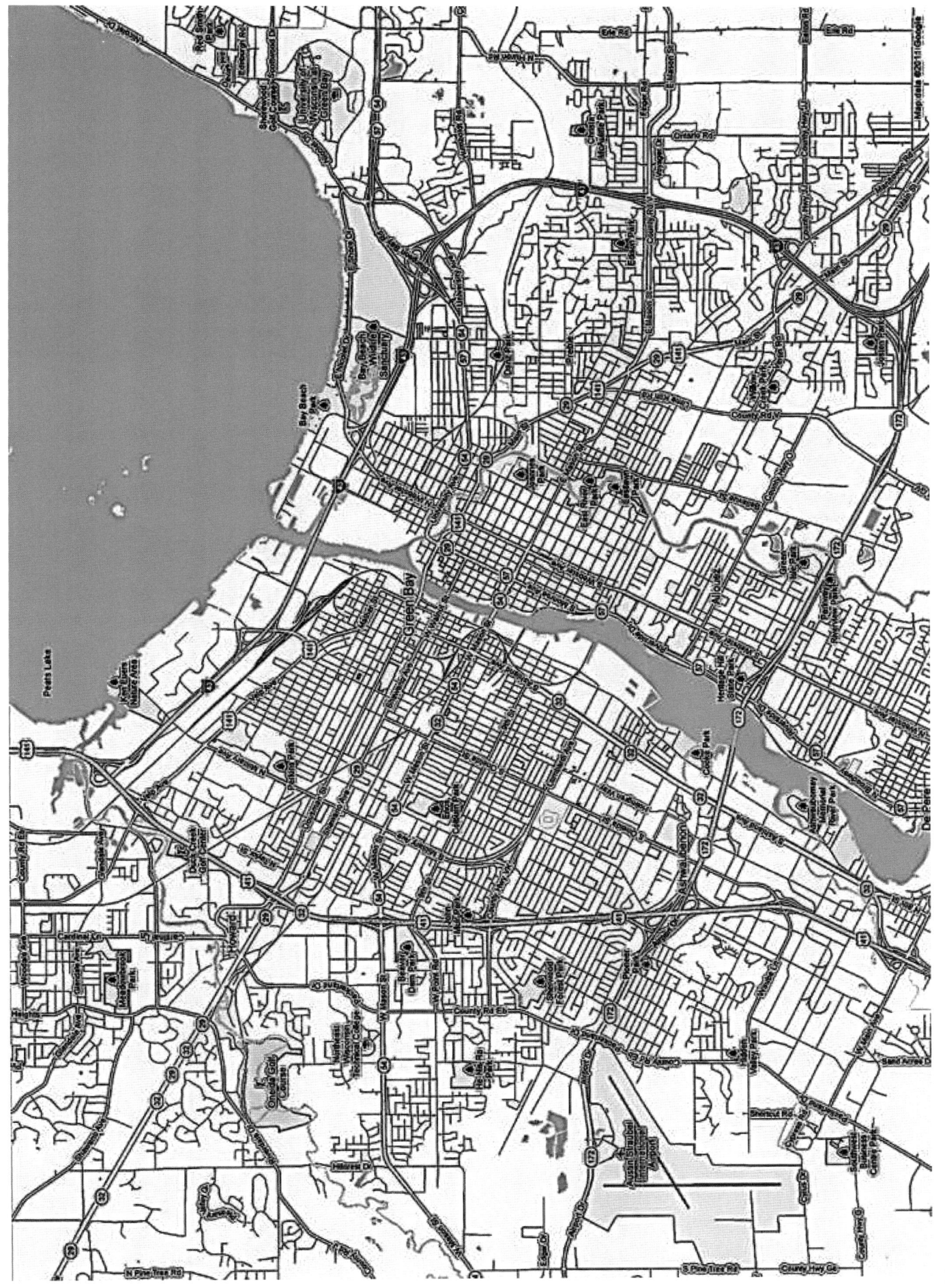

An Overview of Titletown

Before you can understand what it would be like to survive in Green Bay after the zombie apocalypse, you first need to understand a little about life in Green Bay without shambling corpses trying to devour your brains.

According to the federal government the Green Bay Area covers three counties. Many of the smaller, communities in their list are separated from Green Bay by tract of either agricultural or undeveloped land. For our purposes, the Greater Green Bay Area is only going to consist of those cities, villages, and towns closely connected with Green Bay. In most cases, if you didn't see a sign when you went from one to the other, you wouldn't know you were in a different municipality.

Once we've given you a break down the city, its people, its climate, and what life is like without zombies, we'll take a smaller part of the whole, the part where most of the important stuff is located, and discuss it in more detail.

When I describe life in Green Bay to people who don't live here, I tell them that Green Bay is the biggest small town you'll ever visit.

Green Bay is the third largest city in the state of Wisconsin, after Madison and Milwaukee respectively. It is also the smallest city to be home to a professional sports franchise.

The Greater Green Bay Area consists of Green Bay and a number of smaller cities and towns surrounding it. Geography and history have divided these communities between the East side and the West side… which is one of the oldest high school rivalries in the country that began with an unofficial football game in 1895.

The Eastern portion of the Greater Green Bay Area consists of the East side of the City of Green Bay, the east side of the City of De Pere, and the villages of Allouez and Bellevue, and the town of Humboldt. The western portion consists of the west side of the City of Green Bay, the west side of the City of De Pere, the villages of Ashwaubenon, Hobart, Howard, and Suamico.

This division is enforced by the mighty Fox River. I'm not sure what it is about the Fox, but it is a force to be reckoned with. The denizens of Green Bay look at crossing the Fox in much the same way that ancient explorers thought of crossing the Atlantic – surely there is no land beyond this body of water. When we first moved to Green Bay, my wife and I used to make fun of the people who talked about traveling to the west side of town as though they were planning to circumnavigate the globe. (For the record, I still make fun of these people, but now my wife has become one of them.)

Among Green Bay's water ways, this power seems unique to the Fox River. I have not heard anyone discussing the East River or Duck Creek (which is about the same size as the East River) in the same manner.

Together, the Greater Green Bay Area is home to more than a quarter million people. The major ethnic groups represented in this population are Caucasians, Hispanics, Asians, Native Americans, African-Americans, and Pacific Islanders. For the most part, these different cultures get along very well together. The City of Green Bay itself, has just over one hundred thousand people. The part of the Greater Green Bay Area we're going to focus on is somewhere in between.

Greater Green Bay is home to nine high schools, seven institutes of higher learning, five hospitals, three museums, three military reserve centers, two theaters for the performing arts, two malls, a zoo, an animal sanctuary, a botanical garden, an amusement park, a prison, and more taverns than one would than one would reasonably expect.

Like much of Wisconsin, Green Bay experiences two seasons each year – winter and construction. In the fifteen years I've lived in Green Bay, I cannot recall a single year that some part of US Highway 41 has been was not under construction for some period of time between the last snowfall of winter (usually sometime in March, April, or even May) and the first snowfall of the new winter season (sometime in October, November, or December).

The average temperature in Green Bay is 54.3° Fahrenheit. February is the coldest month. The record low, without wind chill, is -33° Fahrenheit. July is the warmest month with a record high 104° Fahrenheit. The city sees an average of 52 inches of snow each year and gets nearly 30 inches of rain when it's too warm to snow.

Temperatures in Green Bay can fluctuate wildly from day to day… or even minute to minute. A few years ago I had the privilege of spending my January working on a loading dock. At noon on Tuesday it was 37° and raining. At noon on Wednesday, it was 30° below zero. Luckily it was not snowing. In twenty-four hours, the temperature changed 67°. (On the flip side, during construction season, the speed limit on the highway can vary just as much.)

Sometimes, because Mother Nature likes to mess with us, it rains and snows at the same time. And sometimes rain never becomes snow and goes straight to ice as it falls. I've actually experienced something we call "thunder snow" – when it snows instead of rains during a thunderstorm. This is a new development. I don't remember seeing or hearing them in my youth. Of course, when I was young, I never uttered the words "it's too cold to snow."

More than the weather or the mystical powers of the Fox, life in Green Bay is governed by one thing – Football. This city lives and breathes football. Many people living here also sleep football and… well, you get the idea… or rather, you will…

While Green Bay is not unique in its love of its professional sports team, that level of devotion… diving over the border of obsession and into a realm psychologists have yet to classify, is unique to Green Bay.

Yes, I know you love <insert local sports team here>. I'm not saying you don't. What I'm saying is that, if Jesus and the Green Bay Packers were both giving out autographs in Green Bay, Jesus would be lonely.

Let me give you some examples of what I'm talking about. In 1996, shortly after we moved to Green Bay, our team won Super Bowl XXXI. Revelers in various states of (un)dress took to the streets. As you can imagine, the police were called to the scene. They proceeded to put up barricades to block off Main Street so that traffic would not injure the revelers.

When the team won Super Bowl XLV in January of 2010, the Green Bay School District closed school early so that the students could greet the returning team. My wife's employer, and many employers throughout the city, also shut down for the team's triumphant return. My own employer at the time constructed a five foot high replica of the Lombardi trophy to commemorate the occasion.

To give you a more recent example, I was called to serve on a jury in November of this past year. Jury selection began Monday morning and the Packers played Monday night. Tension was running high in the jury assembly room, not because of the trial, but because people wanted to go home to watch the game. At nine o'clock in the morning, people were already worried about the game that wouldn't be on for another nine hours.

When the time came, we all filed into the court room to begin the selection process. Before anyone said anything, the presiding judge took a moment to assure everyone that he would be adjourning court that afternoon by four o'clock so that anyone who might have tickets to the game would be able to attend.

For a Sunday game, tailgating begins sometime between Friday after work and two hours before kickoff. People who don't have tickets for the game do not leave their houses on Sundays unless they absolutely have to. Churches have even rescheduled services to avoid conflicts with Packer games.

Once the ball is kicked, Green Bay becomes a veritable ghost town. Nearly all of the more than 250,000 people in the Greater Green Bay Area are either sitting in the stands or glued to their televisions and will remain there for the next three hours.

Businesses that are open on game days furnish televisions for their employees if possible. Stores play the radio broadcast of the game over their public address systems. If the store happens to sell televisions, they are tuned to the game, and most of the employees are in the electronics section watching them.

I once (mistakenly) tried to order a pizza during the game and I was told "it'll be delivered at half time." The thirty minutes or less or it's free promotions they were running at the time did not apply during Packer games.

Season tickets for the Packer games have been sold out since 1960. There are currently eighty-six thousand names on the waiting list for season tickets. The Packers estimate 90 tickets turn over every year, so the waiting list is long…

To put that in perspective for you, if I put my name on the waiting list today, I'd be eligible for tickets in 955 years. Luckily, just as with tickets, you can will your spot in line to your next of kin. Assuming a nice round 25 years per generation, my great grandchildren could inherit my tickets (that's 36 greats).

One last tidbit to show you just how important football is to Green Bay, I'm not really a sports fan, and I spent the better part of two pages talking about it.

As with any good relationship, the team is just as devoted to the community. Players sponsor charities. They work with children to promote education and teach sportsmanship. This team truly appreciates its fans, and we love them for it.

The "Triangle"

Though it is not the official border of the City of Green Bay, most people consider anything found within and adjacent to the area enclosed by the intersections of US Highway 41, Interstate Highway 43, and WI State Highway 172 to be the part of Green Bay. In reality, it's Green Bay, parts of Allouez, Ashwaubenon, Bellevue, Humboldt, and Hobart. Most things south of State Highway 172 is considered De Pere, unless you actually live there and happen to know what village or town you're in.

While this area is affectionately known as the "Triangle", it is actually a rectangle. Interstate Highway 43 forms the eastern and northern sides of the rectangle when it crossed the Fox River to merge with US Highway 41. US High 41 makes up the western side, and WI State Highway 172 makes up the southern side.

Not only do these highways for the effective borders of Green Bay, they are also vital to navigating the city. Though, with the exception of Interstate Highway 43 which is called I-43 just as often as it's called 43, these highways are most often referred to by their number rather than their complete name. Since we're attempting to capture the flavor of the city as well as its geography, that's how we'll be referring to them from now on as well.

Learning the Triangle is essential to living in Green Bay. These highways make it possible to travel from one side of town to the other quickly and efficiently.

Crossing the Fox is possible through the use of the numerous bridges that cross the Fox River. There are six such bridges in the Greater Green Bay Area. However, one of these bridges – the Claude Allouez Bridge - is located in De Pere the part of the area not covered by this tome. With the exception of the highway bridges, all of these bridges are draw bridges, so a passing boat can really mess with your day… and make you late for school or work.

Boats aren't your biggest problem, however. Trains run through the west side fairly regularly… usually when you're in a hurry to get somewhere. The train passes in front of two of the three other bridges… making the remaining bridge extremely busy…

<u>Bridges</u>

1) **Leo Frigo Memorial Bridge**; This bridge was originally named the Tower Drive bridge, and most people, especially outside of official documents, announcements, and directions, still call it Tower Drive. I don't know why it was originally named Tower Drive, but the name was changed to Leo Frigo Memorial Bridge in honor of Leo Frigo, a philanthropist who, among other things, founded Paul's Pantry, one of the largest food pantry programs for feeding the hungry in the nation.

2) **Ray Nitschke Bridge:** This bridge was formerly the Main Street Bridge. It was renamed the Ray Nitschke Bridge in honor of Raymond Ernest Nitschke who played for the Green Bay Packers from 1958 to 1972. It crossed the Fox River at Main Street

3) **Walnut Street Bridge:** The Walnut Street Bridge is the oldest bridge in Green Bay. It crosses the Fox at Walnut Street.

4) **Don A. Tilleman Bridge**: This bridge was named in honor of a former mayor of Green Bay. Most people refer to it as the Mason Street Bridge. There are people who insist on calling it the Tilleman Bridge. They are usually dismayed when the person they're talking to asks "which bridge is the Tilleman?" and are forced to call it Mason Street Bridge like the rest of us. The speed limit is as baffling as the river it goes over. Heading east on the bridge is 30 mph and heading west it's 35 mph. Right in the middle of the bridge the speed limit seems to be "as fast as your car will go" much to the dismay of the Green Bay Police.

5) WI State Highway 172 bridge: This bridge is a six-lane expanse of concrete crossing the Fox River on the southern end of the Triangle.

Getting Around in Green Bay

Once you've learned the sides of the Triangle, there are only a few streets you need to know in order to get almost anywhere in the city.

> ➤ **Navigating on the West Side**

On the West side, there are a few more streets to remember, but that's because the West side is home to more stores and business.

- • *West Side: North-South Streets*
  - ▪ Broadway (this street used to be home to the majority of businesses on the West side. As the city grew, more and more businesses either closed or moved with the people. The majority of the businesses that remained were taverns, and Broadway soon gained a bad reputation for barroom brawls. The city worked to clean up Broadway and succeeded. Now there's not much there.)
  - ▪ Ashland (this is a major thoroughfare connecting Green Bay with the businesses in Ashwaubenon… like Bay Park Square Mall making it one of the busiest streets on the near west side)

- Oneida / Waube (Technically, this street doesn't change names until it passes under 172 and out of the area we're detailing, but I already wrote it, so I guess we'll have to deal with it. Oneida runs from Dousman through Ashwaubenon and passed the front of Bay Park Square Mall. North of Mason Street, however, Oneida is not very busy and runs through a largely residential area.)
- Military (many of the businesses on the west side that are actually in Green bay can be found on Military Avenue… including my favorite barber shop)
- Packerland (this street is technically beyond the western border of our area of concern. However, Green Bay Southwest High School is on Packerland. If you decide to make that the starting point of your campaign, you'll need to know where it is. The post office is also located on Packerland, but I doubt you'll need to mail anything during the zombie apocalypse.)

- ### West Side: East-West Streets
  - Velp (when Broadway was a hub of business, so was Velp. It is home to many half-filled strip malls, empty buildings, and lots of used car… lots…)
  - Dousman (once Main Street crosses the River, its name changes to Dousman. Dousman borders the back of the Green Bay West High School campus.)
  - Walnut / Shawano (as mentioned earlier, Walnut is the only street… other than Mason… that's name doesn't change when it crosses the river. Walnut remains Walnut until it crosses Ashland Avenue.)
  - Mason (Again, technically this is West Mason Street, but you only say that if the person you're talking to doesn't know what side of town you're talking about… so someone who doesn't live here)
  - Lombardi (Lambeau Field is on Lombardi Avenue… and a Shell station that used to be a Sinclair station and still has the Sinclair Dinosaur outside… which does you no good during the zombie apocalypse…)

- ### Navigating on the East Side

On the East side, you need to know the four major north-south streets and the three major east-west streets. There are numerous other streets, but, if you were in Green Bay asking for directions, you'd be directed to them based on the intersection of these streets.

- ### East Side: North-South Streets
  - Monroe / Riverside (for some unknown reason, this street changes its name when it enters the downtown area)
  - Webster (this is the street both Bellin and St. Vincent's Hospitals are located on. As a fictional citizen of Green Bay, remember, people rarely get stopped for speeding toward a hospital.)
  - Bellevue runs from Mason Street to Allouez Avenue providing an alternate root on congested days.
  - Lime Kiln (this is county highway GV and is the fastest way to get from 172 to downtown. My favorite restaurant happens to be a truck stop located at the intersection of 172 & GV / Lime Kiln)
  - University (When Monroe / Riverside turns east, its name changes to University Avenue. The University isn't really located on University Avenue, but it's not really located in Green Bay either, so… I don't know.)
  - Presidential Streets – There isn't a street in Green Bay called Presidential… or, if there is, I've never had a reason to drive on it. However, Green Bay does have quite a few streets named after presidents. They all run north and south. More importantly, they go in order, starting at the Fox River with Washington and working east to Roosevelt. There are one or two street thrown in not named after presidents, and we did skip some of the presidents that didn't do anything really important… and a few that did… but, if you know your presidents, it'll help.)

- ### East Side: East-West Streets
  - Main Street (despite its name, Main Street is not the main street in green bay. That honor is reserved for the only street that's name doesn't really change when it crosses from the east side to the west side.)
  - Walnut (this street runs from the West side to the parking lot of East High School and City Stadium. Walnut is also the only street that doesn't change names after crossing the river, instead it changes when it reaches Ashland Avenue, but we'll get to that when we talk about the west side.)
  - Mason Street (Mason Street stays Mason Street as it passes through Green Bay. Officially, it's called East Mason Street on the east side, and West Mason on the west side, but that's just to help people navigate. Mason Street is the main thoroughfare in Green Bay.)

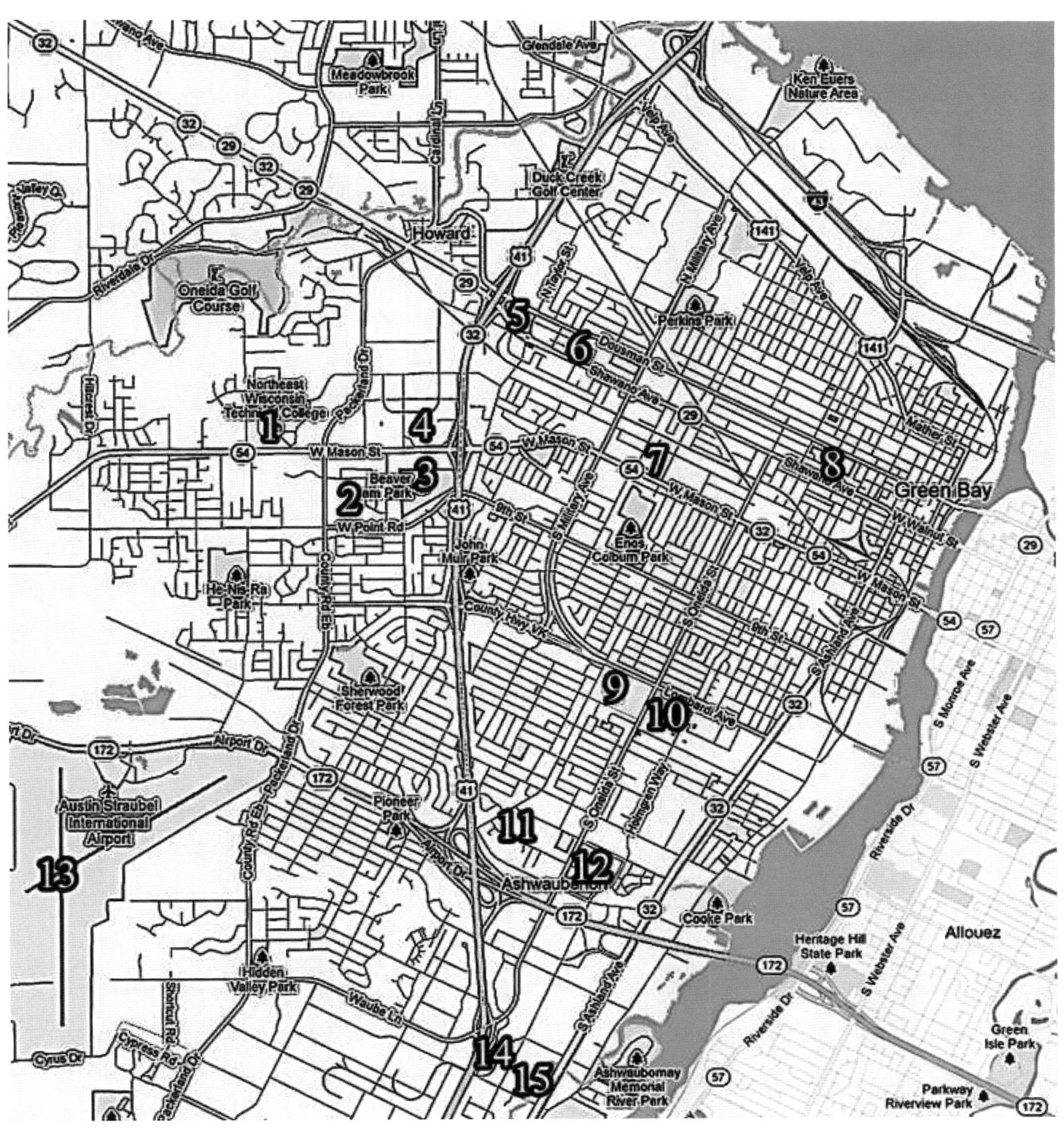

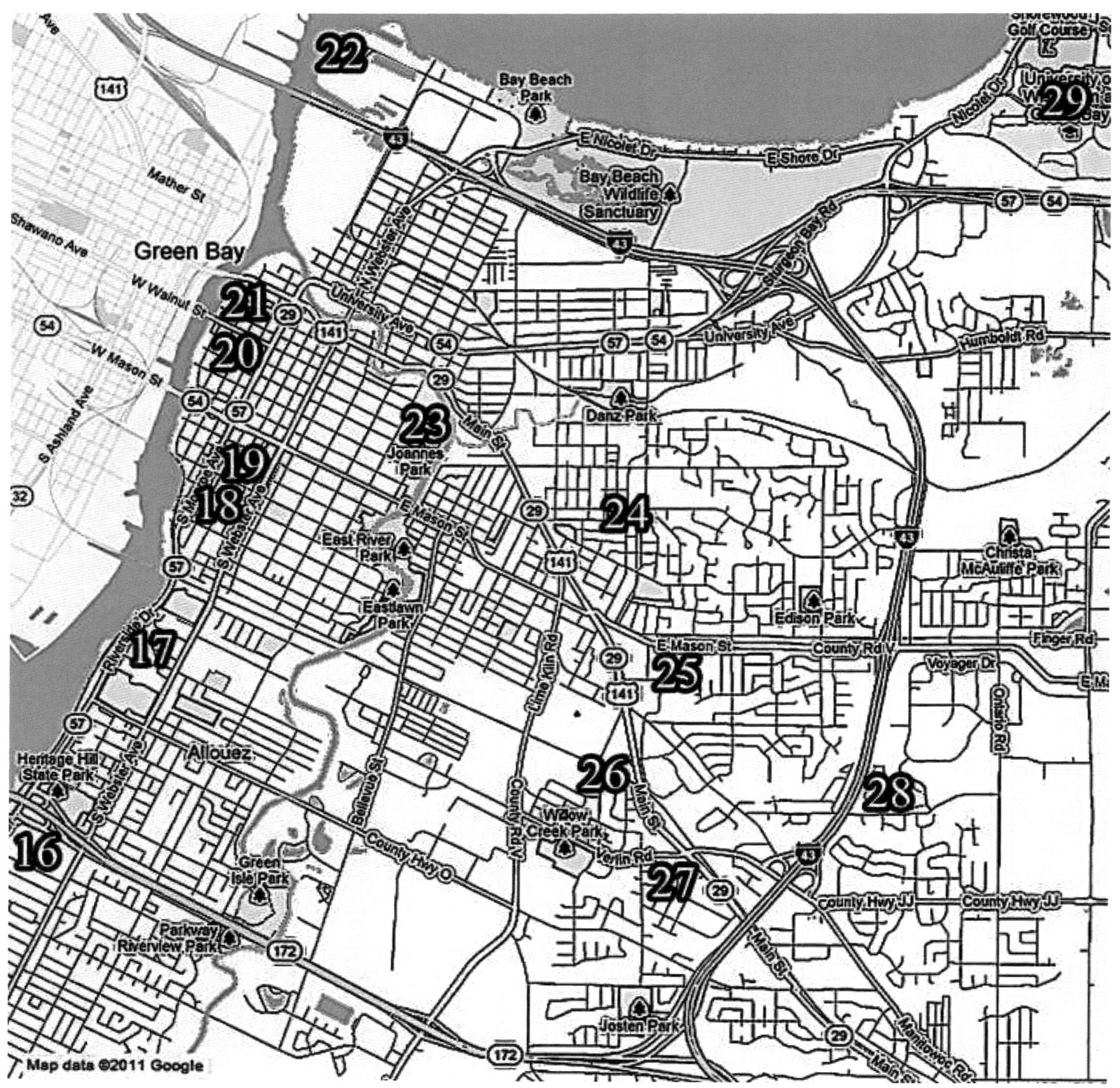

Important Locations

Just knowing how to get around Green Bay isn't enough. Knowing how to get somewhere doesn't matter if you don't know where you're going. To make things easier, we've divided Green Bay into four quadrants. (These are not official divisions of the city.)

Quadrant One: Far West Side

1) Northeastern Wisconsin Technical College (NWTC): NWTC was established in 1912. This institution offers more than 100 Associate Degrees, Technical Diplomas, and Apprenticeships plus 84 certificate programs. Approximately 41,500 students attend classes at NWTC annually.

2) Southwest High School: Roughly 1,400 students attend Southwest High School. Their colors are blue and silver. Their mascot is the Trojan.

3) Aurora Medical Clinic: This facility has doctor's offices, a pharmacy, and a basic medical laboratory.

4) Wal-Mart Super Center: This super center has a sizable grocery section, taking up roughly a third of the building. It also offers clothing and a section of tools, appliances, and sporting goods.

5) Austin Straubel International Airport (GRB): Austin Straubel is technically an international Airport, but the runways are shorter than larger airports making landing larger planes difficult.

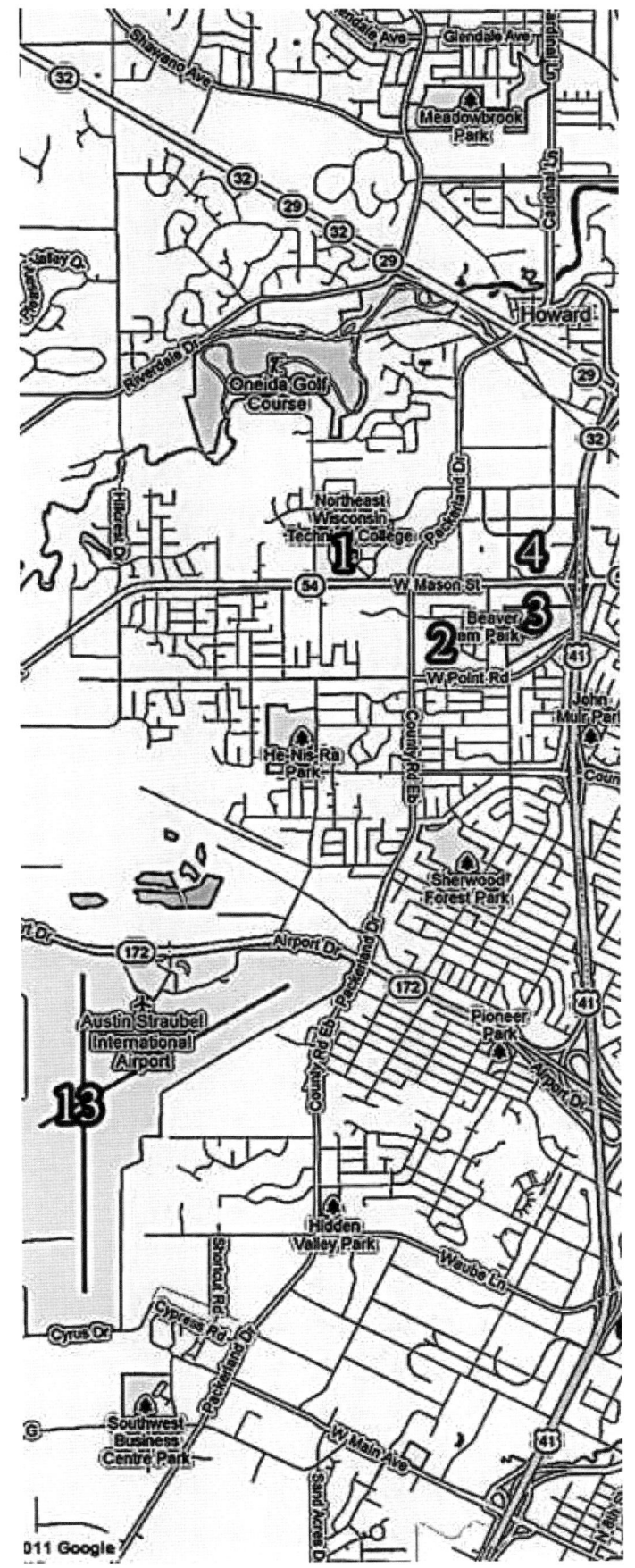

5) Fleet Farm West: Hunting, fishing, and camping equipment plus tools, automotive parts, building supplies, food, and clothing, not to mention the adjacent gas station… Fleet Farm has everything you need to survive.

6) St Mary's Hospital

7) Notre Dame Academy: This is a private high school attended by approximately 740 students. Their school colors are royal blue, Kelly green, and white. Their mascot is the Triton.

8) West High School: Just over `1,000 students attend West High School. Their colors are purple and white, and their mascot is the Wildcat.

9) Lambeau Field

10) Brown County Veteran's Memorial Arena, Resch Center, and Shopko Hall

11) Ashwaubenon High School: Their colors are green and gold. Their mascot is the Jaguar

12) Bay Park Square Mall

14) US Naval & Marine Reserve Centers

15) US Army Reserve Center

16) Brown County Correctional Facility

17) Green Bay Catholic Diocese

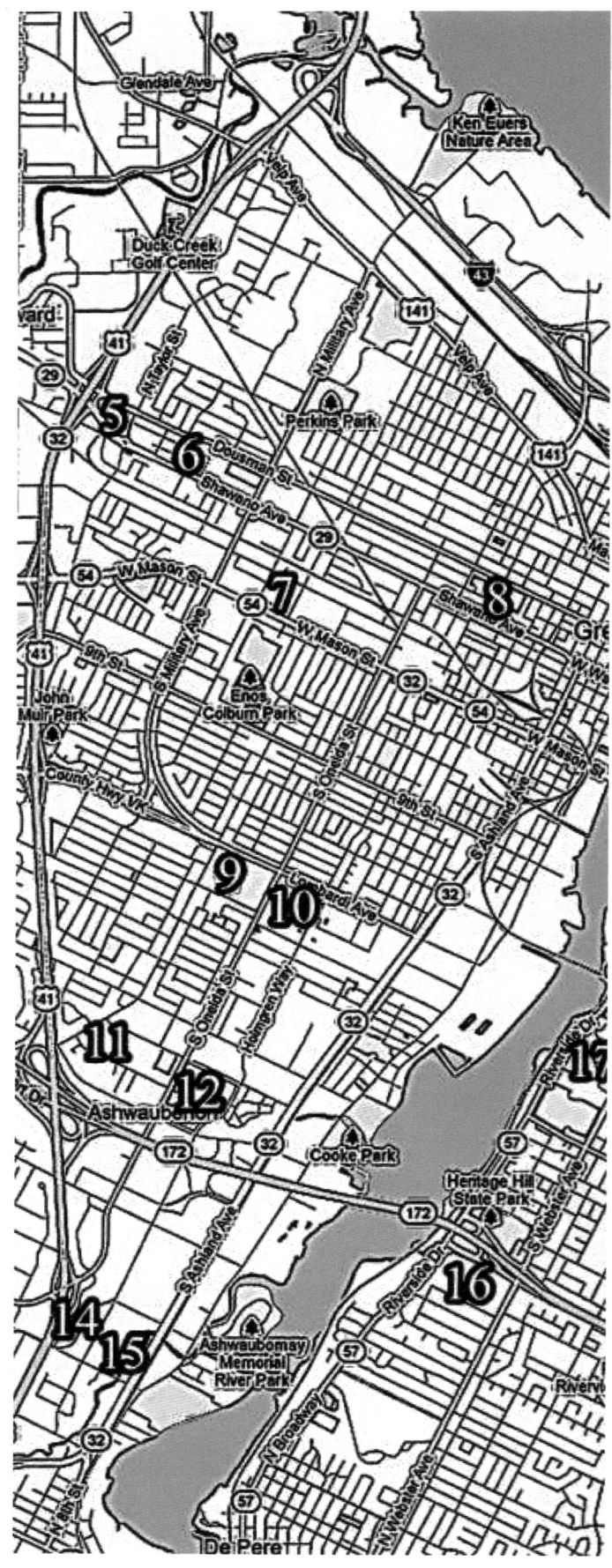

Quadrant Three: Near East Side

17) Green Bay Catholic Diocese
18) Saint Vincent Hospital
19) Bellin Hospital
20) Brown County Courthouse, Green Bay City Hall, Brown County Sheriff's Department, Green Bay Police Department, County Jail
21) Washington Commons / Port Plaza Mall: and abandoned shopping center surrounded by parking ramps. The city is attempting to repurpose this structure.
22) Green bay Coast Guard Station
23) East High School and Old City Stadium: Nearly 1,300 students attend East High School. It's colors are red, white and black. Its mascot is the Red Devil (named for the red clay of the east river, formerly the devil river, which winds around the school). East Stadium was originally known as City stadium and is where the Green Bay Packer used to play before the construction of Lambeau Field.
24) Preble High School: More than 2,200 students attend Preble High School. Its colors are green and gold. Its mascot is the Hornet.
26) Wal-Mart Super Center: This super center is smaller than the one on the west side. It does hold the same variety of merchandise.

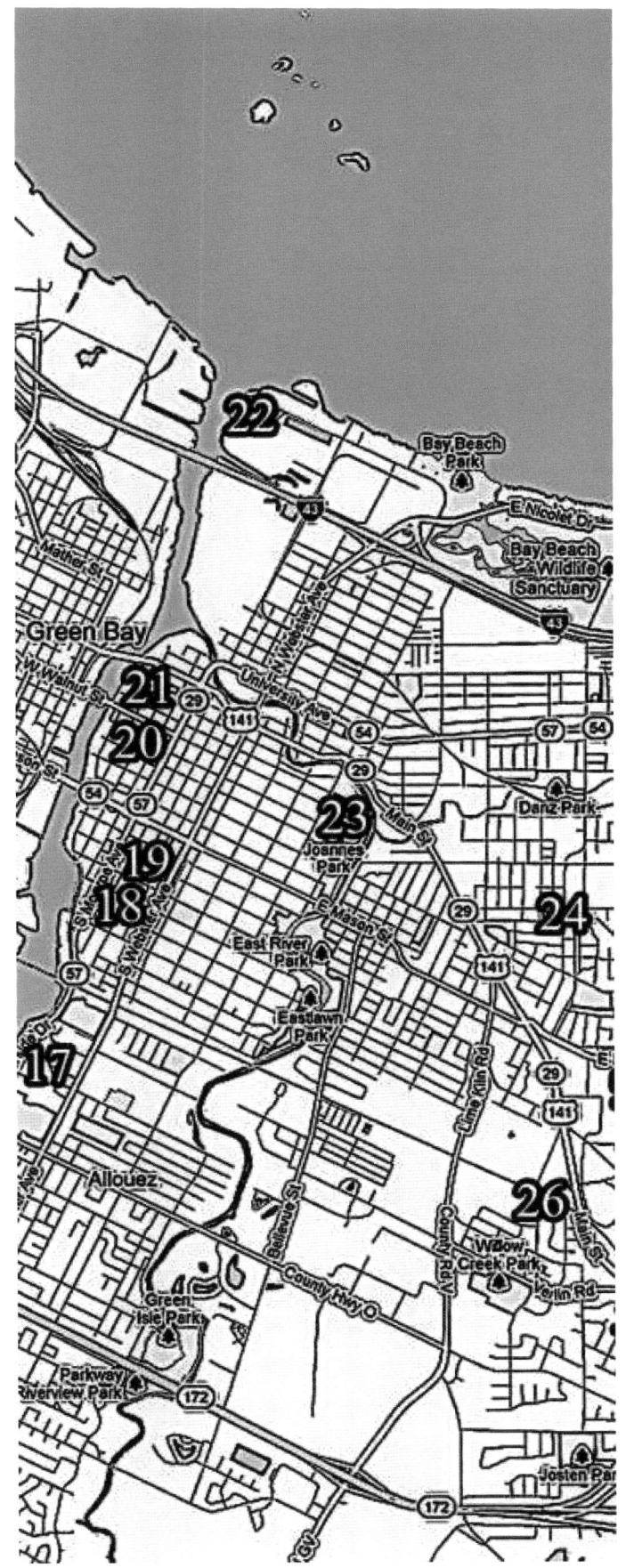

25) East Towne Mall

27) Fleet Farm East: This store has all the same things that the west side store carries. The only difference is that the east side Fleet Farm does not have an adjacent gas station.

28) Aurora Baycare Medical Center (Hospital)

29) University of Wisconsin Green Bay (UWGB). Unlike most state universities in Wisconsin, UWGB is not actually located in Green Bay. Instead the university is nestled in the heart of the Cofrin Memorial Arboretum. UWGB is unique for two other reasons. Its student housing is not located near the classrooms, making it difficult to get to class during the cold and snowy Wisconsin winters. Once you get to the class buildings however, UWGB's other unique feature is a welcome change. All of the school buildings (with the exception of student housing) are connected by subterranean hallways. I'm told they are easy to navigate once you get the hang of them, but, as someone who's gotten lost in this maze on more than one occasion, I'm fairly certain Daedalus was the architect and a minotaur is lurking somewhere within. Approximately 6,665 students attend UWGB. Their colors are green and white. Their mascot is the Phoenix.

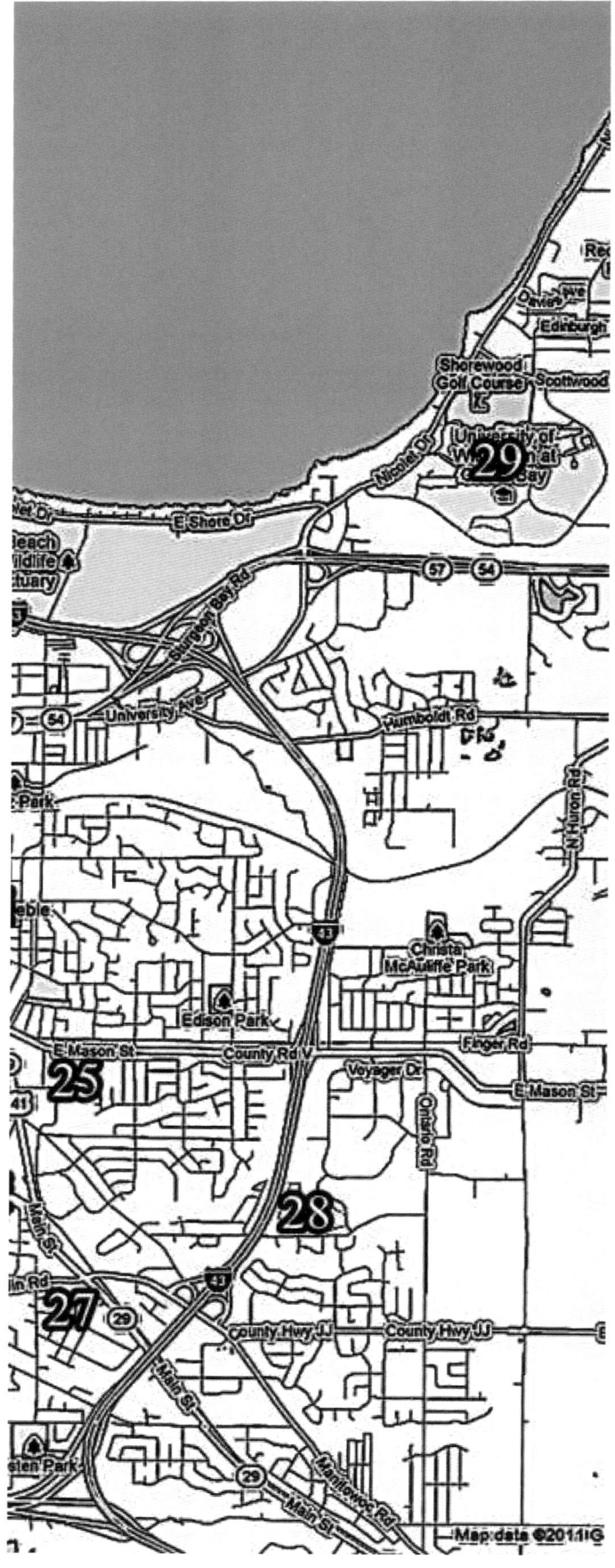

The Timeline of Armageddon

December 7th, 2012

10:05am – The first reports of a mysterious illness are reported throughout Green Bay. Local EMTs and Hospital struggle to keep up with the growing number of 911 calls.

10:55am – People begin to collapse from the strange illness. Hospital officials contact the Centers for Disease Control for help dealing with the strange ailment.

11:51am – The first reported case of transfer of contagion by bite occurs in Green Bay.

12:00am – Someone at the CDC realizes that similar calls have been coming in from major metropolitan areas across the country.

2:57pm – The CDC contacts the Department of Homeland Security and advises that we are experiencing multiple instances of a strange illness with similar symptoms at separate locations in the United States. They suspect that this might be a biological attack.

By the end of the first day, the CDC estimated that more than 135 million people (43.5% of the population) had been infected by the strange disease. They still did not know what originally caused the disease, but reports indicated that it was being transmitted by bite. Researchers suspected some type of toxin in the saliva, but they had not yet been able to confirm their suspicions

December 8th, 2012

9:00am – The DHS reaches out to America's intelligence community to try and determine if there has been any indication of a terrorist threat.

12:30pm – The DHS raises the terrorist threat level to super scary end of the world red. They suggest that people can protect ourselves with black plastic garbage bags and duct tape.

2:45pm – The governor calls a state of emergency and mobilizes the National Guard.

By the end of the second day an estimated 202.9 million people (65.2% of the population) were afflicted with the strange disease which had unofficially been named the zombie flu due to the behavior of those who had succumb to the disease.

December 9th, 2012

10:15am – the Director of Central Intelligence briefs the president on the situation.

11:18am – The White House begins work on a speech to address the American public.

1:00pm - The president addresses the nation from Air Force One. He declares a state of emergency. Thankfully, he does not tell us that shopping can avert this crisis. Sadly, most people are too busy trying to stay alive and unable to hear the government proclaim that we are under a state of emergency.

Estimated Infected: 240.7 million (77.4% of the population... but no one was left in labs to count them...

Life after the Apocalypse

The advent of the zombie apocalypse has changed the face of the once proud city of Green Bay. We started this book discussing life in the Greater Green Bay area. In this section, we're going to talk about how life has changed since the zombies started eating everyone.

In the first three days of the outbreak, almost 80% of the population of the United States had been infected. The rest of the world fared little better. Some isolated parts of the globe seemed to fair a little better, but the Greater Green Bay area was not one of them… no matter how long I've been waiting for 4G speeds…

City streets were littered with cars and trucks abandoned by former denizen trying to flee… denizen now roaming the city as zombies. Most buildings in the city are now mere shells. Their Windows shattered as zombies tried to break in and horrified occupants tried to break out.

The city's hospitals were heavily hit by the lightning pandemic. They struggled to keep up with the onslaught of people suffering from the strange ailments. Their rooms overflowed with people seeking answers. The doctors and nurses did what they could, but they were unprepared for what was to come. It was a matter of mere minutes from the instant that the first patient climbed from his gurney and started to attack the EMTs that were transporting him to the time that the hospital was overrun with zombies. Few made it out alive.

The sudden illness wreaked havoc everywhere. School and businesses closed with the best of intentions, but this decision inadvertently helped to spread the illness.

The city tried to limit the devastation. They raised the Main and Walnut Street bridges and barricaded Tower Drive and 172. It would have worked if Green Bay was located on an island. It's not.

The combat engineers of the city's Marine Reserve unit were asked to help bolster the defenses on Tower Drive and 172. The Civil Affair specialists at the Army Reserve Center were called in to help organize the relief efforts and the medical personnel from the Naval Reserve to aid in those efforts. They had braved wars in countries some school children couldn't find on the map, but the zombie apocalypse halted their progress at the corner of Lombardi and Oneida Avenues

They chose to make their stand in Green Bay's most famous landmark – Lambeau Field. They encircled the stadium with armored personnel carriers and transports to form a defensive perimeter. They couldn't make it to the center of the city, but they could help the survivors trapped in this formal commercial paradise.

Elsewhere unscrupulous looters (as if there was another kind) broke store windows trying to steal televisions they'd never be able to watch. The news crews tried to bring attention to chaos that reigned, but they fell to the zombies… and looters not wishing to be filmed… before they had a chance to break their stories.

Most of the people who remained huddled in their makeshift shelters wondering whether the zombies would find them before or after their hastily gathered supplies ran out. Some people banded together for safety and security… even it is was just a mass self-delusion. Others would strike out… some to leave the city al together… preferring to starve and be eaten further away from the place they had called home.

This is the world where this game takes place.

You're not heroes. You're just kids… high school students. You're not trying to save the world. You're just trying to save yourselves.

The society you've railed against since you became a teenager has fallen to its knees. There is no one to protect you. There is no one to save you.

You've prepared for this day your whole lives. Every video game… every comic book… every anime… every horror movie has led you to this one defining moment.

There is only one question left to ask…

What are you going to do?

BKM·2008

The ABC's of Surviving the Zombie Apocalypse

Now that you know your way around the city and know as much as anybody else how we got to this point, we need to talk about the things you need to know in order to survive. Well stick with the big three – people, places and things because that's what will keep you alive long enough to learn if anything else is important.

People

There are only two kinds of people left after the zombie apocalypse – Friends and Enemies. There are no "frenemies" at the end of the world. You don't have time.

➢ **Enemies**

For the purposes of this discussion, an enemy is anyone who doesn't increase your chances of survival. There are general four categories of enemies you'll encounter. Some of them might not seem like a threat, but the world isn't working like it used to. Anyone who isn't directly aiding in your survival is competition for vital… and increasingly scarce… resources.

Abductors: Abductors are those wonderful people who think it's easier to take your supplies than scavenge for supplies of their own. Abductors will follow you back to your safe haven. If you're lucky, they'll wait until you leave to gather more supplies before sneaking in to steal the things you already have. If you're not lucky, they'll kill your sentries and you in your sleep.

Abiders: Abiders are people who've accepted the fact that the world is over and are just trying to survive. They're resigned to their lot in life, and that's the problem with them. They think about the infected the way the rest of us used to think about mosquitoes or flies.

Amblers: The infected aren't a problem… or they wouldn't be if they didn't travel in packs. One or two semi-intelligent meat bags aren't a threat to a healthy and well-rested human. Of course, as the number of healthy humans has decreased, so have the number of well-rested ones.

Any time you encounter more than two amblers, your best option is to run. Even if you outnumber them, they'll swarm your weakest friend. Killing them won't be much consolation when you have to put a bullet in the head of your closest friend since kindergarten.

Assailers: This class of people is a lot like abductors except that they don't wait for you to be sleeping or away before they try and take your stuff. Assailers will mount a full scale invasion of your haven, kill you & your friends, and then take your stuff.

• *Associations*

Associations are, as you might have guessed, groups of people. Most of these groups fall into one of the general categories mentioned on the previous page. Others are unique and defy categorization other than, if you aren't with them, you're against them.

Apocalytes: The Apocalytes are a group of very devote religious people [read: fanatic nut-jobs] led by a man they call "Father". As far as anyone knows, they aren't affiliated with any particular church, and they welcome members of all faiths and denominations. All that is required is a belief that god sent the zombie apocalypse to punish people for some sin or another… homosexuality seems to be a favorite.

They spend their days screaming from roof tops (if they were on the street, the agents of god's righteous wrath might eat them) telling everyone else to repent of their evil ways. They seem to forget that they're stuck here with us, so they can't be as righteous as they think they are.

Avarites: Avarites are a group of survivors ruled by their greed. The leader of the Avarites, which has changed many times since the onset of the apocalypse, is known as the Plutarch. They believe in one of the oldest version of the golden rule – he who has the gold makes the rules. They want to rule this new world, and they believe the best way to do that to control all the gold. Of course, in this case "gold" is taken to mean anything of value… food, camping equipment, weapons, and anything else you might need to survive.

Avarites gather supplies and store them in secret warehouses hidden around the city. These warehouses are patrolled by an army of armed guards equipped with some of the best hardware the city had to offer. These guards are extremely loyal. After all, with mountains of food, security, and camaraderie… the Avarites offer an attractive package, as long as you don't mind being enslaved by the Plutarch.

Bob's Krewe: Bob's Krewe is a group of former UWGB faculty & students who claim the former campus as their domain and rule it from the David A. Cofrin Library. The core of this group is composed of the former members of the UWGB Gamers' Club. They are led by an individual known as the "Dictator" who is rarely, if ever seen outside his stronghold on the library's upper floor.

The dictator's power is further bolstered by a loyal group of history enthusiast led by a man who calls himself the "Centurion". This honor guard dresses in armor reminiscent of the ancient Roman legions and calls themselves the legionnaires.

When the disease first appeared and the rest of the world was wondering what was happening, these students recognized the signs of the zombie apocalypse. As their fellow students

rushed home to their impending doom, these students prepared for what was to come.

Bob's Krewe is not particularly well-armed. Most of their weapons consist of sporting equipment and truncheons taken from university security. Still, the isolation of campus and the abundance of available supplies make them one of the most secure groups in the city.

Ephesians: The Ephesians are the other side of the religious coin. While the Apocalytes view the zombie apocalypse as a punishment from God, the Ephesians see it as their duty to minister to the remaining survivors. The Ephesians collect food, clothing, and medical supplies and provide them to survivors that they find.

Since there message is one of love and compassion, they are often at odds with the Apocalytes. These two groups wage war against each other over which group had a true understanding of their deity's will.

The Ephesians take their name from the New Testament book of Ephesians. Chapter six verses ten through eighteen, which call for believers to put on the armor of God and wage war against the forces of darkness, hold a special place in Ephesian rituals. The Ephesians are led by someone called the Deacon.

G-Force: The Greater Green Bay Area was home to three military reserve units – Army, Navy, & Marine Corp. When Zombies started plaguing the community, these brave men and women did what they were trained to do… what we've asked

them to do time and time again… They gathered their gear and went to work protecting the people of the Green Bay area.

They chose one of the city's most famous icons to make their stand – Lambeau Field. From the field, the G-Force does their best to protect the survivors that made their way to the field.

Lambeau has become a military encampment. Military vehicles form a defensive circle around the stadium. Armed sentries patrol the gates and concourses to ensure the safety of the people taking refuge on this hallowed ground.

LEOs: The LEOs make their headquarters in the area of the former Brown County Courthouse and adjoining Sheriff's Department and county jail. The LEOs consist of former members of the Brown County Sheriff and the Green Bay Police Departments. Their leader is the former mayor of Green bay who holds court in one of the court rooms in the former Courthouse.

The mayor's chief lieutenants are the Chief and the Sheriff. Each leads their respective departments. With the advent of the zombie apocalypse, the LEOs have given up trying to enforce law. However, they still take their job of serving and protecting very seriously. The LEOs patrol the city searching for survivors and protecting them from zombies whenever possible. Their modified patrol cars are a welcome sight among the few remaining survivors.

Wild Ones: Exactly what the Wild Ones were when they started is anyone's guess. All anyone knows now is that these roving bands of modern day barbarians are just as deadly as a horde of zombies. The most vicious member of the Wild Ones is a woman called the "Amazon." As the deadliest warrior in the tribe, the Amazon is the de facto leader of this group.

If the Wild Ones have a headquarters, no one knows where it is. For all intents and purposes, the Wild Ones are roving bands of crazy people that make the ancient berserkers seem downright civilized.

> ➤ **Friends**

Now that you know who's out to ruin your day, we'll take some time to identify the kinds of people that will aid in your continued survival. Unlike the five types of adversaries you're likely to encounter, there are only three kinds of allies you'll find.

Co-conspirators: Co-conspirators might be friends you've known all your life, members of your family, or people you've just recently met. What distinguishes a co-conspirator from everyone else is the fact that they possess vital skills that directly aid in your ability to continue to exist.

Companions: This category of people is home to those people who do not directly help the cause, but you want to keep them alive for some reason. Girlfriends, siblings, parents, and friends are all candidates for this category. Companions might possess skills that make your miserable existence slightly more bearable. They might know how to cook or tend to your wounds. \

Cannon Fodder: Anyone you keep with you that doesn't fall into one of the previous two categories is a member of this one by default. These are people who drain your supplies and don't really add anything to the group. They might not possess skills of any real importance… or they might just be people who you don't like… In either case, you've found a job that they can do to earn their keep… Feed zombies while you run away. You would risk your life to save a co-conspirator or a companion, but these people are the ones you throw to the wolves to cover your own escape.

The real problem comes in when one person falls into two different categories to two different members of your group. You might want to protect your boyfriend, so to you, he's a companion. To someone else in the group, who isn't even indirectly benefiting from his continued existence, probably classifies him as cannon fodder.

Places

Sleep is one of the most precious commodities during the apocalypse. While food, weapons, and other supplies might seem important, they won't do you any good if you're too tired to use them.

When looking for a safe place to hold up and rest, you have two choices to make. You can stay mobile, sleeping in a different place every night. It's a strategy used by political and military leaders.

While there advantages to remaining mobile, there are disadvantages as well. For starters, every ounce of energy spent trying to find a place to hold up for the night is an ounce you don't have if and when you need to defend yourself. The second, and probably most overlooked, draw-back is the lack of stability and the stress it causes. You're already in a very stressful situation. Can you really afford to add more stress to your life?

Your other option is to find a place to hold up and make your stand. A well-fortified position has also been long used to secure important people and items of value. Green Bay itself was once the location of Fort Howard, a fort intermittently occupied by the US Army in the 19th century.

Of course, there are disadvantages to this approach as well. Staying in one place means that your enemies know where to find you, where you keep your valuable supplies, and where they need to watch in order to learn about your patterns and schedules.

Regardless of which option you choose, there are several important things to keep in mind.

Abandoned: Unless you're already friends with the people already living somewhere, it's best to select a location that no one else is occupying. You could fight for a location, but it better be worth the trouble. More often than not, trying to fight a battle against an entrenched enemy is a waste of your resources and your time. Now that more than ninety percent of the population is ambling around the city thirsting for cerebral fluid, there are plenty of buildings to choose from.

Barricaded: Some places might sound like good ideas… a grocery store is full of food… but you need to be able to block the entrances if you want a good night's sleep. Storefronts tend to contain lots of inviting glass. When it comes to protecting yourself, glass is not your friend. Walls are better than fences. Brick is better than wood. Wood is better than straw. You (and every child who's heard the three little pigs) get the idea.

Concealed: Whenever possible, you should choose a location that doesn't give away your position. Places with signs that turn on when you turn on the lights are a bad idea. Some places might meet all the other requirements on this list, but if just being there alerts people that you're there, find somewhere else to be.

You never want to draw more attention to yourself than you have to. That makes you a target, and targets end up dead. Even if it is defensible, defending it wastes resources, so you don't want to do it if you don't have to.

Defensible: Even if the place doesn't have glass doors and doesn't give away your position by its very nature, it needs to be a place you're capable of defending. A large stone building with steel doors and few windows might seem ideal, but if there are just two of you in your group, you couldn't hope to defend it. Pick a location you can defend. Preferably some of you can defend in shifts so that one of you can sleep while the others stand watch.

Entrenched: Once you've found the ideal location, someplace abandoned, barricade, concealed, and defensible, you need to set up defensive positions. You don't want anyone to breach your defensives, but you need to prepare for when someone does… and, given enough time, someone will. Sentries posted at each entrance are a good start. A sniper on the roof, as long as his presence doesn't give you away, is always a good idea. Set up firing positions and make sure you have adequate cover.

Things

The things you'll find on your journey are just as important as the things and people you'll come to know. Things will help you protect yourself from adversaries, secure places, and keep the friends you have alive as long as you need them to.

There is a large variety of supplies we need to cover, but, let's face it; you're going to skip ahead to weapons anyway. So we're going to start there. Then we'll come back and cover the other things that, while not as interesting as weapons, are just as valuable to your survival.

Weapons

There is no shortage of weapons in the world, and, with Wisconsin's hunting culture, quite a few of them can be found in Green Bay. It's not even a matter of knowing where to look. It's a matter of knowing what the best weapon is to use in the situation you're in. For that, you need to know the four B's – Bullets, Bows, Bats, and Blades.

> **Bullets**

As you've probably guessed, this category covers guns. The right gun in the right hands can be a life saver. The problem is that popular culture has "taught" us that flash is more important than function. The reality of the world is that the weapons that see the most screen time in action movies are also the weapons least likely to help you. It's an almost perfect inverse relationship.

Guns have several advantages, but have just as many disadvantages, especially when it comes to fighting zombies. Since you can only carry so much, you'll have to weigh these advantages and disadvantages in order to decide which firearm, if any, is right for you.

• *Advantages*

Damage: Guns cause a lot of damage. In the right hands, a knife is a deadly weapon. Even in the wrong hands, guns can be dangerous. Throw enough lead at a target, and they'll stop moving. Throw a little bit of lead in the right places, and they'll stop moving even faster.

Range: All firearms can be used against an enemy that's too far away to bite you… or your allies. This is especially important when a bite can quickly turn an ally into an enemy. The odds can quickly turn against you when you start losing allies. When those fallen allies rise again as enemies, the odds swing that much further that much faster.

Portability: Firearms allow you to carry a lot of potential damage. A modern firearm can turn any person into a killing machine. Since the nineteenth century people have noted that God might have created man, but it was Samuel Colt that made them equal.

Ease of Use: Guns have been referred to as the original point and click interface. It might sound like another cute saying for a (de)motivational poster, but it's true. While it may take them a while to become proficient with a gun, most people understand how to use them. All you have to do is point the business end at the bad guy and pull the trigger… reload and repeat until the bad guy stops moving.

• *Disadvantages*

Noise: As any hunter will tell you, noise is your enemy… and all guns make noise. Despite what you've seen on TV and in the movies, it can't be avoided.

A gun fires a bullet using a contained and directed explosion. Explosions make noise. You can muffle the noise, but you can't eliminate it. Noise draws attention, and not all attention is good. More importantly, most creatures, including zombies, know that the sound of gunfire means people are nearby. Zombies are drawn to the sound of gunfire like fat people to an all you can eat steak buffet. (As a fat person, I can tell you that it's the gastrological equivalent of a black hole…)

Not only do you announce your presence to every zombie within earshot, every living human in the area also knows what's happening. If they're the type of people who want to possess the things you have, they're likely to follow the zombies to your location. Then, assuming you survive, they might track you to your lair, and we all know what happens next.

Ammunition: Guns need bullets in order to be of use. Sure, you can swing a rifle or shotgun like a baseball bat if you need to, but you're just as likely to damage the gun as your opponent.

Before the zombie apocalypse, you could afford to shoot at steel targets, aluminum cans, watermelons, and cantaloupes wrapped in seven layers of plastic wrap pulled on a small wagon at eleven miles per hour. They made more bullets every day.

After the zombie apocalypse, bullets are a valuable commodity, so you don't want to use any more of them than you have to. Since firing a gun draws more adversaries to your location, it's a difficult balancing act. The more bullets you fire, the more enemies you'll be facing. The more enemies you face, the more bullets you'll need to defeat them.

> **Type of Firearms**

As mentioned earlier, the flashy weapons you see in movies and on TV aren't the ones you want to be using during the zombie apocalypse. In this section, we're going to list the various categories of firearms and tell you why is each one might be an asset or a liability to your cause.

- *Rifles*

There are several varieties of rifles. Most of the ones you're going to encounter fall into the hunting rifle category. That's lucky for you since these rifles are the ones that do the most to aid your cause.

- Hunting Rifles

A hunting rifle is usually either the bolt action or semi-automatic firearm. They provide excellent accuracy and range, especially when used with a scope of some type.

Because you're firing one bullet at a time, it will limit using more bullets than necessary. It's hard to stress enough how important the conservation of ammunition is going to be for you.

Most importantly, hunting rifles are made specifically to kill something that isn't standing next to you… though they can be used to kill something close by if need be. This long range will help keep you out of danger and give you time to move before more opponents arrive on the scene.

- Sniper Rifles

Truth be told, the sniper rifle is big brother of the hunting rifle. Both fulfill the same purpose, but sniper rifles are designed to do it from further away. This is often, though not always, accomplished using a larger caliber shell. Most sniper rifles incorporate some form of flash and sound suppression system making them seem like the ideal weapon.

Unfortunately, weapons of this type are usually found in the hands of the military and special police units like S.W.A.T., so you're not likely to find them. This rarity also means that ammunition is hard to find.

- Anti-material Rifle

If the sniper rifle is the brother of the hunting rifle, the anti-material rifle is its angry, meaner cousin. These large caliber rifles are to vehicle what sniper rifles are to people. They have all the advantages and disadvantages of sniper rifles… just amplified to take on an armor personnel carrier rather than the personnel it carries.

- Assault Rifles

Assault rifles come in many shapes, colors, and styles. From the M16 and AR15, military and civilian versions of the same weapon to the AK-47 and AK-74, assault rifles are a mainstay of TV, movies, and infantries across the globe.

Assault rifles can be found in three major rates of fire. Civilian versions of these weapons are usually semi-automatic while military versions add burst fire and fully automatic modes. Having civilian versions makes finding ammunition easier, but the idea behind these weapons make them of dubious value to you.

Assault rifles are designed to put as much lead as possible hurling towards your target. This is great if you're fighting a war and your budget is nine figures. It's not as helpful when you're scavenging for bullets.

Since they often lack the range of hunting rifles and the potential exists for wasting ammo, you might want to avoid these weapons. However, in the hands of a disciplined shooter, an assault rifle is still a valuable asset… and even without a disciplined shooter, it's better than throwing rocks at your enemy.

- ### Shotguns

Shotguns are one of the most useful firearms you'll come across. They are versatile, have good to excellent stopping power, and a decent range. When used with buckshot, you don't have to be a good shot to do a lot of damage to your opponent. If you are a good shot, you can to a lot of damage to a number of opponents at the same time. Firing slugs gives you more accuracy and stopping power.

The majority of shotguns come in breach-load, double-barrel, lever-action, or pump-action. Pump and lever actions allow you to fire faster because they carry multiple rounds. However, a double barrel shotgun allows you the option of firing two shells at the same target simultaneously.

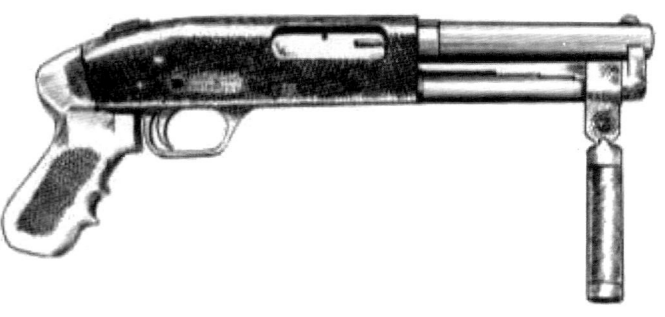

There are some semi-automatic shotguns on the market for civilian use and militaries are fielding fully-automatic varieties of this weapon; however, neither of these will be very common.

- ### Pistols

Pistols are primarily found in two varieties – revolvers and semi-automatics. As a general rule, pistols are closer range than you want to be with a zombie, but it's still not melee combat.

Like other semi-automatic weapons, a semi-auto pistol can fire as fast as you can pull the trigger. Revolvers can also fire as fast as you pull the trigger provided it's a double action revolver, and most are these days.

As a general rule, semi-automatic pistols hold more ammunition and are easier to reload during a fight. Speed-loaders can cut reload time for a revolver, but most don't hold much ammunition. You can't suppress the sound from a revolver either, sorry Hollywood. Due to these drawbacks, unless your revolver has a lot of stopping power, you're probably better off with a pistol.

- *Submachine Guns*

Submachine guns like the Mac-10 are a staple of gangs in movies and in real life. They often have a high rate of fire with both burst and full automatic modes available. However, as with any weapon that throws a lot of lead, they waste ammo. They don't have much more stopping power than a pistol, so it's best to avoid them unless you don't have any other options.

- *Machineguns*

Man-portable machineguns have all the drawbacks of assault rifles, but, with no civilian versions available, these weapons are all fully automatic. Machineguns are usually large caliber weapons, so they have very good stopping power. Unfortunately, they are not very accurate.

Because they are designed to mow down large numbers of opponents, they might seem attractive. However, this wastes ammo, which will be hard to come by because of the rarity of the weapon. All in all, you're better off carrying more useful weapons with easier to find ammunition.

➢ **Bows**

There are quite a few different types of bows, but the ones you're likely to find are compound bows, recurve bows, and crossbows. All bows function under the same basic principles, but different styles transfer different amounts of power to the projectile (arrow for bows or bolts for crossbows).

Bow hunting remains popular in Wisconsin. Many people who participate in gun hunting also go bow hunting. Arrows and even bolts can be found at most sporting goods stores.

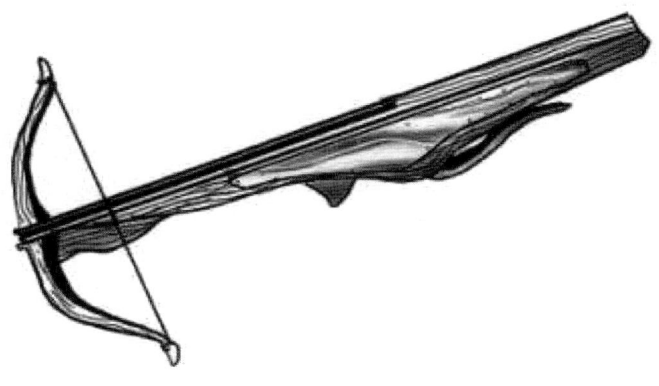

➢ **Blades**

Blades cover everything from pocket knives and tactical folders to machetes and katana and everything else with a sharp edge. Halberds, sharpened garden shovels, and those scraping blades used to scrap manure into the gutter in the barn. Any handheld weapon with a sharp edge counts as a blade.

Though they always look cool in the movies, avoid power tools like chainsaws. They require fuel, and, more importantly, you're just as likely to hurt yourself as anyone else.

The largest functional blade you're likely to find is the machete. These are available at most stores carrying camping supplies. Machete come in all shapes and sizes from the traditional blade to the kukri style. Despite their visual differences, they do the same thing.

Axes are also a common bladed weapon. Most stores that carry sporting goods carry hatchets for chopping and splitting firewood. Hatchets are small axes, so they require you get close to your opponent.

Stores specializing in outdoor activities might carry ice axes. These axes are designed to cut into ice to provide a secure purchase. Take care using them as a weapon. The last thing you want is for your weapon to form a secure purchase in your opponent.

Some stores even carry larger axes for chopping down trees, and fire departments have a decent supply of fire axes. If you're going to wield an axe, a fire axe provides a great combination of weight and effectiveness.

Mail order catalogues make it possible for the average person

to own a weapon that wouldn't normally be available in their part of the world. Few people order these weapons with the intent to use them, and the sellers and manufacturers know it. Some of these weapons are of the highest quality. Others are worth more as scrap metal than as an actual weapon.

Along those same lines, ordering anime and movie replica blades has become extremely popular in recent years. While these blades look very cool, most are designed as show pieces and are not truly intended for combat.

Still, if it's made out of metal, all you need is a whetstone (or a grinder) to put an edge on it. Depending on the actual construction of the blade, it may require considerable maintenance to remain useable. Blades not designed for actual use do not always hold an edge.

The main disadvantage to using blades is that they require you to be close to your opponent. It might look amazing on the big screen, but a sword fight against man-eating zombies quickly loses its appeal when you're the one holding the sword.

> **Bats**

Besides the iconic baseball bat from which this category gets its name, bats include every handheld blunt weapon. While any blunt instrument can be used as a weapon, it's not hard to find a baseball bat, so most people will choose to use them.

Bats come in a variety of sizes and weights. They are traditionally made either of wood or aluminum. Both materials work fine against a zombie, but, like other weapons, there are some things you should keep in mind when selecting a blunt implement of wanton zombie destruction.

Longer bats are, of course, preferable to shorter bats if only to keep the zombies further away from you. If you're into physics, a longer bat is also a longer lever which means you'll get more force at the end of your swing.

Most people assume that a heavier bat will do more damage. However, a bat is really a form of a lever, so the damage you do is all about leverage. If you can't effectively wield a heavy bat, a lighter bat might actually do more damage in your hands.

Vehicles

Many people believe the best thing you can do during the zombie apocalypse is start moving and keep moving. If this is your plan, you need to consider your means of egress from the city.

Even if you don't plan to leave the city, it'll still be helpful to know your options when it comes to getting around within the city… and how to leave it if it comes to that.

As you all know, there are three primary types of transportation – land, air, and water. We'll take a brief look at each of them and consider the different ways each can be used.

> ## Air

Green Bay does boast an international airport, so air travel is certainly possible. However, regular flights to and from the city were grounded as soon as zombies started appearing. Since commercial flights are out of the question, you would need to utilize one of the private aircraft hangared at Austin Straubel.

Many of these private aircraft are owned by corporations. Quite of a few of these aircraft left the city once the true danger became apparent. The Federal Aviation Administration had stopped all air traffic on the country early in the cycle of disease, but money talks. If you can afford a plane, you can afford to bribe a tower official or two and get your plane off the ground anyway.

Still, there are likely to be a few aircraft still sitting in hangars at Austin Straubel. If you can make it to the airport and know how to fly one, one of these craft could take you out of the city. Of course, with every airport in the country closed, landing will be a problem, but the rules are one of the first things to get tossed out the window when survival is on the line.

> ## Water

Piloting a boat is much easier than piloting a plane. Unfortunately, travel on both Green Bay and the Fox River are difficult in winter.

Much of Wisconsin's waterways are filled with ice, which lends itself to ice fishing. Ice does not pose as much of a problem to large ships. These ships require a trained crew. Engineers and pilots are only the first of your concerns. If these ships are capable of leaving port, they're already gone. This leaves you with smaller craft with which to make your water-borne escape. .

Most boats are taken out of the water to ensure that freezing waters do not damage their hulls. Ice along the shore of the Fox River will make getting the boat back into the water difficult. Each winter Green Bay seals itself with ice. In particularly cold winters, even the mighty Fox might freeze over. Fiberglass and aluminum hulled boats are not designed to break ice.

Even the largest charter fishing vessels are not designed to accommodate large numbers of people for a significant amount of time. There is little room for supplies. Being on the water might provide you with a safe haven from zombies, but it just condemns you to a slow death by starvation.

> ## Land

Escape by land is probably your safest path. The problem with this is that you're not the only one who's going to come to this conclusion. Roadways will quickly become gridlocked as people attempt a mass exodus from the cities.

Deep snow and hidden ice make travel off-road difficult, and available vehicles designed to travel off-road aren't designed to carry enough supplies to last you all winter. This means you're going to have to travel from place to place and scavenge for enough supplies to get you to your next stop on an endless journey.

That might appeal to some people, but it's not very practical. Scavenging becomes increasing difficult in unfamiliar locations. Sure, you know where food is likely to be stored, but so does everyone else, so it's easier to search a location you know. It's also easier to notice something out of place in a location that you know. The harsh reality is that moving around just increases your chances of dying in an unfamiliar location.

Even if you opt to remain in a familiar area, you want to move as efficiently as possible. As long as you have fuel to keep them running and time to maintain them, ground vehicles provide a quick and efficient way to move from place to place within the confines of a familiar city. Like most things, every type of conveyance has its advantages and disadvantages.

Bikes: Since you supply the motive force, bicycles do not require additional fuel. Though pedaling around town will tire you out, it will keep you in shape and that might save your life.

However, bicycles are not designed for hauling things you can't carry yourself. Even a basket or rack doesn't offer that much additional cargo.

They offer no protection from the elements. While I cannot say I have never seen a bicycle driving down the snow covered streets of Green Bay, their use is limited during the winter months.

Motorcycles: Green Bay actually has a sizable community of motorcycle riders, so finding a bike in Green Bay isn't that difficult. You might think that Green Bay has a limited riding season, but you'd only be partially right. Saying that riding a motorcycle is treacherous during the winter months is an understatement. All the dangers you face when driving a vehicle seem to increase geometrically as the number of wheels decrease.

If you're a skilled rider, insulated riding leathers make it possible to ride late in the year and start riding again early the next year. (Personally, I park my bike for the year sometime in November and pulled it back out as soon as the snow stops sticking to the roads in March.)

Cars: Automobiles come in all shapes and sizes. Some run on gasoline and some run on electricity. Some have two doors and some have four. They come in convertible tops, Targa tops (T-tops), and hard tops. Most are front wheel drive, but a few are still rear wheel drive.

Cars are one of the most prevalent forms of transportation in the country, and Green Bay isn't much different. They allow you to carry between two and six people comfortably. Their trucks usually offer enough space for luggage if nothing else.

Trucks: Pickup trucks are very common in Wisconsin. They come in both two wheel drive and four wheel drive, but most of the trucks you'll find in Green Bay will be four wheel drives. Pickups can carry between two and five people, depending on whether or not the truck in question is an extended cab.

A pickup truck is defined by its cargo bed. This feature allows you to carry quite a bit of material or carry more passengers. Tanneau covers and truck caps might limit the cargo space, but protect your cargo from the elements.

Sport Utility Vehicles: SUV's are really a cross between a pickup truck and a car. They offer the comfort of a car and the carrying capacity of a small pickup… at the expense of passenger space.

Like pickups, they are available in both two and four wheel drive models. Also like pickups, you'll find a lot more of the four wheel drive variety in Green Bay.

Vans: Whether it's a minivan or a full sized van, these vehicles haul a lot of people and things. Some passenger vans can carry as many as fifteen people. Cargo vans and panel vans can carry a whole lot of cargo. Larger vans are primary rear wheel drive, so some people have difficulty driving them in the snow.

Busses: Between the schools, Green Bay Metro, Lamers Bus Lines, and the Greyhound station, there are lots of busses in Green Bay. Busses are designed for one thing – moving people. Busses are big and bulky making them difficult to drive in high pressure situations. However, if you need to move a lot of people quickly, it's hard to beat a bus.

Semi-Tractor (Big Rig): If you're looking to haul goods rather than people, it's hard to beat a big rig for pulling power. Green bay happens to be home to the largest truckload carrier in the United States, so finding a truck isn't your problem.

Driving a truck isn't easy especially when you're running empty (deadheading) or running without a trailer (bobtailing)

in the winter. These trucks are built to pull loaded trailers. Without that weight on the drive tires, controlling a big rig in winter is just as much fun as driving anything else. Of course, they do have the added benefit of being bigger than most other things on the road. Physics can be a brutal master.

Personal Off-road Vehicles: This category includes everything from ATVs (three to six wheeled personal All-Terrain Vehicles… with the four wheeled variety being the most common) to snow mobiles. These vehicles handle well in snowy conditions. In fact, as is the case of snow mobiles, many were designed to drive in the white stuff.

You can find a lot of these vehicles in or around Green Bay. They're used to bring hunters and fishermen to remote locations or just to drive around. While these vehicles are quick and versatile, they lack the cargo capacity of larger vehicles. This means that many of them will be left behind. It does, however, limit their use largely to patrol and scouting duties. Of course, those are important duties, so do not be quick to dismiss their usefulness.

Recreational Vehicles: RVs hold a special place in apocalypse lore. They are designed to be mobile dwellings, a home away from home. They offer the familiarity of a stable home with the security of moving. Many RVs are capable of holding enough supplies to feed an average family for a week or more. All of that makes them seem like the ideal vehicle to survive the zombie apocalypse. Unfortunately, unless you find an older (less fuel efficient) model, modern RVs are built to be as light weight as possible causing serious security concerns to any discerning survivor.

▪ Vehicle Modifications

As rugged as some SUVs and pickups are, the truth is that owning a vehicle has become a fashion show. Before crumple zones and airbags, cars and trucks could take a lot of punishment and be no worse for the wear. Of course, the occupants were probably dead, but the car was just fine.

Because of this, any ride you plan to use for any period of time will need to be modified and reinforced. Most vehicle reinforcement takes the form of beefed up brush guards (deer pushers) and window plating. Engine enhancements are also very popular.

Glossary of Terms

10-sided die or dice : A polyhedral shape, specifically a decahedron, where the sides are numbered either from zero to nine or one to ten. Traditionally the zero on a ten-sided die is considered a ten. In this system, not only does it represent zero, but, if your die has a ten on it rather than a zero, it too represents a zero

Action Pool : A dice pool that can be used to modify any active skill roll

Armor Value : The amount of protection afforded by a particular type of armor this value is subtracted from the power of the attack

Attack : Rolling dice to represent your character's attempt to damage another character (see character) or NPC (see NPC)

Attack Power : The target number needed to gaff damage from an attack. It is usually equal to the weapon rating of an attack plus 3

Attributes : A series of scores used to represent your character's ability to affect the world around him or her. There are four physical attributes (Strength, Coordination, Quickness, and Constitution) and four mental attributes (Reason, Insight, Psyche, and Charisma)

Body Hit Points : The category of Hit Points representing how much physical damage your character can take before he or she is no longer playable

Build Points : The points you spend to create your character

Character : Any "person" in the game, see "player character" and "non-player character"

Charisma : Your character's ability to relate to other people

Combat : Any time your character is pretending to do damage to an opponent who is, in turn, trying to do damage to them.

Constitution : You character's physical health and toughness

Coordination : Your character's ability to coordinate visual input and movement (i.e. hand-eye coordination)

d10 : A single 10-sided die. If more than one d10 is to be rolled, it will be noted with the number of dice preceding the d10, for example, 2d10 means roll 2 10-sided dice)

Damage Bonus : A set amount of damage added to the total damage of a successful attack after the net number of successes has been determined.

Damage Rating : The amount of damage a given weapon does per success rolled. The actual damage done to the target of the attack is determined by subtracting dodge and gaff rolls from the attacker's successes

Defaulting : When a character does not have the appropriate skill to perform a task he or she might use another skill or even an attribute to attempt to succeed but it will be much more challenging

Dice : Polyhedral shapes with numbers (or sometimes pips) on them to add an element of randomness to the game

Dice Pool : A group of dice that refreshes each time your character rolls initiative (see initiative). Dice from a dice pool can be rolled to augment other dice rolls; however, once a die from the pool is used in this manner, it has been "spent" and cannot be used again until the pool refreshes.

Die : The singular form of dice… also the act of no longer being alive… which sucks in real life, so thankfully this is just a game.

Difficulty : A difficulty is a target number modified for the situation

Director : The person who tells the players how the world reacts to their character's actions. The term is derived from the larger term Game Operations Director which is itself a play on the fact that many of the people in this position suffer from what is known as a "god complex"

DM : A term used in other games for the role taken on by the director. Older gamers tend to use this term regardless of what the title is for a given game

Dodge : Trying to avoid being hit by rolling dice equal to your quickness attribute plus any dice you want to use from your available action pool

Experience Points : Experience points, or XP, are points earned by the character during the course of play. The player can then spend this XP to improve their character's skill & attributes, learn new skills, or, in some rare cases, pay off the debt of a disadvantage

Exploding Die	:	When the highest possible result on the die is rolled (in this case a nine) then the die is rerolled and the second result is added to the first. If the maximum result is achieved on the second roll, then the totals of all three rolls are added together. The same holds true in subsequent rolls result in the maximum possible result. There is no limit to how many times you can reroll and add the results to the original as long as you keep rolling nines
Gaff	:	The act of resisting an attack by rolling dice to mitigate damage
Game Session	:	Anytime your game group gets together to play
GM	:	A generic term used in some games for the director
Hit Points	:	A score used to measure how much damage your character can take before he or she is no longer playable.
Initiative	:	A dice roll done to determine what order people act in a combat round or other round (see round)where the order of action is important
Insight	:	Your character's instincts and intuition
Mind Hit Points	:	The category of hit points representing how much mental and emotional damage your character can take before he or she is no longer playable
Modifier	:	A bonus or penalty applied to a roll to represent circumstances that differ from the ideal
Non-Player Character	:	See NPC
NPC	:	Non-Player Character, everyone in the game not controlled by a player
PC	:	Player Character (see character)
Pen & Paper RPG	:	See Table-top RPG
Phase	:	An abstract unit of time it takes a character to perform a single action.
Player	:	Anyone other than the director who is involved in playing the game
Psyche	:	You character's mental health and toughness
Quickness	:	Your character's ability to move in the world
Reason	:	You character's ability to use logic to reach a conclusion
Role-Playing	:	The act of pretending to be someone else in a fictional or fantastic setting doing things you would not, could not, or hope never to have to do in real life.
Round	:	An abstract measure of time used in the game to manage the actions of PCs and NPCs. It is officially defined as the amount of time it take for everyone involved in a particular scene (see scene) to resolve all the actions gained from an initiative roll. Round are broken down into phases
RPG	:	Role-Playing Game – A game where one role-plays (see role-playing)
Scene	:	Any grouping of related actions taking place (i.e. a combat scene, a negotiation, a car chase, etc.)
Skill Test	:	see test
Soul Hit Points	:	This category of hit points represents your character's soul/spirit/humanity/etc. and how much of it can be lost before he or she is no longer playable
Strength	:	You character's ability to apply force to the outside world
Success	:	A result on a die that equals or exceeds the target number assigned to the task
Success Threshold	:	see threshold
Table-top RPG	:	A role-playing game that takes place in the imaginations of the players and director who are usually, though not always, seated around a table during play… as opposed to a computer based RPG or a MMORPG
Target Number	:	The number which must be met or exceeded in order to successfully complete a task
Test	:	Any time your player rolls dice on behalf of the character, this is called a "test"
Threshold	:	The number of successes required in order for a task to be completed successfully.
Vigor Pool	:	A dice pool that can be used to help your character resist physical attacks
Weapon Difficulty	:	The target number to use a particular weapon
Willpower Pool	:	A dice pool that can be used to help your character resist mental & emotional attacks
XP	:	see experience points

Creating a Character

Getting Started

In order to create your first character you'll need a few things.

- Scratch paper
- Pen or pencil
- Set of Dice
- This book
- Character Sheet or blank paper
- Your imagination

Now set all of these things aside so that you can get to work making your character. Making a character boils down to eight "easy" steps. Well, a seven easy steps and one step that is deceptively difficult.

- Come up with a character concept
- Pick traits the agree with your concept
    a. Choose your clique
    b. Find your character's personality
- Determine your starting build points
- Assign points to your character's attributes
- Assign points to your character's skills
- Select your character's advantages
- Select your character's disadvantages
- Finish fleshing out the Character
    a. Reallocate points as necessary
    b. Determine your dice pools
    c. Determine your character's gaff scores
    d. Determine your character's hit points
    e. List your starting equipment, if any
- Play the game

The truth is that most good characters are created long before the dice hit the table or the pencil touches the paper. This is the deceptively difficult step I mentioned above. Creating a good character starts with coming up with a good character concept.

It sounds easy enough. A role-playing game is journey for your character. Like taking any trip, all you have to do is decide where you're starting and where you want to end up. Though it's not strictly necessary, it also helps to know where you've been.

That is especially true in games like this one that use a "point buy" system for character creation. In order to spend your points correctly, you need to have an idea what you want your character to look like when it's finished. You might not have enough points to get you there right from the beginning, but the journey is the whole point of the game.

You might not think this is important. You might realize its importance in other games, but, in this game, you play a high school student. How much background can a character possibly have at that age, and what difference could it possibly make?

> ➤ **Character Concept**

Where your character comes from is just as important as where he or she is going. We've all sat (and suffered) through a teen movie. We all know about the clichés and stereotypes, but, as much as we hate to admit it, most clichés and stereotypes are based on some kernel of fact… that is usually extrapolated and blown completely out of proportion.

I was a fat kid with glasses when I was in high school… before becoming a fat adult with glasses. I got good grades. I played role-playing games. So I was labeled a nerd and a geek.

Well, I was a nerd and a geek. Today I proudly wear those same labels that plagued me as a child.

Of course, there was so much more to who I was than just a fat nerd with glasses. More importantly, the people in my gaming group were not paper dolls. Even those of us who happened to be overweight and wore glasses were not the same people. We had different motivations. We came from different places. We wanted different things.

As an adult looking back at those days, the differences were trivial at best. Even the differences between the nerds and the jocks weren't all that important in retrospect. As a child, however, those *trivial* things meant all the difference in the world. If you're to role-play a character in high school, you have to start by acknowledging that those differences are very important to your character's development if not their world view.

Though it may have been a while for some of us, high school was likely either wonderful enough (the best years of your life) or terrible enough (a traumatic even that left scars that will never heal) that we remember high school. The clothes you wore, the activities you participated in, the people you talked to, and even your race, color, creed, and gender all played a role in determining how your time in high school would go.

If you don't think any of these things are important, you were probably lucky enough to be a member of the in-crowd or have developed a high enough sense of self not to care.

- ***Character History Questionnaire***

For your convenience, I've made a list of questions that you might want to consider when coming up with your character concept. As a director, these are the questions I'm listening and looking for when I hear or read a character history.

Of course, you don't need to answer all these questions, but you should keep in mind the cardinal rule of character creation – Anything you don't specify is something the Director has free reign to make up for you. As a role-player with years of experience, I can tell you that the Director can (and usually will) use anything you haven't stated to make "life" difficult for your character.

Getting to know where your character came from will help you decide what things are important to him or her when the game begins. These things can (and will) change over the course of game play. The apocalypse is one of the great equalizers. Wealth and political power don't mean much when society and the economy have collapsed, the dollar is worthless (more worthless), and you're struggling for survival.

When answering the following questions about your character, keep in mind the difference between your character's perspective and reality. Things are not always as they seem to a teenager… but try explaining that to one some time. Also keep in mind how these answers would affect your character. Pay particular attention to how they would feel about the answer and whether or not the answer reflects the "real" world or just the character's view of it.

- Family

Family is the foundation on which you'll build your life. Your family doesn't make you who you are, but they are our first exposure to the world around us. As we get older, we can choose to be like the people who raised us or to never become anything like them… or something somewhere in between. In any case, your family has a profound influence on who you are, and, since it's the place where your character's life began, it's the place we're going to start.

Parents
- Were your character's parents married?
- If so, were they married to each other?
- If so, were they married to each other when your character was born?
- If they were not married to each other, were they married to someone else?
- How did this person feel about your birth?
- Were both biological parents involved in raising your character?
- What did your character's parents do for a living?
- How did they treat your character?

- How did your character feel about them?
- Did your character get along better with one parent?
- If so, which one?
- Also, how did the other parent feel about this?
- Does it create tension between the character and the non-favored parent?

Siblings
- Is your character an only child?
- If not, how many siblings does he or she have?
- Where does your character fall in the birth order?
- Are his or her siblings boys, girls, or a combination?
- How does your character feel about his or her siblings?
- Which siblings are they closest to?
- Why is the character close to that sibling?
- Which sibling does the character get along with the worst?
- Why do they not get along?

- ***Socio-Economics***

Socio-economics status is important to many adults who seem to derive some measure of worth to how much crap they can buy and how large of a box they have to put their crap in. (The late great George Carlin once commented that houses are nothing more than boxes we fill with our stuff.)

As important as this is for adults, it seems to be even more important to their children. This might seem counter intuitive. After all, the adults that use wealth as a measure of self-worth view it as a valid measure because they earned the money. Few children are independently wealthy, so children who take this view miss a vital part of the work-income-worth equation.

Social Standing
- How was your character's family viewed in their community?
- Were they respected?
- Were they looked down upon?
- Why was that the case?
- Was it something they did, or something someone else did?
- How did your character feel about it?
- Despite your character's feelings, was it a fair assessment?
- What, if anything does your character do to change this perception?

Affluence
- Compared to the rest of the community, was your character's family wealthy, poor, or somewhere in between?
- How did they come by this money?

- Do your character's parents work?
- Do both parents work outside the home?
- What do they do to earn their money?
- Does the character have a job?
- If so, what kind of job is it?
- How does the family spend their money?
- Do they flaunt the wealth that they have?
- If so, do other resent them for it?
- How does this affect the way that the character views others?

Environment
- What type of house did the character grow up in?
- Was there enough room or was the family cramped for space?
- Was it clean?
- Was it cluttered? (Yes, mom, there is a difference!)
- Was it in good repair?
- Did it have a yard?
- If so, is the yard fenced in?
- Was it in a good neighborhood?
- Did you get along with the neighbors?
- Did the neighbors have any children?
- If so, did your character get along with these children?
- If they don't get along, why don't they?

- *School*

The lessons they learn in class and, more importantly, the things they learn at recess and in the lunch room, will help shape the character's world view.

Friends
- Who were your character's friends? (Names aren't really important. The director will invent them if you don't.)
- Who were his or her best friends?
- How long did the character know these people?
- What interests did they share?
- Were there any conflicts in the group of friends?
- Were they serious conflicts (in the eyes of a high school student)?

Enemies
- Where there any people your character did not like?
- What was the cause of that dislike?
- How serious was it?
- How long has it lasted?

Education
- How did your character do in school?
- Was this important to your character?

- Did they struggle to maintain this level of performance?
- What school clubs did the character belong to?
- Why did they choose these clubs?
- How important were the clubs to the character?
- Did the character play any sports in school?
- If so, which ones?

- *Self-image*

All of these factors help to form the character's self-image. Parts of this self-image are largely superficial, but that does not make them less important in the eyes of a high school student.

Your Character's Appearance
- How old is your character?
- What does your character look like?
- Hair Color
- Eye Color
- Height
- Weight
- What style of clothing does your character wear?
- Where did he or she get that clothing?
- Does your character have good personal hygiene?
- Does your character take time with his or her appearance?
- Is your character happy with how he or she looks?
- Does he or she care about appearances?

Your character's beliefs
- Does your character have any particular religious or philosophical beliefs?
- Does your character have any political beliefs?
- Does your character have any beliefs that would be considered strange by the community?
- Does he or she hide any of his or her beliefs?
- Does your character have any biases against any particular group?
- Where did these beliefs come from?
- How do these beliefs affect your character's world view?

Your Character's Social Standing
- How do the other students view your character?
- Does the character know how others view him or her?
  - If so what affect does this have on your character's self-image, if any?
  - Does your character care what others think of him or her?
  - If he or she does care, does your character let it show?

- How does your character treat others?
- Does this affect how others view him or her?

Life Outside of School
- What does the character do when he or she is not in school?
- What are their hobbies & interests?
- Is there anything the character wants to do, but cannot?
- Why can they not do these things?

Significant Other
- Does your character have a boyfriend or girlfriend?
- If so, how serious is the relationship?
- How long have they been in this relationship?
- Has the character been faithful?
- If not, does his or her significant other know about the infidelity?
- Has the character's significant other been faithful?
- If not, does the character know about it?
- Have there been any rough patches in the relationship?
- Does the character expect the relationship to last?

The Future
- Has the character given any thought to life after high school?
- Does your character plan to continue his or her education after high school?
- If so, what school does the character hope to attend and how does the character expect to pay for this schooling?
- What are the character's career goals, if any?

If may seem foolish to look over all of these things. In truth, you could play the game without them. However, it will be much easier to make your character if you've given even a little consideration to the questions on this list.

For example, when selecting your character's skills, it will be helpful to know your character's interests. It will also make a more believable and fun character. It's not likely that every skill your character possesses will be useful for surviving the zombie apocalypse. Knowing where your character fell in the high school hierarchy will help you choose the right clique, and knowing how your character feels and thinks will help determine his or her personality type.

> ## Choosing a Clique

The first thing you need to do to create your character is to choose the clique that your character belongs to.

People are social creatures. Whether we want to admit it or not, we need other people. Cliques provide both vital social interaction and a sense of belonging.

There are quite a few cliques that high school students can belong to… far too many to list in any single book. For the sake of simplicity, we've grouped these cliques into nine general categories.

The description of each clique will contain the following five things:

- A general description of the clique
- Examples of what stereotypical students might belong to that clique
- A chart of the maximum starting attributes for members of that clique
- Any special advantages gained from being a member of that clique
- Tips for role-playing a member of this clique

- *Academics*

Academics are students who value academic achievement above everything else. These students place a high value on academic achievement.

Academics may participate in extracurricular activities, but these activities are always secondary to their school work. If they have to make a choice between school work and practice, school work will win every time.

Though they tend to get good grades, that is not always the case. A student who works very hard to maintain average grades would still be classified as an academic so long as their school work is the most important thing to him or her.

Who's an Academic: Bookworms, Mathletes, Valedictorians, Teacher's Pets, Nerds, Geeks, and the (secretly hot) girl who spends her time in the library are stereotypical academics.

People who are academics that you might not normally consider part of this group include the student who studies his or her tail off just to make passing grades, the student who gets poor grades because they are not challenged enough in class, and the class clown who gets good grades despite his or her horrendous behavior.

Maximum Starting Attributes			
Strength	3	**Reason**	6
Coordination	3	**Insight**	4
Quickness	4	**Psyche**	4
Constitution	3	**Charisma**	4

Bonus: Academics get 10 points to spend on knowledge skills per point of Reason rather than the standard 7 points.

Role-Playing Tips: An academic is likely to look at everything from a more pedantic perspective than others. If your party were traveling around the area in a psychedelic van with a talking Great Dane, the academic would be wearing an orange sweater and would be blind without his or her glasses.

Avoid jumping to conclusions. Study the facts and strive for logical conclusions based on that evidence.

- **Creators**

Creators are artistic types who revel in the act of creating art. They may be aspiring painters who see the world in a spectrum of colors that the rest of us don't even understand. They might be people who dream of writing music that brings the world together... or captures the angst of their entire generation... or expressed their own feelings without any regard for the world around them.

Creators are defined by their passions and their dreams. They see the world in unique, strange, bizarre, and shocking ways. They have a passion to share this vision with the rest of us.

Sometimes it's as easy as a photograph of a baby sitting in a plastic eggshell wearing a necklace of giant flower petals. Other times it's a painting of blurry people on a river bank. A few times it's been a something resembling a half-completed autopsy frozen in acrylic. We don't always understand it or appreciate it.

Their work need not even be that good. It's the desire to create art that puts them in this category, not necessarily skill in doing it. After all, I've seen some famous paintings that look an awful lot like my third grade art projects, and I'm no artist.

Maximum Starting Attributes			
Strength	3	Reason	4
Coordination	5	Insight	4
Quickness	4	Psyche	4
Constitution	3	Charisma	4

Who's a Creator: Struggling Painters, Aspiring Song Writers, Amateur Novelists, Sketch Artists, Sculptors, and anyone else to create something artistic in nature could all be considered Creators.

Creators can also be people with a passion for robotics or medicine. As long as they dare to dream of something the rest of us only hope for and let their passions guide them to bring it into being, they could be considered Creators.

Bonus: Creators get the *Natural Talent* advantage for Painting, Sculpting, Music, Writing, Drawing, or other artistic skill (approved by the Director. No, shooting guns is not artistic) at no cost to them.

Role-Playing Tips: It's OK to be different. Why march to the beat of a different drummer when you can play the drums yourself? You have a dream and you will not let it be denied by narrow minded simpletons.

- *Drifters*

Drifters are those rare individuals that manage to be welcomed and accepted in nearly every clique, but really don't belong actually to any of them.

Drifters seem like social butterflies, but, in reality, aren't all that social of creatures. Maybe that's how they manage to pull off the seemingly impossible.

Most drifters have some quality that draws people to them. Not everyone will like them, of course, but for some reason, no one thinks they can afford to exclude him or her.

Who's a Drifter: Drifters are actually pretty rare in schools. The most popular kid in school might be able to drift between the various cliques without too much trouble, but they usually have and stick to their own group.

Drifters are people who have something everyone wants. It might be a simply as an infectious attitude or as complicated as the nicest car in school. She might be the hot girl with a soft spot for nerds or the technical genius who grew up next door to the captain of the football team.

Though you probably don't realize it, the people to make this work for them most often are Foreign Exchange Students. Since they're new and different… and only there for a year… people tend to include them in all sorts of activities, even those normally reserved for clique members.

Maximum Starting Attributes			
Strength	3	Reason	3
Coordination	4	Insight	5
Quickness	4	Psyche	4
Constitution	3	Charisma	5

Bonus: Drifters get the *Social Grace* advantage at no cost to them.

Role-Playing Tips: Try not to make waves unless you have to. If you do ruffle some feathers, try to either do it in such a way that the person whose shorts are in a knot can't complain without losing face or make yourself valuable so they can't afford to exclude you.

- ***Gamers***

Gamers used to just be the nerds who met in the library after school to pretend they were elven warrior princesses battling evil armies of orcs. (That's nostalgia, not criticism.)

Today Gamers include all sorts of people… and some people who might better be classified as near-people. The one thing they share is a love of gaming.

For a gamer, the game is more than just a diversion. The game is life. That's not that they're obsessed with a particular game. It doesn't matter what the game is. They want to know the rules and find a way to win.

As crazy (and cliché) as it might sound, Life is a Game to a gamer. They see life in terms of games. These are the people who buy "Level One Human" shirts for their newborns. They use terms like "critical hit" and "critical fumble" in everyday life. (I know, when I found out my wife was pregnant with our first child, my first thought was "Natural Twenty, Baby!")

They might talk about their plans for the weekend like it's a football play. Or claim they tossed the napkin into the garbage from three point range.

Who's a Gamer: As you would expect, Role-players, LARPers, People who play MMORPGs, and members of the Chess Club are all gamers. Those are all easy targets, and honestly, they aren't all gamers in the sense we're using it in this game.

People you might not consider gamers but who definitely fall into this category are sports players who spend their free time contemplating strategies and plays. Seemingly social people who see climbing the social ladder as a challenge to be conquered are also good candidates for this clique.

Maximum Starting Attributes			
Strength	3	Reason	4
Coordination	5	Insight	4
Quickness	4	Psyche	4
Constitution	3	Charisma	4

Bonus: Gamers receive the *Natural Talent* advantage at no charge. This advantage can be applied to both the Strategy *and* Tactic knowledge skills or to either the Firearms *or* Computer Operation active skills. (I'm not too shabby with a pistol, but most of my range time takes place in front of some type of video screen.)

Role-Playing Tips: Pick your favorite game and talk about real life in terms of that game. Talk about screen plays and zone defense. Call out your successes as if they were chess moves. Tell your friend he wouldn't burn toast if he put a few ranks in the cooking skill.

- *Jocks*

Jocks participate in contests of skill, strength, stamina, speed, agility, and willpower. They are gladiators in the modern day coliseum. Like gladiators, no matter how much personal fame and glory they gain, they fight for something bigger than themselves… bigger than the team they belong to… Jocks fight for the honor and glory of their school.

Who's a Jock: Football players, baseball players, track stars, soccer players, softball players, tennis players, and anyone else who engages in contests while wearing a uniform to represent the school can rightly be considered a jock.

There are other students that also strictly qualify for this classification, though don't necessarily come to mind. As long as the participant shares the right mentality, even people who aren't engaged in contest we would normally consider sports might belong to this group. This includes competitive singing groups, debate groups, even mathletes in some schools.

Maximum Starting Attributes			
Strength	4	Reason	3
Coordination	5	Insight	4
Quickness	5	Psyche	4
Constitution	5	Charisma	4

Bonus: Jocks gain their choice between either the *Natural Talent* advantage in the thrown *or* impact weapons skill (thrown weapons is the skill that governs throwing a football or baseball as well as shooting a basketball, and impact weapons is swinging a baseball bat), *or* they may choose the *Tough as Nails* advantage representing the toughness that their devotion fosters.

Role-Playing Tips: This isn't any different than any other competition. You might not have a coach anymore, but you're still part of a team. In this contest, the victor is the group that can stay alive the longest. There are numerous teams hoping for the "W", but there can be only one champion.

- **Outcasts**

Outcasts live on the edges of high school society. The only consistent feature among this group is that they belong to no other group. Some of them choose to exclude themselves from the world of cliques, but most are banished there for one reason or another.

Who's an Outcast: Depending on the demographics of the school you belong to, almost anyone can be an outcast. People who belong to fringe groups tend to gravitate together and form a group of people no one else wants to hang out with.

If your school is relatively isolated (generations of your family have lived and died in the same small town) outcasts might be anyone who wasn't born or grew up here. In most schools, groups like goths and skaters tend to be outcasts. In schools that stress academics or the fine arts, someone normally considered a jock might be an outcast.

Maximum Starting Attributes			
Strength	3	Reason	4
Coordination	3	Insight	4
Quickness	4	Psyche	5
Constitution	4	Charisma	3

Bonus: An outcast chooses one disadvantage, probably the thing that makes them an outcast. They receive double the point value for this disadvantage.

Role-Playing Tips: You live on your terms. Society has rejected you, so reject it. Challenge the people who claim to be in charge. Don't acknowledge their authority until they've earned it.

Performers

More than anything else, performers are entertainers. To the performer, the world is a stage, and we are but actors. They take this role pretty seriously. They enjoy being the focus of attention… even if it is just a bit part in the background.

Who's a Performer: The performer might be a band student or a member of the school's chorus or glee club. He or she might be a drama student or the star in the schools play.

Students who enjoy hobbies that make them the center of attention are also candidates. The front man for a garage band is a typical example of this group. The class clown is definitely a performer as is the basketball player who can't help but showboat on the court.

Graffiti artist could also be in this group as long as the intention is to be noticed rather than just to create art.

Maximum Starting Attributes			
Strength	3	**Reason**	3
Coordination	5	**Insight**	4
Quickness	4	**Psyche**	4
Constitution	3	**Charisma**	5

Bonus: Performers gain the *Poise* advantage at no charge to the player.

Role-Playing Tips: Attention is a drug just as intoxicating as any other. You are an attention junky. Use whatever you have at your disposal to get your fix.

Dance… Tell jokes… Quote movies… Be melodramatic… Never miss an opportunity to show off…

- **_Socialites_**

As we, and every serious and respected behavior psychologist, have said, humans are social creatures. We want to associate ourselves with people we like and / or admire. We want to surround ourselves with friends. The Socialite is an expert at navigating this web of social networks, because of this, they wield untold power, especially in high school where social standing is really the only thing you can call your own.

Who is a Socialite: The "popular" kids at school are probably the best example of socialites. Their approval can open doors and their disproval can just as easily slam them shut one again.

Not all socialites are popular, however. Some members of this group use their powers more benevolently, often earning the ire of their fellow socialites. The cheerleader who likes to hang out with the geeks and nerd (because she understands she will rule their social circle) is also an example of this type of socialite.

Though it might not seem like it, the "playa" is also a master socialite. He or she uses their insight into other people and their powerful charisma to get what they want.

Maximum Starting Attributes			
Strength	3	Reason	3
Coordination	4	Insight	5
Quickness	4	Psyche	4
Constitution	3	Charisma	6

Bonus: A socialite begins play with either the _Presence_ or the _Sex Appeal_ advantage for two points less than listed.

Role-Playing Tips: Remember the power you hold over others. At any given point in time, this power can be a force for good, a force for evil, or a tool for your own selfish gain. Exploit this gift whenever you feel it's necessary. The power is intoxicating, but it is even more potent because you must use it or you will lose it.

- *Technicians*

Technicians are the people who understand how things work. Machines are easier to understand than people. They are designed to perform a specific function or set of functions. If they do not operate as expected, something is wrong and needs to be repaired. Because, unlike people, machines are predictable and consistent, technicians often prefer spending time with them to interacting with people… who do not make much sense most of the time.

Technicians come from a wide variety of backgrounds and socio-economic statuses. They usually collect in groups based on their machine of preference, but there is some overlap between the various groups.

Who's a Technician: Computer geeks, hackers, and gear heads are all examples of technicians.

Members of the Audio-Visual Club, if you school has one, are likely to belong to this group. The students who excel at wood shop and automotive shop, if your school offers these classes, might also fit into this category.

Maximum Starting Attributes			
Strength	3	Reason	5
Coordination	4	Insight	4
Quickness	4	Psyche	4
Constitution	3	Charisma	4

Bonus: Technicians begin play with one *Aptitude* advantage of their choosing at no cost to them

Role-Playing Tips: Try to avoid getting involved with things that don't matter, like measuring egos. Talk is cheap, and doesn't accomplish anything meaningful. Expect people to show you what they can do before you believe in their ability to do it.

Instead focus on the things that really matter, the things you do well. Enjoy the roar of a well-tuned engine or the hum of synchronized case fans.

Personality Types

More than the clique your character belong to, his or her personality will help you decide how your character is going to act in any given situation.

There are sixteen personality types available in High School of the Damned. Each player will select one of these for his or her character. Choose one that you feel you can role-play correctly. As you will see in the health and healing section (see page 118), your character's survival might depend on it.

It is important to keep in mind that a personality type only gives a guideline to how your character behaves the majority of the time. It is not some decree to which your character must slavishly adhere. In reality, we all take on one of more roles as the situation demands.

Reading through the descriptions of each personality may make selection seem daunting. At the end of this section, we have included two flow charts to aid you in selecting the appropriate personality for the type of character you want to play.

Both charts ultimately lead to one of the sixteen personality types, but each looks at the personalities in a slightly different way.

Architect: The architect is a pragmatic person. They tend to observe a situation and gather information before they take action.

Their primary interest is learning how things are structured, built, and / or configured. They tend to think logically about a situation, and base their ideas on factual information rather than speculation.

In social situations, the Architect's tend to be logical. This adherence to logic coupled with the architect's tendency to point out inconsistencies and contradictions can alienate them from the group.

Artists: Artists live in the here and now. They tend to be in tune with their surroundings, including the people they surround themselves with. Artists are individualists. They do not like other people trying to run their lives and do not try to run the lives of others.

In social situations, an Artist will tend to be reserved. They will share information with the group, but only if they think they have something of value to add.

Champion: Champions are passionate individuals. They tend to have strong ethical and moral convictions. They value ideals like justice.

Once a champion chooses a cause they think is ethical, moral, and just, they become enthusiastic proponents of that cause.

In a social setting, the Champion tends to be a warm person whose deep, moving emotions and boundless enthusiasm are contagious. Champions share their thoughts and feelings with the world, using the strength of their convictions to motivate others.

Counselor: The Counselor values harmony and works to maintain peace whenever possible. They work well with others, and tend to put the needs of others above their own.

Despite this desire to contribute to the well-being of others and work harmoniously with the group, Counselors tend to be private people. They rarely share their own emotions. They internalize criticism, sometimes to the point of becoming physically ill because of it.

In social situations, Counselors are excellent listeners. They like to help others through difficult situations. In fact, they are the happiest when helping another. While they are quick to aid an individual, they are not quick to share their ideas with the group, often from fear of rejection. They are, however, quick to step in to try and preserve group unity and promote cooperation.

Crafter: As you may imagine, the crafter excels at crafting things. They tend to use any and every tool at their disposal to get the job done as efficiently as possible. Crafters tend to be introverted, and are not often comfortable spending time with others. They prefer to think and work alone to devise a plan of action once they have all the information.

In social settings, Crafters can be very forceful. They have already examined the evidence, reached a conclusion, and come up with a solution. Further debate or discussion on the subject is an unnecessary and inefficient use of time.

Czar: The Czar is a strategist. They tend to be very good at brainstorming to find a solution. They are pragmatic and decisive, but are open to new information, evidence, and ideas.

Czars tend to theorize about possibilities. They often have contingency plans to handle a wide variety of situations.

Though they make capable leaders, Czars do not enjoy leading others unless no one else is suited for the job. When they do lead, they confident leaders who tend to make decisions quickly… and, though they're are happy to listen to the input of others; they tend to make all of the decisions.

Czars tend to ignore the personal costs involved with implementing a particular plan of action. Once they have gathered the evidence, heard the arguments, and decided that a particular course is best for the group, they will often ignore others points of view.

Defender: The Defender is greatly concerned with the security of others. They find it satisfying to help the less fortunate, downtrodden or disabled. They tend to be uncomfortable being in a position of power, but are equally comfortable working alone or in a group. They tend to have a strong work ethic and can often push themselves too far while performing their duties.

Defenders abhor the squandering of resources. Some may argue that using resources to aid people outside of the group (or group members who are no longer useful to the group) during the zombie apocalypse *is* a waste of resources. That is a good way to make an enemy of a Defender.

Defenders are not comfortable in a world that is always changing. They value tradition and stability. They will tend to hold onto reminders of their past, even to the point of leaving behind vital resources to carry a treasured heirloom.

In social situations, Defenders are shy. They can seem cold, but they are warm people if (and when) you get know them.

Entertainers: Entertainers are the most fun-loving of all personality types. They dislike being alone. This does not present much of a problem because Entertainers seem to attract other people.

They derive considerable pleasure from delighting others, and are constantly in search of new experiences to share with their friends. Entertainers live in the moment, trusting that tomorrow will somehow take care of itself.

In social situations, Entertainers tend to be well-liked. They are eternal optimists, capable of finding the silver lining around any dark cloud. While Entertainers are most likely to succumb to temptation, they will usually not endanger themselves or others seeking new experiences.

General: As their name implies Generals are natural leaders. They are highly skilled at devising strategies and directing people to achieve the goal of that strategy. They also have a natural talent for being able to see the possibilities in an operation and plan for contingencies that might occur. The General is goal driven. He or she has a clear vision where the group is headed and a desire to communicate that to its members.

Despite the fact that they often make excellent leaders, Generals do not always seek leadership roles. If another capable leader is present, the General is happy to let them lead, offering advice when he has something to contribute. However, should this leadership fail or be absent entirely; the General will step up to the plate and take over.

The General values efficiency. They tend to break ideas down into base components and reconstruct them in their simplest forms. If established procedure can be shown to be inefficient, the General will abandon it immediately and work on formulating a new procedure.

In social situations, the General can seem can rub other people the wrong way. They do not often understand why others cannot see the clear goals that they have articulated. While they value the input of others, their logical and theoretical nature causes them to place a higher value on that of other intellectuals (Czars, Inventors, & Architects). They may seek the council of more tactical thinkers in the short term (Promoters, Crafters, Entertainers, & Artists), and may look to Visionaries (Teachers, Counselors, Champions, & Healers) to support their visions. They value the abilities of the Protectors (Supervisors, Inspectors, Providers, & Defenders) to implement their strategies and plans, but do not often seek their input when formulating them.

Healer: Healers, as the name implies, want to bring peace, health, and happiness to the people around them and to society at large. They are compassionate and empathic individuals who want to please others. They tend to be idealists who are passionate about the causes that interest them. This idealism and devotion can cause them to make sacrifices to see their causes grow.

Healers tend to be highly independent romantics. They tend to see the best in others. They are both thoughtful and considerate. Healers are good listeners and their good nature often puts others at ease.

In social situations, Healers are a mix of conundrums. On one hand, they are welcoming and understanding, but they also have high standards. These standards are often higher than the standards of those around them which can lead the Healer to try and take control of the situation.

Inspector: The Inspector carefully and thoroughly examines people and institutions. They are practical and decisive. Though they rarely seek positions of leadership, their thoroughness often sees them placed in these roles.

An Inspector values tradition, commitment, and perseverance. They would never think of dishonoring a contract, whether it's written or verbal. Their devotion to a cause is not dependent on reward, so their dedication can often go unnoticed and unappreciated.

In social situations, Inspectors are loyal and consistent. They take both their personal and professional lives very seriously. More importantly, they expect others to share these qualities. These traits coupled with their quiet demeanors can sometimes give the impression that the Inspector is shy or is a loner. However, once you get past this façade, it is hard to find a more loyal ally than the Inspector.

Inventor: The Inventor seeks new, practical ways to accomplish things. They have a knack for functional engineering, and are adept at discovering effective, pragmatic solutions as the need arises.

Inventors do not value tradition for tradition's sake. Just because something has always been done a certain way does not mean that there is not a better way to do it… or exclude the idea that you've always been doing it wrong.

Inventors are only interested in ideas that can be put into action or used to make or improve something. They do not play in the realm of the hypothetical just for the sake of theorizing. The Inventor's ability to improvise, modify, adapt, and overcome challenging situations make them excellent leaders, but only in situations that can keep their interest.

The Inventor is a non-conformist. In social situations, they tend to be laid back and non-judgmental. In social exchanges they inform rather than direct, making suggestions rather than decrees.

This tends to be one of their most off-putting qualities, however. If the people in charge dismiss a suggestion which the Inventor is passionate about, he or she will continue debate on the issue, promoting their idea while tearing apart that of their opposition. Most Inventors are skilled debaters, and this strategy can backfire, turning a potentially cooperative relationship into a combative one.

Promoter: The Promoter is the consummate salesperson. They are adept at finding what people want or need and selling them whatever the promoter has to sell. They are also king-makers, maneuvering people into positions of power… usually to the benefit of the promoter.

Promoters are very resourceful. They take the time to get to know influential people and use those contacts to their advantage.

In a social situation, the Promoter is always looking for ways to sell themselves and their ideas to others. They can be very persuasive, but are not above using every tool at their disposal to accomplish their goals.

Provider: The Provider is concerned with the health and welfare of those under their care. They are very sympathetic to the feelings of others. This often leads the Provider to be concerned what other people think of them. They are affectionate people who love and want to be loved. They can be easily crushed by criticism.

In social situations, Providers are out-going and friendly. They love to hear news about friends, family, and the community. They will strike up conversations with complete strangers, talking about anything that comes to mind.

Supervisor: Supervisors are civic-minded individuals. They strive to promote and maintain the institutions that keep society running smoothly. They trust in rules, policies, and procedures. They prefer tried and trusted methods over experimental methods.

In social situations, Supervisors are out-going. They clearly communicate their ideas and expectations to others. They are loyal friends and faithful spouses. They tend to be open and honest in their dealings and enjoy ceremony and ritual.

Teacher: Teachers tend to look for the best in people. They believe that everyone has the potential for greatness and expect people to work to reach that potential. They use their genuine belief in others to motivate people to continue to strive.

Teachers like to have things organized. They like to plan their days so that they know what to expect. Once made, they tend to honor their commitments.

Though they can be capable leaders, Teachers prefer educational leadership positions to social ones. They work toward personal growth, and it's often difficult for them to focus on other goals.

In social situations, Teachers often mirror the beliefs, characteristics, and emotions of the people they are interacting with to build rapport. Teachers use the knowledge of what's going on inside of themselves to provide insight into what's going on inside others.

If the Teacher has one major flaw, it is that the Teachers unwavering belief in the potential of others may unintentionally overpower those people, making them believe they are capable of things far beyond their grasp. This can have unintended consequences, and the Teacher must live with those every day of their lives.

Personality Traits

These examples tell us a little about each personality type. They will guide you when you wonder how your character will act in a given situation. They do not, however, explain the in-game effect that your character's personality will have on his or her chances of survival. To understand that, we'll first have to look at what traits make up each personality type.

The chart below shows the primary, secondary, and tertiary traits of each of the sixteen personality types. A brief definition of these traits follows the table below. These traits will be important to your character and his or her chances of continuing to be a playable character in the future.

Personality Category	Personality Type	Primary Trait (+1)	Secondary Trait (+2)	Tertiary Trait (+3)
Visionaries	Teacher	Diplomacy	Develop	Educate
	Counselor	Diplomacy	Develop	Guide
	Champion	Diplomacy	Mediate	Counsel
	Healer	Diplomacy	Mediate	Console
Intellectuals	General	Strategy	Arrange	Mobilize
	Czar	Strategy	Arrange	Entail
	Inventor	Strategy	Construct	Devise
	Architect	Strategy	Construct	Design
Protectors	Supervisor	Coordination	Regulate	Enforce
	Inspector	Coordination	Regulate	Verify
	Provider	Coordination	Support	Supply
	Defender	Coordination	Support	Secure
Creators	Promoter	Tactics	Expedite	Persuade
	Crafter	Tactics	Expedite	Instrument
	Entertainer	Tactics	Improvise	Demonstrate
	Artist	Tactics	Improvise	Synthesize

- ***Primary Traits***

Diplomacy: Diplomacy is the act of negotiation between two parties to reach a compromise.

Strategy: Strategy is a big-picture look at the situation and what you hope to accomplish.

Coordination: Coordination is the proper, orderly, and harmonious action of a group.

Tactics: Tactics are the small steps necessary to bring the big picture into view.

- ***Secondary Traits***

Develop: To develop something is to bring it from one level to the next.

Mediate: To mediate is to find the middle ground between two opposing ideas.

Arrange: To arrange is to organize components into their most useful version.

Construct: To construct is to create something from something else.

Regulate: To regulate is to control or direct by rule, principle, method, etc.

Support: To support is to sustain or maintain some object, plan or goal.

Expedite: To expedite is to speed up or hasten a process.

Improvise: To improvise is to make, provide, arrange, perform, or compose from whatever assets are readily available.

- ***Tertiary Traits***

Educate: To educate is to instruct or teach someone something.

Guide: To guide is to aid another, often by providing advice, to achieve their goal or reach their destination.

Counsel: To Counsel is to provide meaningful advice to another.

Console: To console is to comfort or provide solace to someone.

Mobilize: To mobilize is to assemble or marshal into a state of readiness for action.

Entail: To entail is to cause or involve someone by necessity for the good of the group and its goals even if it could potentially harm the individual so entailed.

Devise: To devise is to contrive, plan, elaborate, or invent something from existing principles or ideas.

Design: To design is to form or conceive of a plan or prepare a preliminary idea for something new.

Enforce: To enforce is to obtain compliance or compel obedience, usually through the threat or use of force.

Verify: To verify is to ascertain, prove, or confirm the truth of something.

Supply: To supply is to furnish or provide someone with what they are lacking or require to accomplish their goal.

Secure: To secure is to make safe by freeing from harm or danger.

Persuade: To persuade is to convince someone of something by appealing to reason or understanding.

Instrument: To instrument is to equip someone or something with tools or instruments.

Demonstrate: To demonstrate is to exhibit to show someone how to do something.

Synthesize: To synthesize is to form something by combining parts or elements.

Personality Trees

Sixteen personality types seems like a lot, but don't worry. On the following pages are two trees to help you choose your character's personality. If you sneak a peek ahead, the charts might seem daunting, but they're very user friendly. You can use either personality tree to reach your character's personality. Both trees lead to the same personalities. They just represent different ways of looking at the information. Just start at the left with the situation. Follow the tree along its path by choosing the branch that best suits your character. When you reach the right side of the tree, you'll know your character's personality.

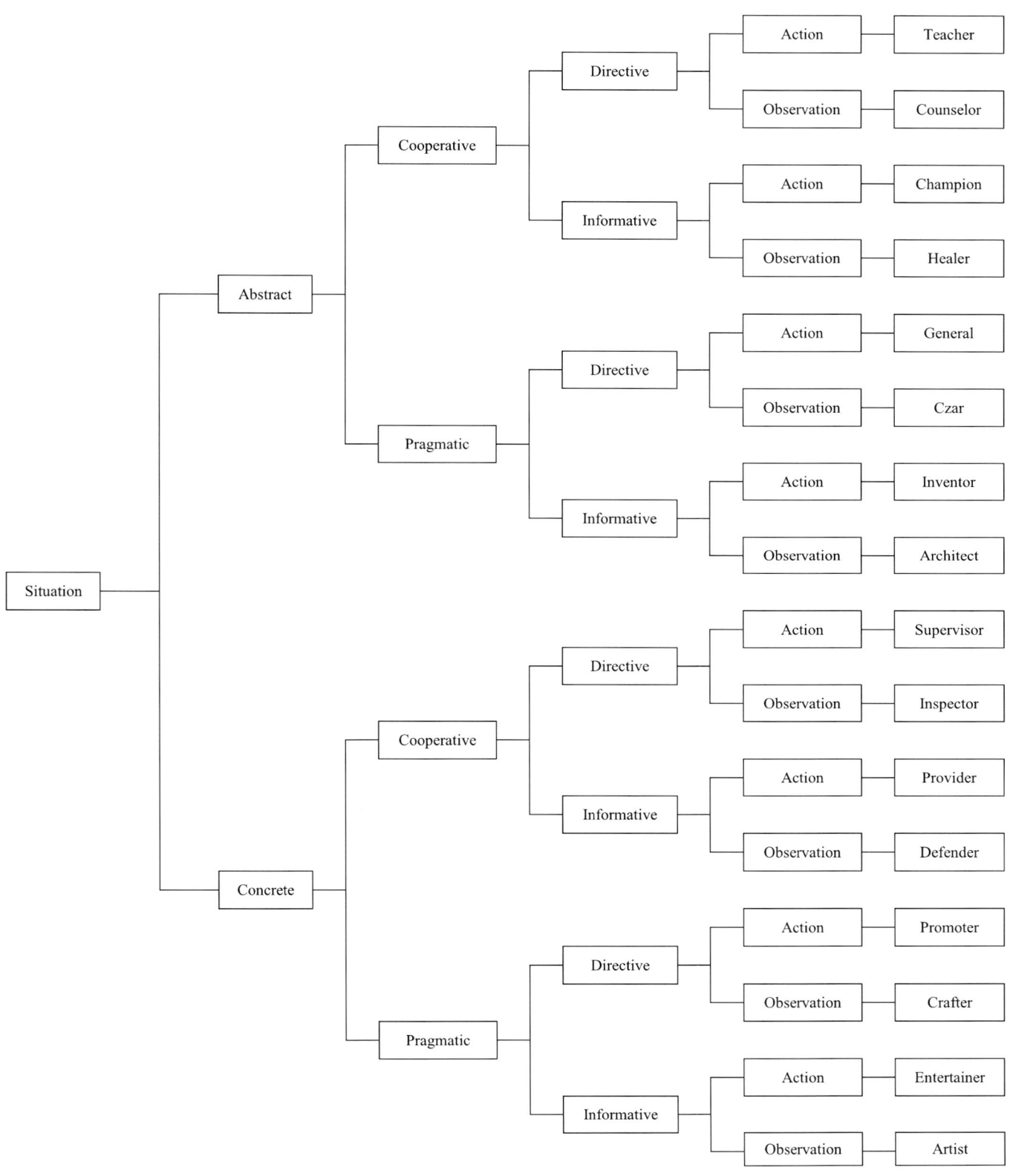

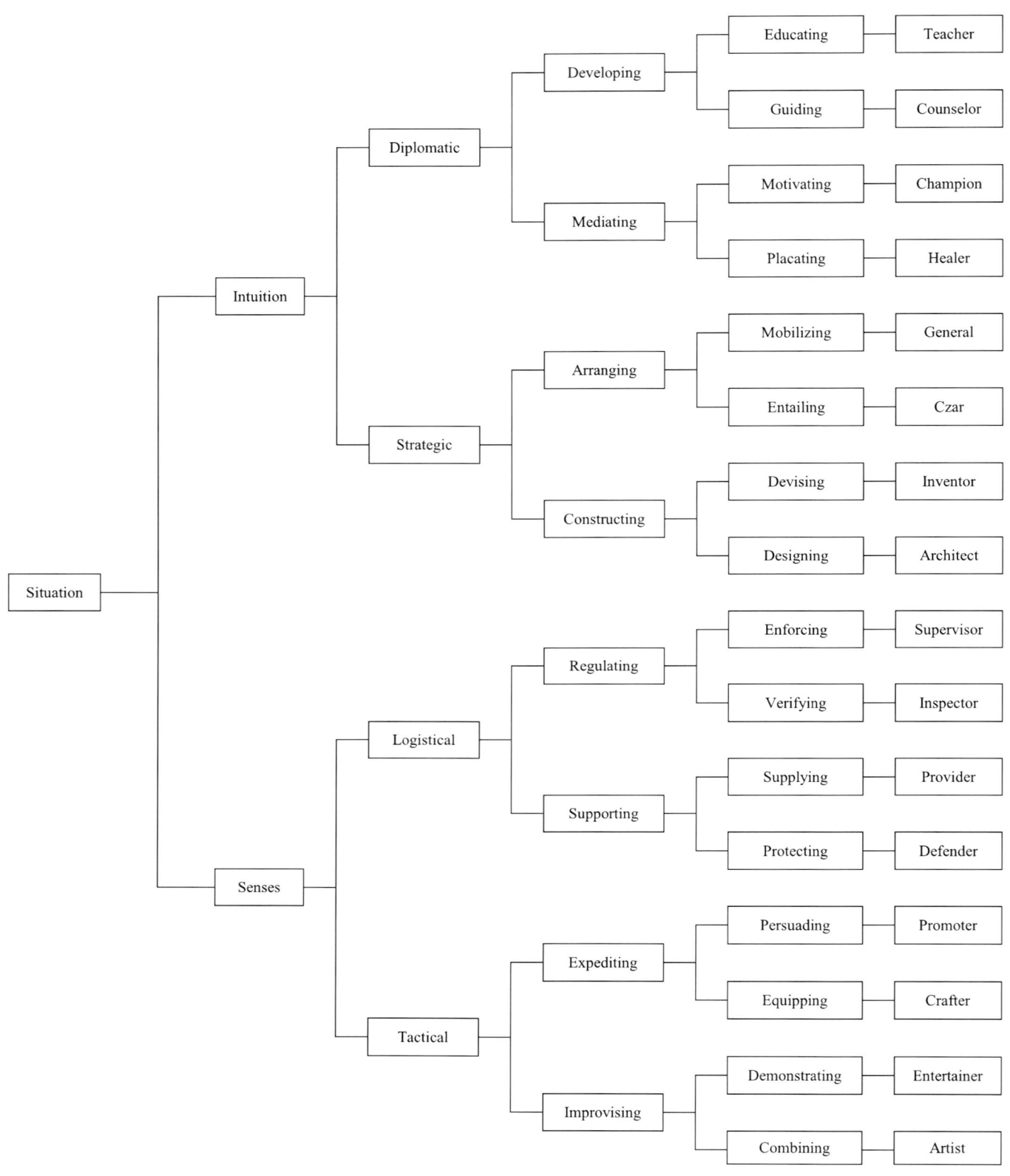

Parts of your Character

There is more to your character than his or her clique and personality. You will also need to determine your attributes, active skills, knowledge skills, advantages, and disadvantages. This is done with build points. We will cover how many build points you get in the next section, but, in order to know how to spend these points, you'll first need to know what you're spending them on.

➢ **Attributes**

Attributes represent your character's natural talents and aptitudes and the character's ability to use them to affect the world around them. Attributes are divided into two categories – Physical & Mental attributes. Beneath each description is a scale so that you know what each point of attribute represents. (The average human score are in bold.)

- *Physical Attributes*

Strength (STR): Your character's strength represents his or her ability to apply force to other people and the world around them. This is physical force and the ability to do work as they would be defined by physics.

1 – Physically Impaired
2 – Minimal Strength Training
3 – Occasional Strength Training
4 – Regular Strength Training
5 – Intense Regular Strength Training
6 – Maximum Human Strength

Coordination (CRD): Coordination represents your character's ability to coordinate movements of the eye to movements of the hand, or hand-eye coordination. It represents your character's natural talent to aim a weapon, throw a football, shoot a basket, and play video games.

1 – Below Human Average
2 – Normal Human Ability
3 – Minimal Practice
4 – Some Practice
5 – Regular Practice
6 – Superior Talent
7 – Superior Talent and Regular Practice
8 – Maximum Human Potential

Quickness (QCK): Quickness is a representation of your character's ability to move about the world. It represents grace, balance, and speed.

1 – Clumsy
2 – Normal Human Ability
3 – Some Regular Practice
4 – Intense Regular Practice
5 – Olympic Level Athletic Talent
6 – Olympic Level Gymnastic Talent
7 – Maximum Human Potential

Constitution (CON): Your character's constitution score represents your character's health and stamina. It is your character's body's ability to resist physical damage and fight disease.

1 – Unhealthy
2 – Minimal Exercise
3 – Occasional Exercise
4 – Regular Exercise
5 – Intensive Regular Exercise
6 – Maximum Human Endurance

- *Mental Attributes*

Reason (RSN): As you might suspect, your character's reason score represents their ability to utilize logic and reason. It represents his or her ability to process and use information.

1 – Below Average Human Intelligence
2 – Average Human Intelligence
3 – Above Average Intelligence
4 – Superior Intelligence
5 – Very Superior Intelligence
6 – Gifted
7 – Genius
8 – Prodigy

Insight (INS): The insight score is a representation of your character's intuition and his or her ability to pick up on things around them. Where reason is your cognitive thought, insight is more of an instinct or gut feeling.

1 – Oblivious to Surroundings
2 – A Little Slow on the Up Take
3 – Normal Human Intuition
4 – Above Average Intuition
5 – A Fine Eye for Detail
6 – Strong Gut Feelings or Intuition
7 – In Tune with the World Around You
8 – Nothing Escapes You

Psyche (PSY): Your character's psyche represents your character's mental endurance. It is your character's willpower as well as their ability to resist mental trauma and stun damage.

1 – Easily Dominated or Influenced
2 – Young or Hampered Sense of Will
3 – Normal Human Will
4 – Strong Personal Convictions
5 – A Personal Code
6 – Highly Developed Self-Esteem
7 – Strong Sense of Self
8 – Indomitable Willpower

Charisma (CHA): Charisma is your character's ability to influence the people around him or her. It represents your character's ability to persuade others to his or her line of thinking. It is also your character's ability to impress and entertain other people.

1 – Socially Impaired
2 – Socially Inept
3 – Normal Human Charisma
4 – Well-Liked or Personable
5 – Influential
6 – Very Influential
7 – Highly Influential
8 – Maybe Too Influential

➢ **Active Skills**

Active skills represent a real and practical understanding of a subject matter. As such, these are the skills your character will most likely depend upon to survive.

Most active skills are the result of some kind of training or intense practice. This is important to keep in mind when you're choosing your skills. There are some skills that a high school student just wouldn't have any training in or ability to practice. Your director is well within his or her right to ask where and why your character learned a particular skill.

When this happens, you should have a plausible answer ready. If you don't, the director might require that you reallocate this skill points. (Of course, between video games and Wisconsin's hunting tradition, almost everyone knows how to fire a gun.)

Active skills provide the best possible chance of success when you're trying to accomplish something. Using a weapon, building or repairing a vehicle, or operating a computer are all examples of active skills.

➢ **Knowledge Skills**

Knowledge skills represent the things your character knows. Knowledge skills don't usually *do* things. Instead they represent an academic understanding of the subject matter. You can gain a rudimentary knowledge of almost anything just by visiting a library or going online.

Do not discount the importance of knowledge skills; however, even an academic understanding of certain skills can help you accomplish certain tasks. In many cases, as those of us who lived through the 80s are well aware, "knowing is half the battle!"

For example, I'm no mechanic, but I understand the science behind an internal combustion engine. This scientific knowledge isn't always enough to help me make the necessary repairs to my vehicles, but it's usually enough to give me a good idea what's going wrong. I generally know how serious the problem is and if the mechanic I'm asking to complete the repairs is trying to rip me off. (See defaulting on a skill check on page 107.)

➢ **Advantage**

Advantages are things that give your character an edge. They usually represent aptitudes or special abilities that will help your character survive and flourish. These might be the result of careful planning on the part of your character, the result of years of conditioning, or the manifestation of a recessive genetic trait.

➢ **Disadvantages**

Disadvantages are things that have a detrimental effect on your character. The represent serious character flaws or other quirks that can (and will) get your character into trouble. You should take care when selecting your disadvantages. The director can, should, and probably will exploit them at every opportunity.

Building your Character

While reading the descriptions of the various cliques you might have noticed statements that certain cliques receive certain advantages at no cost to them. The cost mentioned is the number of build points spent to gain a particular advantage.

Each character starts with a base of 100 character points, and 1-18 bonus build points. To determine the exact number of points you will have to spend on your character roll 2 10-sided dice and add the results. Remember that the 0 (or 10) on your die counts as 0 in the d10 system. This means that every character will begin with between 100 and 118 build points plus the points for his or her race.

These build points will be spent to purchase your character's attribute scores, active skills, and any advantages you might want for your character.

Additional build points can be gained by taking disadvantages for your character. Each of these disadvantages has a real effect on game play and your character. It is not easy to get rid of a disadvantage once it is taken, so disadvantages should not be taken lightly.

The exact number of additional points that can be gained through disadvantages is up to your director. We recommend setting a maximum of 18 points gained in such a manner, though characters would be wise to take much less.

> ➢ **Buying Attributes**

You purchase your character's attributes with his or her available build points. Physical attributes cost three build points per attribute point. Mental attributes cost two build points per attribute points.

Physical Attribute = 3 build pts. per 1 attribute pt.

Mental Attributes = 2 build pts. per 1 attribute pt.

You must purchase at least one point in each attribute. A chart near the clique you chose for your character shows the maximum starting rank for every attribute for each clique. You character's starting attributes cannot exceed this attribute maximum at the beginning of play unless you purchase an advantage that allows it.

A table is reprinted on this page so that you don't have to flip back to the cliques. This table also includes a listing of human minimums and maximums for your consideration.

Clique	STR	CRD	QCK	CON	RSN	INS	PSY	CHA
Academics	3	3	4	3	6	4	4	4
Creators	3	5	4	3	5	5	4	4
Drifters	3	4	4	3	3	5	4	5
Gamers	3	5	4	3	4	4	4	4
Jocks	4	5	5	5	3	4	4	4
Outcasts	3	3	4	4	4	4	5	3
Performers	3	5	4	3	3	4	4	5
Socialites	3	4	4	3	3	5	4	6
Technicians	3	4	4	3	5	4	4	4
Human Min	1	1	1	1	1	1	1	1
Human AVG	2	2	3	2	2	3	3	3
Human Max	6	8	7	6	7	8	8	6

➤ Selecting Active Skills

Once you've purchased your attributes it's time to choose your active skills. When purchasing an active skill, it is important to note which attribute governs that skill. This will determine how much it costs for each level of the skills.

If the skill rank is less than or equal to the governing attribute score, it costs only one build point to raise the skill one level. If the skill rank is greater than the attribute score, it costs two build points to raise the skill one level.

You cannot begin play with a skill ranking higher than twice the score of the governing attribute.

Skill ≤ Attribute: 1 build point per skill point

Skill > Attribute: 2 build points per skill point

For example, if your character has a Quickness attribute of 4 and wants to select the Dance skill, each level of dance will cost one point up to rank 4. After rank for, each rank in the skill will cost 2 points up to the character's starting maximum skill rank of 8.

Let's say that you want your character to have a dance skill at rank 7, one rank below the maximum possible starting rank for the skill. It would cost this character 4 build points to raise the skill to rank 4 and 6 addition points to raise the skill to rank 7.

➤ Selecting Knowledge Skills

Unlike active skills, you do not *need* to purchase Knowledge Skills using build points. Instead, your character is given seven points per point of reason to spend on Knowledge skills. (As their clique bonus, members of the Academic clique get 10 points per point of Reason with which to purchase Knowledge skills.) These points can only be spent on Knowledge skills. However, if you want additional knowledge skills, you're certainly welcome to use build points to purchase them.

Other than this difference, Knowledge skills are purchased and limited in the same way that active skills are. It still costs one point per rank to purchase a Knowledge skill up to the level of the governing attribute (which is the character's Reason score for all knowledge skills) and two points per rank in the skill above the governing attribute score up to a maximum of twice the character's Reason score.

Also, unlike active skills, the list of knowledge skills presented later in this book is just examples. This list is by no means comprehensive. It is simply the knowledge skills we used during play testing. If you want your character to have a knowledge skill we did not list, talk to your director. Use the existing skills as a guideline and create a new knowledge skill for use in your game.

• *Languages & Literacy*

Language and Literacy are important in the modern world. While we use these skills every day, they are knowledge skills rather than active skills, and, as such, are purchased using knowledge skill points.

Language and Literacy skills differ from other knowledge skills is a number of ways. Language will be covered more in depth at the end of the knowledge skill section, but we'll cover the differences here to (hopefully) avoid any confusion later.

First, every character begins play with a language and a literacy skill in their native language at no cost to them. This initial level is determined by the character's reason.

Second, unlike every other skill in the game, raising these skills is not dependent on your reason score.

Third, Language and Literacy skills have a skill level maximum that is not dependent on the character's reason score and does not change as the character improves. (We'll cover improving your character at the end of the player section.)

Fourth, if your character knows more than one language, the second language is capped at a lower level than his or her native tongue.

Fifth, you will rarely, if ever, actually roll your language skill. The skill levels will define your ability to use that language.

Finally, there are languages you can learn that no one speaks. These languages not only cost more to learn, but they have an even lower cap than a secondary language would.

➤ Choosing Advantages

After you've completed all of the above steps, you get to pick advantages for your character if you want them. No character is required to take any advantages. If you wanted to, you could even voluntarily refuse any advantage gained from your clique. Of course, since you would not gain a replacement for a refused advantage, it might not be the wisest decision.

After the name of each advantage is a number representing the build point cost for choosing this advantage. Be sure to read the description of each advantage. Consider not only how this would affect your character from a mechanical perspective, but how it works into your character concept.

As cool as some advantages might sound, they might not fit with your character concept. If that happens, try to stay true to your character concept. After all, there's a really, really good chance that your character will not remain playable during the course of the zombie apocalypse. If (and when) that happens, you can always make a new character and work the new advantage into that character's concept.

You might have already spent all of your available build points by this stage. This leaves you with two options. You can either reassign points you had already spent or choose disadvantages to gain additional build points.

This was not unintentional. Advantages are unique advantages. It's unlikely that any character would have more than a few of them and certainly less than a handful. Allowing the player to select them earlier would have made them more common place.

> **Disadvantages**

To gain additional build points, you can always take disadvantages. Each disadvantage gives you additional points again shown after the name of the disadvantage. Even more than with advantages, it is important to carefully read the description of each disadvantage. Take the time to consider how it will affect your character mechanically, and how it might fit in with your character concept.

In some games there are advantages that don't seem to have a real effect on game play. I assure you that this is not the case in our d10 system. Each of your flaws will have a profound effect on your character. Every disadvantage has real in-game consequences for your character, so be sure to choose disadvantages that you and your character will be able to live with. These disadvantages represent real character flaws for your character. Once they have been chosen, it is extremely difficult (and in some cases impossible) to remove them.

More than one character has met his or her demise because of disadvantages that the player chose without thinking of the consequences because he or she wanted a few extra build points. Do not fall into this trap.

That being said, most people have a flaw or two. These flaws help to make us unique individuals. In many ways, who we are is determined more by our flaws than our virtues. All you have to do is turn on any television news program to find evidence of how true that is. Also, to paraphrase Elizabeth Taylor, the problem with people who have no flaws is that you can be pretty sure they're going to have some very annoying virtues.

➤ Dice Pools

Each character has three different dice pools that can be used to augment certain activities. Most often, these pools will come into play during combat. With rare exception, once the dice in these pools are used, they are unavailable until the character rolls for initiative again or, outside of combat. When used outside of combat, the pools refresh at the end of a given scene. If there is any question as to what a scene is, the director will make the official determination.

There are some exceptions to this rule, however. Dice from one of these pools used to augment a roll to resist fatigue or the effects of sleep deprivation do not refresh until the character either rests or sleeps. In effect, being tired or fatigued reduces the characters dice pools.

Likewise, dice used to activate an *Adrenaline Surge* also do not replenish until after the character has rested. This is done to represent the drain that such a surge has on the body. (see Adrenaline Surge on page 106)

Action Pool: The character's action pool is derived from adding together their coordination, quickness, reason, & insight and dividing the result in half.

For the mathematically inclined, the equation would look like this:

$$(CRD+QCK+RSN+INS)/2$$

Dice from the action pool can be used to augment almost any active skill. Action pool dice are also used to dodge attacks (see dodging on page 111).

Vigor Pool: The number of dice in your vigor pool is determined by adding together your strength, quickness, constitution, & psyche and dividing the result by 2.

For the mathematically inclined, the equation looks something like this:

$$(STR+QCK+CON+PSY)/2$$

The dice from your vigor pool are used to resist physical damage. They may also be used to augment rolls where the character's health comes into play, such as resisting a disease or the effects of alcohol.

Willpower Pool: Your willpower pool is determined by adding all of the character's mental attributes and dividing that result by 2.

For the mathematically inclined, the equation would look like this:

$$(RSN+INS+PSY+CHA)/2$$

Willpower dice are used to resist mental damage. These dice can also be used to resist enervation from casting spells. They may also be used to bolster the character's resistance to seduction, bribery, or other feats of will.

NOTE: Unless indicated by an advantage or decree from the director, even if a particular roll might qualify for augmentation by more than one dice pool, only the dice from one pool can be used.

➤ Determining your Gaff Scores

Gaffing is the act of soaking damage. An attack that you gaff still hits the character. There may even be physical indications that such a wound occurred. A knife will cut you. A bat will leave a bruise. A bullet makes a hole.

When your character gaffs a wound, he or she simply isn't hampered by the damage. It doesn't affect their ability to continue to perform. In the d10 system, we only keep track of damage that actually inhibits your character's ability to accomplish their goals.

For each success on your gaffing roll, your character will gaff or soak a number of points of damage equal to his or her gaff score for that type of damage.

Mental Gaff Score: The amount of mental damage your character gaffs with each success if equal to his or her psyche divided by two. Again, round the way that you learned to round in school.

Physical Gaff Score: Your physical gaff is equal to your constitution score divided by two. Remember to round the way you learned in school

➤ Determining Hit Points

There are three types of wounds in the d10 system. These wounds and the damage that causes them will be discussed at length in the health and healing section (see health and healing on page 118). For now all you need to know is that your character has three different types of hit points and five wound levels.

The five wound levels are – Light, Moderate, Serious, Critical, and Nearly Unconscious or Fatal (though fatal wounds are not always actually deadly, they can be.) For each wound level beyond light damage, the character suffers a cumulative penalty of -1 die to certain dice rolls. Gaffing tests are not affected by wound level penalties.

Body Hit Points: The character has a number of points for *each wound level* equal to his or her *Constitution* score.

Mind Hit Points: The character has a number of points for *each wound level* equal to his or her *Psyche* score.

Soul Hit Points: The character has a number of points for *each wound level* equal to his or her *Charisma* score.

How damage is applied, gaffed, and healed will be covered more in-depth in the Health and Healing section on page 118. For now it is enough to determine your character's numbers for each of the three hit point scores.

➢ **Starting Equipment**

Selecting and purchasing starting equipment is a time consuming process in most games. It often takes longer to equip your character than it took to make the character in the first place. This can be very frustrating to both the director and other players.

Some games attempt to alleviate this problem, some games create packages of starting equipment for you to select. You decide you want to be a warrior, so you take the warrior starting equipment package.

While this does speed up the process, it has some unintended consequences. The most egregious of these consequences is limiting the creativity of players.

This is, after all, a role-playing game. We're asking people to create and take on the persona of a unique character in a game world unlike any they're likely to encounter in the real world. Then, after all that work, we're making the characters all identical if only superficially.

This game is a little different. Since you're playing the role of a high school student, chances are that your character didn't buy his starting equipment anyway. Furthermore, unless your character is lucky enough to be standing at home plate when the zombie apocalypse begins, he or she is unlikely to have any weapons on them. If you've played any video game where zombies are the enemy, you know that scavenging for resources is part of the genre.

To determine your starting equipment, simply make a list of the things you think your character might reasonably carry. Share the list with your director. If he or she doesn't think your character would have something with them when the game begins, he or she will ask you about it. You can explain to the director why you think your character would have the item or items in question, and the director will decide if you are being reasonable.

As with everything else, the director has the final say in what your character can begin the game with.

I, for example, have carried the same basic things with me since before my freshman year of high school.

- Wallet
- Keys
- Pocket Knife
- Handkerchief
- Leather Belt
- Stainless Steel Carbiner
- Steel-toed high-top basketball shoes

When I learned to drive, I added car keys to my key ring. When I got my first pocket-sized cell phone, I started to carry that too. (Yes, I am old enough to pre-date cell phones. In fact, my first cell phone was slightly larger than my wife's purse and the handset was connected to the base by a cord.)

Looking at that list, there are a few questions you (or a director) might ask. Why do I carry a knife? Why do I wear steel-toes shoes, and do they even exist outside of work boots? Why do I carry a lighter? Who carries a handkerchief anymore? Why do you wear a belt if your pants fit? What's with the carbiner?

Each of these questions can be easily answered.

I carry a knife because you never know when you're going to need one. Any knife that is not a switch blade and has a blade of smaller than 3 inches is considered a tool, so there is nothing illegal about carrying one.

I wore (and wear) steel-toed shoes because I've worked a lot of jobs where they were either required or wearing them was highly recommended. Once I learned that they made steel-toed shoes that weren't work boots, I started to wear them almost exclusively. (I still haven't found steel-toed shoes to wear with a tuxedo, but I'm not giving up hope.)

I carried a lighter when I was younger because there was a store in the city where I grew up that sold firecrackers very cheaply. We would save our pennies and buy a brick of firecrackers. (I didn't say I was smart.)

I carry a handkerchief for two reasons. First, they make a quick bandage in a pinch and I carried a knife and played with firecracker. Second, the handkerchief I carry is a monogrammed handkerchief that my great grandfather used to carry.

I always wear a belt because once, when I was much younger, my brother and I were paying by a culvert that allowed the creek to flow through the town. He slid down the hill and couldn't climb back up. I couldn't reach him, so I had to sneak home and get a rope. I got caught, and we got in trouble for playing in the culverts… something about the muskrats that made their nests in them. If I had been wearing a belt, I wouldn't have had to race home, we wouldn't have gotten caught, and, most importantly, I wouldn't have gotten in trouble. I've worn a belt ever since.

Finally, when I was younger, I rode my bike a lot. In a brisk wind, my baseball cap flew off. The carbiner allowed me to attach it to my belt loop so I wouldn't lose it. When I got older, the same held true on my motorcycle, so I still carry one (two if you count the one on my key ring).

Those are all plausible explanations, but, truth be told, I wouldn't have batted an eye at that list of equipment. There is nothing in that list that, by itself, would have any effect on the character's survival. There are items, however, that would help the character get items to aid his or her survival.

Keys have specific functions. The character probably has a key to his or her house. There are definitely supplies located there… since this is Wisconsin, there's a good chance that there's a weapon or three there as well.

A knife isn't just for cutting. They have a wide variety of uses. I've used my trusty pocket knife to pop the locks on a window and get into the house when *someone's* mother got the key stuck in the door. If the knife hadn't worked, the folded handkerchief could have helped protect my hand from the shards of glass when we broke the window.

The wallet might seem useless. The money inside wouldn't be worth much at the end of the world. However, a firm plastic card like a driver's license can make short work of a door without a deadbolt.

Belts make great slings if you don't have another alternative. (It's not a fun lesson to learn, so I don't recommend researching this on your own.)

Steel-toed shoes speak for themselves. Besides protecting your toes if you drop a rock while picking stones, they also protect your toes while you're kicking something or someone.

Skills

Skills represent the things that your character has learned and knows how to do. As you should probably know by now, skills fall into two categories – Active & Knowledge. Your character can, should, and will have skills from each category.

Remember to keep your character concept in mind when you're selecting skills. I know I've said this at least once already, but it's important enough to repeat. Don't just take skills you want your character to have. Take skills that represent your character's interests and areas of study before the zombie apocalypse.

Unless your character was an outcast (and, in this case, a nut-job) who devoted his life to planning for and surviving the zombie apocalypse to the exclusion of everything else, your character is going to have some skills that don't directly pertain to survival. Even someone who's a survivalist will have skills that won't due him or her any good in this scenario.

Keep in mind that skills, to a large degree, are abstract concepts. Their purpose is to provide a mechanic with which to resolve character actions and add an element of chance to the game. They are not intended to represent actual or realistic human abilities.

In the real world, there is a difference between swinging an axe and swinging a sword. In fact, there is a difference between swinging different types of axes and swords. Someone who is skilled at fencing is not necessarily capable of wielding a claymore effectively much less a fireman's axe.

In the game world, all of these weapons fall under the bladed weapon skill. Creating a separate skill for each and every weapon would slow down every aspect of playing the game and wouldn't really add any meaningful differences. Most importantly, the end result of this approach would serious hamper everyone's enjoyment of the game.

Of course, it is possible for someone to choose to practice with and become more adept with a specific weapon. If you want your character to specialize in a specific type of edged weapon, or be better at a more restrictive classification of another skill, skill specialization might be the answer. (See skill specialization on page 79)

What follows is a list of active and then knowledge skills. The attribute that governs each active skill is listed in parentheses after the name of the skill. A brief description of the skill follows. Use this description to help you determine how the skill can be used.

Some skills, particularly knowledge skills, are followed by an "X". When this occurs, the player must specify what the "X" is. For example, if the player chooses the "Build / Craft X" skill for their character, they must specify what the character can build or craft. If there is a question, the director will determine whether the player's choice is appropriate.

Some skills below are preceded with one of two symbols - either a "♪" or a "♫". A "♪" indicates that the skill in question is not common to a high school student and the player must explain why his or her character has a particular skill. A "♫" indicates that the skill is extremely rare for a high school student. Not only must the player explain why his or her character has the skill in question, but the skill character cannot begin play with more ranks in the skill that he or she has points in the governing attribute.

NOTE: The inclusion of a particular skill is only an acknowledgement that such a skill (or close facsimile to said skill) exists in the real world and that players might find it interesting to play characters that possess a variety of skills, some of which they themselves would never have or use in real life. At **NO TIME** should the listing of **ANY** skill under either active or knowledge skills be misconstrued to infer, imply, hint, or otherwise indicate that we, in any way, condone the use of **ANY** skills for **ANY** purpose whatsoever!!!

This is just a game.

Active Skills

Acrobatics (QCK): This skill is used to determine your character's success in acrobatic or gymnastic feats like jumping to grab a swinging chandelier or back flip over a balcony railing to land safely below.

Acting (CHA): Acting is more than just pretending to be someone or something you are not. (That's dating and is covered under the seduction skill.) Acting is becoming someone you are not... it's taking on different mannerisms, different voices, different speech patterns, different accents... and doing it all in a believable way.

Appraise (RSN): The appraise skill allows you to determine the relative quality and value of something (or someone) else. Use this skill to assess the value of an object... giving your character the abilities necessary to begin a lucrative career in any number of reality television shows based on the operation of a pawn shop.

This skill will also help you size up an opponent during a fight. Using appraise your character can tell if is stronger, faster, smarter, and more skilled then he or she is.

Athletics (QCK): Athletics is the skill that governs sports related abilities. It is not the ability to throw a ball, hit a ball, or tackle an opponent. Those are combat skills. It is also not the ability to understand the rules. That is a knowledge skill. This is, however, the ability to catch a thrown ball or a pop fly to center field. It's the ability to run a screen play or get a rebound.

Awareness (INS): The awareness skill represents your character's ability to notice things around them. This skill is used to both spot something out of the ordinary and hear a strange noise.

Beguile: The beguile skill is used when you're trying to deceive someone else. It is specifically the skill you use when you're lying. It doesn't matter if it's a fib (a little white lie) or masterful con used to deceive and defraud people. This skill is a must for anyone sending out emails on behalf of the Nigerian ministry of finance...

♪ Build / Craft X (RSN): This skill is actually a whole bunch of skills. Each time you take this skill, you choose a specific thing your character is capable of building or crafting. It

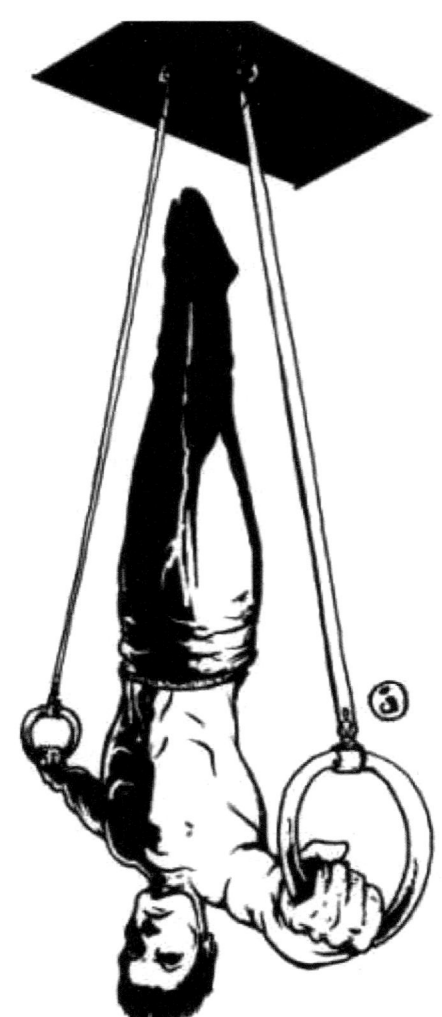

might be building automobile or craft woodwind instrument or anything else you can feasibly imagine your building or crafting.

♪ Cartography (RSN): This is the skill in making maps. Almost anyone at the high school level knows how to read a map, but a person with this skill knows how to make a usable map of a given area. With enough time and information, they could make a comprehensive map of just about anything.

Climb (STR): This skill represents is the character's ability to climb things. Everything from a jungle gym to those ropes that hang from the ceiling of the gymnasium for no explicable reason is covered by the climb skill.

Computer Operation (RSN): The computer operation skill is the character's ability to operate a computer... in case you couldn't tell by the name. This skill governs your character's use of operating systems, ability to navigate menus, using drag & drop applications to create web pages, and aptitude for playing video games not covered by other skills.

♪ Computer Programming (RSN): This skill is your character's ability to read, understand, and write code. While the computer operations skill lets you create a simple web page using a drag and drop application, the computer programming skill will allow you to actually code a web page from scratch.

♪ Cryptography (RSN): The cryptography skill is your character's ability to write and decipher codes of all shapes and sizes. Everything from simple word scrambles to the complex enigma code of WWII is covered by the cryptography skill. (NOTE: As our enemies learned firsthand during WWII, it will not help you decipher an actual language... like Navaho... for example.)

Dance (QCK): The dance skill is your character's ability to move with rhythm and grace to music. Whether your character aspires to be a background dancer in a hip hop video or a prima ballerina, dance is the skill that will get them there.

Dangineering (RSN): Some people call it jury rigging... or a variety of more colorful and less socially acceptable terms. Sometimes you don't have the time, money, or equipment necessary to do the job right, but the job needs to be done nonetheless. When your car needs a $300.00 repair so you can continue to go to work and you only have $12.00 to your name, you danigneer it. It won't look pretty, but it doesn't have to. It just has to work.

♫ **Demolitions (RSN):** Demolitions is the ability to safely and effectively use explosives. Anyone can light a stick of dynamite and throw it at something or someone. A person with the demolition skill understands using the right charge for the job. They understand how to tamp or shape the charge to direct the blast for the optimum effect. Most importantly, they know how to do it while keeping all of their fingers.

Discern Lie (INS): This is the ability to know when someone is trying to lie to your character. This ability won't tell your character exactly what the lie is, but it will let the character know that someone is being less than truthful.

Disguise (CHA): The disguise skill is the ability to change your character's appearance. It covers everything from the proper application of makeup for the school play (or a night on the town) to creating the perfect cosplay makeup for the aliens in your favorite science fiction anime.

Drawing (INS): To most people drawing is simply putting pen to paper and making a picture. That's like saying plopping dough on a metal sheet is making chocolate chip cookies. Drawing is knowing how to bring elements together to create an image. It's using lines of varying thickness to show weight and light. It's as much about what you don't put on the paper as it is what you do.

Drive (QCK): The drive skill governs the use of all land-based vehicles from motorcycles and ATVs to cars and buses. It represents your character's ability to operate and control the vehicle.

Edged Weapons (CRD): The edged weapons skill is used anytime your character is trying to hit an opponent with something sharp that is not thrown, hurled, launched, or fired.

♫ **Escape Artist (QCK):** The escape artist skill allows your character to escape bonds and locations that are not secured by a lock. Slipping out of roles, duct tape, or other bindings is governed by this skill as is fitting through an air duct or small window.

Fast-Talk (CHA): Fast-talk is similar to the beguile skill in many regards. They are both used in similar situations. There is one important difference, however. Fast-talk is your character's ability to worm his or her way out of trouble without actually lying.

Firearms (CRD): The firearms skill is your character's ability to load, aim, and shoot any number of firearms.

Fishing (INS): The fishing skill gives the character the knowledge and ability to use fishing gear and other instruments commonly used in fishing. It does not guarantee that the character will actually catch a fish, however. (In the words of Captain Clarence Pryne, that's why they call it fishing and not catching.)

♪ **Forgery (CRD):** Forgery is the ability to duplicate someone else's handwriting, particularly their signature. This skill comes in handy when writing absence excuses or signing progress reports… among other things.

Gambling (CHA): The gambling skill covers games of chance and wagers placed on those games. It is your ability to know when hold 'em, know when to fold 'em, know when to walk away, and know when to run.

♫ **Gunnery (RSN):** The gunnery skill represents training in firing vehicle mounted weapons. There is not much call to be able to do this in high school, so this is probably the rarest skills in the game. Still, I could come up with a few ways a character might gain some small level of experience in this skill. If you can too, and you can sell it to the director, your character will have a few dice to throw if your party ever comes across an APC with a turret mounted cannon.

Hide (QCK): This is your character's ability to conceal him or her self so that they remain unseen and undiscovered. The hide skill does not help your character move unseen (that's the sneak skill). Hide is specifically finding a hiding place and hiding there.

Impact Weapons (CRD): This skill is your character's ability to hit an opponent with a blunt object like a club or a baseball bat. With blades and bullets available, you might be tempted to ignore blunt weapons, but blunt force trauma is a staple of crime dramas for a reason.

Interrogation (CHA): The interrogation skill is the ability to use fear and intimidation to convince someone to reveal information that they do not want known.

Interview (CHA): Though the word interview conjures up images of reporters, the interviewing skill is not sitting across from someone and asking them questions. Instead it is knowing how to get someone else to give you the information you want without resorting to threats, fear, or intimidation. Often times the target of a successful interview doesn't even know that they were being interviewed.

Intimidation (STR *or* CHA): Intimidation is the ability to strike fear into another person usually for the purposes of eliciting compliance to a demand or obedience to an order.

Unlike most skills, the intimidation skill can be governed by one of two attributes – Strength or Charisma. Each represents a different approach to intimidation. The character might try to intimidate others through a mixture of size and presence (STR) or they might intimidate through precisely worded threats and seeming cold with calculated indifference (CHA).

When selecting this skill, the player must choose which of these two attributes will govern the skill for his or her character. Once this decision is made, it cannot be changed. However, it is possible for a character to possess both versions

of this skill. If the player chooses to take both versions of the intimidation skill for their character, it is considered two completely separate skills.

Jump (STR): The jump skill represents your character's ability to jump. This includes high jumps, long jumps, and the ever popular running long jump.

Launch Weapons (RSN): The launch weapons skill governs your character's ability to use primitive direct and indirect fire siege weapons. Launch weapons have fallen into disuse since the advent of gun powder… except in backyards and playgrounds. Launch weapons include things like catapults and trebuchets.

Navigation (RSN): Navigation is the ability to ascertain, plot, and control the course or position of a vehicle. This skill allows you to read maps, use compasses, and understand what your GPS is telling you to do.

Negotiation (CHA): Negotiation is the art of convincing someone else to give you something you want in exchange for something you don't want anymore. Though your character's goal in negotiations is to gain favorable terms, the negotiations skill is an honest discussion. Dishonest negotiations are governed by either the beguile or fast-talk skills.

Oration (CHA): This skill represents you character's ability to "speechify". Oration is public speaking. This skill can be used to inform or motivate others.

Painting (INS): This skill is not the skill used to paint your character's bedroom walls… unless your character's bedroom walls are a fantastic mural. Like drawing, the painting skill is for creating works of art. It is about composition, perspective, scale, shape, and color.

♪ **Pick Locks (CRD):** The pick locks skill allows your character to manipulate the internal workings of a lock to trick the lock into opening without the key by using a pick and a tension rod. This skill does not cover combination locks, which are the province of the safe-cracking skill.

Pilot Watercraft (CRD): The pilot watercraft skill allows your character to steer a watercraft. This skill provides knowledge and understanding boat operations and the effects of waves, current, and weather on the boat's travel.

NOTE: This skill does not cover the piloting of ships, just boats and personal watercraft. If you do not know the difference, boats are smaller craft used for rivers, inland waters, and littoral waters. Ships, on the other hand, are much bigger with a much longer range. Though it is not 100% accurate, a good rule of thumb is that a boat can fit on a ship, but s hip cannot fit on a boa.

Play Musical Instrument X (INS): This skill allows your character to play a musical instrument. As with other skills followed by an "X", you must select which instrument your character knows how to play when you choose the skill. This skill can be selected multiple times with each skill applying to a different instrument.

Projectile Weapons (CRD): The projectile weapons skill is the character's use of weapons like bows, slingshots, and similar weapons. For the purposes of this skill, a projectile weapon is any man-portable weapon that inflicts damage by hurling an object (projectile) at a target using some type of stored mechanical energy rather than an explosion. Under this definition, firearms and thrown weapons are not projectile weapons.

Repair X (RSN): The repair skill allows you to make repairs to a particular object or class of object. The repair skill need not be as specific as other skills ending with the "X". It is feasible to be skill in small engine repair or automotive repair. It is just as plausible to be skilled in repairing damage to wood work or to repair body work on a vehicle. When selecting this skill, the director will have the final say in whether or not a particular repair skill in acceptable.

Ride (CHA): The riding skill provides a character with the ability to ride animals. While this is a very physical skill, it is governed by charisma because working with closely with any animal is really a function of training and negotiations.

♫ **Safe-Cracking (INS):** The safe-cracking skill is the ability to open a combination lock without knowing what the combination is. If you've ever tried to open a combination lock in this manner, you know that it is not as easy as it looks on television.

Sculpting (INS): Sculpting is the art of taking a quantity of raw material and carving, shaping, manipulating, or molding it into something else.

Search (RSN): Where the awareness skill is more passive in nature, searching is the art of actively looking or listening for something. Your character can use this skill to actively search for a secret door, hidden compartment, or hidden opponent.

Seduction (CHA): When most people think of seduction, they conjure a particular image in their minds. Women often imagine being swept off their feet. Men see the playa who's always hooking up with some beautiful woman. In truth, they're both right. Seduction is enticing or attracting someone. It is leading someone else astray or drawing them away from their principles, faith, or allegiances.

Characters can use this skill to get someone to fall in love with them or convince someone to betray someone or something they otherwise hold dear.

Sense Motive (INS): This skill represents your character's ability to "know" that someone else has some ulterior motive. Given enough information, the character might even be able to guess what that motive is. Sensing motive is more of a hunch or a gut feeling that any concrete evidence of wrong doing.

Sing (CHA): Singing is your character's skill at carrying a tune and impress the judges of their favorite talent competition.

♪ **Sleight of Hand (CRD):** Sleight of hand is normally thought of as the tricks a magician performs at a birthday party. While those tricks are certainly an example of sleight of hand, this skill has far more uses. It is also your character's ability to pick pockets, secretly put something in someone's pocket, or covertly move an object on their person to avoid detection… and making a quarter appear from behind someone else's ear.

Sneak (QCK): The sneak skill is the ability to move quietly and without being noticed. This skill is used when you're trying to move without making a sound… whether that's leaving an area filled with zombies or getting into the house a few hours past curfew.

Thrown Weapons (CRD): The thrown weapons skill covers any object that you throw through the air at your target. It covers everything from passing a football, making a basket, and pitching to knives, hand grenades, and shuriken.

Tracking (INS): Tracking is your ability to follow a trail. This skill is often used by hunters to find deer and other animals that they've shot (who never seem to actually fall over dead on impact like they do in the movies).

♫ **Treat Injury (RSN):** This skill covers all types of medical treatment from basic first aid to setting broken bones and performing emergency tracheotomies.

Unarmed Combat (CRD): Unarmed combat covers a variety of fighting styles, from barroom brawls to more disciplined styles like karate or kung-fu.

Writing (INS): Writing is your character's ability to put their thoughts on paper in a manner that holds the reader's interest.

Knowledge Skills

All knowledge skills are governed by the character's Reason attribute. As such, no governing attribute is listed after the name of these skills.

Agriculture: This is the character's knowledge of modern farming techniques including the proper time to plant and harvest, proper crop rotations to maintain the nutrients of the soil, and the proper use of chemicals like pesticides and fertilizers.

Anthropology: This is the study of cultural development, social customs, and beliefs of humankind over its history.

Archaeology: The study of historic and prehistoric peoples and their cultures through analysis of artifacts, inscriptions, monuments, and other remains.

Architecture: The design of artificial constructs and environments such as buildings or parks.

Area History X: The knowledge of the history of a particular area or community.

Art: A knowledge of art history, famous artists, and other art related topics. This does not include the ability to produce art or appreciate art that someone else produced.

Automobiles: This skill provides a knowledge of the automotive industry as well as an in depth knowledge of popular categories of automobiles such as muscle cars or sports cars.

♫ **Ballistics:** The science or study of the motion of projectiles such as bullets, shells, bombs, etc…

Biology: The study of living organisms, especially their origin, growth, reproduction, structure, and behavior.

Chemistry: The study of the composition, properties, and reactions of substances and elementary forms of matter.

City Ordinances X: Knowledge of laws unique to a particular city, or town.

Comic Books: Knowledge of the comic book industry and comic book characters, including their origins, powers, allies, enemies, etc…

Computer Programs: The knowledge of computer programs and their history. This is not the ability to actually write code. It is just the knowledge that code exists, that there are different languages, what those languages are used for currently, what they've been used for in the past, and what might be possible in the future.

Conspiracy Theories: This skill represents knowledge of the vast number of conspiracy theories floating around. It covers everything from the Illuminati, Free Masonry, and Rosicrucians to aliens, Area 51, and Roswell… and everything in between.

Criminology: The study of criminal behavior and crimes.

Ecology: Technically a branch of biology, ecology is the study of the relationship and interactions between organisms and their environment.

Economics: The study of production, distribution, and consumption of goods and services.

♪ **Engineering & Design X:** This skill is the knowledge of the principles of design and engineering of a particular item, product, or thing.

Etiquette: This skill represents knowledge of the conventional requirements of social behavior and conduct in ceremony or other formal observances.

Federal Law: Knowledge of the laws enacted by the federal government and applicable in all fifty states.

♫ **Forensics:** The study of the legal application of science. This skill does not cover the use of the various sciences. It does, however, convey an understanding of crime scene investigations and the admissibility in a court of law of any scientific evidence gathered.

Fringe Cults: This skill represents knowledge of the beliefs and customs of a variety of cults operating in the world today. For the purposes of this game (as in the real world), cults are any religious belief that has not gained mainstream acceptance.

Geology: The study of the earth, its dynamic and physical history, and the elements from which it is composed.

♫ **Linguistics:** Linguistics is the study of languages.

Livestock: This skill represents knowledge of what is required to raise livestock.

Local Businesses X: Knowledge of the local businesses, their hours of operation, and he goods and services they provide.

Local Gangs X: The knowledge of the gangs that are active in a particular area, their respective territories, customs, signs, and tags.

♪ **Local Underworld:** Knowledge of the local underworld, including organized crime, places to buy and sell ill-gotten items, and popular criminal hangouts.

Logistics: Knowledge of the planning, implementation, and coordination of an operation, especially the procurement, supply, and maintenance of equipment.

Movies: A knowledge of the film industry including and the movies that they produce. This skill provides knowledge of actors and actresses and the roles they've played. It also provides knowledge of movie plots and famous lines from movies.

Mythology: Knowledge of religious beliefs held by people in the ancient world that few, if any, people currently believe to be true.

♪ **Narcotics:** This skill provides the character with knowledge of illegal drugs, where to get them, and how to use them.

Occult Lore: Knowledge of various things once held to be secret and believed to offer knowledge beyond the range of ordinary human understanding, including astrology, alchemy, magical spells and rituals, and a horde of other things that few people pay attention to anymore.

Pharmaceuticals: This skill provides knowledge of prescription medications, their uses, and effects.

Philosophy: The rational investigation of the truths and principles of being, knowledge, or conduct.

Physics: The study of matter, energy, motion, force, and their relationships to each other.

Politics: Knowledge of how governments work and interact with each other and the people they govern.

Psychology: The study of the mind, mental processes and states, behavior, and characteristics thereof.

Quasi-Legal Substances: This skill provides knowledge of substances that are not illegal and do not need to be prescribed by a doctor, but that it is not legal for high schools to possess or use such as alcohol and tobacco.

Religion: This skill provides knowledge of religious beliefs, ceremonies, and customs that are accepted as mainstream.

Robotics: Knowledge of the field of robotics including the history of robotics, latest developments, and the people working on the cutting edge of the field.

♫ **Seamanship:** The knowledge of the operation, navigation, management, safety, and maintenance of a ship.

Sociology: the study of the origin, development, organization and functioning of human society including fundamental laws, social relationships, institutions, etc.

Sports X: Knowledge of the history, rules, and players of a particular sport.

State Law X: Knowledge of the laws adopted by and governing a particular state within the nation.

Strategy: The art of combining and employing tactics in planning and directing larger scale operations to achieve a goal.

Tactics: The art of disposing your assets and maneuvering them to best accomplish your goals

Television Programs: Knowledge of popular television programming, the plots involved in such programs, the people who star in them, and the time and channel on which they air.

Theology: The study of religious truths, especially divinity, its attributes, and its relationship to the universe.

US History: The history of the United States, including wars it has fought in, political upheavals, social unrest, and other important events that helped shape the nation.

Video Games: This skill provides knowledge of video games. A character with this skill knows game titles, plots, and goals. They know the general layout of setting, controls for the game, and tricks or cheats to the game. Of course, knowing how to rocket jump and being able to rocket jump are two very different things.

➢ **Language & Literacy**

Language and Literacy skills are a subset of knowledge skills and purchased using the same point pool. However, language skills and literacy skills are used in a somewhat different manner.

You rarely, if ever, roll for a language skill. Instead, your rating in a skill determines your level of ability within that skill. Your character is unable to perform at a higher level than the one indicated unless he or she raises his or her skill level.

Each language or literacy skill your character possesses will have a rating from one to six. This rating defines their level of proficiency with the language.

Level	Spoken Language	Literacy
1	Elementary Proficiency	Emergent
2	Limited Working Proficiency	Below Basic
3	Professional Working Proficiency	Basic
4	Full Professional Proficiency	Intermediate
5	Bilingual Speaker	Proficient
6	Native Speaker	Fluent

▪ Spoken Language Ratings

Elementary Proficiency: At this level of proficiency the character is able to use and understand basic speech. Their vocabulary is only large enough to convey the most basic needs. Slower speech and repetition are often required to aid in understanding. Hand gestures may be required to convey some ideas.

Limited Working Proficiency: At this level of proficiency, they can handle most basic social situations with some confidence. They understand how to make introductions and can carry on a casual conversation. They can give simple answers to questions, but may have to respond to some questions in a more round about fashion to answer some questions, especially those that are complex. For example, if you wanted French fries, you might have to describe them as thin fried potatoes or you might refer to a hamburger as a cow sandwich. Slower speech and repetition may still be required.

Professional Working Proficiency: At this level, the character will be able to speak with sufficient structural accuracy to handle more practical, social, and even professional conversations. They will be able to discuss topics of interest with relative ease. There vocabulary will be broad enough that they will rarely grasp for words, and they will have little difficulty understanding normal rate of speech.

Full Professional Proficiency: Once the character reaches this level, he or she will be fluent enough in the language to understand and participate in conversations within their own range of personal and professional experience.

Bilingual Speaker: This is the highest level of proficiency possible for most people (those who do not have the bilingual advantage). At this level the speaker has an excellent grasp of structure and grammar. Their vocabulary is broad enough to handle even unfamiliar situations. The character will still not be mistaken for a native speaker due to his or her accent.

Native Speaker: At this level of proficiency, the character speaks the language as if it were their own. Even their accent isn't noticeable.

▪ Literacy Levels

Emergent Literacy: A character with this level of literacy is just starting to learn words. He or she has only the most simple and concrete literacy skills. At this level, the pictures in a book are important to convey the meaning of the words even when the story is being read aloud to them.

Below Basic Literacy: A character with basic literacy understands that words tell a story themselves. Instead of letting pictures tell the story, the pictures support the words that the character is reading and help them to define unfamiliar words.

At this level, characters have a better concept of how words are spelled. They may make attempts to use more complex words with unconventional spelling based on rhyming, blending, and other words that the character knows.

Basic Literacy: At this level, the character has an extensive vocabulary of words they can identify on sight. They have started to understand and use literary language like "once upon a time" and "the end".

Intermediate Literacy: With a limited proficiency, characters demonstrate the ability to make inferences from short passages. They have the skills to read unfamiliar words and try to decipher their meaning using the context in which they appear. At this level, the character is able to understand information contained in relatively long or dense text. This is considered the minimum level of proficiency to function in a society.

Proficient: At full proficiency have a sophisticated understanding of the complexities of written language. Given time, characters at this level of literacy have the tools to comprehend nearly any written information.

Fluent: At this literacy level, the character is so proficient in reading that he or she can read aloud at the same rate at which he or she speaks with minimal errors.

➢ World Languages

It would be nearly impossible (and entirely too time consuming) to list every language ever spoken in the world in this book. Honestly, we're not even going to try. Instead, understand that it is possible for your character to know or learn almost any language.

That being said, we have divided languages into three basic categories that can your character can be proficient in.

♪ **Spoken Languages:** If you're using the default setting, the most common languages spoken in the Greater Green Bay area are English, Spanish, and Hmong. Of course, like much of the United States, English is the primary language. Green Bay schools have excellent English as a Second Language programs, so most students has a high degree of proficiency in English.

In addition, high schools in the area offer a variety of foreign language classes. West High School for example, offers classes in Spanish, German, French, Chinese (Mandarin), and American Sign Language.

♪**Slanguages:** Slanguages are languages all their own within another language. They consist of jargon and slang used by different professions or groups during their normal activities.

Examples of slanguages include the following: Military Jargon, Police Jargon, Legalese (the language lawyers speak so the rest of us don't know what they're talking about), l33t (the language spoken by that guy that pwn'd you), and Medicalese (the language doctors speak when they are talking to a nurse in the presence of a patient).

♫ **Dead Languages:** Dead languages are ones no one speaks anymore, but we still like to learn so that we can feel superior to others. Latin, Aramaic, and Sanskrit are wonderful examples of dead languages.

▪ Limits on Language

Unless the character has an advantage that allows it, a character can only have one language at a rating of 6 in spoken language and literacy. This language should be his or her native tongue. (Character's with the bilingual advantage are allowed to have two languages at this level.)

- *Native Languages*

Your character begins play knowing how to speak and literate in one language representing his or her native tongue. The character gains both the spoken language and literacy skills in this language at a rank equal to his or her reason score. Additional proficiency in both the spoken language and literacy skills for this language can be purchased at a cost of one point per level above his or her reason score to a maximum of twice the character's reason attribute.

Some people may be confused by the notion of having a character is is a native speaker of a language that does not have ranks in the spoken language skill to equate to the native speaker level. I understand and empathize with their concerns.

However, one need only turn on the television and watch "reality television" for a few minutes to learn the sad truth. The vast majority of "native speakers" do not possess spoken language skill in their native tongue at anywhere near level six.

Likewise, a simple web search for adult literacy rates will quickly reveal that most adults (43% to be precise) in this country only have an "intermediate" level of literacy in their native language. Twenty-eight percent of adults have only basic literacy skills, and 16% are considered at the below basic level. That leaves only 13% of adults living in the US would qualify for the "proficient" or "fluent" level of literacy!

Skill Specialization

Sometimes players want their characters to narrow their character's areas of expertise. There are very legitimate reasons for doing this. They might want to use a particular type of weapon rather than have a generic skill in all weapons with the same basic properties – swords rather than any edged weapon, for example. Since most skill represent broad categories, most skills can be specialized.

In order to specialize, the character must have at least three ranks in the base skill. If this criterion is met, the player reduces the score of the base skill by one and adds the specialization as a separate skill at one level higher than the base skill was before the reduction.

For example, Tommy's character has an edged weapons skill of 3. Tommy doesn't want his character to wield any old edge weapon. He wants his character to wield a sword. His character is in possession of a sword, so Tommy decides to specialize in sword. He reduces the level of his "edged weapons" skill to 2 and adds a new skill recorded as "edged weapons – swords" at a rank of 4.

Specialization does not change the way that the skill works in play. It does, however, make it easier to improve the skill once play begins. (See improving your character on page 122).

Specialization is not without its costs, however. Because he chose to focus on swords, Tommy's character is less capable with other edged weapons (represented by the reduction in skill rank). If, at any time, Tommy increases character's edged weapons skill to equal the level of the specialization, Tommy's character loses the specialization. The character gains no points or other benefit for a specialization lost in this manner.

➢ Concentration

A concentration is a further refinement of a specialization. Just as a specialization narrows down your character's expertise to a particular subset of thing covered by a skill, a concentration further narrows the character's focus to a subset of the specialization.

Still using Tommy's character as an example, let's say that Tommy watches an anime one night and falls in love with the idea of using a katana. If he decides that his character is only going to use a katana, the character would concentrate on the katana. This would be a skill concentration.

In order to concentrate, the character must first have a specialization at least two ranks higher than the base skill it was derived from. If this criterion is met, the character reduces the level of his or her specialization by one and adds the new concentration at one level higher than the specialization was. If either the base skill or the specialization ever equals the rank of the concentration, the concentration is lost and the character gains no points or other benefits from this loss.

Again, sticking with Tommy's character, the character already has the "edged weapons" skill at rank 2 and the "edged weapons – swords" at rank 4. If he then concentrates in the katana, Tommy would reduce his specialization to rank 3 and record the new skill of "edged weapons – swords (katana)" at rank 5.

As with specialization, a concentration doesn't work any differently than a base skill (or a specialization). However, it is even easier to improve a concentration.

This may seem like a great deal. The player purchases a base skill for his character at rank 3 and gains a concentration at

rank 5. It is a good deal, provided you can actually use the concentration.

What would happen is Tommy's character never finds a katana and has to rely on a sword, or never finds a sword and has to use another edged weapon? Worse, what happens if Tommy finds a katana, improves the concentration, and then loses it forcing the character to wield an axe? If Tommy decides to improve the character's edged weapons skill, the character might lose both his specialization and his concentration.

If Tommy ever raises his character's edged weapons skill to 3, without first raising his character's specialization, he will lose the specialization. If he raises the specialization to 5 without first raising his character's concentration, he will lose the concentration. Also, if he raises the edged weapons skill to 5 without first raising the specialization and concentration, he would lose them both.

Advantages & Disadvantages

The next step in creating a character is completely optional, though highly recommended. Selecting advantages and disadvantages adds depth to the character, but they should not be selected lightly. As with skills, the advantages and disadvantages you choose for your character should fit with (or be worked in to) your character concept.

Every advantage and disadvantage has a point value assigned to it based on the impact that it has on game play. Advantages can be purchased using build points. If you run out of build points, you can acquire more by taking disadvantages.

Unless it is specifically listed in the description, any given advantage or disadvantage can only be taken once by a particular character.

Advantages

Academic Aptitude (3): A character with this advantage has a knack for knowing things. He or she gains an additional die whenever their character makes a knowledge skill check. This die applies even if the character is defaulting to a knowledge skill.

Acute Hearing (2): A character with this advantage has really good hearing. He or she gets an additional die to any tests that specifically pertain to hearing something.

Acute Vision (2): Character's with this advantage have better eyesight than other characters. The character gains an additional die for any checks specifically related to noticing visual details or things other people might have overlooked.

Adeptness (3 or 5): This advantage makes it one level easier for a character to improve a specific skill and any specializations or concentrations of that skill (see improving your character on page 122). The character must choose the skill that this advantage applies to when the advantage is taken. If that skill is an active skill, this advantage costs 5 points. If it is a knowledge skill, its cost is 3 points. This advantage can be taken more than once, but must apply to a different skill each time is chosen.

Ambidexterity (5): Unlike most of us who are either right or left handed (well, most of us are right handed), a character with this advantage is able to use both of his or her hands with equal aptitude. This provides several advantages, not the least of which comes when using two weapons simultaneously (see fighting with two weapons on page 116).

Bi-Lingual (2): A character with this advantage blessed with knowing two languages at character creation rather than just receiving one. Additionally, unlike other characters that speak and read multiple languages, a character with this advantage can improve both of their starting languages to level 6 in both spoken language and literacy.

This advantage is particularly suited to characters who speak one language at home and another in public. This is the case with many Native American and immigrant households who want to maintain their own culture and language while still integrate into society.

Bland Appearance (2): This character's appearance is perfectly average making it difficult to distinguish this character from other people of similar height, weight, and skin color. Anyone attempting to identify the character has their target numbers to do so increased by 3.

NOTE: The bland appearance advantage cannot be taken if the character has other advantages that make them stand out from the crowd such as presence, sex appeal, or popular.

Brave (4): The character with this advantage isn't fearless, but being brave isn't about not being afraid. It's about acting even when you are afraid. A character with this advantage has all target numbers to resist fear cut in half.

For example, let's say your small band of survivors encounters a horde of zombies. You're out numbered and were taken by surprise. Your target number to resist the fear caused by the zombies is 6, so you need to roll sixes or take a +3 penalty to all your target numbers. While everyone else is rolling against a six, a character with the brave advantage is rolling against a 3 to resist the fear.

Common Sense (5): Common sense, as you've probably noticed by now, is becoming decidedly less common every day. A character with this advantage gains an important edge. Whenever a player says that the character with this advantage is going to do something that is likely to cause harm to the character, party, or their goals, the director will ask the player if he or she is sure that they want the character to perform said action. This should give the player pause to consider the actions. If the player confirms the action after this warning, the player's been warned and the character must suffer the consequences of his or her actions.

Computer Aptitude (3): The character with this advantage gains an extra die for any tests involving a computer.

Cunning Linguist (1): A character with this advantage has a gift for languages. It is easier for him or her to improve a language skill, both spoken language and literacy (see improving character on page 122). The character still must pay the normal cost to learn a new skill at rank one and is still limited to a maximum rank of 5 in any language other than his or her native language.

Eidetic Memory (5): A character with this advantage has what is commonly referred to as a photographic memory. However, their ability to vividly recall details is not limited strictly to things that they have seen. These characters can recall in vivid detail anything they have sensed.

To use this advantage, the player tries to recall some factoid from a previous adventure or encounter. If the player cannot recall, he or she can ask the other players. If they cannot recall the detail, the player rolls a number of dice equal to his or her character's willpower pool against a target number assigned by the director. Every success the player achieves is a question that the player can ask the director about the fact that the director must answer honestly.

Exceptional Attribute (5): Purchasing this advantage gives the character an additional point in the attribute of the player's choosing. This advantage is the only way a character can exceed the maximum starting attribute for his or her clique. It cannot, however, exceed the physical limitation of the human body… in other words it can't be used to exceed maximum human attributes.

Exceptional Peripheral Vision (2): A character with this advantage gains an additional die to any test to notice something with their peripheral vision. The bonus die gained from this advantage stacks with the bonus die from the Acute Vision advantage if the character has both advantages and both advantages apply (like noticing the name on the shirt of a mechanic that strolls past your car while you're talking to a passenger in the car).

Focused (3): When the character takes the focused advantage, they choose the skill to which this advantage applies. Anytime the character makes a skill test using that skill, he or she gains an additional die to roll for that test.

Good Reputation (2): A character with this skill has a favorable reputation. People believe that the character is honest and trustworthy. This results in an extra die that the character can roll for any negotiation tests.

High Pain Tolerance (8): A character with this advantage is less susceptible to pain than other people. In game terms, your character suffers one less die penalty at each wound level.

Hyper-Immune System (7): When a character with this advantage attempts to resist the effects of disease he or she gains an automatic success in addition to any gained from the actual resistance roll

In Tune (3): A character with this advantage is more in tuned to the world around them than others. The character gains an additional die on any awareness, discern lie, search, or sense motive test they make.

Internal Compass (3): This advantage grants the character an innate sense of direction. The character gains an automatic success to any navigation test he or she makes. Additionally, they can spend an action pool die to learn which direction is north… and therefore which direction is east, south, and west. Action pool dice spent in this manner refresh normally.

Light Sleeper (3): A character with this advantage maintains some (possibly subconscious) awareness of his or her surroundings even when asleep. As such, they do not suffer the usual penalties to awareness tests while asleep (see sleep and fatigue on page 120).

Mechanical Aptitude (3): A character with this advantage gains an additional die to any test involving a mechanical device.

Natural Talent (4 or 8): A character with this advantage has a natural talent for a particular skill making it easier for the character to improve that skill. The skill must be declared when this advantage is purchased. If it is an active skill, then this advantage costs 8 points. If it is a knowledge skill, the cost is only 5 points.

Perfect Time (2): This advantage grants the character an almost preternatural sense of timing. They are able to estimate the actual time with surprising accuracy. A casual estimate might only be off by a few minutes; however, if they are actively concerned about the passage of time, their accuracy improves to a matter of a few seconds.

Poise (4): When someone has poise, they have self-confidence and bearing that allows them to quickly recover from missteps. Once per gaming session, a character with this advantage can reroll a single roll the results of a failed roll.

Poison Resistance (3): A character with this advantage gains an additional die to resist the effects of poisons and toxins.

Popular (3): Popular kids don't always have it easier, but it sure seems that way. Even outside of school their lives appear blessed. Someone with this advantage he or she gains an automatic success to any social skill test. This is in addition to any gained from the actual skill dice rolled.

Presence (2, 4, or 6): There is just something about some people that draws others to them. A character with the presence advantage is one of those people. Of course, once people get to know the character, this mystique seems to wear off, but the character can accomplish a lot in the meantime.

When a character with the presence advantage makes a social skill test involving people who do not know them very well, they receive one bonus die for every 2 points spent on this advantage to a maximum of 3 dice. For the purposes of this advantage, people who don't know them very well are people with the following relationships to the character: Positive Acquaintance, Just Met, Never Met, and Negative Acquaintance. If the other person involved in the test falls into any other relationship category, this advantage does not apply. (See social skill tests on page 107)

Quick Healer (3, 5, or 8): A character with the quick healer advantage recovers from injuries at twice the normal rate (see health and healing on page 118). For 3 points, the character recovers from mind damage at a faster rate. For 5 points, the character recovers from body damage at a faster rate. For 8 points, the character recovers from both mind and body damage at a faster rate. There is no way to recover soul damage faster!

Quick Study (2): Some people need to learn by doing while others can gain a decent understanding simply by reading a book. A character with the quick study advantage is one of those people. This advantage reduces the cost of learning a new knowledge skill from the standard 10 experience points to a mere 7 experience points.

Scientific Aptitude (2): A character with this advantage gains an additional die to any test involving a scientific knowledge skill.

Sex Appeal (2, 4, or 6): A character with this advantage is extremely attractive. When a character with the sex appeal advantage makes a social skill test involving people who find them attractive, they receive one bonus die for every 2 points spent on this advantage to a maximum of 3 dice.

It is up to the discretion of the director whether a particular NPC is attracted to the character. Players get to choose for their own characters.

Social Grace (3): A character with this advantage suffers only half the normal penalties for defaulting on a social skill test. When defaulting to another active social skill, the character takes only a +1 penalty to target number. When defaulting to an applicable knowledge skill, the penalty is only +2 to target number. If the character must default to his or her charisma attribute, they suffer only a +1 penalty to target number and count two successes for every three successes achieved on the roll. (See defaulting on a skill test on page 107)

Tough as Nails (6): It isn't that a character with this advantage is less susceptible to damage. It's that the damage they do take has less of an effect on them. The character suffers one less point of damage from each attack that injures them. Additionally, the character can choose to derive his or her physical gaff score using their strength attribute rather than their constitution score. Once this choice is made it cannot be changed.

Will to Live (7): A character with this advantage has a drive to survive. To reflect this, the character can choose to use dice from his willpower pool to augment a physical gaffing test. Only one dice pool can be used to augment any one roll, so, if the character uses dice from his or her willpower pool, they cannot also augment the same roll using dice from their vigor pool.

Disadvantages

Addiction (Varies): The character is addicted to some substance. The cost of this disadvantage is based upon the substance that the character is addicted to and the frequency with which they must indulge their addiction. The sum of the substance rating and the frequency rating is the total rating of the addiction.

A common substance is one that is readily available and can be easily obtained in civilized areas. Wheat and sugar are examples of common substances.

An uncommon substance is one that is more only slightly more difficult to find. Caffeine is an example of an uncommon substance.

A restricted substance is something that is legal, but there are laws regulating it. The berries of the blood vine are an example of a restricted substance. Their transportation and sale is regulated in an attempt to stop this plant from spreading further. Cigarettes and alcohol fall into this category as well.

Illegal substances are things that cannot legally be purchased. Narcotics and prescription drugs are just examples of illegal substances.

The character with the addiction must use the substance to which they are addicted at least once in the time allotted. If you use the substance multiple times within the allotted time frame, you still must take it at the next interval. If you could store up uses of an addictive substance, I wouldn't need another cigarette until I'm 153 years old.

Points	Substance	Points	Frequency
1	Common	1	1 / CON Weeks
2	Uncommon	2	1 / CON Days
3	Restricted	3	1 / CON Hours
4	Illegal	4	1/ CON ½ Hours

If the character fails to use the substance at the prescribed interval, they must make psyche check verses a target number equal to the total rating of the addiction and score a number of successes equal to the dosage(s) missed. If they succeed, their Constitution drops by one point. If they fail, they go into immediate withdrawal and suffer a penalty to all target numbers equal to the frequency rating of the addiction. In addition the character still loses a point of Constitution. This roll repeats itself each time the character fails to use the substance. The penalty does not increase, but the character continues to lose Constitution. Constitution scores cannot fall below one… unless you're dead. Continue to keep track of lost constitution point below one, however. They will play a role in the next phase of recovery.

Once the character begins to indulge their addiction again, their constitution points return at a rate of one for each interval in which the character uses the substance he is addicted too. Additional uses do not increase the rate at which these points return. If the character suffered loss that would have brought their constitution score below one, these points must be "regained" before any actual constitution points are recovered.

If, and only if, the character chooses to end his addiction they must stop using the substance and make the requisite will test as described above. They must continue not to use the substance for a number of weeks equal to the frequency rating of the addiction. If they manage to survive this withdrawal period, the player must spend a number of experience points equal to five times the total rating of the addiction in order to be considered "clean & sober".

Even after they have conquered their addiction, they're still not clear of danger. If they ever use that substance again, they must make a Psyche test versus a target number equal to their original addiction rating. If they fail, their addiction returns in full force.

Addiction is a dangerous thing. It isn't funny or fun. It destroys families and lives. And, more often than not, the addicted person is consumed by their addiction. It is included as a disadvantage for the sake of realism. Both players and directors are strongly cautioned about using this disadvantage in the game.

Allergy (varies): As with addiction, the strength of an allergy depends on the severity of the allergy and how common the substance is. Unlike addiction, however, the more rare the allergen, the less debilitating the allergy and the less points it's worth.

Allergies develop for a variety of reasons. Once an allergy develops, most people remain allergic to a given substance for the rest of their lives, though medication may help alleviate the effects of the allergy.

Points	Substance	Points	Severity
1	Rare	1	Mild
2	Uncommon	2	Moderate
3	Common	3	Severe

When choosing a substance for an allergy, some care must be taken. While this disadvantage provides less additional points for more rare substance, there must still be a chance to encounter the substance otherwise the allergy is not a disadvantage… and therefore worth nothing.

A rare substance is something that a character is unlikely to encounter during the regular course of their day. Prescription medications are an example of a rare substance.

Uncommon substances are things that a character has a fair chance of encountering, but, for the most part, can be easily avoided. Allergies to certain foods are an example of uncommon substances.

Common substances are things that it is very difficult to avoid. Unless the character takes the utmost care in their daily lives, they are bound to encounter a common substance on an almost daily basis. Allergies to pollen, the chemicals used to clean the municipal water supply might be common allergies.

The one thing that I haven't mentioned is allergies to animals. Such allergies are quite frequent in the real world, and there is no reason to exclude them from you game. Just how many points an animal allergy is worth depends on the type of allergy and where your game is located. An allergy to cat dander might simply rate uncommon… or even rare in a more urban setting. An allergy to animals in general is likely to be common, especially in more rural areas like the default setting of Green Bay, Wisconsin.

The severity of an allergy is another story each level of severity results in a +1 penalty to *all* of the character's target numbers while the substance is *present* (i.e. +1 for mild, +2 for moderate, and +3 for severe).

Bad Reputation (2): Whether it's deserved or not, the character with this flaw has a bad reputation. People always assume the worst of the character. In social settings, people tend not to trust the character. In game terms, a character with this disadvantage always considers people 3 categories toward Nemesis on the relationship scale and they get two less bonus die for consequences… which makes their scale +1 to -5 rather than +3 to -3. (See using social skills on page 107)

Berserker (5): While most characters enjoy combat, a character with this flaw is obsessed with it. A character with this disadvantage is easily overtaken by bloodlust and finds it difficult, if not impossible, to withdraw while there are still enemies who need killing.

Whenever the character enters melee combat, he or she cannot willingly disengage from the conflict unless they succeed on a Psyche test with a difficulty equal to 5 plus 1 for every 3 enemy combatants. Each success achieved on this test allows the character to spend an action disengaging from combat. It does not, however, stop his or her opponent(s) from chasing them and reengaging.

Blinders (5): A character with this disadvantage tends to focus on one thing to the exclusion of all others. Once something draws the character's attention, they only gain half their dice to any awareness checks made until they are done examining the object of considering the notion. Additionally, the character only receives half their normal initiative dice if they are already engaged in an activity (a quarter of their initiative dice if they are taken by surprise).

Blowhard (2): No one likes a braggart… except the braggart themselves. Character's with this disadvantage tend to brag, name drop, and do other things to make themselves seem important and annoy the rest of us. Because of this, these characters suffer a +2 penalty to all target numbers for social skill tests.

Color Blind (1 or 2): Contrary to popular belief, a character with this disadvantage doesn't see in grayscale. However, they do have trouble distinguishing between different colors (usually red & green or blue & green). If your character has one of these conditions, this disadvantage is worth a single point. If they have both, it's worth 2 points.

Aside from having trouble picking clothes that match, a color blind character encounters additional difficulty when they have to make a skill check requiring color… like cutting the blue wire when there is a green wire right next to it… or don't shoot the one guy wearing a green hat in the parade of people wearing red hats. Whenever the character needs to make a skill check and color is an important factor, the target number of that test is increased by a penalty of +5.

I know this may seem like a high penalty for relatively little cost, but the truth is that, aside from dressing, color comes into play in our lives a lot less often than you think. When it does come into play, it is usually easy to remedy the situation. All you have to do is ask someone who isn't color blind to remove color from the equation.

Combat Paralysis (4): A character with this disadvantage tends to freeze up in a combat situation. The character only gains half of his or her initiative dice for the first round of combat. Thereafter, the character rolls initiative normally.

Deep Sleeper (4): A character with this disadvantage sleeps very deeply and often has trouble waking. When he or she is sleeping, they only receive half of the normal dice available to notice their surroundings when asleep. (As a normal sleeper only gets half of their dice when sleeping, a character with this disadvantage receives only a quarter of their normal dice pool to notice events around them while sleeping. See sleep and fatigue on page 120.)

Frail (5): A character with this disadvantage is wounded more easily than others. Whenever the character suffers damage (is unable to dodge an attack or gaff the damage dealt by the attack) he or she suffers and additional point of damage above and beyond that inflicted by the weapon.

Horrible Secret (varies): It might be hard for most of us to imagine a secret so horrible that it would still be relevant during the zombie apocalypse. A character with this disadvantage has no such trouble. They have some secret that they do not want others to learn.

Exactly what the character is hiding and what lengths they will go to keep it hidden is up to the player. Work with your director to devise a suitable secret. Tell the director how far the character would be willing to go to protect that secret. The director will assign a value based on what this discussion. We recommend a point value of between 1 and 5. A secret that might cause embarrassment the character would like to avoid, but that the character will do nothing to protect might be worth a single point at most if any at all. It should go without saying that an extremely terrible secret that the character would go to any lengths to keep hidden would be worth the most points.

Impulsive (5): Some people speak without thinking. A character with this disadvantage has a similar problem. They act because the player controlling them spoke without thinking. If you choose this flaw for your character, everything you say or do is assumed to be in-game. In other words, the character does whatever comes out of his or her player's mouth and then deals with the consequences. Even off-hand comments and announcements to the group are taken in-game.

If two players are arguing and one players flippantly says "I'm going to kill you" to the other player, then the character belonging to the player speaking attacks the character belonging to the player being spoken to. If an important non-player character insults the character and the player retorts, then the player's character also retorts. Likewise, if you're exploring an old house deep in the woods and the player says "Let's burn this place down," then the player's character starts trying to build a fire and burn the building down. This doesn't just apply to in-game situations. If the player announces that he or she has to use the restroom, the character just made a similar announcement in-game.

We recommend going so far as to require that the player whose character has this disadvantage does something special before they can speak out of character. Raising their hand and waiting to be called on or putting on a special hat to speak and act out of character are examples of things we've used during play-testing.

Inept (3 or 5): A character with this disadvantage has more difficulty improving a particular skill than other characters. The skill is considered one level worse for purposes of improving it (see improving your character on page 122). You must choose which skill the disadvantage applies to when taking it. The character must have at least three ranks in the chosen skill in order to gain any points from this advantage. A knowledge skill is worth three points while an active skill is worth 5 points.

Lazy (2): A character with this advantage hates to do anything… Unless their life is in immediate danger, every task they do takes at least twice as long as it would take another character… and is usually accompanied by quite a bit of whining and complaining.

Low Pain Tolerance (7): A person with this disadvantage feels the effects of injury more acutely than others. This character is one of the people who stubs their toe and swears it's broken or skins their knee and believes they have broken their leg. In game terms, the character suffers an additional die penalty at each wound level – including the first (see health and healing on page 118).

Lowered Immunity (5): A character with this disadvantage is more susceptible to disease than other people are. He or she gets one less success than the dice indicate when attempting to resist the effects of disease.

Mood Swings (5): We all have mood swings, but a character with this disadvantage has wild mood swings. They can go from being suspicious and brooding to abnormally agreeable for seemingly no reason.

Whenever the character experiences trauma, conflict, or some other event… or whenever the director feels like it, the director rolls on the following table. The player must play his or her character according to the result otherwise they earn no experience for the gaming session.

Roll	Effect
0	Character Takes on the Mood of Those Nearby
1	Reclusive, Surly, & Emotionally Cold
2	Irritable & Bitter
3	Indecisive & Noncommittal
4	Open to New Ideas & Willing to Explore
5	Positively Gleeful & Sickeningly Optimistic
6	Happy & Understanding
7	Abnormally Reasonable
8	Depressed & Suspicious
9	Player's Choice

Night Blindness (3): The character with this disadvantage sees more poorly in darkness than other characters. Any target number penalties to vision from darkness are increased by +2. (See vision modifiers on page 114)

Phobia (Varies): The character with this disadvantage has an irrational fear of something. The number of additional points earned by this disadvantage varies depending on the object of this fear and the frequency in which this object would be encountered.

Keep in mind, if there is no chance of encountering the object of the character's fear, then the fear isn't worth any points at all.

For the purposes of this disadvantage, a rare object is anything that the character is very unlikely to encounter during the course of a typical day. Animals not native to an area, but which may be displayed in nearby zoos are a good example of a rare substance.

An uncommon object would be something that is unlikely to be encountered during the normal course of the day or something more common that the character could easily avoid by taking the most rudimentary of precautions. Heights and deep water are examples of uncommon items. Hospitals, doctors, dentists, and other members of the medical profession are common items that would fall into this category.

Common objects include indigenous animals and other things that the character is likely to encounter every day. The character can take precautions, but he or she will still have to face his or her fear periodically.

A very common object is something you have no hope of avoiding. These are usually larger categories of common items. A squirrel is a common object in the default region. Rodents are very common… Squirrels, chipmunks, field mice, voles, and a horde of other rodents abound (hopefully) just outside your front door.

Points	Object	Points	Severity
1	Rare	1	Mild
2	Uncommon	2	Moderate
3	Common	3	Severe
4	Very Common	4	Crippling

For each level of severity, the character loses one die to any roll they make while in the presence of the object of their fear. For example, I suffer from a severe fear of heights. This is worth 5 bonus points to me, but I suffer a penalty of 3 dice to any roll that I make while I'm somewhere high above ground.

Poor Vision (Varies): The character with this disadvantage is either near-sighted or far-sighted. This disadvantage is worth 1 point for every two points of penalty that the character incurs. This cost may seem disproportionate, but keep in mind that this disadvantage can be easily overcome through the use of corrective eyewear. Near-sighted characters suffer a penalty to any action where they must see something further away than their score in yards. Far-sighted character's, meanwhile, suffer a penalty to any action where they must observe something closer than their Reason score in yards.

Sanctity of Life (7): Most character's value life…especially their own. A character with this disadvantage values all life.

In fact, he values it so much that he will not take a life – _any life_ – unless there is absolutely no other choice. A character with this disadvantage can only take up arms in defense of himself or others. Even if history proves that a potential opponent is normally aggressive… a zombie, for example… the character must still wait until that opponent tries to attack someone before he or she can engage it. Even then, he or she must act to stop the attack… shooting limbs to slow the zombie or extricating its intended victim from the situation… and reserve trying to kill it only as a last resort.

Uncouth (2): An uncouth character is crass, rude, and often lewd. They say the wrong things all the time without concern for the company that they're keeping. This has a tendency to put off anyone who doesn't know the character. A character with this disadvantage suffers a +2 penalty on all social skill check target number for interactions with anyone whose relationship with the character is not rated intimate, friend, ally, or positive acquaintance. Even these people can often grow irritated with the character's crass comments. While intimate relationships and friends tend to be immune to their boorish behavior, the character still suffers a +1 penalty to target numbers for those people rated as allies or positive acquaintances.

Underachiever (4): While other characters were studying, the character with the underachiever disadvantage was slacking. As such, the character only receives 5 points to spend on knowledge skills per point of reason attribute rather than the normal 7 points. If the character belongs to the academic clique, he or she only receives the normal 7 points per point of reason rather than the 10 points provided from their clique bonus.

Vindictive (5): Most characters in role-playing games tend to have a vindictive streak in them. A character with this disadvantage takes this one step further. They are compelled to even the score for any slight on their honor, reputation, or self-image. Whether the slight is real or imagined makes no difference to the character. Until the character gets even, he or she earns only ½ their experience award for any gaming session he or she participates in. These experience penalties are cumulative, so, if the character receives two unanswered slights, they receive only ¼ of the experience that they earned… half of the half… Because you always round the way that you learned in school, it is possible for the character to not earn experience for a gaming session because of this disadvantage.

Weak-Willed (8): A character with this disadvantage is easily swayed by others. The character finds it difficult to refuse to do what he or she is asked. Unless the character or attempting to influence the character with this disadvantage is known to be an enemy, personal foe, or nemesis all penalties for interacting with this character are halved and all bonuses for dealing with the character are doubled.

Weapons, Armor, & Equipment

If you've been creating a character as you've been reading this, your character is already finished. All that's left is to assign statistics to the starting equipment that your director agreed to. As a fellow player, I'm sure you'd also like to know what some of the things you'll find along the way do in the game. Naturally, you found your way to this part of the book.

There are a few things I'd like to discuss with you before we actually get into weapons, armor, and equipment.

First, it would be impossible to list every possible weapon you could find and use. The availability of weapons will depend on where your game takes place, your character's background & concept, and how many other survivors are scavenging in the now finite equipment pool. Rather than try to cover everything, we're going to provide a list that will encompass a wide variety of weapons. We'll cover the most common weapons – baseball bats and tools that can be used as weapons. We'll also touch on some items that would be extremely rare – anti-material rifles and hand grenades. Then we'll pepper the list with some of the things found in between. Our hope is that, if you're players use something as a weapon that isn't on the list, we will have provided something similar that you can tweak to represent the new instrument of zombie death.

We took the same approach for armor. Using the default setting as a basis, we tried to cover most of the armor you might encounter if you used the default setting. Using this list and a little common sense, you should be able to create any armor we didn't specifically include.

Equipment is the one thing we that ignores this basic procedure. In fact, we didn't list any equipment at all. The reason for this is very simple – there's no need to do it.

In a normal role-playing game, equipment is listed for two reasons.

First, you need to know how the equipment functions in the game. Since this game is set in the real world during the current era, you already know how most of this stuff works. Even if you don't understand the particulars, you know enough to use it in the game. I don't need to know exactly how the "jaws of life" works to know that I can use them to open a car like a tin can.

The second reason has to do with the in-game economy. When you go to a shop carrying a particular type of merchandise, you need to know how much it's going to cost your character. Since society, and therefore the economy, is one of the first casualties of the zombie apocalypse, there are no stores. Instead, your characters will have to find items or barter with other people who have already found them.

Bartering is a unique economic model that depends on the needs of the seller rather than any intrinsic value the items being traded might hold. An apple is worth much more to a starving man than it is to someone with an ample food supply. A starving man might trade ammunition for the apple, especially if he has a disproportionate amount of ammo.

In any case, you'd use your character's social skills in order to make the trade… usually the negotiation skill, but other skills like seduction or intimidation are not out of the question. The rules for dealing with social interactions cover these things, so there is no need to pretend to assign value. (See using social skills on page 107)

As such, including a list of equipment beyond weapons and armor (which need concrete statistics for use in the game) would only serve to artificially inflate our page count… and cost you more money. Some companies might find this acceptable, or even desirable, but we are not one of them.

Weapons

Weapons are key to your survival during the zombie apocalypse. In most cases, the charts include everything you need to know in order to use the weapon.

Some of the things might not make sense to you at this point, especially if you've never played one of our games before. A detailed example of how to use this information during combat can be found in the combat section of the rules. (See combat on page 109)

Weapon: This column gives the name of the weapon.

Skill: This column gives the weapons or combat skill that the character uses in order to wield the weapon.

Hands: The number of hands normally required to use the weapon effectively.

Target Number: This is the target number for the attack test. It is the number that the character needs to meet or exceed on his or her skill test in order to hit his or her target.

Damage Rating: This is the damage that the weapon does per success on the attack test. If the attack is successful, this number is multiplied by the net successes of the attacker to determine the damage done to the target.

Damage Bonus: The damage bonus is extra damage dealt by the weapon. This bonus damage is added to the total amount of damage done, after the damage from the damage rating has been applied.

Damage Type: This column shows what type of damage the weapon does. There are four types of damage used in High School of the Damned.

P = Piercing
I = Impact (bludgeoning)
E = Energy (fire/cold)
S = Slashing

Range Increment: This column tells you the effective range of a given weapon. There are three basic types of range increment that you will see – melee, reach, and a numeric value given in feet.

> Melee – A weapon with a range of melee can only be used to attack adjacent opponents.
> Reach – a weapon with a range of reach is still a melee weapon, but, due to its length, these weapons can be used against opponents up to 5 feet away.
> Numeric Value – a numeric value is given for actual ranged weapons. When a numeric value is given it represents the length of each of five range categories for the ranged weapons. At each range increment, it becomes harder to hit your target. This is represented by a penalty to target number based on range. (See range increment on page 97)

Special Rules: Some weapons have special rules that apply to their use. If such rules exist, there will be a "Yes" in this column. The rules will be found in the weapon's description.

- ***Weapon Descriptions***

Baseball Bat: A baseball bat is a smooth wooden or metal club no more than 2.75 inches thick at its thickest point and no more than 42 inches long. A typical baseball bat weighs 33 ounces, but other weights are available.

Baton: A baton is a small club, less than arm's length, made of metal or wood (and sometimes plastic). Batons are commonly used by law-enforcement, corrections officers, and security guards for forced compliance and / or self-defense purposes.

Bow (Compound): A compound bow is a modern bow that uses a levering system, usually of cables and pulleys (cams) that allow a more efficient transfer of energy than other bows.

Bow (Recurve): A the tips of a recurve bow turn away from the archer when the bow is strung. This allows the bow to store (and transfer) more energy than an equivalent straight-limbed bow.

Brass Knuckles: Brass knuckles are a piece of metal shaped to fit over the knuckles of the wearer. This concentrates the force of a punch on a smaller and harder contact area causing more tissue disruption. *Special: a punch made while wearing brass knuckles does physical (body) damage rather than stun (mind) damage like a normal unarmed strike.*

Broad Sword: A broad sword is basket-hilted sword used by the military during the late middle ages. The name "broad sword" served to distinguish it from the much thinner rapier, also known as a "slim dueling sword", which was worn with civilian dress during the same period.

Chainsaw: a chainsaw is a portable mechanical saw that uses sharp blades attached to a rotating chain to cut. *Special: chainsaws are devastating weapons. Unfortunately, they often cause as much damage to its wielder as it does to its target. You do not get a bonus to damage due to your character's strength when using a chainsaw. Additionally, any ZERO rolled on the attack roll is considered a success against the wielder. These successes cannot be dodged… you're holding the chainsaw, after all. The damage can be gaffed normally.*

Cleaver: A cleaver is a large knife with a flat, rectangular blade designed to chop through thick meat, cartilage, and even bone.

Crossbow: A crossbow consists of a horizontal bow mounted on a stock. It is fired in much the same way as a rifle. Crossbows resemble a handheld version of a ballista.

Fire Axe: A fire axe is an axe with a pick shaped poll (the area of the axe head opposite the cutting edge). They are often decorated in vivid colors to make them easily visible during an emergency. The fire axe is designed to quickly break down wooden doors and open windows. *Special: A fire axe is actually two weapons in one. It can be used as an axe doing slashing damage or as a pick doing piercing damage. The wielder can easily switch between the two types of damage by rotating the axe, something that can be done as a free action. (See action types on page 110).*

Flare Gun: A flare gun is a pistol-shaped device used to fire a signal flare to indicate both distress. Flare guns are not designed to use as weapons. Instead they are intended to be fired into the air to mark the location of distressed people. *Special: A target hit with a flare takes damage normally from the attack. At ranges further than the short range increment, even if all the damage is gaffed, the target catches fire (see catching on fire on page 116).*

Hatchet: A hatchet is a small, single-handed striking tool used to cut and spit wood. A hatchet looks like a smaller version of an axe.

Katana: A katana is traditional Japanese sword often referred to as a "samurai sword". A katana has a moderately curved blade approximately 23 ½ inches long. It has a single edge and a handle that can accommodate two hands, so the weapon can be used either one or two-handed. Additionally, the unique properties of the blade make it particularly well-suited to parrying other weapons. *Special: A katana can be used with either one or two hands. Furthermore, when a katana is used to parry another weapon, the damage rating is considered to be one higher than it normally would be. The damage rating is for parrying is listed in parentheses -- a 4 rather than a 3. (See parrying on page 111).*

Knife: Knife covers a wide variety of cutting tools with exposed blades. Modern knives are generally found in both fixed-blade and folding varieties. *Special: Knives can be used either to stab (piercing damage) or cut (slashing damage). Additionally, even a knife not specifically designed to be a throwing knife can be thrown. Because a normal knife isn't weighted or balanced for throwing, the target number to throw them is increased by a penalty of +3 (increasing the target number to a 7). The range increment is equal to the thrower's strength score in feet.*

Kukri: A kukri is a Nepalese knife similar to a machete but with an inward (forward) curved blade.

Long Sword: A long sword is a type of European sword with a double-edged straight blade and a grip capable of two-handed use. *Special: A long sword can be used with either one or two hands.*

Machete: A machete is a cleaver-like cutting tool with a blade between 13 and 24 inches.

Machine Gun: A machine gun is a fully automatic mounted or portable firearm designed to fire rounds in rapid succession from a belt of large magazine. Machine guns typically have a rate of several hundred rounds per minute. *Special: Machine guns always fire in full automatic mode using 5 per shot fired.*

Pistol (Revolver): A double-action revolver is a firearm designed to be held, aimed, and fired with one hand. The revolver gets its name from the revolving cylinder containing multiple chambers that each holds a round of ammunition. Revolvers typically hold five or six rounds of ammo, but some revolvers hold ten or more.

Pistol (Semi-Automatic): A semi-automatic pistol is also a firearm designed to be held, aimed, and fired with one hand. Unlike the revolver, a semi-automatic pistol has only one chamber. When a round is fired, some of its power is used to cycle the action, ejecting the spent cartridge and loading a fresh shell into the chamber.

Pistol Whip: A pistol whip isn't really a weapon. A pistol whip is simply whipping someone with the butt of a pistol's grip.

Pitchfork: A pitchfork is an agricultural tool with a long handle and long, thin separated pointed tines (also called prongs). Pitchforks are often used to lift and pitch loose material such as hay, leaves, grapes, dung, and other agricultural materials. Pitchforks typically have two or three tines, though some have as many as six tines.

Rapier: A rapier is a long, slender pointed sword used predominantly for thrusting attacks. Rapiers often had complex, sweeping hilts to protect the sword hand. These eventually gave way to the cup hilts of later rapiers. A large pommel served as a counter weight to the long slender blade.

Rifle (Anti-Material): An anti-material rifle is a rifle designed for use against military equipment rather than personnel.

Rifle (Assault): An assault rifle is a selective rifle that uses an intermediate cartridge and a detachable magazine. They are the standard infantry weapon of most modern militaries and falls somewhere between a light machine gun and a submachine gun. *Special: An assault rifle is capable of firing in one of three rates of fire – single shot (1 bullet, standard damage), burst fire (3 bullets, +1 damage bonus), and fully automatic (5 bullets, +3damage bonus).*

Rifle (Bolt-Action): A bolt action rifle is one where the weapons bolt is operated manually by the use of a small handle. When the bolt is opened, the spent cartridge ejects. The firing pin cocks either as the breach is opened or as it is closed after the new round is chambered.

Rifle (Semi-Automatic): As with a semi-automatic pistol, A semi-automatic rifle harnesses some of the energy of the previous round to cycle the action ejecting the spent cartridge, cocking the firing pin, and chambering a fresh round… assuming one remains in the magazine.

Rifle (Sniper): A sniper rifle is a precision rifle used to ensure a more accurate placing of projectiles at longer ranges than other weapons (with the exception of the anti-material rifle). Sniper rifles can be found in both bolt-action and semi-automatic varieties.

Rifle Butt: Like a pistol whip, a rifle butt is not an actual weapon. It's the act of using the butt of the rifle's stock to strike an opponent.

Sap: A sap is a leather clad device, often a metal rod fitted with a spring handle or a pouch of lead pellets, designed to spread its impact across a wide area to render the target unconscious without breaking bones.

Scythe: A scythe is a two-handed agricultural implement used to cut long grasses and reap crops. It consists of a long wooden handle and a curved blade sharpened on the concave end. In the modern world it is most often seen in museums, history textbooks, and depictions of the grim reaper.

Short Sword: A short sword is a bladed weapon falling somewhere between a dagger and a sword. Short swords first saw use in the Iron Age with the Roman gladius and the Greek xiphos, and was issued to members of the U.S. Army's foot artillery regiments until 1872. _Special: Though the short sword was designed primarily as a thrusting (piercing) weapon, it's also capable of cutting (slashing)._

Shotgun: A shotgun is an almost iconic weapon that used the energy of a fixed cartridge to fire a number of spherical projectiles (shot) or a single solid projectile (slug). Shotguns can be found in several of configurations including single-barreled and double-barreled and use a wide variety of mechanisms to cycle the action including pump-action, bolt-action, lever-action, semi-automatic, and even fully automatic. _Special: If you're firing buckshot or birdshot from a shotgun, the target number to dodge is increased by +3 (from 10 to 13)._

Sickle: A sickle is a one-handed agricultural implement consisting of a crescent-shaped blade attached to a handle. It was originally used to harvest grains and cut forage for feeding livestock.

Sledgehammer: A sledgehammer is a tool consisting of a large, flat head, usually made from metal, attached to a long handle. The long handle and large striking head allow more force to be applied to each blow.

Slingshot: A slingshot is generally made from two rubber strips joined by a pocket and attached to a Y-shaped frame.

The projectile is placed in the pocket which is then drawn away from the frame to generate the desired power.

Speargun: A speargun is a rifle designed to fire a spear-like projectile into a target. They are usually intended for use underwater and are found in two basic varieties – (rubber) band-powered and pneumatic (air-powered). _Special: The projectile from a spear gun can be attached to a small, high strength line creating a tether between the weapon (and its user) and the target. These lines can serve a variety of purposes depending on what the other end is attached to._

Submachine Gun: A submachine gun is an automatic carbine designed to fire pistol ammunition. _Special: Submachine gun can operate in one of three firing modes – single shot, burst fire, and fully automaticSpecial: Submachine gun can operate in one of three firing modes single shot (1 bullet, standard damage), burst fire (3 bullets, +1 damage bonus), and fully automatic (5 bullets, +3damage bonus)._

Taser: A taser is an electroshock weapon that relies on Electro-Muscular Disruption technology to incapacitate an opponent. _Special: a Taser replies on contact between the target and two points of electrical contacts fired from the weapon. As such, 2 successes are required (one for each contact) before the Taser does any damage to its target. If at least two successes are achieved, the Taser does damage normally. Damage done by a Taser is stun damage._

Throwing Axe: A throwing axe is a small, hatchet-like weapon that is weighted and balance so that is can be effectively thrown at a target.

Throwing Knife: A throwing knife is a knife that is weighted and balance so that is can be effectively thrown at a target.

Tonfa: A tonfa is a baton with a perpendicular handle located closer to one side of the baton (approximately ⅓ of the way from the "short" end of the weapon). _Special: When a tonfa is used to parry another weapon, the damage rating is considered to be one higher than it normally would be. The damage rating is for parrying is listed in parentheses -- a 3 rather than a 2. (See parrying on page 111)._

Unarmed Kick: An unarmed kick is exactly what it sounds like… kicking your opponent. _Special: An unarmed kick normally does stun (mind) damage, but it is resisted by the impact damage rating of armor (see armor on page 100)_

Unarmed Punch: An unarmed punch is a regular punch. _Special: Like a kick, a punch normally does stun (mind) damage, but it is resisted using the impact damage rating of armor (see armor on page 100)._

Weapon	Skill	Hands	Target Number	Damage Rating	Damage Bonus	Damage Type	Range Increment	Special Rules
Baseball Bat (metal)	Impact	2	6	3	+2	I	Reach	No
Baseball Bat (wood)	Impact	2	6	3	-1	I	Reach	No
Baton (metal)	Impact	1	5	2	+1	I	Melee	No
Baton (wood)	Impact	1	5	2	-1	I	Melee	No
Bow (compound)	Projectile	2	6	2	+3	P	45 ft	No
Bow (Recurve)	Projectile	2	6	2	0	P	30 ft	No
Brass Knuckles	Unarmed	1	4	--	0	I	Melee	Yes
Broad Sword	Edged	1	6	3	+1	S	Melee	No
Chainsaw	Edged	2	8	4	+2	S	Melee	Yes
Cleaver	Edged	1	5	2	0	S	Melee	No
Crossbow	Projectile	2	5	2	-1	P	40 ft	No
Fire Axe	Edged	2	6	3 / 2	+1 / 0	S / P	Reach	Yes
Flare Gun	Firearms	1	8	1	0	Fire	30 ft	Yes
Hatchet	Edged	1	5	2	0	S	(STR) ft	No
Katana	Edged	1 / 2	5	3 (4)	+1	S	Melee	Yes
Knife	Edged	1	4	1	0	S / P	Melee	Yes
Kukri	Edged	1	5	2	0	S	Melee	No
Long Sword	Edged	1 / 2	6	3	0	S	Melee	No
Machete	Edged	1	5	2	0	S	Melee	No
Machine Guns	Firearms	2	6	5	+1	P	100 ft	Yes
Pistol (revolver)	Firearms	1	5	3	+2	P	30 ft	No
Pistol (Semi-auto)	Firearms	1	6	3	+1	P	40 ft	No
Pistol Whip	Impact	1	6	1	0	Stun	Melee	Yes
Pitchfork	Edged	2	7	2	+1	P	Reach	Yes
Rapier	Edged	1	5	2	-1	P	Melee	No
Rifle (Anti-material)	Firearms	2	6	6	+3	P	150 ft	No
Rifle (Assault)	Firearms	2	6	4	+1	P	80 ft	Yes
Rifle (Bolt-Action)	Firearms	2	5	4	+2	P	90 ft	No
Rifle (Semi-Auto)	Firearms	2	6	4	+2	P	70 ft	No
Rifle (Sniper)	Firearms	2	6	5	+2	P	125 ft	No
Rifle Butt	Impact	2	6	1	+2	Stun	Melee	Yes
Sap	Impact	1	5	1	0	Stun	Melee	Yes
Scythe	Edged	2	7	3	+1	S	Reach	No
Short Sword	Edged	1	6	2	0	P / S	Melee	Yes
Shotgun	Firearms	2	6	4	+3	P	30 ft	Yes
Sickle	Edged	1	6	2	0	S	Melee	No
Sledgehammer	Impact	2	7	4	0	I	Reach	No
Slingshot	Projectile	2	6	1	-1	I	50 ft	No
Speargun	Firearms	2	6	2	+1	P	10 ft	Yes
Submachine Guns	Firearms	1 / 2	6	3	+1	P	50 ft	Yes
Taser	Firearms	1	6	3	0	Stun (P)	5 ft	Yes
Throwing Axe	Thrown	1	6	1	+1	S	(Str x 2) ft	No
Throwing Knife	Thrown	1	5	1	0	P	(Str x 3) ft	No
Tonfa	Impact	1	5	2 (3)	0	I	Melee	Yes
Unarmed Kick	Unarmed	--	5	2	0	Stun (I)	Melee	Yes
Unarmed Punch	Unarmed	1	4	1	0	Stun (I)	Melee	Yes

➤ Ammunition

While we've discussed firearms a little in our discussion of weapons, we have not discussed ammunition. The modern cartridge provides both the projectile that strikes your enemy and the energy necessary to propel that projectile. The weapon that fires the projectile provides accuracy and range by efficiently transferring the explosive energy of the cartridge into kinetic energy.

Even though we've listed damage in the description of the firearms, the damage dealt has just as much to do with the bullet you're firing as it does with the gun it fires from.

• *Caliber & Gauge*

Not every pistol is identical. Some handguns use larger bullets than others. Your character might want to be all gansta and carry a D'Eagle. Obviously this weapon does more damage to its target than a 9mm pistol. Likewise, your character might be unlucky and the only pistol he or she finds is a .22 caliber handgun which does less damage than a 9mm.

Creating any of these specific weapons is simple using our system. The 9mm is, by far, the predominant handgun in the United States. As such, it is our "standard" pistol. If you want to use a weapon with a larger cartridge, simply consult the chart below and adjust the weapon's properties accordingly.

Caliber / Gauge (Size of the Bullet)	Damage Rating	Damage Bonus
Low Caliber/Gauge	-1	0
High Caliber/Gauge	+1	0

This same chart works for different calibers of rifle and, though it is less common, different gauges of shotguns.

• *Magazine Capacities*

The next consideration for using a firearm is how much ammunition it can carry. The size of the magazine varies, but not as much as you might think. All non-specialty pistols are roughly the same size and shape. Some pistols are a little larger to accommodate larger cartridges, but making them too large would make them unwieldy and therefore less effective as weapons.

Astute observers will notice that we never listed how much ammunition any of the firearms on the weapons table could hold. This isn't an oversight on our part. Rather than list capacities for our generic weapons, we created a chart that will allow you to select the correct capacity for the caliber or gauge of the firearm your character is using.

Since all firearms of the same type are approximately the same basic size, if a firearm uses a larger cartridge, then there are naturally going to be less of them. Likewise, smaller cartridges allow for more of them in the same basic space. Once again, simply consult the table below to determine how many bullets your weapon can carry.

Type of Firearm	Size of Magazine (Number of Bullets)			
	Standard	Low Caliber	High Caliber	Extended Magazine
Machine Guns	100	150	100	Double Capacity
Pistol (revolver)	6	8	5	Double Capacity
Pistol (Semi-auto)	15	20	9	Double Capacity
Rifle (Anti-material)	5	7	3	Double Capacity
Rifle (Assault)	50	50	50	Double Capacity
Rifle (Bolt-Action)	1	1	1	Not Applicable
Rifle (Semi-Auto)	30	45	25	Double Capacity
Rifle (Sniper)	7	10	5	Double Capacity
Shotgun	8	10	5	Not Applicable
Submachine Guns	45	60	30	Double Capacity

- ***Types of Ammunition***

In addition to different calibers of bullets, you can also use different types of projectiles. Each type of ammunition has benefits and drawbacks.

- Standard Ammunition

Armor Piercing: Armor Piercing bullets are specifically designed to penetrate armor. *Special: Armor piercing bullets reduce the armor value of armor struck by the shell by ½ for determining how much the power of the weapon is reduced.*

Flechette: A flechette round is a pointed projectile with a vaned tail for stable flight.

Frangible: Frangible rounds are bullets designed to break apart on impact and bounce around inside your body to cause lots and lots of damage. *Special: Because frangible rounds are designed to break apart on impact, the armor value of the target is doubled for the purposes of gaffing damage from frangible bullets.*

High Explosive: A high explosive round is a round designed to trigger an explosion on impact with a solid object firing a secondary projectile at even higher forces into the target. *Special: The armor value of any target is reduced by ½ for the purposes of reducing the power of a high explosive round.*

Rubber: A rubber bullet changes is just like a normal shell except that the projectile is replaced with rubber rather than steel or lead. *Special: Rubber bullets change the damage type of the weapon from physical (body) to stun (mind). Additionally, the damage is resisted by the armor's impact value rather than its piercing value.*

Subsonic Rounds: Subsonic ammunition is ammo designed to travel as less than the speed of sound so that you don't hear the sonic boom. *Special: Target numbers to hear the sound of subsonic gunshots is increased by +5.*

Tracers: A tracer round is ammunition with a small pyrotechnic charge in its base. The pyrotechnic charge is ignited by the burning powder creating a tail of phosphorus that burns brightly. This allows the shooter to quickly adjust his or her aim to more easily hit the target. *Special: The first shot fired from a tracer doesn't provide any bonuses. However, subsequent shots at the same target receive a -1 bonus to the weapons target number. This is the total bonus received from tracers. It does not continue to increase with additional shots. Also note that tracers work both ways. Someone trying to locate the shooter can follow the trajectory of the tracer back to the shooter.*

White Phosphorus: White phosphorus ammunition has white phosphorus placed on the tip. This causes serious burns to the target on impact resulting in additional damage. *Special: A target wearing flammable material risks catching fire if struck by a white phosphorus round. (See catching fire on page 116)*

- Shotgun Ammunition

Beanbag: Beanbag ammunition replaces the shot with a small beanbag. *Special: Beanbag ammunition changes the damage type of the weapon from physical (body) to stun (mind). Additionally, the damage is resisted by the armor's impact value rather than its piercing value. Perhaps most dangerously, due to the spread of the shot as it leaves the shotgun, the target number to dodge this type of shell is increased by +3 (from 10 to 13).*

Ammunition Type	Target Number	Damage Rating	Damage Bonus	Range Increment	Special Rules
Standard Ammo					
Armor Piercing Rounds	--	--	-3	--	Yes
Flechette Rounds	+1	+1	--	--	No
Frangible Rounds	--	+1	--	--	Yes
High Explosive Rounds	--	+1	+1	--	Yes
Rubber Rounds	--	--	--	--	Yes
Subsonic Rounds	--	--	-2	- 20 ft	Yes
Tracer Rounds	-- (-1)	--	--	--	Yes
White Phosphorous Rounds	--	--	+2	--	Yes
Shotgun Ammo					
Beanbag Shells	--	--	--	--	Yes
Birdshot Shells	--	-1	-3	45 ft	Yes
Buckshot Shells	--	--	--	--	Yes
Slugs	--	+1	--	60 ft	No

Birdshot: Birdshot is made up of smaller pellets than buckshot. As such it flies farther, but does less damage on impact. *Special: Due to the spread of the shot as it leaves the shotgun, the target number to dodge this type of shell is increased by +3 (from 10 to 13).*

Buckshot: Buckshot is assumed to be the standard ammunition for a shotgun. As such, there is no change in the statistics for a shotgun using this type of ammunition. It is included only because of its special properties. *Special: Due to the spread of the shot as it leaves the shotgun, the target number to dodge this type of shell is increased by +3 (from 10 to 13).*

Slug: A slug is a large, heavy lead projectile intended for use in a shotgun, often for hunting large game. The slug has more range than beanbag shells, birdshot, or buckshot and does more damage than any of those three types of shotgun ammunition. However, unlike the three other types of shotgun ammo, it is no more difficult to dodge a slug than it is any other bullet.

- ● *Range Increment*

The last thing we need to discuss about firearms is range increment. Most people would agree that it is more difficult to shoot something that is further away from you. In addition to being more difficult to see, even a small error in aiming can equate to a large miss at a distance.

To take these factors into consideration, each ranged weapon has a range increment listed in number of feet. This represents the distance of each of four range increments – close, short, medium, and long. The fifth and final range increment – extreme – is equal to the double the long range increment.

Range Category	Length of Range	Target Modifier
Close	0 to RI	+0
Short	RI+1 to 2 x RI	+1
Medium	(2 x RI)+1 to 3 x RI	+3
Long	(3 x RI)+1 to 4 x RI	+6
Extreme	(4 x RI)+1 to 8 x RI	+10

For example, a machine fun has a range increment of 100 feet. Its range would look like this.

Close Range…... 0 to 100 feet
Short Range…... 101 to 200 feet
Medium Range.. 201 to 300 feet
Long Range…… 301 to 400 feet
Extreme Range.. 401 to 800 feet

Beyond 800 feet, characters are unable to successfully hit their targets with a machine gun.

- ▪ Range and Target Numbers

The target numbers given on the weapons chart are for the close range increment. When attempting to fire at a target beyond this range increment, the target number to successfully use the weapon increases. Use the chart below to help you determine the range increment and target number modifier for each ranged weapon.

Scopes can be used to mitigate some of these modifiers. To determine how much effect a scope has, simply divide the distance to the target by the magnification of the scope. Use this new distance to determine the modifier. So looking at a target 120 feet away through a scope with a magnification of "x6" would be the same as targeting something 20 feet away. *NOTE: This does not change the effective range of the weapon.*

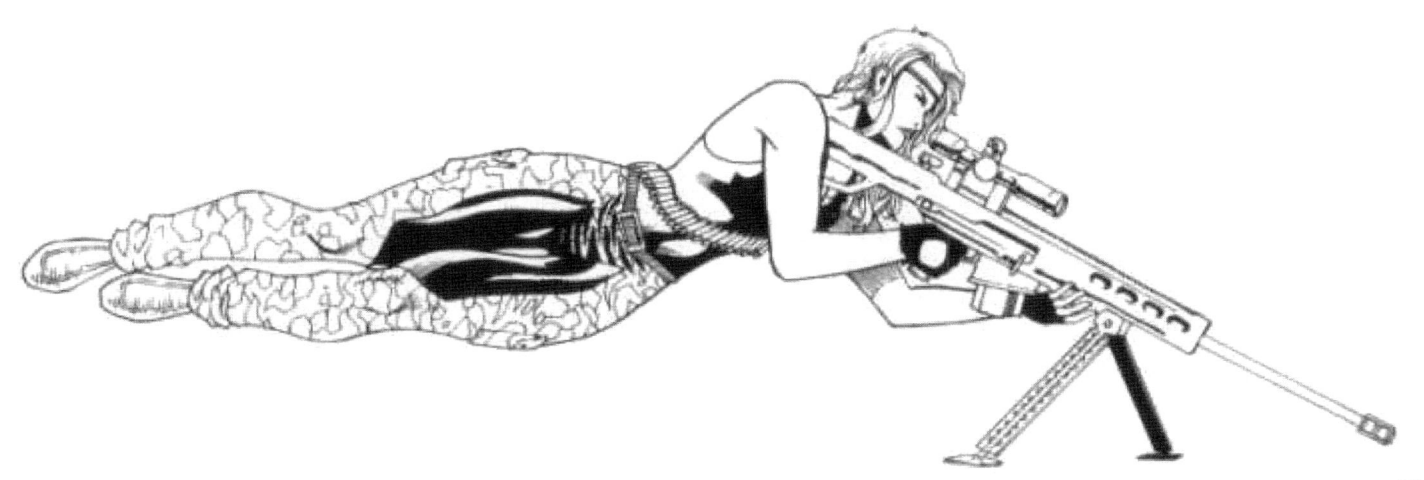

Explosives

Eventually, someone will want to find and use explosives. Explosives are extremely dangerous and should be used with extreme caution. Despite the extreme caution one should use in the real world, in this game they are treated like any other weapon. The one difference is that explosives add a new column to the weapons chart, however – Damage Radius.

- ***Damage Radius***

Damage radius works much like a range increment. Anyone trapped within this radius when the explosive goes off takes damage. (See dodging on page 111).

> **Types of Explosives**

You might thing explosives are not something that the average person could easily get their hands on, even during the zombie apocalypse. I shared this misconception until I started doing the research for this book. I was surprised to learn how many explosive were not that difficult to come by… even without the internet.

For simplicities sake, we're going to cover the seven explosives found in the default area that are most often used in role-playing games.

Det Cord: Det cord (short for detonation or detonating cord) is a high-speed fuse composed of a high-speed explosive material (4 miles per second) encased in a plastic tube. *Special: Unlike most explosives on this list, det cord is set rather than thrown. The statistics given on the chart are for a single strand of det cord running through a 5 foot area. It is, of course, possible to run several passes of det cord through the same 5 foot area. Each additional strand adds +1 to the damage bonus for det cord up to a maximum bonus of +5. Additional strands do not increase the damage any further. You can only blow someone up so much.*

Dynamite (¼-stick): Dynamite is actually fairly common. It's used by local farmers (especially older farmers) for everything from digging holes to removing stumps. Dynamite was invented by Alfred Nobel (of peace prize fame). Dynamite has changed significantly since Nobel first created the explosive. A stick of dynamite is a cylinder about 8 inches long and about 1 ¼ inches in diameter. *Special: More than one stick of dynamite can be used at a time. The first ¼ stick added increases the damage bonus by +1. The second ¼ stick added increases the damage rating by +1. A third stick added increases the damage radius by 5 ft. This pattern continues*

until 12 ¼-sticks are used. Beyond that, you run into the "can't blow someone up any more" issue. Like playing with real dynamite, it gets a bit tricky. Because that's a lot of math (and we're lazy), we made a chart that we'll share with you.

Frag Grenades: Frag grenade is short for "fragmentation grenade". While frag grenades certainly explode, it is the shrapnel (fragments of the grenade's casing) for which they're named that make them so deadly. When a frag grenade explodes, its shell is shredded and these shards of casing are propelled by the explosion tearing, cutting, punching, and piercing anything they come upon. *Special: A fragmentation grenade does both piercing and slashing damage. A character unfortunate enough to be in the damage radius of one of these explosives uses the worst of the two rating for the armor he or she is wearing. (See armor on page 100)*

¼ Sticks of Dynamite	Damage Rating	Damage Bonus	Damage Radius
1	2	+1	5 ft
2	2	+2	5 ft
3	3	+2	5 ft
4	3	+2	10 ft
5	3	+3	10 ft
6	4	+3	10 ft
7	4	+3	15 ft
8	4	+4	15 ft
9	5	+4	15 ft
10	5	+4	20 ft
11	5	+5	20 ft
12	6	+5	20 ft

Molotov Cocktail: A Molotov cocktail is an improvised explosive consisting of a breakable container such as a glass bottle filled with a flammable liquid and plugged with a rag. The rag is lit on fire and the container is thrown creating a fireball when it strikes an object. *Special: A Molotov cocktail does +3 points of bonus damage if it strikes a target. Anything hit by a Molotov cocktail is in danger of catching fire (see catching fire on page 116).*

Plastic Explosive: Plastic explosive comes in a brick weighing approximately 1 pound. It resembles a brick of hard, translucent wax when cold. Once it has been kneaded, the plastic explosive warms and is easily shaped. *Special: Each additional brick of plastic explosive used beyond the first adds +4 bonus damage to the attack and increases the damage radius by 2½ feet.*

Weapon	Skill	Target Number	Damage Rating	Damage Bonus	Damage Type	Range Increment	Damage Radius	Special Rules
Det Cord	Demolitions	5	2	+1	Energy	--	5 ft	Yes
Dynamite (¼ Stick)	Thrown or Demolitions	6	2	+1	I	10 ft	5 ft	Yes
Frag Grenades	Thrown	6	3	+4	P / S	10 ft	20 ft	No
Molotov Cocktail	Thrown	6	2	0 (+3)	Fire	10 ft	5 ft	Yes
Plastic Explosive (1 lb.)	Demolitions	5	2	+4	I	--	10 ft	Yes
Thermite (1 lb.)	Demolitions	6	9	0	Energy	5 ft	10 ft	Yes
White Phosphorus Grenade	Thrown	6	2	+3	Energy	10 ft	20 ft	Yes

Thermite: Technically, thermite is not an explosive since it does not actually explode. Instead thermite produces an exothermic oxidation-reduction reaction. In English that means it burns really, really hot... somewhere in the vicinity of 4,500° Fahrenheit... possibly high depending on the recipe used to make the termite... That's a big number, so big, in fact, that it's hard to imagine, so I'll try to put that into perspective for you. Thermite burns roughly 3 times hotter than molten lava... When a spacecraft renters Earth's atmosphere, it encounters temperatures around 3,000° Fahrenheit... If you parked your car on the beach and ignited thermite on the hood, it would burn through the hood, melt the engine and turn the sand under the car to glass as it burned its way into the earth.

It isn't just temperature that makes thermite dangerous. Unlike the other explosives on the list, thermite contains its own fuel and oxygen supply. It can't be smothered making traditional firefighting equipment useless against it. Thermite will burn underwater. It will burn in the vacuum of space. It will continue to burn until it has exhausted its fuel, and there is nothing you can do about it.

This, of course, makes thermite an ideal way of dealing with hardened military targets... like tanks... and destroying things you don't want your enemies to be able to use against you... or touch for a while... or identify afterwards...

It should go without saying that getting caught inside the radius of a thermite reaction is not conducive to your continued existence. Short of a miracle, you will die.

So, you might ask yourself, if this stuff is so dangerous why is it included on this list at all? The answer might surprise you. Thermite is very easy to obtain... and would make just as short work of a zombie as it would you.

CAUTION: ***DO NOT,*** *for any reason, attempt to obtain or use thermite. It's a good way to get yourself killed. If you genuinely have such little regard for your own life, get a job in a high-risk profession like pararescue jumper, volunteer to test experimental medication, or join a circus and* *apprentice to some death-defying act. At least then you'll serve a purpose.*

Special Because you can't stop the thermite reaction, anyone caught in the damage radius takes the same damage indicated by the attack roll each round until you leave the damage radius or the reaction ends. How long the thermite burns depends on how much is used. Again, because we're such nice people, we've made a nice chart for you.

Pounds Used	Duration In Rounds	Damage Radius
1	2	5
2	4	10
3	6	15
4	8	20
5	10	25
6	12	30
7	14	35
8	16	40
9	18	45
10	20	50

Unlike other explosives, using more thermite doesn't increase the damage rating. However, thermite burns hot enough to melt armor your character is going to find. As such, armor provides no protection against thermite. In fact, as the armor melts, it will cause more harm. In the second round your character takes additional bonus damage equal to the highest damage rating of the armor your character is wearing after which the armor is either a molten puddle at your feet or vaporized.

White Phosphorus Grenade: A white phosphorus grenade using an explosive charge to rain burning phosphorus in the damage radius. *Special: Anything within the damage radius of a white phosphorus grenade is in danger of catching on fire (see catching on fire on page 116). Additionally, a white phosphorus grenade creates a lot of smoke. Within 5 feet of the detonation point is considered "thick smoke" and there is ring of "light smoke" in a 10 foot radius around that. (See visibility on page 114)*

Armor

The last thing we'll need to discuss is the armor that your character wears. Most people don't wear armor every day… at least most people don't realize that they're wearing armor.

Again, making an exhaustive list of armors would be impractical and… exhausting. So, rather than do that, we once again turned to the types of armor that could be found in the default setting. Using these armors as examples, you should be able to make any type of armor found in whatever setting you choose to use… unless you use the default setting, in which case it should cover nearly all of them.

- Reading the Armor Chart

Every kind of armor in this game has four armor values – Slashing, Piercing, Impact, and Energy. The weapons listed on the weapons table all include a damage type.

Slashing Value: Slashing damage is any damage that involves cutting into something rather than piercing it. Knives, swords, and chainsaws are all examples of slashing damage.

Piercing Value: Piercing damage is puncture damage. Bullets, arrows, crossbow bolts, and teeth are all examples of piercing damage.

Impact Value: Impact damage covers anything that causes damage by hitting you rather than slashing or piercing. Bats, batons, punches, and kicks are all examples of impact damage.

Energy Value: Technically all damage is done by the transfer of energy. The energy rating of armor specifically covers those damages that are not related to kinetic energy. It covers heat (from fire) and cold (from a Wisconsin winter) damage.

As with weapons, after the statistics is a column to indicate whether there are special rules that govern the use of the armor. If you find a "Yes" in this column, see the description of the armor to learn what special rules apply.

➢ **Types of Armor**

Attack Dog Training Suit: This thick, padded suit is designed to protect someone from attack by a guard dog. Though this armor is usually used in the training of said dogs, it has an expanded usage during the zombie apocalypse. *Special: Attack Dog Training Suits are bulky and limit movement. Anyone wearing such a suit has their movement rate cut in half (see movement on page 118)*

Bomb Squad Armor: This armored suit is normally worn by bomb disposal technicians and is designed to protect the wearer from an explosion should a device detonate while it is being disarmed. *Special: Bomb squad armor is bulky and heavy. Anyone wearing such a suit has their movement rate cut in half (see movement on page 118)*

Chainmail Shirt: Though you might not think it, quite a few people have made chainmail shirts that are now hanging in their closets. While it's not ideal armor, it sure beats a cotton shirt for protection from zombie bites.

Fireman's Fire Suit: A fireman's fire suit is designed to protect the fireman from heat and flame. Because of its construction, it also provides some protection from slashing, piercing, and impact damage.

Football Pads: Football pads are designed to protect you from impact. They generally consist of shoulder, elbow, thigh, and tail bone pads, a protective cup, and a helmet. *Special: While they do provide some protection, this protection is very limited. Football pads do not protect against any injury to your torso... which is where most people will try to hit you.*

Forced Entry Armor: Forced entry armor is the armor worn by S.W.A.T. entry teams. It provides considerable protection against bullets, blades, and even bats. It even grants descent protection against energy damage. *Special: Forced Entry armor is heavy and bulky limiting movement. Anyone wearing one of these suits has their movement rate halved. (See movement on page 118)*

Hazmat Suit: A Hazmat suit is a protective garment as protection from hazardous materials (that's where the name "hazmat" comes from) and substances. This suit covers the entire body and usually contains its own breathing apparatus. *Special: If a character wearing a hazmat suit is hit by a slashing or piercing attack (fails to dodge said attack) the suit no longer provides any protection.*

Linothorax: Linothorax is a type of upper body armor used in the ancient Greeks. The art of making this armor was lost to time. Only written descriptions and images on pottery remained until its secrets were unlocked once again by UW-GB's Linothorax Project. Because of its unique properties and special link to our default setting, we'll discuss this amazing armor in more detail at the end of this section.

Leather Jacket: A leather jacket is exactly what it sounds like – a jacket made of leather.

Armor Type	Slashing Value	Piercing Value	Impact Value	Energy Value	Special Rules
Attack Dog Training Suit	2	3	3	2	Yes
Bomb Squad Armor	3	3	5	6	Yes
Chainmail Shirt	4	2	3	1	No
Firemen's Fire Suit	2	1	1	5	No
Football Pads	0	0	2	0	Yes
Forced Entry Armor	3	4	3	2	Yes
Hazmat Suit	0	0	0	6	Yes
Linothorax	2	2	3	0	No
Leather Jacket	1	1	1	1	No
Light-duty Vest	2	2	2	1	No
NBC Suit	2	2	2	7	Yes
Reenactment Plate Armor	3	1	2	0	No
Riding Leathers	2	1	2	1	No
SCUBA Dry Suit	1	1	1	4	Yes
SCUBA Wet Suit	1	1	1	3	No
Snowsuit	2	1	2	4	Yes
Special Response Vest	3	3	3	2	No
Tactical Vest	2	3	2	1	No
Undercover Shirt	1	1	0	0	Yes
Undercover Vest	2	2	1	0	Yes

Light-Duty Vest: A light-duty vest is a lightweight tactical vest used by law-enforcement and military forces.

NBC Suit: An NBC (Nuclear, Biological, & Chemical) suit is a combination hazmat suit and bomb disposal armor designed to protect disposal technicians who disarm nuclear, biological, & chemical devices. *Special: Like other suits of this type, a NBC suit is bulky, so it reduces the character's movement rate by half (see movement on page 118). Additionally, if the character suffers damage from a slashing or piercing weapon, the suit's ability to withstand radiation, biological agents, or chemical agents is compromised. The suit still protects from energy attacks like fire and cold.*

Reenactment Plate Armor: A resurgence of renaissance fairs and medieval reenactments has created a new breed of knights wearing gleaming armor. Advances in metallurgy and technology have made this armor lighter… but less protective than its predecessors.

Riding Leathers: Riding leathers is either a one-piece suit or a two piece outfit consisting of a leather jacket and leather pants or chaps.

SCUBA Dry Suit: A dry suit is a diving suit used for cold water dives in temperatures from 28° to 59° Fahrenheit. The dry suit protects its wearer from this temperature by maintaining a pocket or pockets of insulating air between the wearer and the water. *Special: If this suit is cut or pierced (if the wearers fails to dodge such an attack) the suits protection from energy is negated until the suit has been properly repaired.*

SCUBA Wet Suit: A wet suit is a diving suit made of foamed neoprene worn by surfers, divers, windsurfers, canoeists, and other people engaged in water sports. The suit provides some minor protection against injury, but its most important feature is its ability to protect the wearer from cool waters.

Snowsuits: A snowsuit can be a one-piece jumpsuit or a two-piece in the form of a heavy jacket and matching insulated pants. These suits are designed to keep your body warm while you engage in winter sports and activities… which in Wisconsin can be anything from trick-or-treating to skiing and snowmobiling. *Special: Snowsuits are somewhat bulky, so they quarter the movement rate of any character wearing one.*

Special Response Vest: A special response vest is heavy version of the tactical vest. It incorporates groin and neck protection.

Tactical Vest: A tactical vest is the standard body armor for police tactical forces and military units.

Undercover Shirt: An undercover shirt is a T-shirt with bands of light protective material sewn into the lower torso used when an undercover operative must not appear armored. *Special: An undercover shirt does not count as an additional* *piece of armor for terming movement penalties for wearing more than one type of armor at a time.*

Undercover Vest: An undercover vest is an armored vest (commonly referred to as a bullet proof vest despite the fact that it is not truly bullet proof) that is designed to wear beneath clothing. *Special: An undercover vest does not count as an additional piece of armor for terming movement penalties for wearing more than one type of armor at a time...*

- Stacking Armor

In some cases it is possible to wear more than one kind of armor at a time… and players are going to try to do it. When this occurs, the character gains full benefits for the highest armor value worn. The armor with the second highest value provides ½ that value to the character's overall protection. A third suit, if added, provides ¼ its value to the total. Remember to round the way you learned in school. Additional suits provide no benefit.

This added protection comes at a price. The character's action pool is reduced by 1 for each suit of armor worn beyond the first. This reduces not only the number of additional dice the character can bring into play to augment his or her actions during a given round, but also reduces the number of dice he or she gets to roll to determine initiative (see combat on page 109).

Further, each suit of armor after the first reduces the character's effective quickness by 1 point, reducing his or her ability to dodge attacks. This would also reduce the character's movement rate, which is derived from his or her quickness (see movement on page 118). This is in addition to movement penalties for bulkier armors (which also take their full effect), and is subtracted from the character's quickness before normal movement penalties for bulkier armors have been applied. Each movement penalty is applied separately in turn rather than all at once. (This is important because of the way you round. Reducing a quickness of 1 by ½ twice will result in a ½ and a ½ both of which are rounded back up to a 1. Reducing a quickness of 1 by ¼ will result in a ¼ which is rounded down to 0… meaning a character is immobile. (No one wants to play a turtle… at least one that wasn't secret mutated by ooze, named after a famous artist, and trained as a ninja by a mutated rat.)

For example, a character with a quickness of 5 find a hazmat suit that fits over the snowsuit they are already wearing. The addition of the hazmat suit won't change the slashing, piercing or impact values of the armor. It will, however, increase the energy value by 2 (the value increases by ½ the lower value, in this case, the snowsuit's energy value of 4 becomes an increase of 2 to the hazmat suit's energy value of 6 giving the character a total energy value of 8).

However, the character's effective quickness is reduced from a 5 to a 4 because he or she is wearing two suits of armor. This reduces his movement rate from 25 feet per action to 20 feet per action. The snowsuit and hazmat suit each normally reduce movement by ½, and both need to be applied. The snowsuit reduces the character's movement from 20 feet per action to 10 feet per action. The hazmat suit further reduces it from 10 feet per action to 5 feet per action.

- *Linothorax*

When we study ancient history, we study the artifacts that were left behind. We have wonderful examples of stone work, metal work, and even some wood work from the ancient world. We do not have many examples of their clothing, however. Cloth just doesn't stand up well to centuries of exposure. Most of what we know about the clothing and cloth used in the ancient world comes from the artwork and documents that survived.

Professor Gregory Aldrete and his students working on the Linothorax Project have found approximately two dozen accounts in ancient literature and approximately 700 visual examples of linen armor we've come to know as linothorax.

Using these ancient references, the Linothorax Project was able to reconstruct a viable linen-based armor from materials available during the period. Their discovery is nothing short of amazing. They have managed to rediscover something that was lost to time… and our own preconceptions of what the ancient world was like. It changes our perception of the ancient world, or at least it should.

Linothorax was constructed from numerous layers (between 11 and 18 depending on the thickness and weave) of laminated linen. UW-GB's Linothorax Project experimented with different types of linen. It was found that fine or course weave was not an important factor. Test have shown no notable difference between linothorax made from full sheets of fabric or patches of fabric. What seems to matter most is the thickness of the final product. Tests have shown slightly less than ½ inch (12mm to be precise) to be optimal balance between protection and flexibility. Since scraps can be used to produce this amazing armor, the only real constraint is time.

The extensive tests on this armor by the Linothorax Project have yielded amazing results. Linothorax has proven surprisingly effective at protecting its wearer against both slashing and piercing blows. In addition, the flexibility of linothorax allows it to efficiently dissipate force from bludgeoning weapons as well.

Not only is linothorax extremely durable, it was significantly lighter than comparable metal armor. Linothorax made with period linen and glue weighed ⅓ the weight of metal armors

of the day. As the linothorax is worn, the body heat of the wearer warms the material causing it to conform to the body… unlike metal armor, which forced the wearer to conform to it. Linothorax also tends to be cooler than similar metal armor.

While those things are incredible traits if you're a Greek or Roman soldier, what, exactly, do they have to do with surviving the zombie apocalypse?

I'm glad you asked.

Because linothorax is made from laminated layers of linen adhered together with glue, it can be made into any shape or size. Any body part you could cover with linen could conceivably be covered by linothorax. Torso armor, shin guards, and helmets have been made and tested. Forearm and upper arm guards are certainly plausible even if they have yet to be constructed in the modern world.

The reconstructions done by the Linothorax Project showed some revealed some important points when producing this armor. First, each layer of lamination must be allowed to dry before a new layer was added, otherwise the interior layers would begin to mold. Second, the linen was much easier to

cut prior to laminating them together. In fact, the first "slab" of laminated linen they produced was a single sheet they hoped to cut once it had fully cured. This proved to be more difficult than they had anticipated requiring the use of a jigsaw equipped with a metal cutting blade.

However, because the methods of construction are incredibly simple, anyone with access to cloth and glue can produce linothorax (given enough time to allow the layers to dry). This makes it an extremely viable option for people with few other ways of protecting themselves. It also makes the armor easy to repair or replace.

Additionally, ancient documents record the use of linothorax as protection while hunting, and its effectiveness against the bites of wild animals with far more bite force than humans (roughly five times the bite force if you can believe National Geographic). Since zombies were once human, they have a similar bite force quotient to normal humans. Therefore it stands to reason that linothorax would provide protection from their bites as well.

The citation is the second century A.D. author Pausanius, Description of Greece, 1.21.7. The passage reads "Linen breastplates are not much used by fighters for they let steel pass through when driven with great force, but they are useful for hunters because the teeth of lions or leopards break off in them."

Lastly, though it might not seem like an advantage, because linothorax is made from linen, it can easily be decorated. In a world were zombies are not your only enemies, being able to readily identify friend from foe is not an advantage to be summarily dismissed.

Bob's Krewe makes extensive use of this type of armor. Student housing at UW-GB provided a vast supply of bed linens to use and glue was not that hard to come by on campus.

For more information about this amazing armor that you can make in your own home… and to see some videos of linothorax in action, please visit the Linothorax Project website. As someone who's had the opportunity to examine this unique piece of recovered history personally, I can tell you that it's well worth looking into.

http://www.uwgb.edu/aldreteg/Linothorax.html

The Rules

Rolling Dice

Before we can explain how to adjudicate a skill test (see the Skill Test section that follows) and ask you to choose skills for your character, we must first explain how and why the dice are used in the d10 System.

As mentioned earlier, one of the primary purposes of using dice is to add an element of randomness to the game. In a table-top role-playing game, there is no "win condition". Instead, success is measured by not losing. In order for "not losing" to be meaningful, there has to be a chance of failure. Dice allow for that chance.

➢ Ten-sided Die and Dice

This game uses a ten-sided die to resolve actions and tests. There are other games that use a 10-sided die; however, the d10 System uses them in a slightly different way.

Most ten sided dice are numbered zero to nine with the zero understood to represent a ten if it is rolled. Rather than counting the die from one to ten, in the d10 System, we count the die from zero to one just as it is shown. If your dice are actually numbered one to ten, the ten will count as a zero. If you're dice are numbered for use in determining percentages (i.e. double zero through ninety), then ignore the final zero.

• Rounding

Any time you divide a number and come up with a fraction, that number is rounded the same way you learned to round in school (i.e. to the nearest whole number).

• Successes

A particular die is considered to be a success when it meets or exceeds the target number for the test in question.

This does not necessarily mean that the task measured by the test was successful. For some tasks multiple successes are required for the task to be accomplished. This is known as the success threshold.

• Exploding Die

This term does not mean that your dice explode. Instead, it refers to the act of rerolling a dice and adding the results of the second roll to the first to determine the final result.

In the d10 system, every time you roll a nine on a die, you reroll that die and add the results to the initial roll. If another nine is rolled, you reroll the die again and add the results to the first two rolls. This continues until something other than a nine is rolled on that die.

Because the die is counted from zero to nine, this method allows you to, in theory, roll any whole number zero or greater. In practice, it becomes increasing harder to roll higher and higher numbers. The highest result that I've personally witnessed on a single die is a 70… which was pretty impressive… more so because it was a crucial negotiation test.

• Critical Successes

Anytime *all of the dice rolled* for a particular test achieve a result that is equal to or higher than the target number, this is considered to be a critical success.

A critical success is the best possible outcome for a given situation. Usually this is left up to the director to decide, but there are some circumstances where the results are defined. The most important of these situations (to most players) is going to be combat.

NOTE: a character can never get a critical success when pulling their punch (see pulling your punch on page 105).

▪ In Combat

Attack Roll: A critical success on an attack roll increases the damage rating of the weapon by one for determining damage from that particular attack.

Dodge Roll: A critical success on a dodge means that the dodge does not cost the character an action.

▪ Repair Tests

When a critical success is achieved on a repair test, the interval for the repair increases by one interval of time (i.e. from minutes to hours, from hours to days, etc.).

• Critical Failure

Conversely, if all the dice rolled for a test come up *ZERO*, then a critical failure has been rolled. This represents the worst possible result for the character. They might move into the line of fire making an otherwise normal attack into a more lethal attack. They might cause more damage to something while they attempt to repair it.

➢ Pulling Your Punches

Sometimes you do not want to do a lot of damage to your target. Sometimes you want the thing you're fixing to work, but not well or not for long. In these cases you pull your punch. To pull your punch in the d10 system, simply roll less dice than your skill would otherwise allow.

For example, let's say your character has an unarmed combat skill of six. The character has a fellow party member who's being unruly, and you decide that your character wants to punch him or her. You don't want to seriously injure another player's character (in this example anyway), but you want to get their attention. So, rather than roll all six of your unarmed combat dice, you choose to pull your punch and only roll three of them.

Easy, right? The only downside to this is that you cannot add more dice once you've rolled. If, in the example above, the three dice don't do the job, you'll have to wait for your next action before you can swing again (see combat on page 109).

> **Adrenaline Surges**

The human body is an amazing machine. In times of crisis, it can perform beyond what any of us ever imagined. Mothers lift cars off of their children. People push fear aside to rush into flaming buildings to rescue people they've never met. Someone ignores near fatal injuries to save a friend.

All of this is done with the help of adrenaline… and endorphins… and some other chemicals that escape me at the moment. When the chips are down, characters can tap this amazing potential too, but it is not without cost.

If you believe your character to be in a situation where adrenaline, endorphins, and other chemicals I can't name would kick his or her body into overdrive, simply declare what you believe would trigger such a surge and sacrifice an action pool die to initiate the surge. Once the surge is initiated, the character can sacrifice additional dice (up to one from each dice pool) to gain the desired effect.

Duration: The adrenaline surge lasts until the scene ends or the crisis that triggered the surge is removed. This may be the entire duration of a fight or just until a particular character is out of harm's way. The director will establish this ending condition when the player initiates the surge.

After Effects: Once the surge has ended, the character is fatigued. To represent this, the character suffers one point of physical (body) and mental (mind) damage for each initiative round that the adrenaline surge lasted. This damage cannot be gaffed or resisted in any way; however, such damage does not bleed over into the next category in the damage hierarchy like normal damage does. (See Health and Healing on page 118)

Additionally, dice sacrificed from dice pools spent to initiate the surge _do_ _not_ refresh until the player has rested. (See Healing Damage & Fatigue on page 120)

- *Possible Effects of an Adrenaline Surge*
  - When making a skill test, *in addition* to the skill dice that they would normally roll, the character can also roll dice equal to the attribute score that governs that skill. Activating this ability costs one action point.
  - The player can choose to spend a die from his or her vigor pool to ignore modifiers caused by physical damage for the duration of the adrenaline surge.
  - The player can choose to spend a die from his or her willpower pool to ignore the effects of mental damage for the duration of the adrenaline surge.

Skill Tests

Any time a player rolls dice on behalf of their character, this is a "test". Skill tests are, by far, the most common tests you will be asked to make for your character. There are four basic types of skill tests you'll come across during play. Each type applies to specific type of situation in the game. Each type of skill test is detailed later in the Skill Test section. It is up to the director to decide which type of skill test is required for a particular situation.

Standard Test: A standard test is a test where a player rolls dice equal to his or her skill rating against a target number assigned by the director.

The standard test is most often used when the character is attempting to accomplish a task without any direct opposition from another character. Searching the internet, picking a lock, or repairing a car are all examples of situations where a standard test *might* be the most appropriate choice.

Open Test: An open test is a test where the character is performing an action that is likely to be directly opposed by another character. In an open test, the player rolls dice equal to his or her character's skill rating. The highest result achieved on the roll becomes the target number for the opposition's skill test should it become necessary.

This type of test is often used when your character is attempting to hide or sneak. The result of the open test then becomes the target number for sentries and other guardians to notice your character sneaking or hiding.

Direct Test: A direct test usually occurs when two characters are directly competing against each other. It is one of the few times attributes come into play outside of defaulting on a skill test.

In a direct test, the character's roll their skill dice against a target number that is usually the attribute of the other character. The object of the test is to determine which of the two characters involved gains the most successes.

This type of test is most often used in conjunction with social skills. The character rolls his or her appropriate skill dice against a target number equal to the one of the target's attributes (usually reason, insight, or psyche). The target then rolls either skill dice (if there is an appropriate counter-skill) or attribute dice equal to their opponent's charisma. (If there is an appropriate counter-skill and the opponent does not have it, they are considered defaulting. See defaulting on a skill check on page 107).

Parallel Test: The last type of test is a parallel test. This test comes when two characters directly oppose each other to achieve a goal, but there is some outside factor that determines the actual difficulty of the test.

For a parallel test, both character's roll dice equal to their respective rankings in the appropriate skill against a set target number. Again, the winner is determined by which of the characters achieves the most successes.

An example of a parallel test would be two players competing against each other in a video game. Each player would roll dice equal to his or her applicable skill against a target number representing the difficulty of the game. The player that scores the most successes on the parallel test would be the character that wins the contest.

- ***Defaulting on a Skill Test***

Sometimes a character doesn't have the necessary skill to accomplish a task. This does not mean that the character cannot still attempt the task. Sometimes knowledge of a different subject provides insight that allows you to do something you're not technically trained to do. Swinging a baseball and swinging a sword are similar skills… except for the fact that the sword has a sharp end. Knowledge of electronics and circuitry, for example, can help you try to defuse a bomb even if you don't know the first thing about explosives.

Even if you don't have a knowledge skill, you can sometimes use a related active skill to accomplish a task. If that is not an option, you can always relay on a combination of natural talent and dumb luck by defaulting to the attribute that would normally govern the skill.

Of course, someone defaulting on a skill will never be as capable as a trained professional… or a trained amateurs for that matter… but it's better than nothing. (And, in the case of the bomb, you're probably going to die anyway, so why not try. After all, what's the worst that could happen?)

Defaulting to another Active Skill: When defaulting to another active skill, the character takes a +2 penalty to the target number for the test.

Defaulting to a Knowledge Skill: When defaulting to a knowledge skill, the character suffers a +3 penalty to the target number of the test.

Defaulting to an Attribute: When defaulting to an attribute, not only does the character suffer a +2 penalty to the target number, they need to achieve twice as many successes to accomplish the same result. In other words, one success is counted out of every two successes rolled on the test.

➤ **Using Social Skills**

Just like in the real world, using a social skill depends on three things – your ability, your relationship with the person you're talking to, and the potential risks and rewards for that person.

Most social interaction skill tests will be direct tests. One character will roll his or her skill against one of the target's attributes. Meanwhile, the target will roll either a counter skill or an attribute against the applicable attribute. Whoever gains the most successes wins. The chart below will help you determine what skills and / or attributes are appropriate.

Social Skills	Target Number	Counter-Roll	Counter Target Number
Beguile	Insight	Discern Lie	Charisma
Fast-Talk	Reason	Reason	Charisma
Interview	Insight	Sense Motive	Charisma
Interrogation	Psyche	Psyche	Charisma
Intimidation	Psyche	Psyche	Charisma or Strength
Negotiation	Reason	Negotiation	Charisma
Seduction	Psyche	Sense Motive	Charisma

It seems easy enough, and it would be if people weren't involved. We tend to complicate things by adding extraneous details into the mix like risk and reward. If the rewards outweigh the risks, you're more likely to encourage someone to do something… unless you're threatening them. In that case, the exact opposite is true. The more horrific the perceived threat, the more likely someone is to comply with it.

In this game, the extra influence exerted by risk and reward are represented by bonus dice. As you explain the risk and reward to your target, the director decided the *net influence* that it will have on them and assigns bonus dice accordingly using the following chart as a guideline.

Perceived Consequences	Encouragement Bonus Dice	Threatening Bonus Dice
Fantastic	+3	-4
Favorable	+2	-2
Agreeable	+1	-1
Neutral	0	0
Unpredictable	-1	+1
Unfavorable	-2	+2
Horrific	-4	+3

Again, it's not overly difficult to understand. If you promise something of great value for minimal risk, you get bonus dice to cajole me into doing what you want me to do. Likewise, if you threaten the people I care about to get me to do what you want, as long as that threat is credible, you've got my attention.

This, of course, brings us to the one element of social interactions that always throws a wrench into the situation – relationships. Nothing confuses a situation faster than throwing emotion into the mix, and human emotion, for good or ill, invariably results in a relationship of some kind.

To take relationships into consideration, we must first define some terms that people tend to toss about without much care for their actual meaning.

When you're using these relationships, you always use what the target considers the character to be. That doesn't necessarily match with how the character views the relationship. I might consider you a friend, but you might only consider me a (hopefully) positive acquaintance.

Intimate: Despite the common use of the word, not every intimate relationship involves sex. In fact, many sexual relationships occur with people who have no intimate knowledge of one another. In an intimate relationship is one where the person knows the character very well. This person knows your character's darkest secrets… and still talks to you.

Friend: A friend isn't just someone who accepts your request on some social network website. A friend is someone your character feels he or she can count on and someone who can, in turn, count on your character. When you help a friend and tell them "you owe me one", you don't really mean it. You're not keeping score… you don't have to…

Ally: An ally is very close to a friend. Your character might hang out and do things with an ally. You even call on each other from time to time when you need a hand. The big difference is that with allies, unlike friends, you keep score…

Positive Acquaintance: A positive acquaintance is someone you get along with. It's someone you might even help… if it's not too much of an inconvenience.

Just Met: Someone with this level of relationship is someone you've met recently. They really haven't had time to form an opinion of you, but are often willing to give you the benefit of the doubt.

Never Met: People don't generally remain in this category for very long. This level of relationship only applies the first time you meet someone. Once you open your mouth, people are quick to form opinions about you.

Negative Acquaintance: This is someone that you know, but who really only tolerates your character's presence. They may act cordial and courteous. They may still be polite. They might even provide aid, depending on why you're acquainted in the first place. They just don't really like your character. This might be a party member who doesn't like you… or the significant other of one of your friends or allies.

Frenemy: This is someone who adheres to the old adage, "Keep your friends close and your enemies closer"… (Or, as my father often said "it's better to have a skunk inside your tent pissing out than outside pissing in). In any case, despite all appearances… and a frenemy works hard to keep up

Target Number Modifier							
Relationship	Beguile	Fast-Talk	Interview	Interrogation	Intimidation	Negotiate	Seduction
Intimate	-1	-1	-3	+3	+2	+5	--
Friend	-2	-2	-3	+2	+3	+3	0
Ally	-2	-1	-2	+1	+2	+2	-1
Positive Acquaintance	-1	0	-1	0	+1	+1	-2
Just Met	-1	0	0	-1	0	0	-1
Never Met	0	0	0	0	0	0	0
Negative Acquaintance	+1	0	0	+1	-1	+1	+1
Frenemy	+1	-1	+1	+2	-1	+1	0
Enemy	+2	-2	+2	+1	-1	+2	+2
Personal Foe	+2	-2	+3	+2	-2	+3	+4
Nemesis	+3	-3	+5	+3	-2	+4	+6

appearances… this person is not your character's friend… but the character isn't likely to know that… or has done an equally good job keeping up the façade for similar reasons.

Enemy: An enemy is someone who dislikes your character for some reason. They aren't likely to go out of their way to show their dislike, but they have no reason to hide it either. If you have to describe an enemy's feelings toward your character cold indifference would sum it up nicely.

Personal Foe: A personal foe actively dislikes your character. Unlike an enemy who won't go out of his or her way to show their dislike of your character, a personal foe will… unless they have something more important to do. The cold indifference of an enemy is a welcome respite from the hot ire of the personal foe.

Nemesis: A nemesis is someone who not only actively hates your character; he or she is someone who has made it their mission in life to make you suffer. Where a personal foe will show their dislike of the character only if they have nothing better to do, the nemesis *has* nothing better to do. Where the enemy is coldly indifferent and the personal foe is hot anger, the nemesis is boiling rage. They will make you pay for whatever it is you've done to them if it's the last thing they do.

➤ **Build & Repair Skills**

Your character's skill level is just one of several factors involved in repairing (or dangineering) something. The availability of tools and the conditions under which the character is working also play a large role. When a character needs to make a repair (or dangineering) test, consult the table below to determine any modifiers to the repair target number due to these factors.

The Working	Modifier to Target Number	
Conditions are…	Repair	Dangineer
Terrible	+5	+3
Very Bad	+3	+2
Bad	+2	+1
Not Good	+1	+0
Good	+0	-1
Very Good	-1	-2
Tools are…	Repair	Dangineer
Unavailable	Not Possible	Not Possible
Improvised	+4	+2
Inadequate	+2	+1
Available	0	0

These modifiers stack, so, if your character is trying to make a repair with improvised tools under terrible working conditions, they would incur a penalty of +8 to the target number for the test.

When your character makes a repair (or dangineers) something, the number of successes achieved has a direct correlation to how long that repair lasts. The more successes you get on the repair (or dangineering) test, the longer the repair holds out.

To do this, the character rolls the test normally. The repair last for a number of units of time equal to the attribute that governs the skill used. Consult the table below to determine the correct unit of time for the number of successes. Successes beyond five are added to the governing attribute to determine the length of the increment.

Number of	Time Increment	
Success	Repair	Dangineer
1	Hours	Minutes
2	Days	Hours
3	Weeks	Days
4	Months	Weeks
5+	Years	Months

For example, Dan (for whom dangineering is named) attempts to repair a non-functioning headlight. He gets 10 successes on his dangineering roll. (He's really good at it. That's why it's named after him.) Dan has a reason score of 3. The table says that it should last for three weeks. However, Dan has five additional successes which are added to his reason score of three to make a time interval of 8 weeks. After this time period elapses, the dangineered item ceases to function once again.

Combat

Many people seem to think that role-playing games are about combat and that the actual role-playing part of it serves only to string together the different battles. Combat is generally the most rules-intense portion of any role-playing system, but combat isn't just about beating your opponent with a big stick. Other forms of interaction can (and, in my opinion, should) be considered combat If reading the Art of War has taught me anything, it's that everything is a battle. If experience has taught me anything, it's that a well-timed barb can hurt just as much, and often more, than a well-timed punch.

Of course, treating everything like a combat situation is somewhat impractical. A negotiation, for example, is (usually) a straight forward back and forth exchange. Even though you're engaged in a battle of wits with your opponent, rolling initiative makes little sense. Etiquette requires certain behaviors and having the upper hand is more about how you conduct yourself than anything else. Each party involved is probably going to wait for his or her turn to speak. To act early would tip your hand and put you at a disadvantage.

➢ How Combat Works

Like most role-playing games, combat in the d10 system is handled cyclically. Each cycle is called a round. A combat round begins once initiative is rolled and ends when the last combatant uses his or her last action. This is done in order to make combat more manageable for the players and the director. It is not, however, the way combat takes place. Contests of arms are a chaotic whirlwind of activity happening simultaneously… or nearly simultaneously. Keep this in mind while imagining the course of the battle.

The round is divided into a number of imaginary units called phases. The exact number of phases in a round can vary widely and can even change after the round has begun based on the actions that the combatants take during the round. Phases exist only to help the director know who gets to act when.

• Initiative

Initiative is used to determine the order of action of all combatants, the number of actions that each combat can take in a round, and the number of phases that will take place during the round.

To roll for initiative, each potential combatant rolls dice equal to his or her action pool against a target number of 5 and informs the director of the number of successes achieved.

• Actions

Each success achieved on an initiative roll is a potential action that can be taken by a character. There are three types of actions – free actions, standard actions, and special actions.

Standard Actions: Standard actions are, by far, the most common. They include most things that the character will do during a combat round. Examples of actions are as follows:

- Attacking someone
- Dodging an attack by someone
- Parrying a melee attack (Combatants receive 1 free parry each round. Subsequent parry attempts cost an action)
- Drawing or sheathing a weapon
- Readying a new arrow or crossbow bolt.
- Reloading a firearm
- Moving up to the character's movement rate (see movement on page 118)
- Dropping to or rising from crouched position
- Rising from a prone position

Free Actions: Some things that a player will want his or her character to do during a round are simple activities that should not cost one of the character's actions. These activities are called "free actions." Examples of free actions are the following:

- Speaking (up to one sentence can be allowed each phase without spending an action) _unless_ speaking would require any type of skill or resistance test. You _cannot_ use a free speaking action to intimidate an opponent.
- Dropping an item
- Dropping to a prone position

Special Actions: Special actions are not actually actions. Instead they are ways that the combatants can change where they action in the initiative order. There are two types of special actions – Holding & Rushing.

> **Holding Your Action:** When a character holds his or her actions, they are choosing to act later in the round that their initiative would otherwise allow. This is usually done to wait and see what your opponent does. Actions not take while the character waits are "banked" and can be used only for defense (dodging and parrying). Any banked actions not used at the end of the round are lost.

> **Rushing Your Action:** Sometimes your initiative roll indicates that you act later in the round than you need to. When this occurs, the combatant's only choice is to rush his or her action. Rushing an action allows the character to act on the desired initiative phase; however, doing so is not without its drawbacks. First, the combatant does not receive additional actions based on their new phase. (A character with 3 successes still gets 3 actions even if they rush their action to act on phase 7 rather than phase 3.) Additionally, the character takes a penalty to all dice tests equal to the number of phases they moved up in the order. This penalty lasts for the entire round. (So the person moving from phase 3 to phase 7 would suffer a +4 penalty to all target numbers. This penalty would remain in effect until the round ended and a new initiative roll was made.)

▪ Attacking

Attacking costs the character an action. The player simply declares his or her target and rolls a number of dice equal to the appropriate weapon or unarmed combat skill against the target number for using the weapon in question (listed on the weapons chart). Each success is potential damage you deal to your target. If you are using a one-handed melee weapon, you get to add your strength score as an additional damage bonus. If you are using a two-handed melee weapon, you get to add one and a half times you strength score as a damage bonus.

Like other active skills, attacking can be augmented by action pool if the player desires.

Charging: A variation of the melee attack is the charge. In order to charge, you must move at least five feet toward your opponent. The attack is resolved normally. Charging does not increase the damage that your attack does to your opponent. It does, however, increase the power of that attack making it more difficult for your opponent to gaff the damage that you've done. Increase the power of the attack by your character's quickness attribute.

Called Shots: Sometimes you don't just want to hit someone. You want to hit them in the hand… or in the head… for whatever reason. When these situations arise, a modifier is applied to the target number to use the weapon. Use the table below to determine what modifier applies to a particular shot. *Note: the target number to dodge the attack does not change.*

Target	Modifier
Body	+0
Leg	+1
Arm	+2
Head	+3
Hand or Foot	+4

- **Head Shots:** If a character makes a called shot to the head of a target, that target suffers mind (mental), body (physical) and soul damage from that hit.

- *Dodging*

Dodging also costs the character an action. To dodge, a character rolls dice equal to her quickness against an appropriate target number based on the type of attack being dodged.

Type of Attack	Dodge Target Number
Melee	6
Projectile	8
Firearm	10

Each success achieved on the dodge test negates one success from the attack test. If you fail a dodge test, you can choose to parry the remaining damage, but this costs you an additional action even if you have not yet used your free parry for the round.

- Dodging Explosives

In order to dodge an explosive, a character *must* have enough movement rate to get out of the damage radius from his or her position when the explosive explodes. It should stand to reason that, if you can't get out of the blast radius, you risk being damaged by the blast.

In most cases, if the character was the target of the explosive, simply divide the damage radius by 5. If this is less than or equal to the character's effective quickness score, they can dodge. Keep in mind, however, that some armors reduce

movement rate, and stacking armor can drastically reduce movement rate (see stacking armor on page 102).

It is, of course, possible, and perhaps more feasible, to try and gain cover from the blast rather than try to outrun the explosion. If there is cover available, a player can use a banked action or reach cover. If they manage to find such cover, simply use the cover rules presented later in this book.

- *Parrying*

Everyone receives one free parry each round provided the following conditions are met.

- The character wishing to parry is being attacked with a melee weapons. (Despite what you see in the movies, you can't parry an arrow or bullet.)
- The character wishing to parry is holding a weapon suitable for parrying.
- Each character gets one free attempt to parry each melee round. Each additional parry in the same round costs an action.
- You can only try to parry a given attack once.
- If you fail to parry all the damage from an attack, your only remaining option is to gaff that damage. You *cannot* choose to dodge an attack after you've attempted to parry.

Parrying a melee attack is simple. Simply make an attack roll and calculate the damage you would do if you were attacking. Subtract the damage that you would do from the damage that your attacker would do. If the result is zero or less, you have successfully parried the blow. If the result is greater than zero, you have managed to deflect a portion of the blow. Apply the difference as damage. This damage can be gaffed normally.

Because parrying uses an attack skill, it can be augmented by action pool like any other attack roll.

NOTE: It is possible to use a rifle or shotgun to parry a melee attack. However, when you do so, rather than using your rifle skill, you use your impact weapons skill (after all, you're using the weapon as though it was a baseball bat rather than a firearm). Resolve the parry attempt normally calculating damage as if the firearm was, in fact, a baseball bat.

Doing this is very bad for the weapon. It causes damage that will make the weapon unusable until it is repaired. However, sometimes it's better to sacrifice a weapon rather than lose your life.

- Gaffing

Once you've done everything you can to avoid the attack all that is left for you to do is hope you can take it like a champ and suck up the damage.

To gaff damage, simply roll dice equal to the appropriate attribute (Constitution for physical / body damage and Psyche for mental / mind / stun damage) against a target number equal to the damage rating of the weapon plus 3. This is called the *power of the attack*. Each success you achieve on this test reduces the amount of damage you record by your character's appropriate gaffing score.

If your character is wearing armor that protects against the damage dealt by the attack, you can reduce the power of the attack by the appropriate armor value of the armor.

For example, if you are being struck by a metal baseball bat, the power of that attack would be a 6. If you were wearing a leather jacket which has an impact rating of 1, your target number to gaff damage from that attack would be reduced to a 5.

- ### *Sequence of Combat*

Step 1 – Roll Initiative: The person controlling each character involved in combat rolls a number of dice equal to his or her initiative score against a target number of 5 and counts the number of successes. This determines not only the order they take in combat, but the number of actions they get during that particular round of combat. Each success represents an action that the character could potentially take during this round of combat.

Step 2 – Declare Action: Once the character with the highest number of successes states what his or her character is going to do, the person controlling that character rolls to determine the results of his or her character's actions. This is the first phase of the combat round. *NOTE: The other players have not yet rolled for their character's actions. This will come in later phases.*

Step 3 – Resolve Action: Determine the potential results of the character's actions. This is usually the amount of damage possible if the attack succeeds.

Step 4 – Resolve Reaction: The targeted character has the option to take defensive action. This could be parrying a

melee attack (see parrying on page 111), dodging the attack, (see dodging on page 111), or just taking the blow and trying to gaff the damage (see gaffing damage on page 111).

Step 5 – Apply Results: Apply the results of the action as adjusted by the reaction to the target character.

Step 6 – Next Phase: Once the first phase is resolved, continue on to the next phase. When multiple combatants act on a single phase, something that happens a lot at lower phases, those who have not yet acted get to state and resolve their actions first. If two or more combatants have not yet acted and act on the same phase for the first time, the combatant with the highest quickness attribute goes first.

- #### Sample Combat Round

Three characters meet in an alley all hoping to get their hands on a rare prize found within. Tom is carrying an aluminum baseball bat. Joe is holding a katana. The third, Eric, is seemingly unarmed, but he's wearing a long trench coat. They eye each other warily for a few moments before the director calls for an initiative roll. Each player rolls dice equal to his or her character's action pool against a target number of five and informs the director of the number of successes achieved.

Tom has 5 successes. Joe has 3 successes. Eric has 7 successes. Each success rolled is a potential action that they can take during the combat round.

Because 7 is the highest number of successes rolled by a combatant, this round will have 7 phases, though, as you will see, action may not take place on all of them.

Eric has 7 potential actions during this round. Tom has 5 potential actions. Joe only has 3 potential actions.

Phase 7: Eric holds his action and banks it for defense later.

Phase 6: Tom uses a free action to tell Joe he's going to die. Eric holds his action another phase and banks a second action for defense.

Phase 5: Tom has not had an opportunity to act yet, so he gets to make his move before Eric. He attacks Joe with his metal baseball bat. Tom rolls his impact weapons skill against a target number of 6 and achieves 6 successes on his attack roll. He has a strength of 3, so the attack has a damage potential of 25 points of physical (body) damage (6 Successes multiplied by the damage value of 3 plus the damage bonus of +2 from the bat, plus one and a half times Tom's strength score of 3 because he's wielding the bat with both hands)..

Joe has a constitution score of 3, so 23 points of damage could kill him. He uses his free parry, bringing up his katana to block the blow. He rolls his edged weapons against the katana's target number of 5 and gets 4 successes. He has a strength score of 2, so his damage potential for parrying with the katana is 19 (4 successes multiplied by the damage rating of 4 [due to the Katana's special properties], plus the damage bonus of +1, plus Joe's strength score of 2 as he is wielding the sword one-handed). He has managed to deflect the majority of the blow, but is still looking at 4 points of damage.

Joe attempts to gaff the damage. He rolls his dice equal to his constitution of 3 against the power of Tom's attack. Joe is wearing a leather jacket, so the power of the attack is reduced by one, bring the target number to 5 (the bat's damage rating of 3 plus the standard +3 to give it a total power of 6 as a target number for gaffing minus 1 for the armor value of the leather jacket).

Joe does not get any successes with his constitution dice, so he chooses to roll four dice from his vigor pool to augment the roll. He gets two successes, each of which allows him to soak 2 points of damage (his physical gaff score). Though the attack hits him, the damage is superficial.

Eric still has a chance to act this phase, but decides to bank another defensive action. He'll let these two idiots kill each other and deal with the victor… who he assumes will be wounded already and an easy target.

Phase 4: Once again, both Tom and Eric can act in this phase. Tom has the higher quickness, so he gets to act first. He attacks Joe again. This time he uses all 7 dice from his action pool to augment his attack. With the extra dice from his action pool, Tom manages to get 13 successes against the target number of 6 for his bat. The damage potential this time is 46 points of physical (body) damage ($13\times3+2+(3\times1\frac{1}{2}$ rounded according to the standard rules of math).

Obviously, if 23 points was enough to kill Joe, 46 is enough to cause some serious harm. Joe (wisely) chooses to attempt to dodge Tom's attack. He really needs to succeed here if he is going to have a chance to survive this battle, so Joe decides to use his entire action pool to augment his dodge roll. His target number to dodge the attack is 6. He manages to get 9 successes on his dodge attempt reducing the damage he's facing from 44 points to 17. While that's easier to digest, with only 3 points of constitution, Joe can only take 15 points of body damage before he's dead, so this is still a potentially deadly attack.

Joe will need 7 successes against a target number of 5 to gaff the damage. He's already used most of his vigor pool, so he doesn't even have that many dice to roll. He chooses to spend another action to parry the remaining damage. He rolls 5 successes to parry making his damage potential 23. He manages to parry the remaining damage, but he is down to one

action remaining. He's out of action pool dice and only has half his vigor pool.

This round Eric acts. He pulls out the shotgun he's had hidden under his trench coat.

Phase 3: Since Joe hasn't acted yet, he gets to go first this phase. Since he only has one action remaining, only half his vigor pool, and no action dice, Joe chooses to hold his action and bank one for defense against Tom's next attack.

Tom comes through with the feared attack. He rolls his edged weapons skill once again against the bat's target number of 6 and gets 4 successes. His potential damage is 17, which is still enough to kill Joe.

Joe only has one action left, so he can either dodge or parry this attack. He chooses to parry because he'll get more dice to roll… since his action pool is gone. He rolls his edged weapons skill against the target number of 5 for the katana. Joe scores 4 successes giving him a damage potential of 19 points. This deflects all of Tom's damage.

Eric takes this opportunity to deal with his foes. Since Joe has taken a beating already, Eric levels his shotgun at Tom. He rolls his firearms skill against his shotgun's target number of 6 and gets 9 successes. This gives Eric's attack damage

potential of 39 points.

This is almost enough damage to kill Tom twice. Since you can't parry a firearm, Tom decides to try and dodge. It's a long shot, but it's the best chance he has. At most, Tom only has 11 dice to roll to gaff (4 dice from hi constitution and 7 dice from his vigor pool). At most, he could gaff 22 points of damage, leaving 17 points which would be a near fatal wound.

Tom rolls to dodge and miraculously gets 2 nines. He rerolls these and adds the results to his initial rolls getting 2 successes of 13 or more and negating 2 of Eric's successes. This reduces the damage he has to deal with to a *mere* 31 points of damage. Tom's going to have to gaff a lot of damage if he's going to survive.

He invests all of his vigor pool into the gaffing roll. The power of Eric's attack is 7, but Tom's wearing an undercover vest reducing his target number to a 5. He gets 6 successes negating a further 12 points of damage. The remaining 19 points of damage brings Tom all the way to the "near fatal" category. He will suffer a -4 dice penalty on all his future skill checks.

Phase 2: To recap where our combatant's stand… Joe isn't hurt, but he's out of attacks and both his action and vigor pools are completely expended.

Tom is suffering from a near fatal injury. He has completely expended both his action and vigor pools as well, and he only has one action remaining.

Eric hasn't used any of his dice pools yet, nor has he suffered any damage. He has two actions remaining and 4 actions banked for defensive actions.

Tom has the highest quickness, so he gets to act first. He knows Eric is going to kill him this round if he doesn't do something, so he charges Eric. Toms rolls dice equal to his impact weapons skill minus 4 dice due to his wound penalty. He gets 5 successes. He has the potential to do 17 points of damage to Eric.

Eric chooses to use one of his banked actions to dodge Tom's attack. He rolls his quickness dice against a target number of 5 and gets 3 successes. He rolls 3 dice from his action pool to get the last success he needs to avoid damage.

Having avoided Tom's blow, Eric rolls his attack and decides to add half of his remaining action pool to the effort. He scores 13 successes. The 55 points of potential damage are enough to kill Tom's character who only has 2 points of body damage remaining. There is no way Tom can dodge the attack or gaff the damage. Tom falls to the ground at Eric's feet.

Phase 1: Eric is the only one with actions remaining. He sets his sights on the last remaining combatant – Joe. Since this is the end of combat, Eric uses the rest of his action pool in his attack on Joe. He gets 6 successes, but there is no way for Joe to dodge or gaff the 27 points of potential damage. Joe's lifeless body drops to the ground.

Eric smiles at his victory. The bushel basket of apples they had been fighting over are his for the taking.

Unfortunately, firing three blasts for the shotgun drew the attention of every zombie in the area. They tend to be attracted to loud noises, and shotguns tend to be loud. They've crowded both ends of the alley trapping Eric. The director allows Eric to spend his banked actions to reload his shotgun… because it isn't going to matter anyway.

Eric may have won the battle, but he still managed to lose the war.

- ### *Miscellaneous Combat Modifiers & Rules*

The rules listed above will be enough to get you through most combat situations. Once is a while something comes up that throws a wrench into the mix. This section will try to deal with the most common of these occurrences.

- #### Visibility Modifiers

As anyone who has ever attended a birthday party with a piñata can tell you, being able to see a target makes it much easier to hit said target. Visibility modifiers do not really make the target more difficult to hit. The target still has the same dimensions and it is still in the same place doing the same things. Instead, how visible a target is affects the character's ability to hit it. As such, the modifiers for visibility do not increase target numbers (make the target harder to hit). Instead they decrease the number of dice you can use to fire at the target (decrease the character's ability).

Visibility Modifiers	Dice Penalties		
	Normal Vision	Thermal	Low-Light
Complete Darkness	-4	-1	-4
Minimal Light	-3	-1	-2
Dim Light	-2	-1	-1
Partial Light	-1	-1	0
Glare	-1	-2	-1
Mist	-1	0	0
Light Fog, Rain, or Snow	-1	0	-1
Heavy Fog, Rain, or Snow	-3	0	-2
Light Smoke	-1	-1	-1
Thick Smoke	-2	-2	-2
Very Thick Smoke	-4	-4	-4

Complete Darkness: As you might have guessed, "complete darkness" is the absence of any light source. In the real world this doesn't happen all that often. Even being outside at night you have some light from the moon (reflected sunlight) and stars. As long as the building has windows, being inside a dark building at night isn't much different from being outside at night.

Complete darkness usually occurs underground, in buildings or rooms without windows, and outside in the wilderness on really overcast moonless nights.

Minimal Light: Minimal light is the conditions you find yourself in when you're inside a dark building at night. It's also the condition of a moonless night far away from civilization that isn't overcast.

Dim Light: Dim light is the normal conditions outside at night away from civilization. It's dark, but not so dark that you can't function, albeit at a lesser aptitude than you function during the day.

Partial Light: To experience partial light one need only go out into the city at night. Street lamps provide enough lamination that you can't see the stars. It's not as bright as daylight, but it's a heck of a lot brighter than being trapped in a windowless basement without a flashlight.

Glare: Glare covers any sudden increase in the brightness of light, whether the flash of on-coming headlights or a bright room suddenly becoming dark. It also covers firing into the sun and other instances where bright light hampers vision.

Mist: Mist is caused by small droplets of water suspended in the air. It occurs naturally as part of the weather. It can also be caused by volcanic activity, though not in the default setting.

Light Fog, Rain, or Snow: Fog is a slightly thicker form of mist, though its impact is nearly the same. However, while mist is droplets of water suspended in the air, rain is actual precipitation. Snow, of course, is rain that has frozen and crystallized on its way down to Earth.

Heavy Fog, Rain, or Snow: This is just a heavier version of the pervious entry. It causes more visual impairment than the lighter variety.

Light Smoke: Light smoke is no heavier than a light fog. Still, it differs in that smoke derives from something burning rather than water droplets. Campfires made from dry wood tend to generate light smoke.

Thick Smoke: Thick smoke falls somewhere between light and heavy fog. This level of smoke is often generated by campfires made from wet wood or grasses and foliage.

Very Thick Smoke: Very thick smoke is even more impairing than complete darkness. It is usually found resulting from chemical fires or burning buildings.

- Cover

Cover is another issue that tends to pop up from time to time. In the d10 system, cover is more about what you're hiding behind than how far behind it you are. Let's face it, either you have cover or you don't. In the real world there is no partial cover, half cover, three-quarters cover, or full cover.

If I'm hiding behind a table but legs are sticking out, then the person shooting at me needs to be able to hit my leg. If he or she doesn't specifically target my leg, then the shot targets something behind the cover.

Because cover is functions in the same way that armor does, cover is treated exactly as armor is. Simply find the material that the cover is made of on the chart below… or something close to it. The object rating is treated as an armor value for all types of damage.

Material	Object Rating
Cloth	0
Glass	0
Safety Glass	1
Bullet Resistance Glass	2
Thin Wood	2
Thick Wood	3
Reinforced Wood or Soft Stone	4
Concrete	4
Hard Stone	5
Reinforced Concrete	5
Reinforced Hard Stone	6
Soft Metals	6
Metal Alloys	7
Hard Matel or Hardened Metals Alloys	9
Reinforced Metals	10

- Grappling

Characters can grapple with one another. To do this one character must make a successful hand to hand attack against the other. If a grappling attack is not dodged, it succeeds. The grappled character can attempt to break the grapple. To do this, the grappled character rolls dice equal to his or her strength score against a target number of the grappler's strength. The grappler also rolls his or her strength against the strength of the grappled character. Whoever gets the most successes wins. These rolls can be augmented by dice from action pool if either character desires.

- Fighting with Two Weapons

Characters can only fight with two weapons at the same time if they have a ranking of two or higher in the applicable skills for each weapon held and are using two one-handed weapons. The target number to use the primary weapon is increased by +2 and the secondary weapon's target number is increased by +3. The character receives full skill rating with his primary weapon. The character rolls ½ his or her skill dice for the second weapon up to his or her coordination score.

If the character is using melee weapons, he or she only adds ½ of their strength score to the damage from the weapon in his or her primary hand and no strength bonus to the damage for the second weapon.

A character fighting with two weapons can choose to engage two targets simultaneously. The difficulty for the primary weapon increases by +1 and by +2 for the secondary weapon. This makes a total modifier of +3 for the primary hand and +5 for the secondary weapon. (Like everything else, shooting two different targets at the same time is a lot more difficult than it seems in the movies.)

Since a character with the ambidexterity advantage can use both hands equally well, it is easier for them to fight with two weapons. Both weapons are considered primary weapons, so the target number for each is increased only by +2. If they are using melee weapons they get their ½ their strength bonus on each melee attack.

The character must still decide which weapon is their "secondary" however as the number of dice they can roll for this weapon is still limited for game balance. The limit, however, is increased to twice their coordination score. It's a small price to pay for being able to make two attacks in a single action.

- Surprise

If your character is surprised… or surprising someone, the person or people being surprised only roll ½ of their action pool to determine initiative in the first round of combat. Initiative in subsequent rounds is determined normally.

- Catching on Fire

If a character is exposed to fire in a bad way… say as part of an explosion, then the character risks catching fire. There is no active roll on the character's part to avoid this. He or she already had their chance to dodge the attack.

To determine whether or not a character, catches fire, simply roll a number of dice equal to the damage rating of whatever caused the fire against a target number equal to the energy value of the armor. If the object in question is not armor, roll the same dice against the object rating of the item in question.

If the material that the object is made out of is not on the material chart, use what is listed as a guide.

Each success achieved on this roll is a round that the fire continues to do damage to the target. The damage done is equal to the damage rating of the weapon that started the fire.

- Noise

Zombies seem to be attracted to loud noises. Zombies have been known to home in on the sounds of a battle, but there are certain weapons that draw their attention faster than others. Using weapons like firearms and explosive might dispatch zombies quickly, but it also tends to attract new zombies. This makes the snipers modus operandi of "Acquire, Fire, & Displace" almost mandatory for anyone fighting zombies.

If characters fight using firearms or explosives or a chainsaw or any other weapon that makes a lot of noise, they risk drawing the attention of zombies not yet in the fray. Any zombie… or other people… in the area might hear the sound of the battle.

To determine if other anyone hears the battle, look at all the weapons used in battle that make the most noise. Take the highest damage rating from among these weapons and add one for each additional noise-making weapon used during the previous round. Roll that number of dice against a target number equal to the distance in city blocks from the nearest zombie. If you're not in the city, one city block is roughly 500 feet. Each success is a zombie that starts toward the source of the noise… in other words, the place where you're shooting.

Zombies do not move quickly, so it will take them a while to reach the site of the battle. Humans will get there much faster. Of course, not knowing which direction that they're coming from is the biggest problem you'll face. You could run into them trying to leave the scene of the battle before they arrive.

Using a sound suppressor (there is no such thing as a silencer) doubles the target number for this test, but it also applies a penalty to the weapons damage bonus of -2 and decrease the range increment by 5 feet.

- Dodging Bullets

In the d10 system, a character that has available actions can always spend one of those actions to dodge an attack. This is part of game mechanics and is not always "realistic." Of course, you're playing a game where zombies are eating everyone, so you shouldn't get too high up on the realism horse…

Some of those people will argue that you shouldn't be able to dodge a bullet. Honestly, those people are right. However, this is just a game. Remind them. If they continue to object, inflict damage upon their character… always their character… no matter how much rage you might feel.

Others might, erroneously, claim that their character should be capable of this feat of superhuman dexterity. These people are idiots. Tell them… often…

If that doesn't work, here is the math behind dodging a bullet. Explain it to them… slowly… use small words… I'll type it slowly just in case they're reading it themselves…

First, according to the 1998 edition of *World Book Encyclopedia*, the average speed of a bullet is between 600 and 5,000 feet per second. As a general rule, pistols have a lower muzzle velocity (bullet speed) than rifles. Most of us can't think in feet per second, so let's translate that into something that's easier to imagine shall we?

A bullet traveling at 600 feet per second travels 36,000 feet in a minute (600 feet x 60 seconds in a minute). That means in an hour it travels 2,160,000 feet (36,000 feet per minute times 60 minutes in an hour). Since here are 5,280 feet in a mile, we can determine that the bullet is traveling at 409 miles per hour… on the low end. On the high end, using the same basic equations, we see that a bullet can travel as fast as 3,409 miles per hour. That's more than 4 times the speed of sound and pretty fast. I don't care who you are.

The M9 Beretta, a 9mm pistol that officially became standard issue for the U.S. Marine Corps in 1982, has a maximum effective range of 152.5 feet and a muzzle velocity of 1,200 feet per second (approximately 818 miles per hour).

Even at the furthest edge of its effective range watching the shooter pull the trigger, you don't stand a chance. It would take the bullet approximately 0.13 seconds to cover that distance. Since the hand to eye reaction time of the average human being is 0.16 second, the bullet would tear through your flesh 3 hundredths of a second before you even realized it was coming. It would take another 0.16 seconds for your muscles to react to the signals from your brain and try to get out of the way. Of course, you would have already been bleeding for 0.19 seconds.

That's pistols, but what about rifles? The longest confirmed kill by a sniper was set by a Canadian sniper team in Afghanistan at just under 7,973 feet. The gun they were using was an M107 with a muzzle velocity of 2,800 feet per second (approximately 1,909 miles per hour). That gives you 2.8475 seconds to get out of the way… oh wait… 2.6875 seconds… I almost forgot it takes a little bit of time for your mind to react. Sorry… 2.5275 seconds… I forgot that your mind needs time to tell your body what to do.

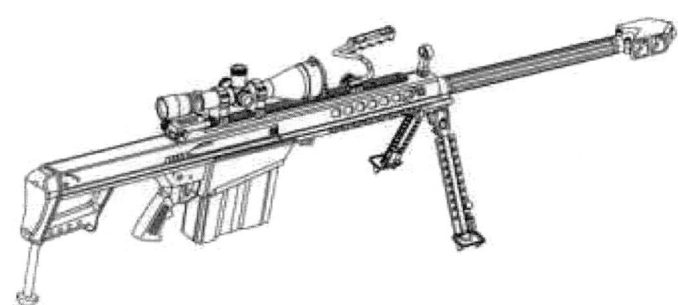

Of course, that's assuming that you notice the sniper lying prone just over a mile and a half away from you. The bullet is traveling somewhere around mach 2.5 so it would hit you before you even heard the shot… Of course, with the sound suppressor that any competent sniper would use, you probably wouldn't even hear the shot at all. Flash suppressors would make the muzzle flash a moot point, though at that distance, it's questionable whether you'd recognize it anyway.

As you can see it is simply unreasonable for anyone to believe that they can dodge a bullet. In the real world, if someone is shooting at you with a ballistic weapon, your only real hope is that either the shooter is incompetent or that your armor does its job.

Your character, however, is lucky enough to get a dodge roll. In fact, there is roughly a 9% chance that any die dropped will result in a 10 (a 10% chance of rolling a nine on the initial roll and then a 90% chance of rolling a one or higher on the second roll). Your chances of multiple successes decrease dramatically, but, frankly, we're still being extremely generous.

Movement

Knowing that your character can move as an action is only useful when you know how far your character can move.

Walking: In a normal action, a character can move five feet per point of quickness. If you're using miniatures and a tactical map, this is convenient (and no accident). Scale on such maps is usually 1 square = 5 feet. This means the character could move one square per point of quickness in an action.

Running: Sometimes walking doesn't get you where you want to go fast enough. In these situations, I like to use my car, but others might opt to run. Your character can make that same choice. All the character must do is declare that he or she is running. Once that declaration is made, the character can spend up to his or her constitution score in actions for movement in a single phase.

Quadrupeds:

Though players do not have the option of playing quadrupedal characters, such creatures do exist in the world. I know. I've seen them.

Four-legged (that's what quadrupedal means… just in case you thought I was making up words) animals tend to be quick. The rules for adjusting their movement rates is simple, however. Simple multiply the standard movement by the number of pairs of legs that the animal has.

For example, an average human with a quickness of 2 can move 10 feet in one action. A dog with a quickness of 2 can more 20 feet in one action. A three-legged dog can move 15 feet in one action.

Like other creatures, quadrupeds (and unfortunately animals like the three-legged dog in our example) can also run. They follow the same rules that humans and other bipeds do.

Health & Healing

During character creation we mentioned that there are three types of hit points used to represent the durability of your character's mind, body, and soul. We also talked about how to determine how much of each of these hit points your character had.

Keep in mind, if your character does not dodge (or parry) an attack, your has been hit by that attack. However, in the d10 System, we only keep track of damage that adversely affects your character. Growing up with three brothers, I can attest to the fact that not every blow your opponent lands hampers you. Some blows just motivate you… usually to teach your opponent the error of their ways and put an end to the fight.

> ➢ **Hit Points**

As we've already mentioned earlier, your character has three different types of hit points – Mind, Body, & Soul. Each keeps track of a different kind of damage that can be done to your character.

Mind Hit Points: Mind hit points represents your character's mental health. It's mental endurance, sanity, and ability to remain conscious all rolled into one.

Body Hit Points: Body hit points represent the physical punishment that your character can take. It represents your ability to take physical damage and your ability to resist the effects of diseases and toxins. In short, it's your health.

Soul Hit Points: Soul hit points represent your character's tie to the material world. It also represents their humanity. Having a lot of soul hit points doesn't mean that you are more humane. It just means you are capable of understanding humanity, human interaction, and human emotion.

A different attribute governs each type of hit points. Mind hit points are governed by your character's psyche attribute. Body hit points are governed by your character's constitution attribute. Soul hit points are governed by your character's charisma attribute.

- • **Wound Levels**

There are five wound levels – Minor, Light, Moderate, Serious, & Critical. Your character has a number of hit points at each wound level equal to the governing attribute for the type of hit points in question. If you have a constitution of 3, then you have 3 hit points in the minor wound level, 3 in the light wound level, 3 in the moderate wound level, 3 in the serious wound level, and 3 in the critical wound level. This would give your character a total of 15 body hit points.

Of course, there is no reason to divide hit points into wound levels if wound levels don't have some effect on the game. Since I hate keeping track of things that don't matter, wound levels have a direct effect on your character's abilities.

Minor Wounds: At this level of wounds, you character's activities are unhampered. They're likely in pain, but it's not enough to slow them down.

Light Wounds: Light wounds are where you character starts to feel the effects of the choices that they've made. When you've suffered a light wound, you take a penalty of -1 die to certain skills. If the light wound is mind damage, you suffer the penalty to any skills governed by mental attributes. If the light wound is physical, the penalty applies to any skill governed by physical attributes.

Moderate Wounds: A moderate wound hurts enough to give pause while you contemplate those questionable decisions that led you to this point. At this wound level, your injury has a primary and a secondary effect on your character. The primary effect is that the wound penalty suffered for the light wound increases from -1 die to -2 dice. The secondary effect is that the other skills (physical skills if it is moderate mental wound and mental skills if it is a moderate physical wound) begin to feel the affects as well. Your character now suffers a -1 die penalty to these skills as well.

Serious Wounds: Serious wounds are natures way of telling you that you need to slow down. Once again there is both a primary and a secondary effect. The primary penalty increases from -2 dice to -3 dice. The secondary penalty increases from -1die to -2 dice.

Critical Wounds: Critical wounds are called "critical wounds" for a reason. At this point your character is on the cusp of something he or she is not going to like. If it's a critical mental wound, the character is about to fall unconscious. If it is a critical physical wound, the character is about to die. At this wound level, the primary effect increase by another die, going from -3 dice to -4 dice. The secondary effect, however, remains at -2 dice.

Condition Monitor

Minor Wounds

Light Wounds

Moderate Wounds

Serious Wounds

Critical Wounds

- Hierarchy of Damage

If a character takes more damage in a certain hit point category than he or she has points remaining in that category, the extra damage bleeds into the next category of damage.

Blood, like water, always flows down hill, so damage can only bleed in one direction according to a strict hierarchy. Extra mental damage is applied as physical damage. Extra physical damage is applied as soul damage. There is no such thing as extra soul damage. A sample condition monitor is shown below. There is a condition monitor for each of the three damage types on the official character sheet. Simply black out the boxes that you're not using for your character.

- Multiple Wound Levels

If a character is unfortunate enough to suffer both mental damage and physical damage, the penalties _do not stack_. Only the highest of the applicable penalties apply.

For example, if your character has taken a serious mental wound, he or she suffers a -3 dice penalty to all skills governed by mental attributes and a -2 penalty to all skills governed by physical attributes.

If that same character later suffered a light physical wound, it would impose a -1 die penalty to all skills governed by physical attributes. However, since the -2 penalty imposed by the mental wound is larger than the -1 die penalty imposed by the physical wound, only the -2 penalty from the mental wound applies.

Now, if that same character takes additional physical damage bring them to a serious physical wound, the -3 penalty imposed on skills governed by physical attributes would replace the -2 penalty to the same skills imposed by the mental wound. The secondary penalty from the physical wound is ignored because it is less than the penalty already in effect from the previous mental wound.

- ***Soul Damage***

Our descriptions of wound levels thus far have not included soul damage. That isn't an oversight, and it's not because we're lazy… though we are… it's just not the reason we haven't done this.

The reason we haven't discussed soul damage is because soul damage is handled a little differently than the other two types of damage. There are still five wound levels and they're even named the same as the others. However, soul damage doesn't cause pain to your character. It doesn't impair limbs. It doesn't hamper your concentration. What it does do is slowly strip away your humanity. The more charisma damage you take, the more cold and detached you appear.

This has two in-game effects on your character. First, starting at the light wound level, you take a -1 die penalty to any social interaction… whether offensive or defensive. This penalty continues to increase by -1 at each wound level.

Additionally, and perhaps worse, starting at the minor wound level, everyone you interact with is shifted one level on the social interaction target number table (see using social skills on page 107). The direction of this shift depends on which modifier is more detrimental to the character. Like the other penalty, this one also increases with each wound level, so when your soul damage condition modifier is filled, even an intimate relationship is no different to the character that a relationship with someone they've never met.

The character does not lose knowledge of the relationship. He or she still know who their friends and allies are… or at least who they were. It's just that the character can no longer relate to them the way that they once did. They simply don't care.

> **Fatigue & Exhaustion**

It should go without saying that running and fighting for your life is very tiring. You run and fight to find a safe place to sleep so that you have the energy to run and fight your way to another place to sleep. It's a vicious cycle; one that you're afraid to break.

Fatigue and exhaustion are really just forms of damage, albeit damage that isn't usually as painful as a bullet to the chest. Since we already have rules in place to deal with damage, we can adapt the same rules to accurately represent the effects of fatigue.

At the end of every battle, character's that participated in the battle take one point of mental and physical fatigue damage.

Outside of combat, fatigue and exhaustion can still sneak up on you. Whenever your character engages in strenuous activity they become fatigued. If the character's contribution was physical, the character suffers a point of fatigue damage for every hour spent doing the activity. If the character's

120

contribution was mental, then they suffer an additional point of mental damage. Fatigue damage should be applied to the appropriate condition monitor – Physical to the body condition monitor and mental to the mind condition monitor.

Lastly, every 6 hours your character's awake, he or she takes a point of both mental and physical damage. This represents the effects of being awake during the day (or during the night depending on when you're character is awake). Stimulants can be used to mask the effects of fatigue, but only for a short periods of time. (You can use a stimulant like caffeine to negate the penalties incurred from fatigue, but the damage remains. The director will tell you when it's effects start to wear off.)

Fatigue damage cannot be gaffed. Unlike combat damage, fatigue damage does not bleed into the next category on the hierarchy and can be healed even if unconscious or passed out.

> **Healing Damage & Fatigue**

There are two parts to healing… technically three, but we'll get into that a bit later.

Physical damage is healed when the character rests. For every hour of uninterrupted rest, your character heals a number of points equal to his or her physical gaff score. In order to be considered at rest, the character must not be engaged in any activities that would require a skill test to perform.

It is not necessary to sleep in order to recover from physical damage. Of course, you do rest when you sleep, so physical damage is healed while sleeping.

Sleep, however, *is* necessary to heal mental damage. For every hour of uninterrupted sleep the character gets, he or she heals a number of points equal to his or her mental gaff score.

Unlike the real world, all the character needs to do in order to sleep is declare that he or she is going to sleep. While asleep the character receives only ½ of their skill dice to make any awareness checks or insight skill when defaulting for awareness. They are unable to use their dice pools in any way.

For each hour spent resting, the character heals a number of body hit points equal to his or her physical gaff score. For each hour spent sleeping, the character heals a number of points of mind hit points equal to his or her mental gaff score. Remember, if you're sleeping, you're resting.

- Waking from Sleep

Anything that occurs around the character while sleeping results in an awareness test… or defaulting to insight if the character lacks the awareness skill. The director will determine the target number and / or umber of successes needed.

If combat occurs, sleeping characters still roll initiative. They are, however, considered surprised and receive only ½ of their action pool to roll initiative. They do not get to do anything on their initiative except roll a new awareness test.

Once the character awakens, he or she can use any remaining actions to act normally in the combat round if they desire. If the combat continues for more than one round, characters who remain asleep gain an additional die to roll for the awareness test for each round of combat that they've slept through.

- ### *Death & Dying*

Exactly what happens to your character when his or her condition monitor is filled depends on which monitor is full… and what type of damage filled it.

If a character's mind condition monitor fills, the character falls unconscious. He or she is no longer able to take any action other than lying still and drooling. Fortunately, being unconscious allows the character's mind to start recovering. Unconsciousness and sleep are effectively the same thing for the purposes of this game.

If your character's body condition monitor is filled, he or she is "mostly dead". Whether or not the character survives depends on the character. The character's body has shut down, and, without medical treatment, he or she will die.

Unlike being unconscious, the "mostly dead" character cannot heal himself. He is not sleeping, and he is not resting. He's dying.

In game terms, the character whose body condition monitor has been filled looses a point of soul damage for each hours that they remain mostly dead. If their soul condition monitor reaches zero, the character's status changes from "mostly dead" to "all dead". When this happens, all that's left to do is go through their pockets for loose change.

If the character's soul condition monitor reaches zero, his or her humanity is gone. The character doesn't die… though a character whose soul condition monitor is at zero when his or her body condition monitor falls to zero, the character passes "mostly dead" and goes straight to "all dead".

- #### Treating Injuries

As mentioned above, a dying character doesn't heal himself. Someone has to do the healing for him. This is where companions and co-conspirators come in handy.

A character wishing to try and heal another roils his or her treat injury skill against a target number equal to the wound level that the character has suffered plus all applicable modifiers from the table below.

The Working Conditions are…	Modifier to Target Number	
	Healing Self	Healing Others
Terrible	+5	+3
Very Bad	+3	+2
Bad	+2	+1
Not Good	+1	+0
Good	+0	-1
Very Good	-1	-2
Tools are…	Repair	Dangineer
Unavaible	Not Possible	Not Possible
Improvised	+4	+3
Inadequate	+2	+1
Available	0	-1

Every success achieved is an hour's worth of healing that the dying character is capable of despite their condition. If the character is not dying when you treat his or her injuries, each success is an hour that the character heals twice what he or she normally wound.

If the character's sleep/rest is interrupted… if they awaken or if they take additional damage before awakening… then this accelerated healing stops. Any successes not used are lost.

You must roll to treat physical and mental wounds separately.

- ### *Healing Soul Damage*

Healing soul damage is both easier and more difficult than healing mental or physical damage. Your character regains lost soul damage every time he or she acts according to the personality you chose during character creation.

If you recall the chart of personalities shown earlier, you might have notices primary, secondary, and tertiary traits for each personality. On the chart beneath each of these column titles there was a +1, +2, and +3 respectively. This probably didn't make much sense at the time, but this is what those numbers are for.

When you in accordance with these traits, you recover lost soul damage. It's that simple. If your character has "teacher" for his or her personality, they regain 1 point of soul damage when they use diplomacy. They recover 2 point when they help develop another character. They regain 3 points when they educate another character.

You can only regain points for each trait once per hour. Points *cannot* be regained while sleeping no matter what you want to claim your character dreams about

If you don't recall the chart, we'll reprint it on this page so that you don't have to flip back to the character creation section.

Personality Category	Personality Type	Primary Trait (+1)	Secondary Trait (+2)	Tertiary Trait (+3)
Visionaries	Teacher	Diplomacy	Develop	Educate
Visionaries	Counselor	Diplomacy	Develop	Guide
Visionaries	Champion	Diplomacy	Mediate	Counsel
Visionaries	Healer	Diplomacy	Mediate	Console
Intellectuals	General	Strategy	Arrange	Mobilize
Intellectuals	Czar	Strategy	Arrange	Entail
Intellectuals	Inventor	Strategy	Construct	Devise
Intellectuals	Architect	Strategy	Construct	Design
Protectors	Supervisor	Coordination	Regulate	Enforce
Protectors	Inspector	Coordination	Regulate	Verify
Protectors	Provider	Coordination	Support	Supply
Protectors	Defender	Coordination	Support	Secure
Creators	Promoter	Tactics	Expedite	Persuade
Creators	Crafter	Tactics	Expedite	Instument
Creators	Entertainer	Tactics	Improvise	Demonstrate
Creators	Artist	Tactics	Improvise	Synethsize

For example, if I use the personality tree to determine my own personality, I'm an inventor. This means I regain 1 point of soul damage when I think strategically, two points when I construct something, and 3 points when I devise something. That means I regain 6 points of soul damage for every hour I've spent sitting here writing this game… Well, 5 points for the setting & character creation sections and 6 points while I wrote the rules. (Just don't tell my boss otherwise "healed soul damage" will be added to my benefits.)

Improving Your Character

In the d10 System, you earn experience for playing. Your director will issue experience either at the end of each gaming session or at the beginning of the next session. These experience points are spent to improve your character.

Raising an attribute cost a number of experience points equal to the desired attribute score multiplied by 10. So raising an attribute from a 3 to a 4 costs 40 experience points.

Raising a skill is easier… and by that I means less costly. To determine exactly how much it costs to increase a skill, you need to know what attribute governs the skill. Compare the skill ranking to the attribute find the appropriate row on the chart.

The first time you spend experience points, most of your character's skills will fall into one the bold categories on the table below. However, certain advantages reduce the

difficulty of improving a skill. Other options like specialization and concentration also reduce the difficulty of improving a skill. To find out how many experience points it will cost to improve these skills, simply find the category that the skill would fall into without any special benefits and then move one category closer to the top of the table.

Cost of Raising Skills

Attribute Score	Active Skill	Knowledge Skill
--	$(C-1) \times C$	$(C-1) \times (C-1)$
--	$C \times C$	$(C-1) \times C$
--	$C \times D$	$C \times C$
$\leq A \times 2$	$D*D$	$C \times D$
$> A \times 2$ but $< A \times 3$	$(D+1) \times (D+1)$	$D \times D$
$> A \times 3$ but $< A \times 4$	$(D+2) \times (D+2)$	$(D+1) \times (D+1)$
$> 4 \times A$ but $< 5 \times A$	$(D+3) \times (D+3)$	$(D+2) \times (D+2)$
$> 5 \times A$ but $< 6 \times A$	$(D+4) \times (D+4)$	$(D+3) \times (D+3)$

A = governing attribute score
C = the current level of the skill
D = the desired level of the skill

If your character would like to learn a new skill, the character can purchase this new skill using experience points. A new active skill costs 15 experience points to learn while a new knowledge skill costs 10 experience points to learn.

➤ Training

It is possible for someone else to train you in the use of a particular skill. This will make improving that skill easier, but does not make it less costly to learn a new skill.

In order to train someone you must meet all of the following criteria.

- You must have at least three levels in the skill to be trained.
- You must have at least 2 more level in the skill that the person you are intending to train.
- If you are using a specialization to train a base skill or a base skill to train a specialization, your skill must be at least 5 levels higher than the skill of the person you are training. (Concentrations count as specializations for the purposes of training.)
- You must spend one uninterrupted hour training per point that the skill will be after the improvement in order to gain any benefit from training.

Once the training is complete, the person who was trained can improve the skill at a cost on category higher on the table (less expensive) than he or she would otherwise improve it.

THE DIRECTOR'S CUT

Warning: *Continuing to read this section of the book, unless you are the director, could greatly reduce your enjoyment of the game. We strongly encourage you to stop reading now! If you are the director, please turn the page and get started learning the other things you need to know to run the game.*

Seriously. Put down the book. You're only hurting yourself.

I'm not joking. Stop reading. Let me guess, you're the kind of guy who buys the strategy guide and searches for cheats online before you've played through a game even once.

My eleven year old is the same way. I mean… What's the fun in that? Is winning really that important to you? Do you want to claim victory so badly that you're willing to cheat to do it? What are you going to do when you finally move out of your parents house and have to live in the real world? There are no cheat codes for real life, and most of the strategy guides are terrible… or at least written by complete idiots who probably think you can dodge bullets if you just believe in whatever it is they're trying to sell… usually self-esteem these days. Of course, if they have to sell it to you, it isn't "self" anything. But you're not going to understand that because, as we've clearly established, you lack the reading comprehension skills necessary to understand pretty much anything.

On the bright side, if and when the zombie apocalypse does occur, assuming robots haven't gotten to us already, I can clearly put you down in the "cannon fodder" category without losing too much sleep… and by that I mean "without a second thought or moment's hesitation."

Whatever… We already have your money, so it's no skin off my teeth. Go ahead; ruin it for yourself… You're going to do what you want anyway. There is just no talking to you! Now I sound like my mother. I hope you're happy!

Running a Game

By far the most daunting task for any perspective… or seasoned… director is actually running the game. This task is viewed with such dread that some games devote an entire book to the topic. Countless magazine articles have been written about the topic (and by that I mean I haven't counted them) that provide a myriad of tips, tricks, and advice… some of which is mutually exclusive.

The issue is further complicated by the titles given to the person who runs the game. Titles like game of dungeon master give the mistaken impression that the person running the game is the adversary of the players. Titles like administrate imply that players are something to be managed. It sets a bad precedence.

Even the title of storyteller, is deceptive. The person running the game isn't telling the story. How could they? They don't have any idea what the main characters are going to do. Narrator might be a better title. After all, that's really what you're doing. You're narrating the player's story.

We, of course, use the title "director". I'd like to pretend that there's a good reason for this, but there isn't. It's actually short for "Game Operations Director"… which abbreviates to G.O.D.. It seemed fitting since most people who run games seem to develop a god complex over time… sometimes as little as a few minutes.

> I own all the books, I created the adventure, I wrote up all the NPCs, and I know ever rule in this game. So I ask you; when someone fails a roll and their head hits their hands and they pray to God that the zombies don't notice them or that their character doesn't die or that one of their party members can get to them in time, who do you think they're praying to? Now, go ahead and read your Bible, Player, and you go to your church, and, with any luck, you might win the annual raffle, but if you're looking for God, he's sitting at the head of the table, and he doesn't like to be second guessed. You ask me if I have a God complex. Let me tell you something: I am God.

(That's a paraphrase from the 1993 movie *Malice* starting Alec Baldwin, Nicole Kidman, and Bill Pullman in case you didn't get it.)

Running a game seems difficult because people like to overcomplicate things. People write articles telling the person running an RPG how to handle every problem from a derailed adventure to an adventuring party that doesn't work well together. In reality, neither of those things is your problem.

The most important thing to remember when running a game is this – your job is to tell the players how the world reacts to their actions or inaction. That's it. Everything is either not important or not your job.

Keeping the party together? Not you job. Advancing the plot? Not your job. Creating a compelling story? Believe it or not… Not your job.

Trust me. I've been doing this for a long time, and I learned from some of the best. I can tell you unequivocally that the biggest problem directors (or whatever you want to call the person who runs the game) have is trying to do too much. They take on responsibilities that they shouldn't and the game suffers for it.

Our website contains an entire section on how to run a game, but I'll give you a quick overview here. There are only five easy steps to running a successful game.

Step 1 – Decide what is going to happen if the players do nothing.

Step 2 – Modify that plan based on the actions that the players do take.

Step 3 – Describe the results to the players from the perspective of their characters.

Step 4 – Rinse

Step 5 – Repeat.

That doesn't seem very difficult. That's because it isn't. The part of the job that really gets to most people is drawing maps and creating non-player characters for the players to encounter. This task gets even more daunting when you spend a few hours detailing an encounter and creating a unique NPC, and your players avoid the encounter all together.

When this happens, some directors like to (metaphorically) grab their players by the nose and lead them to the planned encounter. A better plan… one the players will create a more vibrant experience for the players and a lot less work for you… is to not make the encounter in the first place.

This game takes place in the real world… albeit a version of the real world undergoing the zombie apocalypse. You live in the real world. You've been in buildings before… or at least seen some on TV. They don't change a whole lot. Whether it's a one room shack on the outskirts of town or a luxurious mansion high on a hill, a house is a house. They have kitchens, bathrooms, bedrooms. They might have a den or dining room. Some might have a home office or study. If you're really rich (or an old role-player… and those seem to be mutually exclusive), you might have a library.

Schools aren't that much different wherever you go. They have gymnasiums, classrooms, offices, and bathrooms. Junior and senior high schools tend to have locker rooms and auditoriums or theaters, but schools are schools.

The same holds true for offices, factories, stores, malls, restaurants, police stations, gas stations, prisons, hospitals, nightclubs, taverns, and any other building you can imagine. We define these buildings based on their functions and their functions are defined by the rooms that they contain.

You can make a map of a special location – the building where your players choose to make their home during the zombie apocalypse, for example – but for most buildings they'll visit, your memory of buildings you've been in and places your seen on TV or read about in a book or wandered through while playing a video game will do just fine.

That leaves non-player characters. Making believable NPCs is important to any game. Luckily for you, you come pre-equipped with a database of hundred, if not thousands, of readymade NPC personalities just waiting to encounter your players.

Consider this… NPCs are just people. How many people do you know? How many characters have you seen on TV or in the movies? How many have you read about? Each and every one of those is a possible NPC complete with mannerisms, motivation, and everything else you could hope for.

Here's the best part… basing your NPCs on the people mentioned above ensures consistency… and consistency makes NPCs believable.

It's hard to know what Skippy the Scavenger might do when the players meet him. It's even more difficult to remember how Skippy the Scavenger is supposed to act when the players haven't seen him for a month. However, if Skippy the Scavenger has the same personality as your brother Dan, for example, the problem goes away. You know how your brother acts. You can guess what he's going to do. That isn't going to change. It doesn't matter how long it is between meetings.

By tweaking the personalities in your database, you can create even more NPCs that are ready for use. Accentuating certain personality traits and ignoring others can create an entirely different person… without having to come up with an entirely different person. You can even combine two or more people's personalities to make someone new… or excise part of someone's personality entirely.

This brings me to my first tip for running your game – TAKE NOTES!

When your players meet Skippy the Scavenger for the first time, make a note of it. Write down whose personality you're using for Skippy, where they met Skippy, and how Skippy would feel about the encounter.

Skippy the Scavenger (Brother Dan) – abandoned car dealership. Player traded a case of bottled water to Skippy for two gallons of gas. Skippy agreed because he thought Sara's character was cute. She left, and Skippy is hurt… and feels cheated.

Next time your players run into Skippy, you'll have a good idea how he'll react… He'll behave just like your brother Dan would if he was tricked into making a bad trade because of a cute girl.

I don't have a good lead in for my next tip, so I'll just tell you – LISTEN TO YOUR PLAYERS.

Players are devious. They will come up with horrors you could not even begin to imagine. Fortunately, most of them do not know when to keep quiet. If you pay attention, they'll do all the hard work for you.

If you're new to role-playing, it won't take long before you understand what I'm talking about. If you're not new to role-playing and don't know what I mean, it's because directors are sneaky too. If your director is any good, he or she has been using this trick for a long time. You just haven't realized it.

Players will tell you what they want to happen and what they hope doesn't happen… well… they might not tell you, but they will say it out loud to their fellow players while you're sitting at the table. You'll describe a dark, dank passageway and some player will say something like "I bet it's a trap. Any minute now <insert horrible fate> is going to happen!"

Use this information. If their idea if better than yours, use their idea. Or better, use enough of their idea to lull them into a false sense of thinking they know what's going on and then hit them with something unexpected at the last minute.

If you want more tips, tricks, or examples, feel free to visit our website. Each of the things mentioned here are discussed more thoroughly… and there are some more tips and tricks… like how to deal with someone who's being a jerk at the gaming table.

On a similar note, if you have a tip or trick that works for you, send it in to us. If we like it, we'll post it. The more people who know how to run games, the more play time the people who normally run them will get…

Rewarding Players

Rewards to player actually take many forms. Sometimes those rewards are monetary in nature, sometime they take the form of items, and other times they are merely the gratitude of the non-player characters. Of course, earning experience points to use to improve your character doesn't hurt either.

Treasure

Loot is an important part of the role-playing experience. Other than poor people (like me), most people carry some money on them at all times. During the zombie apocalypse money isn't that important, but mementos of better times are always important to the survivors. Players who vanquish a foe and loot the body can and should receive this treasure… as well as any items the foe had on them. There is nothing wrong with this expectation. In fact, if you ignore the players' expectations too often, they may decide to ignore your gaming night.

Social Rewards

Keep in mind that the gratitude of non-player characters can be a very important reward, especially if you are playing a campaign in which the party will encounter those NPCs again at some later point in time.

A grateful NPC might provide food, shelter, of weapons to the player characters. The people they save from a horde of zombies today might save them from horde tomorrow.

Experience Points

Some RPGs make experience a function of how many kills the character's score. Others have rejected this idea in favor of a "threat" system. While all of these methods provide a nice means of gauging experience, they tend to put emphasis on one particular aspect of the game. Players naturally want to see their characters advance, so they do the things that bring in experience.

So how do you issue experience in a way that keeps the game interesting, but doesn't focus too much on any one aspect of it? Like many things, the answer is so simple it might amaze you. You issue experience based on story and to reinforce behaviors you want players to continue.

Showing Up to Play: Every player who shows up to play deserves to earn some experience, give it to them. Just showing up to play earns the characters a point of experience.

Advancing the Story: Advancing the plot is important. After all, if the story doesn't advance, the game doesn't go anywhere. Issue some experience to everyone if the party manages to move the story forward. If a particular character does something important that significantly advances the story, issue that player extra experience unless that character did something that was completely out of character. A laconic character has no business leading a negotiation. If this happens, that character should not be rewarded for bad role-playing even if he advanced the plot.

Role-playing: Since this is a role-playing game, role-playing should be a determining factor in issuing experience. Unfortunately, as I said earlier, it tends to be forgotten in most campaigns. To reward role-playing, anyone who puts forth *any* effort in this regard should earn some experience. Additional experience should be issued if they are able to role-play consistently. Issue more to anyone whose character acts "in character" despite the fact that the player knows that the behavior is not in the best interests of the character or that some other course of action might lead to better results.

Keep in mind that not all role-playing is social in nature. I once played in a group with a player whose character was a mute & illiterate barbarian. Anytime the player communicated with members of the party or NPCs he drew pictures on a sketch pad to convey his message. This was superb role-playing. Unfortunately, the person running the game, for reasons I cannot fathom, thought that not being able to speak was a "cop out" and refused to issue any "role-playing" experience points to the character. The player eventually quit playing in that game because of this lack of experience.

Intelligence Awards: Players should be rewarded when they come up with a good idea, especially if that idea saves the group or allows the group to avoid a potentially deadly situation. Again, experience should only be awarded if the idea was in-character.

Surviving: Any character that lives through a role-playing session should earn something simply for not dying.

Threat Awards: Characters that face a significant threat to their lives and well-being and survive may be issued more for surviving that particular threat. However, you should avoid issuing extra experience for each and every combat that the party participates in. If experience starts to become "kill based" your game becomes no different than countless console RPGs available. Players can play console games whenever they feel like it. They aren't likely to set aside one night each week or month to show up and accomplish the same thing at your house that they could in their own.

Experience Point Award Table

~General Awards~	
Showing Up to Play	1
Surviving to Play Another Night (or Day)	1
~Plot Related Awards~	
Moving the Main Story Along	1
Moving a Personal Story Line Along	1
~Role-Playing Awards~	
Good Role-Playing	1
Staying In Character	1
Good Role-Playing at a Detriment to the Character	2
Showing Bravery	1
Being Down Right Heroic	2
Demonstrating Intelligence	1
Avoiding Unnecessary Violence	1
Clever Idea that proves futile	1
Clever Idea that proves useful	2
Clever Idea that Saves the Party	3
Clever Idea that Saves Numerous People	4
Quick Thinking	1
Making the Other Players Laugh or Cry	1
Making the Director Laugh or Cry	2
~Threat Awards~	
Defeating a Minor Threat	1
Defeating a Major Threat	2
Defeating a Great Threat	3

Assigning Target Numbers

Assigning target numbers isn't really that difficult. All you have to do is consider how difficult the task would be for the average person. Look on the chart below, find that difficulty, and announce the target numbers. Simple, right?

Players who read further in the book than they should… or who peak at the book while you're not looking… will eventually argue that a particular task isn't "challenging" to his or her character. Do not give in!

Target numbers aren't about players. That's where skills come in. Target numbers represent the intrinsic difficulty of performing a task. Change the target number only when a task itself becomes more difficult.

For example, let's imagine that my children are surfing the interwebs one day and a virus infects my computer. Not wanting to have to explain what happened, they try to fix the problem themselves. They lack the knowledge to remove the virus, so I'll have to give it a try when I get home.

The virus isn't magically easier to remove because I'm sitting at the keyboard. It's still the same virus. The only thing that's changes is the skill level of the person trying to deal with it. When I fail to remove the virus, I'll call their uncle. His skill with a computer exceeds mine, but the virus is still the same.

Difficulty of Task	Target Number
Very Easy	1
Easy	2
Simple	3
Routine	4
Average Difficulty	5
Above Average Difficulty	6
Moderately Difficult	7
Challenging	8
Difficult	9
Very Difficult	12
Extremely Difficult	15
Strenuous	18
Intense	21
Heroic	24
Nearly Impossible	27+

The difference in skill level is represented by the dice that the players roll. The more skill you have in a particular subject, the more dice that you get to roll. If your ability to perform a task is hampered, this is represented by a reduction in the number of dice the character gets to roll. If you're sleeping or surprised, you only have access to ½ your normal action pool. If a character takes damage and the pain, mental or physical, hampers their performance, the penalty is assessed in dice.

These are the guiding principles behind the d10 system.

Zombiology

Zombiology is the branch of biology that relates to zombies, including classification, physiology, development, and behavior. It's a science that humanity will scoff at and ignore until it's too late… but that's part of what makes us human…

> *"Man is the only animal in whom the law of self-preservation is enacted only after he has willingly subjected himself to the machinations of his destruction."* (ASL, TDN)

When people think about zombies, they tend to place them into one of two categories – the living dead or diseased humans. Whichever of these answers your players assume to be true is perfectly fine. Let them guess. Let them learn over the course of play. It'll be both realistic and challenging.

The truth, as far as this game is concerned is that zombies are both… and neither… at the same time. Of course, humanity won't figure that out for a year… or two… At this stage of the game, the powers that be are just as worried about survival as the players. They don't have time to learn the truth. Truth-seeking is a luxury one normally engages in only once one is no longer concerned with being eaten alive.

Zombies in this game differ from "traditional" zombies in a number of important ways. We'll try to cover all of them here, but keep in mind that this is information that players are supposed to learn through play. Knowing it won't make the game impossible to play, but it'll certainly take some of the fun out of it…

Zombie Physiology

Zombies were once human, so you would expect them to have human physiology. You would be sadly mistaken.

The disease that causes zombism also causes some drastic and important changes to the human body. These changes result in an organism that is both more and less than human.

The physiological change that most often comes to mind is the insatiable hunger for human flesh… particularly human brains. This is actually a myth stemming from a number of phenomenons.

First, zombies crave any type of flesh, not just humans. The problem is that we, as a species, are so ego-centric, that we think the world revolves around us. Think about it, sharks kill fish all the time. Lions, tigers, and bears prey on other animals every day. As soon as one of these eats a human, there's a man-eater on the lose! It's because we (mistakenly) think we're special and exempt from the food chain because we invented grocery stores.

Second, we're creatures of habit. We like to be around people and things we know. If a forest starts on fire, animal run. If a house starts on fire, people try to fight the fire until they realize that fire usually wins. Then they call the fire department to continue the fight while they stand nearby and watch. Animals don't do that. When their habitat becomes a danger to them, they move to somewhere less dangerous.

When a predator shows up in the woods, animals hide. Chipmunks do not show up at city hall demanding the rodent police arrest the local owls. Rabbits don't peak out of the burrows watching to see if the hawk is attacking the field mouse next door. They hide, and they stay hidden until the danger has passed. If they can't hide, they run.

People do not do that. We might go into our homes… so they we're neatly packaged with all our valuables. We call the police, and the mayor, and the local news demanding that they apprehend the person or persons that infringe upon our feeling of safety. When the powers that be cannot make us safe, we expect, and in some cases demand, that they lie to us… and then we believe the lie… because we want to…

Just hide under your wooden desk kids. That will protect you from a nuclear bomb. Go shopping and buy duct tape to save yourself from anthrax. I'm from the government, and I'm here to help.

Zombies are after us because a) we're food b) we're here, and c) we don't really want to leave.

I know what you're thinking… But, Ben, they moan the word "BRAINS!" as they plod toward us.

No they don't. You just think they do because that's what TV and movies have told you that they do. You hear what you expect to hear because that's the way our brains are wired.

Think about it for just a moment. Why would a zombie want to eat your brain? There are other organs in your body that aren't protected by roughly ½ inch of bone plating. This is simply your mind feeding off your fears… just like it used to when you were little and thought an evil monkey lived in your closet.

The first real change to zombie physiology is that higher brain functions are severely inhibited. Zombies aren't mindless, but they're not intelligent either. They're more along the lines of really, really, dumb animals, but we'll cover that more when we discuss zombie psychology.

The second important change is that zombies no longer feel pain. Whether this is caused by somehow blocking the neuro-receptors for pain (nociceptors) or whether the nerves cease functioning all together is unknown as this point. What we do know is that zombies seem to have no idea that they're being harmed. You can shoot them…you can hit them... you can stab them… Until the zombie is no longer capable of motion, they keep moving.

The third change, and probably the most notable, is that zombies do not appear to heal. Our bodies naturally repair and replace damaged cells when we rest and sleep. When we are cut, platelets in our blood clot and for a protective scab over the wound while out body repairs the damage. While a zombie's blood will clot and scab, no healing takes place. If and when the scab is removed, the bleeding begins again.

In addition to ignoring wounds, zombies also seem ignorant of (or at least unhindered by) changes in temperature and weather conditions. Neither snow… nor rain… nor gloom of night…

Fourth, though zombies still need air to breathe, they seem capable of breathing underwater. There are several reasons that this may be. Our lungs are perfectly capable of removing oxygen dissolved in water in much the same way that a fish's gills do. The reason we can't breathe underwater is that our lungs lack the surface area to collect enough oxygen to support our bodily functions. (Air has something like 20 times more oxygen than the same volume of water.)

Because zombies do not appear as warm as humans when viewed through a thermal-imaging device… like a thermal rifle scope… some surmise that they are no longer warm-blooded. Fish are cold-blooded and require less oxygen because of it. Since we do not see zombies sunning themselves on rocks and in streets, we can probably dismiss this hypothesis.

Another hypothesis is that zombies are still warm-blooded but require a lot less oxygen then humans to maintain their limited function. This may tie into difference number three. Repairing and replacing cells take a lot of energy.

The last physiological change for zombies, at least the last noticeable one, is that zombies seem to have decreased motor function. They don't walk, they trudge. They don't attack so much as flail. They lack the motor skills and hand-eye coordination to utilize firearms effectively. They are not very dexterous. They don't have to be. They see you as food, not as a threat.

Are you threatened by your food? Do you run away from it? Face it, we eat food we know is going to hurt us. Your local pharmacy has shelves devoted to antacids and anti-gas medication for just such emergencies. The CDC estimates that at least 128,000 people are hospitalized and 3,000 people die from food poisoning each year. Yet we continue to eat. Zombies don't feel pain, so even the Super-Red-Hot-Atomic-Fireball-Melt-the-Spoon-and-then-the-Toilet-While-It-Eats-Your-Stomach Chili doesn't faze them… and, honestly, it sounds pretty tasty right now to me too.

Zombie Psychology

The most dangerous psychological trait of zombies may be that zombies do not seem to identify one another as competition for resources. Because zombies do not view other zombies are threats, zombies often travel in packs... at least that's the hypothesis.

Humans tend to form groups for a variety of reasons, none of which seem to apply to zombies. Zombies do not appear to have a social hierarchy. They do not seem to have meaningful communication with one another… or any communication whatsoever.

In reality, zombies don't even appear to actively cooperate with one another. Groups of zombies just seem to be packs of creatures individually try to accomplish the same thing, but show no hostility or animosity toward one another when one of them achieves the shared goal.

A second important psychological trait of zombies has to do with the way they process information. As humans, we tend to rely on our sight more than any other sense. Only if we lose our sight, do we start to rely on our other senses.

Zombies do not share our visual prejudice. They rely on information from all of their senses equally. This makes them particularly dangerous in situations where sight is impaired. Humans are naturally at a disadvantage because of their reliance on sight. Zombies easily compensate for their impaired vision by using their other senses. Some people believe that this reliance on the other senses help zombies to identify one another, but exactly how zombies do it remains a mystery.

The most misunderstood part of zombie psychology is zombie intelligence. Contrary to popular belief, zombies are not mindless automatons. It is true that zombies are not intelligent in the same sense that humans are intelligent. They even lack the cunning often associated with predators in the wild. This does not mean that zombies lack intelligence all together.

Zombies are roughly as intelligent as a very dumb and feral dog. Like a feral animal, zombies are driven by instinct. Like a dog, they tend to see the world as a dichotomy. Also like a dog, they tend to be single-minded… until something else draws their attention.

A dog understands time in terms of right now and forever. When you leave the house, your dog thinks you're going to be gone forever. When you return from the mailbox, they act as though you have been gone for an eternity. Dogs are either starving to death or full. If you leave for a weekend, you can't just leave an ice cream pail of food for the dog because he'll eat it all at once and then wonder why you've left them starving, near death for an eternity.

Zombies are very similar. They are either starving or satiated. There is no middle ground. They exist in the here and now without any concern for tomorrow, yesterday, or even the rest of today. They don't consider the consequences of their actions or dwell on their past. In fact, they don't seem to have any memory whatsoever.

A zombie faced with a barrier like a wall will try to walk through the barrier. When that fails, they will try to walk around the barrier. Trying to climb the barrier or trying to tunnel under it won't cross their primitive minds. If a zombie is trying to walk around said wall and sees, hears, or smells signs of another food source, they will stop trying to overcome the barrier to pursue the new food source.

Likewise, a zombie that manages to catch a source of food begins feasting immediately. They do not continue to fight when they can feed. Other zombies in the pack who are not eating will, of course, continue to fight so that they can feed.

Khymera Pestis

When people finally get around to trying to determine that actual cause of zombism, they'll discover a family of interlinked microorganisms they will dub Khymera Pestis. Khymera Pestis is not a virus, a bacteria, or a biological toxin. It's all three.

Khymera Pestis is originally named "Chimera Pestis" for its ability to rapidly mutate. The name is soon changed to Khymera Pestis to stop people from mispronouncing the name... something that infuriated the people who discovered it.

Once the pathogens are identified, the following entry is added to the U.S. Armed Forces Nuclear, Biological, and Chemical Survival Manual.

B.4.1 Khymera Pestis

Signs and Symptoms: The disease caused by Khymera Pestis begins after an incubation period that varies widely between its victims. The victim experiences tremors and chills. The victim's skin begins to pale and eventually takes on a sickly green-gray hue as the disease progresses. Eyes become bloodshot, and eventually the sclera (white of the eye) turns red with blood. Breathing becomes shallow and the victims develop pneumonia-like symptoms, except the fluid in the victim's lungs tends to be blood. Victims often cough up a combination of phlegm, spit, and semi-coagulated blood. All of these substances may contain traces of the disease and facilitate its spread.

Unlike many diseases, Khymera Pestis does not have a period of contagion. Victims are contagious through all stages of the disease; however, the disease is less contagious during its initial stages.

Diagnosis: Khymera Pestis should be suspected in any situation where otherwise healthy people begin to exhibit any of the above symptoms.

Prophylaxis: Asymptomatic persons who have come in contact with a source of Khymera Pestis should be isolated immediately. Isolation should continue for seven days or the term of the exposure plus one week. If no signs of the disease are present after this period, it is generally safe to release the person from isolation.

Isolation and Decontamination: Use standard and respiratory droplet precautions when dealing with any potential infection. Khymera Pestis can survive for varying periods, but is susceptible to heat and exposure to sunlight. Traditional disinfectants have not been effective in containing the disease, but good hygiene and frequent disinfection with soap and water and other disinfectants should still be observed.

Overview

Khymera Pestis is a virus that attacks bacteria. These bacteria are capable of infecting humans, animals, and plants. The infected creature then produces a bio-toxin that mutates those exposed causing them to create new strains of the bacteria. Both the original bacteria and those created in a host exposed to the bio-toxin are extremely resistant strains. They mutate quickly making infection impossible to fight with antibiotics. The virus is also capable of infecting hosts other than bacteria. It also mutates too rapidly for vaccines to be effective. Khymera Pestis can be transmitted by exposure to infected bodily fluids including blood, saliva, sweat, and waste. No open wound need be present.

The Khymera Pestis organism can remains viable in water, moist soil, and plant or animal matter for several weeks. At temperatures near or below freezing Khymera Pestis will remain alive for month or even years. It is susceptible to heat, however, and is killed after 15 minutes of exposure to temperatures over 150° Fahrenheit. It also remains viable for quite some time in dry sputum, feces, and buried bodies but such specimens are killed within several hours of exposure to sunlight.

History and Significance

The first known case of Khymera Pestis infection of a human was reported in December 7th, 2012. By the Mayan prophesized end of the world on December 21st of that year, most of the world's population was infected. Researchers have since discovered that the infection likely began two weeks earlier. It seems that the disease may have infected its first human on Thanksgiving Day and spread rapidly during the Black Friday shopping frenzy.

It is now believed the Khymera Pestis virus infected a strain of Yersinia Pestis (the bacteria responsible for the Bubonic Plague). How or why this strain of Yersinia Pestis was released is still not known. The Department of Homeland Security suspects it was a terrorist plot, and that the terrorists themselves were the first victims of Khymera Pestis.

Medical Management

Use standard precautions for Khymera Pestis patients. Suspected infection requires strict isolation with droplet precautions for the entire term of the isolation or until sputum cultures are negative. If competent vectors and reservoirs are present, measures must be taken to prevent the spread of the disease. These may include use of insecticides and other pest control measures. Great care should be taken to limit contact between infected patients and any local vectors or reservoirs.

At this time, there is no treatment for Khymera Pestis. Infected patients should be kept comfortable and measures should be taking to support other bodily functions while the disease runs its course.

Any materials that come in contact with infected patients should be placed in special containers and incinerated as soon as possible to kill any remaining contagion.

Should the patient succumb to the disease, his or her corpse should also be incinerated immediately as the infectious agent is known to be able to survive for periods of time in plant and animal matter, including the bodies of the deceased.

Prophylaxis

Vaccine: No vaccine is currently available for prophylaxis of Khymera Pestis. The U.S. Army Medical Research Institute of Infectious Diseases is currently working on a potential vaccine. Because the pathogen mutates so rapidly, developing a vaccine may be impossible.

Antibiotics: No antibiotic treatment for Khymera Pestis exists at this time. Agents capable of combating Khymera Pestis have proven fatal to humans and other animals.

More Rules

Most of the rules governing zombies are the same as the rules governing players. After reading about the physiology and psychology of zombies, you can probably already guess which rules have changed.

Zombie Subspecies

What most people do not realize, and the government won't realize for at least two more years, is that not all zombies are the same. There are actually 6 subspecies of zombie running around on the earth… and one group of delusional humans who think that they're zombies. For your benefit, we've divided them into 4 different categories based on the likelihood of encountering them – common, uncommon, rare, and very rare.

Wight (common): The wight (plural wightes) is the zombies everyone thinks of when they think of the zombie apocalypse. These are the zombies that we discussed in the Zombiology section. Most of the encounters players have during the game will be with this subspecies of zombie.

Nachzehrer (uncommon): The Nachzehrer is the scavengers of the zombie world. For whatever reason, they are less capable than their wight kin. Small bands of Nachzehrers tend to follow larger packs of wightes and pick through the carcasses left behind as the wightes move on to fresh prey.

Drekavac (rare): Though it will be uncommon for players to encounter a drekavac, players will know that they exist. Drekavac are able to release a mournful wail that is capable of chilling the blood of even the most hardened warriors. Even if the players never encounter one, they'll probably be awoken by a drekavac's baleful scream from time to time.

Draugen (very rare): Draugen are the elite shock troops of the zombie world. They are stronger and more resilient to physical injury that is humanly possible. They are almost always armed and armored, which begs the question… who outfits them and why…

Nosferatu (very rare): When most people hear the word "nosferatu" they think of vampires. The origin of the word is a mystery (all we know is that it isn't really Romanian like Bram Stoker said). One theory is that it is derived from the Latin phrase "we prey on you". That seems fitting since the nosferatu are the assassins of the zombie world. Who sends these zombie ninjas on their missions is a mystery players are better off not knowing.

Cotards (not rare enough): Cotards aren't really zombies… they just think they are.

The name of this group derives from the Cotard delusion or Cotard's syndrome (also known as "Walking Dead Syndrome"). Jules Cotard, a French neurologist first described the condition where people believed that they were dead. Cotards are people who think that they are zombies and therefore act the way they think zombies should act.

Many Cotards are survivors of a zombie attack that defeated their attacker, but where bitten. Though their bodies managed to fend off the disease, the Cotard believes they have become a zombie, possibly due to depictions in popular video games, movies, TV shows, and books that make this transformation seem inevitable.

Cotards are extremely dangerous. Despite the fact that they believe themselves to be zombies, they are still fully human. They are just as smart and agile as normal humans and capable of doing everything a normal human can do.

Worse yet, though they are unaffected by its presence, many Cotards still seem to be carriers for the Khymera Pestis. Perhaps because they are carriers of the disease, other zombies do not seem to attack Cotards. Since zombies travel in packs, Cotards usually travel with them.

When people actually get around to studying zombies, scientists will theorize that this phenomenon has something to do with how long it took for the person to fight off the Khymera Pestis infection. For now, just know that they exist, and use them as something unique and different to throw at your players once in a while.

Zombie Special Qualities & Abilities

Since we've explained most of these special qualities and abilities previously, we won't go into detail for most of these abilities… except the ones that require new rules like spreading the Khymera Pestis.

- Zombies are not undead.
- Zombies still digest the food they eat.
- Zombies still expel waste (though they are more animalistic in their approach… Zombies do not use bathrooms.
- Zombies still breathe.
- Zombies need less oxygen than normal humans.
- Zombies can breathe underwater.
- Zombies do not crave human flesh. Humans are just the most prevalent available food source.
- Zombies do moan. It is a function of air from their lungs traveling over their otherwise unused vocal cords. Zombies do not, however, moan the word "brains". People just think they do because people have been programmed to think that they do by games, movies, TV, books, and other media.
- Zombies do not seem to sleep or rest.
- Zombies do not heal.
- Zombies do not feel pain (Zombies suffer no penalties to skill checks or initiative rolls due to damage).
- Zombies do not fall unconscious when they've filled their mind condition monitor.
- Zombies do not pass out when they've filled their physical condition monitor, though their movement rate is cut in half when this occurs.
- Zombies have no charisma, so their soul condition monitor is a function of their constitution just like their body damage is effectively giving them two body condition monitors that are filled separately.
- Zombies do not dodge attacks unless they have a subspecies specific special ability that allows them to do so.
- Zombies do not suffer penalties for visual impairment.
- Zombies still can and do gaff damage.
- Zombies suffer twice the defaulting penalty when defaulting to their (limited) coordination attribute to use a firearm.

➤ Zombie Fear

Most zombies have the ability to cause fear. This isn't so much a special ability as something that happens when a horde of nearly unstoppable creatures that want to eat you marches toward you like a somewhat mobile wall of impending doom.

One, two, or even three zombies aren't much of a threat to a semi-conscious human. They're easy enough to avoid and easy enough to kill if they can't be avoided. It's an entirely different ball game once five or more of the ambling little death machines start heading in your direction.

When faced with five or more zombies, characters need to roll a psyche test to see how the fear affects them. The target number is 5 +1 for every three zombies over five there are in the group. If you get no successes on this roll, your character will suffer a penalty of +3 to all target numbers (other than gaffing) while the zombies are present… even if they manage to kill most of them. Each success you do achieve on this test reduces this penalty by one.

For example, if a group of 10 zombies is coming at your party, everyone would roll against a target number of 7 (5 for the initial 5 zombies and then 2 more for the remaining 5 because 5 divided by 3 is 1 and ⅔ which rounds up to 2). If no successes are achieved, all of the character's target numbers would increase by +4 (7 divided by 2 is 3 and a ½ which rounds up to 4). Each success achieved would reduce this target number by one.

Characters with the brave advantage would still risk the penalty of +4 to all target numbers, but they would roll against a target number of 4 to resist the fear giving them a much higher chance of getting some successes.

➤ Becoming Infected

All zombies have the ability to infect others. The potential to become a zombie yourself is one of the most terrifying aspects of fighting zombies.

Each zombie has two Virulence Ratings – Wound & Exposure. Wound virulence is (usually) equal to the zombie's constitution score. This is the target number to resist the disease if you are wounded by a zombie attack.

Exposure virulence is (usually) equal to ½ the zombies constitution score (which happens to be their physical gaff score). This is the target number anytime a character is exposed to zombie matter such as bodily fluids, rotting zombie flesh, zombie waste, etc. Since this zombie matter is no longer attached to a host organism, it become less infectious over time losing one point of its exposure virulence rating for each hour it is exposed to sunlight or dying immediately if exposed to temperatures in excess of 150° Fahrenheit.

When the character is wounded or exposed to zombie matter, the character takes a number of points of soul damage equal to the target number. Soul damage cannot be gaffed. You resist a by not getting wounded. You resist exposure by not exposing yourself to the harmful substance.

Next he or she rolls his or her constitution score against the pertinent virulence target number. This roll can be augmented by vigor pool if desired, but vigor pool spent in this manner will not refresh until the character has rested.

The character needs three successes to hold his or her ground against the Khymera Pestis. Subtract the number of successes the character achieves from the number of successes needed for the character to hold his or her ground (three when the character is first infected). Compare the results to the chart below.

Difference	Effect
+3 or More	Zombified... Practice your limp & Moan
+2	Target successes Increases by 1
+1	Target Number Increases by 1
0	No Change
-1	Target Number Decreases by 1
-2	Target Successes Decreases by 1
-3 or More	Disease Eradicated

The table will tell you whether the target number for the roll and the number of successes needed to hold your ground against the infection increases to decreases. If you fail by 3 or more (get a difference of +3) you become a zombie within the hours. If you succeed by a margin of 3 successes of more (get a difference of -3) then your body has manage to fight off the disease. You're still contagious for an hour, but after that you're back to your lovable self... depending on how much soul damage you've taken, of course.

This roll is repeated every hour until the character either succumbs to the disease and become a zombie that tries to devour his or her former comrades or manages to neutralize the disease.

If the character manages to neutralize the disease, he or she is safe... this time. However, there are still viable pathogens that must be flushed from the character's body. Anyone coming in contact with this waste material risks exposure with a virulence rating equal to ½ of the no-longer-infected character's constitution score (which also happens to be his or her physical gaff score).

Until their fellow party member succumbs to the disease, he or she might appear pale or feverish, but they are still themselves. It is possible for someone to hide the fact that they have been bitten... for a while anyway. Since most people don't want to die, it's not uncommon for someone who's infected to hide that fact as long as possible... even before the party learns that you have a chance to fend off the disease.

This may seem complicated, so here is an example of how combating Khymera Pestis might look. (The chart used in this example will be reprinted in the back of this book for your use. Feel free to make photocopies if you need or want to.)

Time Elapsed	Target Number	Successes Needed	Successes Achieved	Difference
Infected	5	3	3	0
1 Hour	5	3	4	-1
2 Hours	4	3	3	0
3 Hours	4	3	2	+1
4 Hours	5	3	2	+1
5 Hours	6	3	1	+2
6 Hours	6	4	2	+2
7 Hours	6	5	4	+1
8 Hours	7	5	2	+3

When the character is initially wounded by the wight (common zombie), he takes 5 points of soul damage. He rolls his constitution score and throws in half of his vigor pool for good measure. He gets only three successes, so he doesn't lose any ground to the disease, but he doesn't gain any ground on it either.

From this point forward, the character is a carrier for Khymera Pestis. His bodily fluids and waste carry the disease. His bite can cause infection. He, however, is not a zombie... yet. Whether he is allowed to live long enough to fight the disease depends on the people around him.

One hour after the initial infection, the zombie is long since destroyed, but the disease it harbored is alive and well inside the character. He takes 5 more points of soul damage and rolls again, using the rest of his vigor pool in an attempt to neutralize the disease.

He manages to get 4 successes this time, so his body's immune system is fighting off the Khymera Pestis. In an hour when he rolls again, he'll only suffer 4 points of soul damage and his target number for the roll will be a 4 as well.

His vigor pool is exhausted and will not refresh until he has rested. He'd love to take time to rest right now, but the party is starving & they need to scavenge for food.

Two hours after the infection, the character takes his 4 points of soul damage. He's almost out of boxes on his soul condition monitor, but he won't die simply from taking soul damage. He rolls his dice and gets 3 successes even without his now-exhausted vigor pool. There is no change in his status other than the soul damage that he suffered.

Three hours after he was infected, the character takes 4 more points of soul damage. This actually fills his soul condition monitor. Excess soul damage is just ignored… once you don't have any humanity, you can become more of a cold and callous jerk.

He only scores two success on this roll. The Khymera Pestis fights back and regains the ground it had previously lost.

Four hours after the initial infection, the character doesn't have any boxes left on his soul condition monitor, so it doesn't pay to worry about the damage. He rolls his constitution dice and gets only 2 successes. He still hasn't had a chance to rest, so he doesn't have any vigor pool to use to augment this roll. The disease is starting to win the war. When he rolls again in an hour, his target number will be a 6.

Five hours after the infection, the character rolls his dice again and only gets a single success. His next roll will require 4 successes just to maintain his current state. He's starting to show signs, so he tells the rest of the party that he desperately need to rest (so that he can regain his vigor pool). His friends find a somewhat safe place and take turns watching over their sick comrade.

Six hours since he was infected. The character needs 4 successes of 6 or more to keep from falling closer and closer to a cognitively challenged individual with below average motor skills. He rolls his constitution dice and uses ½ his vigor pool in an effort to regain lost ground. He gets only two successes. His next roll will be even more difficult.

The roll at hour seven is going to be tough. He needs 5 success of 6 or more. He uses the rest of his vigor pool and hopes for the best. He gets four successes, which he would have been happy for any other time. This time it's just enough to raise his target number to seven for the next roll… and he's going to need 5 of them. He goes back to sleep. Without his vigor pool, he doesn't have a chance of succeeding.

Hour eight arrives and the character rolls. He throws everything he has into the roll, but it's not enough. He only gets 2 successes. He's missed the threshold by 3 successes. His future is going to entail a lot of moaning, limping, and trying to eat other people. Within the hour, the character is going to be a zombie.

Of course, his friends who are standing watch over him might have no idea that they're currently guarding something that views them as dinner. If they aren't vigilant, he could take them by surprise and the cycle might begin again.

- Treating Khymera Pestis

As discussed in **B.4.1 Khymera Pestis**, all know cures for this disease are fatal to its host. You can try to make the host comfortable. You can take measures to stop the spread of the disease. You *cannot* do anything to help someone fight off this disease.

You can, however, make a treat injury test to see how the person is doing. The target number for this test is 5. The more successes you get, the more you know about the state of the infected person. A single success might confirm that the character is still contagious (a state the persists for an hour after the character has beaten the disease). A few successes might tell you whether the character or the disease is winning the fight. A phenomenal roll might go so far as to tell you the specific game mechanics involved in the roll.

- ***Subspecies Specific Abilities***

Maddening Howl: Some zombies have the ability let forth a mournful wail that steals the resolve from even the most hardened of hearts. Any who hear this maddening howl must make a psyche test against a target number of 7 (5 plus the insight score of the zombie) . If they score no successes, they suffer a -3 dice penalty to all skill test and initiative rolls. Each success that they achieve reduces this penalty by 1 die.

If the howl is heard during a zombie attack, this test is resolved before any rolls are made to resist fear. If the howl is heard in the middle of an attack, this test is resolved and a new fear test is rolled immediately.

Sense of Self: Zombies with the sense of self ability understand that being hit with a weapon causes injury even if they do not feel pain. These zombies are capable of parrying or dodging attacks made against them following all the same rules that players follow when making such rolls.

Sickening Stench: Some zombies exude the smell of death. The range at which this scent can be smelled is equal to 5 feet per point of the zombie's constitution score (40 feet for the default zombie with this ability).

Character's trapped within this radius are overwhelmed by nausea. They are only able to use ½ of the actions that they earned on their initiative test. If the stench is encountered during combat, the character loses ½ of their remaining actions.

A character can resist this effect by making a constitution test against a target number equal to the zombie's constitution score (8 for the default zombie with this ability). Each success is an additional action that the character can take up to the normal number of actions that they would have remaining.

For example, if a character has 6 actions and encounters the Sickening Stench, the would only get three actions despite their initiative roll. If they score 2 successes on the initiative test they would get two additional actions for a total of 5 this round. If they had rolled 4 successes, the character would have 6 actions (because 3 + 4 from the successes is greater than 6 actions that the character earned on the initiative roll).

Creatures Affected by Khymera Pestis

As noted previously, because of its unique biology Khymera Pestis can both infect and affect humans, animals, and even plants. We've encountered diseases before that can travel from one species to another, but a disease that has virtually the same effect on all species of life is unheard of.

The threat from other humans and animals might seem obvious, but consider this… not all animals see each other as food. An infected wolf or bear would readily attack a group of humans. We know this because diseased animals without access to their regular food supply are often driven to attack humans. Rodents like raccoons, squirrels, and rats don't usually see humans as food, but they certainly attack humans when cornered.

I know what you're thinking, if that was the case, human zombies wouldn't be a threat to other humans. After all, we don't (generally) eat other humans.

True. However, even though we do not routinely eat other humans, we all know that we could if we needed to… say when the plane carrying our rugby team crashes in the mountains. We also know that (most) people like to eat meat… I remember my parents telling me to eat my vegetables, but I have never once been told that I had to eat all the bacon on my plate. The same held (and still holds) true for my own children.

With the exception of attacks by other humans, most infected animals don't pose an overt threat to humans… at least not until predators outnumber their normal prey. The real threat posed by infected animals (and plants) is a contaminated food supply.

As long as there is plentiful food, an infected livestock isn't much of a danger to an uninfected human. Once you attack

that livestock, things change, and the danger is twofold. First, zombies are instinctual creatures, so fight or flight kicks in. The livestock will try to run unless it can't escape. Then is will try to kill you if only to get away from you.

Second, if you kill the livestock for food, something people often do… just walk through your local grocery store's meat section… or, if you live in the default setting, visit one of the numerous meat markets… you risk getting infection due to exposure from infected meat.

If you take precautions against infection due to handling the meat, you still have to make sure you cook it enough to kill the Khymera Pestis. Remember, temperatures of 150° Fahrenheit or more are necessary to kill the pathogen. This makes a food thermometer one of the most important survival tools you can carry.

Rare steaks are a serious health concern during the zombie apocalypse… no matter how good they taste. Over cooked is better than disease laden. Other foods that come from animals can be just as dangerous as the meat. Milk from an infected cow or eggs from an infected chicken risk infection by exposure.

Animal waste is another danger. Like other zombie material, waste remains infectious for hours after it is expelled by the host. Since material is less contagious than a wound and animals behave according to their instincts until their needs are no longer being met, farmers could be caring for herds of zombie cows or a flock of zombie chickens and not realize it.

Pigs are not mentioned because pigs will eat you even if they aren't diseased. (Just ask Mister Wu.) This would make it difficult for pig farmers to know if their pigs are carrying the disease, but, by the time anyone knows that the disease exists, there aren't many farmers left. It still means that there could be food on store shelves that will make you a zombie if you don't cook it enough.

Fish can also carry the disease, and might be a more plentiful food supply with zombie farmers eating their livestock and abandoning their farms to eat other people.

Plants can also carry the Khymera Pestis. Fortunately, plants don't run around killing people… usually. Pollen does not seem to spread the disease. Later on scientists will surmise that the Khymera Pestis located in the pollen is destroyed by factors like sunlight before the pollen is released.

Plants are normally infected by exposure to animal waste. The greatest threat posed by plants is as a food source for people and animals. A human or animal that eats an infected plant runs the risk of getting infected. This is especially true for animals since they don't cook their food before eating it.

Wight – Human (common zombie)

Attributes

Attribute	
Strength (STR):	4
Coordination (CRD):	2
Quickness (QCK):	2
Constitution (CON):	5
Reason (RSN):	1
Insight (INS):	1
Psyche (PSY):	1
Charisma (CHA):	0

Weapon	TN	DR	Type	RI
Claw	4	2	S	M
Bite	4	2	P	M

Armor	S	P	I	E
None				
Total				

Dice Pools

Action Pool:	3
Vigor Pool:	6
Willpower:	2

Skills (Attribute)

Skill	Rank
Unarmed Combat (CRD)	6
Awareness (INS)	4
Edged Weapons (CRD)	4
Impact Weapons (CRD)	3

Gaffing Scores

Body Gaff:	3
Mind Gaff:	1

Special Abilities

Cause Infection
Cause Fear
No Modifiers for Wound levels
No Modifiers for visual impairment

Virulence

Wound:	5
Exposure:	3

Mind Damage

Minor

Light

Moderate

Serious

Critical

No Effect

Body Damage

Minor

Light

Moderate

Serious

Critical

Half Movement Rate

Soul Damage

Minor

Light

Moderate

Serious

Critical

Neutralized

In combat a wight will press its attack on the nearest potential prey. They will attempt to claw other creatures until they are able to grapple with them. Once grappled, wightes will begin trying to eat their prey resulting in a bit attack. They can use primitive melee weapons, but rarely do so. Wightes are relentless in their attack until easier prey becomes available. When this happens, the wight veers off in search of the easier prey giving no thought or having no concern for its previous target.

Wightes tend to travel in packs. They do not actively cooperate with one another. Instead they appear to be individual creatures attempting to achieve the same goal at the same time. They do not normally view other zombies as threats, and will not fight with other zombies over food. If there is not enough room for them to feed on a fallen foe, they simply choose a new target.

Nachzehrer – Human (uncommon zombie)

Attributes

Strength (STR):	1
Coordination (CRD):	1
Quickness (QCK):	1
Constitution (CON):	3
Reason (RSN):	1
Insight (INS):	1
Psyche (PSY):	1
Charisma (CHA):	0

Weapon	TN	DR	Type	RI
Claw	4	1	S	M
Bite	4	1	P	M

Armor	S	P	I	E
None				
Total	0	0	0	0

Dice Pools

Action Pool:	2
Vigor Pool:	3
Willpower:	2

Skills (Attribute)	Rank
Unarmed Combat (CRD)	3

Gaffing Scores

Body Gaff:	2
Mind Gaff:	1

Special Abilities
Cause Infection
Cause Fear
No Modifiers for Wound levels
No Modifiers for visual impairment

Virulence

Wound:	3
Exposure:	2

Mind Damage	Body Damage	Soul Damage
Minor	*Minor*	*Minor*
Light	*Light*	*Light*
Moderate	*Moderate*	*Moderate*
Serious	*Serious*	*Serious*
Critical	*Critical*	*Critical*
No Effect	**Half Movement Rate**	**Neutralized**

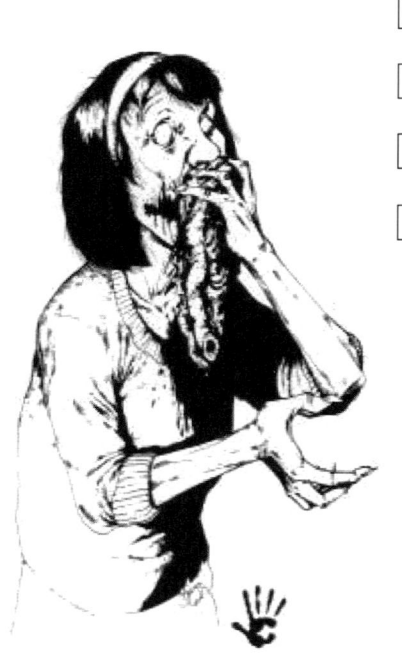

Nachzehrer are the scavengers of the zombie world. They rarely engage in combat on their own. Instead small groups of nachzehrer tend to follow the larger and more capable packs of wightes feasting off the remnants of the wightes fallen prey.

When forced to fight, nachzehrer are only slightly less deadly then their wight kin. They possess many of the same abilities, and, though they are not as formidable in combat, their ability to instill fear in their foes is not diminished in the least.

In addition to their poor combat abilities, the strain of Khymera Pestis that they carry is considerably less potent. Groups of survivors often test the mettle of newer members by pitting them up against these scavengers.

Drekavac – Human (rare zombie)

Attributes

Attribute	
Strength (STR):	3
Coordination (CRD):	2
Quickness (QCK):	2
Constitution (CON):	4
Reason (RSN):	1
Insight (INS):	2
Psyche (PSY):	1
Charisma (CHA):	0

Weapon	TN	DR	Type	RI
Claw	4	2	S	M
Bite	4	1	P	M

Armor	S	P	I	E
Light-Duty Vest	3	3	2	1
Total	3	3	2	1

Dice Pools

Action Pool:	4
Vigor Pool:	5
Willpower:	2

Skills (Attribute)	Rank
Unarmed Combat (CRD)	4
Awareness (INS)	5
Edged Weapons (CRD)	4
Impact Weapons (CRD)	4
Hide (QCK)	5
Sneak (QCK)	5

Gaffing Scores

Body Gaff:	2
Mind Gaff:	1

Special Abilities

Cause Infection
Cause Fear
No Modifiers for Wound levels
No Modifiers for visual impairment
Maddening Howl

Virulence

Wound:	4
Exposure:	2

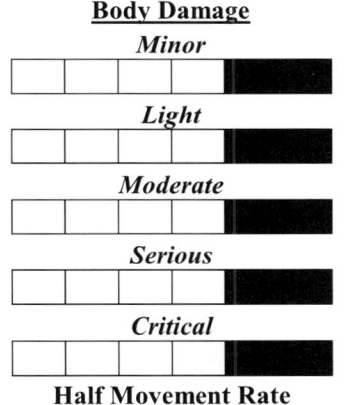

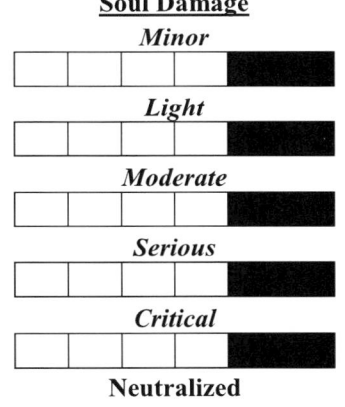

Mind Damage	Body Damage	Soul Damage
Minor	*Minor*	*Minor*
Light	*Light*	*Light*
Moderate	*Moderate*	*Moderate*
Serious	*Serious*	*Serious*
Critical	*Critical*	*Critical*
No Effect	**Half Movement Rate**	**Neutralized**

Drekavac serve as the bloodhounds and scouts of the zombie world. They do not do this intentionally, but they tend to wail when they encounter prey which alerts other zombies to the presence of food.

Though drekavac rarely travel with other zombies, they also do not attack foes that outnumber them. Instead they wait for other zombies to arrive and even the score before attacking. This may be a sign of latent intelligence and planning… or it might just be some fluke… or people might not be able to tell a drekavac from a wight from a nachzehrer… They all look the same. I can't tell them apart. Seriously, if you've seen one man-eating corpse, you've seen them all.

Nosferatu – Human (very rare zombie)

Attributes

Attribute	Value
Strength (STR):	2
Coordination (CRD):	8
Quickness (QCK):	8
Constitution (CON):	6
Reason (RSN):	1
Insight (INS):	3
Psyche (PSY):	1
Charisma (CHA):	0

Weapon	TN	DR	Type	RI
Claw	4	3	S	M
Bite	4	2	P	M

Armor	S	P	I	E
Riding Leathers	2	1	2	1
Total	2	1	2	1

Dice Pools

Action Pool:	10
Vigor Pool:	9
Willpower:	3

Skills (Attribute)

Skill	Rank
Unarmed Combat (CRD)	9
Awareness (INS)	9
Edged Weapons (CRD)	9
Impact Weapons (CRD)	6
Acrobatics	7
Tracking	7
Hide (QCK)	8
Sneak (QCK)	8

Gaffing Scores

Body Gaff:	3
Mind Gaff:	1

Cause Fear

- Cause Infection
- Induce Fear
- No Modifiers for Wound levels
- No Modifiers for visual impairment
- Ambidextrous
- Sense of Self

Virulence

Wound:	6
Exposure:	3

Mind Damage	Body Damage	Soul Damage
Minor	*Minor*	*Minor*
Light	*Light*	*Light*
Moderate	*Moderate*	*Moderate*
Serious	*Serious*	*Serious*
Critical	*Critical*	*Critical*
No Effect	**Half Movement Rate**	**Neutralized**

Nosferatu are zombie ninjas... Well, they don't wear pajamas, so maybe they're just zombie assassins. They creep through the post-apocalyptic landscape hunting down their prey for their mysterious masters. Nosferatu usually work in groups of two or three. They wait until their prey is alone and then strike from the shadows. They rarely take on groups of humans, not because they're not capable warriors, but because their dark masters only dispatch them on missions requiring stealth.

Unlike wightes, nachzehrer, and drekavacs, nosferatu are quick and agile. They are adept at using melee weapons, favoring versatile blades like the kukri.

Draugen – Human (very rare zombie)

Attributes

Attribute	Value
Strength (STR):	8
Coordination (CRD):	2
Quickness (QCK):	2 (1)
Constitution (CON):	8
Reason (RSN):	1
Insight (INS):	1
Psyche (PSY):	1
Charisma (CHA):	0

Weapon	TN	DR	Type	RI
Claw	4	3	S	M
Bite	4	4	P	M
Metal Baseball Bat	6	3+2	I	M

Armor	S	P	I	E
Leather Jacket	2	1	1	1
Chainmail Shirt	4	2	3	1
Total	5	3	4	2

Dice Pools

Action Pool:	3
Vigor Pool:	9
Willpower:	2

Skills (Attribute)	Rank
Unarmed Combat (CRD)	9
Awareness (INS)	6
Edged Weapons (CRD)	7
Impact Weapons (CRD)	8

Gaffing Scores

Body Gaff:	4
Mind Gaff:	0.5

Special Abilities

Cause Infection
Induce Fear
No Modifiers for Wound levels
No Modifiers for visual impairment
Sickening Stench
Sense of Self

Virulence

Wound:	8
Exposure:	4

Mind Damage

Minor
Light
Moderate
Serious
Critical

No Effect

Body Damage

Minor
Light
Moderate
Serious
Critical

Half Movement Rate

Soul Damage

Minor
Light
Moderate
Serious
Critical

Neutralized

Draugen are the elite shock troopers of the zombie world. They specialize in the "slash & burn" theory of the "shock & awe" camp. Luckily they are very, very rare. Like the nosferatu, draugen only get dispatched to perform important mission, but, unlike the nosferatu who work in small groups, Draugen are sent out in large squads to destroy anyone and anything that stands in their way.

Draugen are no more agile than your average wight. In fact, draugen are generally heavily armored making them less agile than a wight and more on par with a nachzehrer. They make up for this lack of agility with strength, fortitude, and numbers. In addition to being armored, draugen are almost always armed. They show a noted preference for weapons that do a lot of damage, with baseball bats, sledgehammers, and fire axes being favorites.

Wight – Rat (common zombie)

Attributes

Attribute	
Strength (STR):	1
Coordination (CRD):	5
Quickness (QCK):	2
Constitution (CON):	1
Reason (RSN):	1
Insight (INS):	1
Psyche (PSY):	1
Charisma (CHA):	0

Weapon	TN	DR	Type	RI
Claw	4	1-2	S	M
Bite	4	1-1	P	M

Armor	S	P	I	E
Total	0	0	0	0

Dice Pools

Action Pool:	5
Vigor Pool:	3
Willpower:	2

Skills (Attribute)

Skill	Rank
Unarmed Combat (CRD)	6
Awareness (INS)	4
Hide (QCK)	10
Sneak (QCK)	12

Gaffing Scores

Body Gaff:	1
Mind Gaff:	1

Special Abilities

Cause Infection

Cause Fear

No Modifiers for Wound levels

No Modifiers for visual impairment

Virulence

Wound:	1
Exposure:	1

Mind Damage	Body Damage	Soul Damage
Minor	*Minor*	*Minor*
Light	*Light*	*Light*
Moderate	*Moderate*	*Moderate*
Serious	*Serious*	*Serious*
Critical	*Critical*	*Critical*
No Effect	Half Movement Rate	Neutralized

As we've mentioned several times, the Khymera Pestis doesn't just attack humans. The rat wight is a perfect example of an animal zombie. They prowl through the sewers preying on other rats. When they come up from the damp, dank tunnels they tend to prey on birds, other rodents, and the occasional cat. (Cats are the cocky bullies of the animal world. What rat wouldn't dream of avenging their fallen brothers and sisters?)

A single rat… or even a small group of rats… doesn't pose much threat to even one armed person, but rats like to travel in swarms… especially when they're attacking humans. Then it's a war of attrition, and even a well-armed band of humans who've fended off packs of human wightes might fall to their beady little eyes, razor-like claws, sharp teeth, and skinless tails.

Drekavac – Dog (rare zombie)

Attributes

Attribute	Value
Strength (STR):	3
Coordination (CRD):	4
Quickness (QCK):	2
Constitution (CON):	5
Reason (RSN):	1
Insight (INS):	2
Psyche (PSY):	1
Charisma (CHA):	0

Weapon	TN	DR	Type	RI
Claw	4	1+1	S	M
Bite	4	2+1	P	M

Armor	S	P	I	E
Total	0	0	0	0

Dice Pools

Action Pool:	5
Vigor Pool:	6
Willpower:	2

Skills (Attribute)	Rank
Unarmed Combat (CRD)	6
Awareness (INS)	9
Tracking (RSN)	8
Hide (QCK)	4
Sneak (QCK)	4

Gaffing Scores

Body Gaff:	3
Mind Gaff:	1

Special Abilities

Cause Infection

Cause Fear

No Modifiers for Wound levels

No Modifiers for visual impairment

Maddening Howl

Virulence

Wound:	5
Exposure:	3

Mind Damage

Minor
Light
Moderate
Serious
Critical

No Effect

Body Damage

Minor
Light
Moderate
Serious
Critical

Half Movement Rate

Soul Damage

Minor
Light
Moderate
Serious
Critical

Neutralized

The canine drekavac is one of those instances when the animal version is more dangerous than its human counterpart. Unlike human zombies whose behavior is only compared to a pack, canine zombies actually have a pack mentality. A canine drekavac will stalk its prey driving it into the waiting jaws of its pack mates. Tireless, fearless, and relentless… there are few things as terrifying as a pack of drekavac dogs chasing your through the dark streets and alleys of a city you used to call home.

Additionally, because humans seem to innately fear vicious dogs, the "cause fear" ability of these zombies is increased. Only one need be present to invoke a fear response, and the target number increases by +1 for every two canine drekavacs beyond the first.

Making Your Own Zombies

Since every zombie was once an actual person or animal, you might want to change other people and animals into zombies during the course of your game. The steps for creating your own zombie are easy enough.

First what type of zombie you're going to create. You can choose to make any zombie that you'd like to create. Keep in mind that some zombies are more rare than others. For whatever reason, Khymera Pestis infections tend to create more of some kinds of zombies and less of others.

On the following chart, the letter "C" represents the character or creature's original attribute scores. Remember that you round the way that you learned in school and that no attribute can be less than zero… except charisma, which is a special exception for zombies… Additionally, all active skills are reduced by half. Skills requiring hand-eye coordination, like firearms, are reduced to zero as are all knowledge skills. The zombie retains any armor, weapons, and equipment it possessed when it turned, though it might not know how to use any of it anymore.

Zombie	STR	CRD	QCK	CON	RSN	INS	PSY	CHA
Wight	C	C/2	C/2	C	1	C/3	C/4	0
Nachzehrer	C/3	C/4	C/4	C/3	1	C/4	C/4	0
Drekavac	C	C/2	C/2	C	1	C/2	C/3	0
Nosferatu	C	C+3	C+3	C	1	C/2	C/3	0
Draugen	C+3	C	C	C+3	1	C/2	C/3	0

Once you've assigned the zombie's adjusted the zombie's attributes and skills, recalculate the zombie's dice pools. Remember the soul damage condition monitor for zombies is determined by constitution just like their body damage condition monitor. All that is left to do is give it special abilities based on the type of zombie you made. Then you have a zombie, ready, willing, and able to attack your players.

Animals can be turned into zombies as well. To make a zombie out of an animal you follow the same steps as you would for a normal humans. You can use the chart on the bottom of the page to help you determine the attributes of the animal in question.

Not every animal is listed on the chart. Of you can make up your own attributes. You don't have to be exact. There is a lot of variation in the world and zombies have hefty modifiers that will cover most of the mistakes you make.

The real trick to making zombie animals is to play off the animal's strengths and weaknesses. A canine drekavac makes sense because the drekavac's memorable howl lends itself nicely to a canine. Feline nosferatu would work just as well since the cat's natural stealth plays into the assassin-like abilities of the nosferatu.

It is just as useful to put together combinations that do not readily make sense. A nosferatu cat might be terrifying, and rightly so, but imagine what would go through your character's heads if a loan human Cotard was followed by a herd of Nachzehrer cats… a truly crazy cat lady…

You can also use zombism to offset the weaknesses of a species to throw your players for a loop they'll not soon forget. A draugen spider might be the stuff of insurance commercials, but a draugen Chihuahua could be downright terrifying… especially if that Chihuahua lived in the purse of a formal television personality turned wight.

Use your imagination. Zombies don't discriminate, so why should you. In fact, their lack of discrimination is one of the things that make them so scary.

Creature	STR	CRD	QCK	CON	RSN	INS	PSY	CHA	Action	Vigor	Willpower
Bat	1	5	5	1	1	5	2	1	8	5	5
Cat, House	1	7	4	1	1	4	2	3	8	4	5
Cat, Wild	2	7	4	2	1	4	2	2	8	5	5
Raven	1	6	6	2	2	4	3	2	9	6	6
Dog, Large	3	3	4	3	1	3	1	3	6	6	4
Dog, Small	1	3	4	1	1	3	2	3	6	4	5
Bird of Prey	2	5	5	2	1	5	3	2	8	6	6
Fox	1	6	4	2	2	4	2	2	8	5	5
Goat	2	2	3	2	1	2	2	1	4	5	3
Weasel	1	5	4	1	1	3	2	1	7	4	4
Owl	1	4	4	2	1	4	3	2	7	5	5
Rat	1	3	5	1	2	4	3	1	7	5	5
Spider	1	2	6	1	1	3	1	1	6	5	3
Toad	1	2	1	1	1	2	1	1	3	2	3

Type of Zombie: _____

Attributes	Weapon	TN	DR	Type	RI
Strength (STR): ___	_____	_____	_____	_____	____
Coordination (CRD): ___	_____	_____	_____	_____	____
Quickness (QCK): ___	_____	_____	_____	_____	____
Constitution (CON): ___					
Reason (RSN): ___	**Armor**	**S**	**P**	**I**	**E**
Insight (INS): ___	_____	_____	_____	_____	____
Psyche (PSY): ___	_____	_____	_____	_____	____
Charisma (CHA): ___	Total	_____	_____	_____	____

Dice Pools

Skills (Attribute) .... **Rank**

Action Pool: _____

Vigor Pool: _____

Willpower: _____

Gaffing Scores

Body Gaff: _____

Mind Gaff: _____   **Special Abilities**

Virulence

Wound: _____

Exposure: _____

Mind Condition Monitor

Minor Wound Level

☐☐☐☐☐☐☐☐☐☐☐

Light Wound Level

☐☐☐☐☐☐☐☐☐☐☐

Moderate Wound Level

☐☐☐☐☐☐☐☐☐☐☐

Serious Wound Level

☐☐☐☐☐☐☐☐☐☐☐

Critical Wound Level

☐☐☐☐☐☐☐☐☐☐☐

The Zombie is Angry

Body Condition Monitor

Minor Wound Level

☐☐☐☐☐☐☐☐☐☐☐

Light Wound Level

☐☐☐☐☐☐☐☐☐☐☐

Moderate Wound Level

☐☐☐☐☐☐☐☐☐☐☐

Serious Wound Level

☐☐☐☐☐☐☐☐☐☐☐

Critical Wound Level

☐☐☐☐☐☐☐☐☐☐☐

Zombie is at ½ Movement Rate

Soul Condition Monitor

Minor Wound Level

☐☐☐☐☐☐☐☐☐☐☐

Light Wound Level

☐☐☐☐☐☐☐☐☐☐☐

Moderate Wound Level

☐☐☐☐☐☐☐☐☐☐☐

Serious Wound Level

☐☐☐☐☐☐☐☐☐☐☐

Critical Wound Level

☐☐☐☐☐☐☐☐☐☐☐

Zombie is Neutralized

Notes on this Particular Zombie:

People of Green Bay

Even during the zombie apocalypse, there are movers and shakers. Someone has to step in and fill the power vacuum left when society collapses. This section will talk about some of the people who continue to survive and thrive in this horror.

- ## *Apocalytes*

The Father: The Father is the undisputed leader of the cult known as the Apocalytes. His real name is Francis J. McCall. Before the beginning of what he believes is the end, Francis McCall was a minister. He filled his sermons with messages of love and forgiveness. He preached peace and understanding. All that changed when the pandemic started.

Reverend McCall saw the disease as a sign from God. Humanity had once again grown decadent. Once again we had abandoned God's will. Once again, humanity would pay for their hubris.

God had promised never to flood the earth, but the book of Revelation was clear about the end times. God would unleash four horsemen upon the Earth. There would be famine, pestilence, war, and death[1].

On that Friday afternoon, Reverend McCall looked out his window and saw all four horsemen riding through his city. God's love had not been enough to steer us evil, so God, in his love, sent down his wrath to cleanse us of our evil ways. God was testing the righteous and punishing the sinful. More importantly, he was calling on Reverend McCall to lead his people from this valley of the shadow of death.

Reverend McCall contact his superiors in the church, but he alone had been called by God. He denounced them for the sinners that they were and set out to form a new church filled with true and righteous believers. He named his church the Disciples of the Apocalypse. The people of the city dubbed them Apocalytes.

- ## *Avarites*

The Plutarch: The Plutarch casts a long shadow over the city. He and his followers exist for one reason and one reason only – to make money.

The way that the Plutarch sees it, it's just a matter of time before Washington and Madison pull their collective heads out of their posteriors and handle this zombie thing. Until then, he's going to take what's rightfully his… which is everything.

After all, people abandoned their stuff. Other people are looting too. They're just pretending it's about survival. It is, and always has been, about getting your piece of the pie. No one's going to serve you up a slice. You need to get it for yourself. The police and the military are busy trying to survive and rescue survivors, so who's going to do anything about it.

FDR took us off the gold standard. The zombies put us on the lead standard. The golden rule doesn't apply anymore. Now we're practicing the leaden rule – He who has the lead gets the gold and makes the rules.

---

[1] We know Pestilence, Famine, War, and Death are not the biblical horsemen of the apocalypse. It's one of the reasons we're not followers of Reverend McCall.

- **Bob's Krewe**

The Dictator: Few people outside of Bob's Krewe have actually seen the one they call "the Dictator". Based on the used by the Krewe, he is believes to be a man dressed in robes and wearing a conical hat.

By all accounts, the Dictator believes is life, liberty, and happiness for all… so long as those people live on his turf, exercise their liberty in areas that are of no concern to him, and find happiness in serving something greater than themselves… and do not, under any circumstances, discuss cheese.

The Dictator holds court in the upper reaches of the Cofrin Library. He surrounds himself with his inner circle of trusted friends and advisors and is always guarded by a handful of legionnaires.

If he ever ventures from the protection of his cylindrical citadel, no one speaks of it. Those under his careful protection are simply grateful that he exists.

Centurion: The Centurion cuts an imposing figure as he strides through the Cofrin Library. He is always seen wearing his personal suit of linothorax and wearing a flowing blue cape emblazoned with the symbol of the Krewe.

The Centurion leads the Legionnaires, a band of elite warriors clad in linothorax and loyal to the Dictator. They are sworn to defend his life and enforce his will among those under his protection… which he considers anyone who happens onto the old UWGB campus.

The Centurion is responsible, not only for the defense of the Dictator, but for the defense of the whole campus as well. He organizes groups to perform necessary tasks, like regularly sweeping the tunnels for zombies and making sure the enclave has a ready supply of their favorite ancient armor.

- **Brown County Correctional Facility**

Inmate 1021: One of the safest places in all of Brown County is the old Brown County Correctional Facility. It seems that building a place to keep criminals in has the fortunate side effect of keeping zombies out.

With the fall of the constituted government of the state of Wisconsin, Brown County, and the city of Green Bay, Brown County Correctional Facility found itself without support from the outside. They had food, but the small group of guards could not hope to defend the prison walls against attempts to breach them from without and within. The situation grew dire and tension ran high. The prisons wall provided protection, but, with no hope of release, their prison became a death sentence.

Inmate 1021 changed all of that. He negotiated a treaty between the (understandably) skeptical guards and the prisoners they had guarded. The guards knew they could not hope to protect the prison from the zombies forever. The prisoners knew that the prison offered the best chance to survive the horrors that raged outside its walls.

Soon orange jumpsuits could be seen next to blue-gray guard uniforms manning the towers. Inmate 1021 even managed to organize foraging mission into the nearby city… first to replenish supplies and later to rescue nearby survivors.

- **Ephesians**

The Deacon: After the Roman Catholic Church re-established the Order of Deacons, Pope John Paul II declared that the deacon serves as Evangelizer, Sanctifier, and Witness and Guide. He tasked deacons with the ministries of the Word, the Liturgy, and Charity and Justice. It is no wonder the head of this order goes by this name.

The Deacon was appointed by the Diocesan Bishop of Green Bay to minister to the faithful still living in the city. She takes this role very seriously.

The Deacon knows that God is love. She knows that God did not bring about the zombie apocalypse. Like most tragic losses of life on our planet, this was man's doing. The Deacon also know that, in times of trouble such as these, God calls upon his people to love and support one another as he loves and supports us.

- **G-Force**

CWO Speight: When the zombie apocalypse began, Chief Warrant Officer Thomas Speight was not the highest ranking officer serving in a reserve unit in Green Bay, but he was the longest serving. His bravery in the battle at the corner of Lombardi and Oneida that saved many of the men and women now under his command, and his face bears the scars to prove it.

Speight leads by example. He values the lives of the soldiers serving under him, and he would not ask them to do anything he would not do himself. He still makes the tough calls, and sometimes people die, but this is war. His soldiers love him. More importantly, they respect him.

The members of G-Force haven't heard from anything resembling a command structure in quite some time, but that doesn't matter. Each and every one of them swore an oath, and, as far as Speight's concerned, that's all the orders they need.

Under Speight's command, Lambeau Field has been turned from a sports stadium to an veritable fortresses. Barricades set up in the atrium funnel the zombies into the "kill zone" to keep his soldiers ready for battle without risking their lives. Sure, shooting zombies from the safety of a balcony isn't the same as fighting with them on the ground, but it's better than wasting ammunition shooting at targets.

G-Force makes regular patrols of the area searching for survivors as well as gathering supplies. They monitor communications channels on the off chance someone else has survived.

Though they have a strong desire to help those around them, Speight knows that they can't help anyone if they're dead. He won't risk the lives of his people on a fool's errand. It's not an easy choice, but it's better to let a few die so that many can live.

- **LEOS**

The Mayor: The person calling themselves "the Mayor" never actually held that office, not while the city existed as a city at any rate. He may be one of the judges that used to preside in the courthouse that serves as the LEOs' headquarters. He might be a member of either the Green Bay Police or the Brown County Sheriff's Department. Or he might just be some guy who happened to have a good idea when people needed one and got the job.

Whoever he is, the person calling themselves "the Mayor" leads what is left of the Green Bay Police and Brown County Sheriff's departments.

Detective Braddock: Jim Braddock always dreamed of being a police officer. He studied criminal justice after high school and jumped at the chance to be a patrol cop in his hometown of Green Bay. He worked his way up through the department until he made detective. Then the world came to an end proving there was more than a little truth to those down and out detective shows he used to watch when he was a kid.

He doesn't do much detecting these days, but he still wear the trench coat and hat. After all, he earned them both.

Officer Mueller: Officer Sarah Mueller began her carrier as a dispatcher for the Sheriff's Department before earning a spot in a patrol car when she graduated from the academy. She'd

like to be a by-the-book deputy, but the book doesn't have a chapter for the end of the world.

She's the rookie on the force, so Mueller gets stuck with most of the job no one else wants. That suits her just fine. The more crap they pile on her, the sooner they'll see she's just as capable as any one of them.

Sergeant Wyler: Officer Wyler is a veteran on the Green Bay Police force. He would have made lieutenant long ago if it wasn't for his attitude… the topic of many of his performance reviews.

Wyler learned his trade as a Military Police Officer in the U.S. Marine Corps. There was a lot less politics in the Corps. It wasn't about writing tickets. It wasn't about how many "contacts" you had during your shift. It was about doing your job.

Alright, so maybe "yes" is not the correct response when your boss asks if you think he's an idiot. If he didn't want to know the answer, why did he ask the question?

Though you'll never hear him admit it, there is a part of the sergeant that is glad the zombie apocalypse is here. It saves him from having to spend half his day filling out paper work.

- **Wild Ones**

The Amazon: The reason that the Amazon leads the Wild Ones is simple, she killed the guy who was the leader before her. The title is hers until someone else can lay claim to it. So far four people have tried and failed to dethrone her. She wears their ears around her neck as a not-so-subtle reminder to anyone else  with delusions of grandeur. Oh, and that's not a tattoo on her neck either. It's a scar left from when a challenger tried to strangle her with barbed wire. Rumor has it that she fed him parts of his body before she took his ear.

The Amazon is a stereotypical post-apocalyptic warlord, or she would be if she wasn't a woman and if the apocalypse was already over. She rules the Wild Ones with an iron fist... and a loaded shotgun. That's no mean feat considering the Wild Ones are not that many steps removed from animals. In fact, that might be an insult to animals.

Happy: Happy served as a lieutenant to the last leader of the Wild Ones. He's the only member of the gang who retains

that distinction. All of the other former lieutenants were put to the axe... Happy's axe. It was the show of loyalty the Amazon demanded in exchange for his life.

Happy has faithfully served the Amazon since he watched her tear the ear off his boss with her teeth. He serves as her enforcer and unofficial protector. Wherever the Amazon goes, Happy is right beside her... which is why she doesn't trust him.

The Gimp: The Gimp is a pistol-totting members of the Wild Ones and one of the Amazon's first recruits. She serves as the Amazon's aide-de-camp, though persistent rumors claim there is more to their relationship. If there is any truth to the rumor, it does not bode well for one of them. The Amazon's last lover happened to be the Wild Ones' former leader.

Hands: The Wild One known as Hands claims to be from Austria. He speaks with a thick German accent.

There is a good chance that his real name is Hans, but the members of the Wild Ones either don't know, or, more likely, don't care.

The Hands moniker does seem fitting, however, as the Austrian is known for dual wielding a pair of revolvers. He is an excellent shot with both weapons and has been known to perform trick shots to entertain people just before he kills them.

- **Independents**

Not everyone roaming the city is a member of some gang, but most do band together to form small groups for mutual defense... there is safety in numbers, after all.

Next we'll take a look at a few of the more famous independent denizens of zombie-laden Green Bay.

Cleopatra Jameson: Cleo is one of a handful of former students from Green Bay West High School that now make their home in the old Fleet Farm building on the corner of Shawano Ave and Taylor Street next to U.S. Highway 41 on Green Bay's west side.

Cleo's mother brought her to Green Bay the summer before Cleo's freshman year of high school. She had only lived in the city for seven months when the zombie apocalypse began. She has since proven herself a capable warrior.

Eric Gibson: Eric has been hunting zombies since he was 12 years old. His tools have changed considerably since he started, but the principles remained the same. His target hasn't changed and the reticule still looks the same, but now instead of clicking a mouse he squeezes a trigger.

Eric was in his sophomore year when zombies started eating people. He and a small group of friends made their way to Fleet Farm to gather supplies. They've been their ever since playing the most realistic and high stakes video game of all time.

Jonathan McCall: Jon used to spend his free time trying to dominate the world. Then he came to the realization that ruling the world wasn't nearly as fun as conquering it. Jon was a sophomore when Eric introduced him to the world of first person shooters. He was never as good at it as his friend, but he excelled at formulating strategies.

When the zombies sprang up during his junior year, Jon helped lead his friends to the relative safety of Fleet Farm.

Lincoln Carter: Linc is a born leader. Just ask him. He's happy to tell you why he should be in charge. Now he leads the ragtag band of students held up at Fleet Farm.

Linc had planned to join the Navy and work on nuclear reactors after high school, but the zombie apocalypse began midway through his senior year. Now he is more concerned about surviving than what he's going to do with the rest of his life.

Linc knows that it's just a matter of time before the government and the military get their act together and put an end to the zombie threat. Unlike the rest of the people trying to survive in Green Bay, Linc isn't sure he wants the apocalypse to end. The end of the apocalypse means going to back to be a normal person, and Linc's not ready to give up his little kingdom just yet.

Miss Fortune: Miss Fortune moved to Green Bay from Las Vegas seven months ago with her daughter to get away from an abusive boyfriend. She took a job doing the only thing she knew how to do – dancing at a local gentlemen's club.

When the zombie apocalypse changed from mysterious illness to zombies eating people, Miss Fortune was at the Brown County Courthouse. The judge was about to set bail when the bailiff decided to take a bite out of the clerk.

Miss Fortune raced out of the courtroom, but the city was already in chaos. She wanted to find her daughter Cleo, but the bridges had already been raised cutting her off from the west side. She didn't know what to do, but she knew she couldn't stay at the courthouse. She ran to the gentlemen's club a mere six block from the courthouse and took refuge in its windowless interior.

After a few days of hiding, Miss Fortune risked venturing out of the building. The same structural features that made the club suitable for its former purpose had kept Miss Fortune safe. Her goal now is to find a way across the river so she can find her daughter.

Misty: Misty has been alone for as long as she can remember. She has parents, but they always treated her like she's a burden. She embarrassed them with her behavior and her interests.

Other young people in her position find solace in their friends, but Misty never had any friends. She was different, and the kids in school picked on her for it.

No one understood her. No one ever had. Life was unbearable, and Misty might have ended it all if it had not been for the zombie apocalypse.

When the zombies appeared, Misty saw them as liberators. She led a pack of them to her house, unlocked the door, and let them inside. Her father was in his study working at his computer when they set upon him. They caught her mother pouring wine from a box. Misty listened to their screams as she packed her backpack and climbed out her bedroom window.

The Professor: There is a large healthcare company in Green Bay that runs a hospital, a nursing college, and a psychiatric hospital. Before the onset of the zombie apocalypse, the Professor was a psychiatrist specializing in psychopathology working at the psychiatric hospital. When the outbreak hit the city, the Professor was asked to come to the main hospital to help learn the cause of the mysterious disease that caused such drastic behavioral changes in people. (The citizens of Green Bay did not regularly try to eat each other...) It was a once in a lifetime opportunity that he could not pass up.

The main hospital has long since been overrun by voracious zombies, but the Professor managed to escape. In the chaos he made his way back to the psychiatric hospital where he continues his work.

War & Piece: War & Piece are a strange father-daughter duo.

War was a member of a local motorcycle club. He was at the clubhouse when the zombies showed up. The bikers managed to fight off their attackers.

When the dust settled, the club members that survived left to gather their families. The plan was to bring them back to the safety of the clubhouse. War was the only one who returned. He's been searching for his brothers and fighting to avenge the fallen ever since.

Piece is War's daughter. She's cut from the same cloth as her father, so she's something of a wild child. She'd grown up around the club. Though she wasn't a member, the club was her family too. She fights alongside her father.

Zombies don't bother coming to the clubhouse anymore. Maybe the zombie heads hanging from the fence scare them away. So War & Piece bring the fight to them. The roar of their exhaust is a welcome sound for human survivors.

Index

Humanity destroys the Earth… a real stretch of the imagination, I know. Our only hope is to reach for the stars and find a new world to pillage and plunder. That's when we learned the truth. We were not alone.

Our little corner of the Milky Way is home to a system-spanning empire… an empire humans founded… and destroyed. Our subjects rebelled against us and banished us to a pale blue dot we came to believe was our home. We became third-class citizens of our own empire… until we rebelled against our former subjects and through the entire galaxy into chaos. Here's your chance to be big damned heroes… or die trying…

After Earth, a science-fiction role-playing game by Erisian Entertainment.

Coming to your favorite retailers in 2013… unless the world does end in 2012, but then we won't care…

Name: _____

Clique: _____

Personaltiy: _____

	Primary Trait	Secondary Trait	Tertiary Trait

Age: ___ **Year in School:** ___
Height: ___ **Hair:** ___
Weight: ___ **Eyes:** ___
Gender: ___ **Orientation:** ___

Attributes

- Strength (STR) ___
- Coordination (CRD) ___
- Quickness (QCK) ___
- Constitution (CON) ___
- Reason (RSN) ___
- Insight (INS) ___
- Psyche (PSY) ___
- Charisma (CHA) ___

Dice Pools

- Action Pool: ___
  (CRD+QCK+RSN+INS)/2
- Vigor Pool: ___
  (STR+QCK+CON+PSY)/2
- Willpower Pool: ___
  (RSN+INS+PSY+CHA)/2

Dice Pools

- Psychical (Body) Gaff: ___
  (CON/2)
- Mental (Mind) Gaff: ___
  (PSY/2)

Active Skills

Acrobatics(QCK) | Interrogation(CHA)
Acting(CHA) | Interview(CHA)
Appraiser(RSN) | Intimidation(CHA)
Athletics(QCK) | Jump(STR)
Awareness(INS) | Launch Weapons(RSN)
Bogulie(CHA) | Navigation(RSN)
♪Build / Craft X(RSN) | Negotiation(CHA)
♪Cartography(RSN) | Oration(CHA)
Climb(STR) | Painting(INS)
Computer Operation(RSN) | ♪Pick Locks(CRD)
♪Computer Programming(RSN) | Pilot Boat(CRD)
♪Cryptography(RSN) | Play Musical Instrument X(CRD)
Dance(QCK) | Projectile Weapons(CRD)
Dangineering(RSN) | Repair X(RSN)
♪Demolitions(RSN) | Ride(QCK)
Discern Lie(INS) | ♪Safecracking(RSN)
Disguise(CHA) | Sculpting(INS)
Drawing (INS) | Search(RSN)
Drive(QCK) | Seduction(CHA)
Edged Weapon(CRD) | Sense Motive(INS)
♪Escape Artist(QCK) | Sing(CHA)
Fast-Talk(CHA) | ♪Sleight of Hand(QCK)
Firearms(CRD) | Sneak(QCK)
♪Forgery(CRD) | Thrown Weapons(CRD)
Gambling(CHA) | Tracking(RSN)
♪Gunnery(RSN) | ♪Treat Injury(RSN)
Hide(QCK) | Unarmed Combat(QCK)
Impact Weapons(CRD) | Writing(INS)

Knowledge Skills

Agriculture(RSN) | Movies(RSN)
Anthropology(RSN) | Muscle Cars(RSN)
Archeology(RSN) | Music(RSN)
Architecture(RSN) | Narcotics(RSN)
Area History(RSN) | Netiquette(RSN)
Art(RSN) | Occult Lore(RSN)
♪Ballistics(RSN) | Pharmaceuticals(RSN)
Biology(RSN) | Philosophy(RSN)
Chemistry(RSN) | Physics(RSN)
City Ordinances(RSN) | Politics(RSN)
Comic Books(RSN) | Psychology(RSN)
Computer Programs(RSN) | Quasi-Legal Substances(RSN)
Conspiracy Theories(RSN) | Religion(RSN)
Criminology(RSN) | Robotics(RSN)
Ecology(RSN) | ♪Seamanship(RSN)
♪Engineering & Design X(RSN) | Shopping Centers(RSN)
Etiquette(RSN) | Sociology(RSN)
Federal Law(RSN) | Sports Cars(RSN)
♪Forensics(RSN) | Sports X(RSN)
Fringe Cults(RSN) | State Law(RSN)
Geology(RSN) | Strategy(RSN)
♪Linguistics(RSN) | Tactics(RSN)
Livestock(RSN) | Television Programs(RSN)
Local Businesses(RSN) | Theology(RSN)
Local Gangs(RSN) | US History(RSN)
Local Underworld(RSN) | Video Games(RSN)
Macro-Economics(RSN) | World History(RSN)
Micro-Economics(RSN)

Weapon	Skill Rating	Hands Required	Target Number	Damage Rating	Damage Bonus	Damage Type	Range Increment	Special Rules

Advantages

Academic Aptitude | Hyper Immune System
Acute Hearing | In Tune
Acute Vision | Internal Compass
Adeptness | Light Sleeper
Ambidexterity | Mechanical Aptitude
Bi-Lingual | Natural Talent
Bland Appearance | Perfect Time
Brave | Poise
Common Sense | Poison Resistance
Computer Aptitude | Popular
Cunning Linguist | Presence
Eidetic Memory | Quick Healer
Electrical Aptitude | Quick Study
Equilibrium | Scientific Aptitude
Exceptional Attribute | Sex Appeal
Exceptional Peripheral Vision | Social Grace
Focused | Tough as Nails
Good Reputation | Will To Live
High Pain Tolerance

Disadvantages

Addiction | Lethargic
Allergy | Low Pain Tolerance
Bad Reputation | Lower Immunity
Berserker | Mood Swings
Blinders | Night Blindness
Blowhard | Phobia
Color Blind | Poor Vision
Combat Paralysis | Sanctity of Life
Deep Sleeper | Uncouth
Frail | Underacheiver
Horrible Secret | Vindictive
Impulsive | Weak-Willed
Inept

Armor Type	Slashing Value	Piercing Value	Impact Value	Energy Value	Special Rules

Total Armor Values:

Action	Roll	Against	Results
Initiative	Action Pool	TN 5	1 Action per success
Attack	Weapons Skill	Weapon TN	DR x Net Success = Damage done to target
Dodge	QCK	TN 5	reduces attacker's success by 1 for each success
Parry	Melee Weapon Skill	Weapon TN	damage is reduced by "damage" done by parry
Gaff	CON or PSY	Power of Attack	reduces damage done by appropriate Gaff Rating per success

Condition Monitors

Mind Condition Monitor

Light (No Modifiers)

Moderate (-1 Die for all rolls)

Serious (-2 Dice for all rolls)

Critical (-3 Dice for all rolls)

Fatal (-4 Dice for all rolls)

Unconscious (- All Dice for all rolls)
Your character is Unconscious.
Any additional damage is applied as
Body Damage

Body Condition Monitor

Light (No Modifiers)

Moderate (-1 Die for all rolls)

Serious (-2 Dice for all rolls)

Critical (-3 Dice for all rolls)

Fatal (-4 Dice for all rolls)

Dead (- All Dice for all rolls)
Your character is "Mostly Dead."
Any additional is applied as
Soul Damage.

Soul Condition Monitor

Light (No Modifiers)

Moderate (-1 Die for all rolls)

Serious (-2 Dice for all rolls)

Critical (-3 Dice for all rolls)

Fatal (-4 Dice for all rolls)

Dead (- All Dice for all rolls)
Your Character is "All Dead."
The only thing left to do is to go through
his clothes and look for loose change.